THE HOOP OF THE ALEKŠU'IN

is off to an amazing start!

REVIEWS FOR
BLOOD INDIGO

"Sullivan's commitment to creating a world unlike any we've ever experienced is astonishing... It is hard to write about this book; one must really read it to understand its power and gorgeous complexity."
Ulysses Dietz

"Sullivan drops you right into the action in this book."
Library Journal

BLOOD INDIGO

TALULAH J. SULLIVAN

Forest Path Books
Independent Publishers of
Divergent Speculative Fiction

Copyright Information

BLOOD INDIGO
Published by
FOREST PATH BOOKS

Forest Path Books publications may be purchased for educational, business, or sales/promotional use. For information, please email the publishers at:
info@forestpathbooks.com
or address:
Forest Path Books, LLC
P. O. Box 847, Stanwood, WA 98292 USA

Stay informed on our releases and news!
Join the reading group/newsletter at:
https://forestpathbooks.com/into-the-forest/

Cover design by James T. Egan of Bookfly Design
Cover content is for illustrative purposes only, and any person depicted on the cover is a model.

Library of Congress Control Number: 2020920942
ISBN: 978-1-951293-25-3 (trade paper)
ISBN: 978-1-951293-24-6 (e-book)

For my grandmother,
who taught me about our People long before I even realised
I was being taught.

Yakoke, svpokni.
Chim anoli shukanumpa sv bvnna.

Buíochas, seanmháthair.
Lig dom scéal a insint duit.

BLOOD INDIGO

THE STORYKEEPER SPEAKS...

"When Grandmother grows weary of us, grows tired of the ever-creeping, cloying moss upon Her many-tiled belly, She has but to draw into Her shell and gather unto Herself. And wait, through beginnings into endings..."

Listen, my cousins, for this is all true! These, the words of our Ancestors, had their beginnings from the words of a'Šaákfo, spoken as the tailed Star danced over Grandmother's belly. The stories passed down over wintering counts, told and repeated even as I tell and sing these stories now. Once, so long yet not so long ago, after Winnowing tilted our lands into a dark and insular time, but before Reckoning showed us the error of our fears, there was a beginning. There are always beginnings, you might say, and a'io, everything begins, everything ends, riding the Hoop as we ride our grazingKin beneath Sun's grace. But this beginning? Ša came stalking-quiet, and we had our backs turned, foolish. Frightened. Like chukfi in ša's burrow, we lingered content, safe and ignorant, digging new warrens, making pellets and babies...

Ah! You ask! But answers are always layered like Earth beneath our feet. Changing *kindles* beginnings. Little changes, they seem, at the first. Singular motions, ripples in cavern pools, new footprints upon a well-worn path. Singular motions, each revealing a new path. Recognise them, my cousins. Remember them.

See them:

Here is one of the Beloved shrugging off complacency and fear, grasping the mane of a spoiled horse to sing ša calm. Here is a daughter feeling betrayal and rebellion beneath ways long twisted and hidden—forbidden! Here is one made outlier and outcast, who Saw in Stars what others feared to. Here is a chieftain's son, changing into something he was taught to fear and hate. Here is a child captured in the raiding, loosed to find her true Clan and set her People free. Here is a too-proud elder who believes he alone knows the secrets, yet merely clasps sand in open fingers. Here is a changing-spirit youth, callow yet powerful enough to shield ša's People. Here is a son of two worlds, craving the belonging but having to turn away, accept instead of deny, believed Shaper when he was, instead, Catalyst.

All these our People, all of them our cousins—and with so many paths it would seem they'd never converge, a'io?

Yet all these paths, all these singular motions, one then the other, falling like drops of Rain to gather and runnel, feeding River. We might act alone, we might take a solitary path, yet every act cannot help but come together and inform the whole. Enrichment, or betrayal, all affects all. We know this. We are one with our Kin, be they two- or four-footed, winged or finned or footless, rooted or carried upon Wind. Our People wander the plains, settle into Forest boughs, glide across deep-packed snow, ride River and brave Sea... but all of us remain together on Grandmother's belly. Our separate motions are as one. We are made one even as we travel the Hoop like those of our own tribe ride our Kin into Wind's blessings.

These ones we See, these ones whose singular, seemingly insignificant motions we will remember? Ah, those were indeed the beginning, my cousins.

They were the beginning of the ending...

◊ ◊ ◊

I
ALEKŠU

"Listen! It is time to Dance!"

It was not the first time Palatan had stood upon the Breaking Ground to challenge.

Deliberate, stripped to clout with the copper and malachite banding his arms, while waves of heat whispered his name and glided across the dried grass and red dust, setting the surrounding hillocks a-shimmer. Dry, reflecting parch and gilt against his eyes, scorching shivers across the oiled, deep bronze whipcord of his shoulders, prickling the numerous, narrow plaits gracing his left temple. Waiting, with blood striping the Marks upon his cheekbones and long dried into skim and flakes; spilt from over his heart and onto the hard, sandy ground, it had likewise baked into sludge.

Palatan welcomed the blaze, humming sweet behind his ears and flaring tendrils to swathe his heart.

He knew Fire.

"Come out, Alekšu! The Dance must be made. It is our way."

His voice rang against the hide several strides away. The door didn't so much as quiver.

Silence. Sun rose higher, and in Her wake trailed a faint, ghostly triad: Brother Moon with younger siblings clinging to one hip. Still Palatan waited, unmoving. Circuit blooded, ceremony observed, with their tribe gathering, albeit sluggish.

Not many dared test Alekšu. All who had? Had failed.

Yet hope began to speak: first one drum, then another, a gravid heartbeat of necessary support. Physical prowess, after all, merely whet one edge of this blade. The Dance was beginning, whether acknowledged or not...

"Come out, old one!" Palatan called. "Lest I Dance without you."

Without me? You do not even know the steps. Mockery curled silent behind his eyes, the soul-talk more yawn than acknowledgement. *I grow tired of sending you back to your dam's tipo, little cur.*

He answered in kind. *You've not had the privilege since Everwintering Mountain sent Fire across Sky. Nearly fifteen winters past.*

A snort. *Has it been so long, son of my brother's daughter? Ai, but you've spent the time like a good horseClans dog, hunting game and siring whelps upon your mate. It seems she must squat every third Hoop to drop her litter, naked in the dust.*

A'io! Harsh affirmation. *I have something to fight for!*

His chieftain Aylaniś, who with her own hands had girded her spouse in sacred oil and smoke. Their three children, standing with her. The clans, gathering, beginning to sway to the drums like Wind-brushed grass.

Palatan stepped forwards; into the Circuit where every member of his tribe—two- and four-legged—was blessed at birth, breaking, and bereavement. "It is time to Dance, Alekšu!" The honorific bore respect; its undertone purled demand. "A challenger waits."

Come out, she-viper. I do not stand alone, this time.

And the door flap heaved open and fell against the taut sides of the tipo.

Grey hair, at the first, close-cropped save for the honour of numerous and tiny braids at one temple, with a flare of beaded quills further proving age and status. Dark eyes faded to milky amber squinted in the brilliance; more and more she found Sun an enemy rather than the ally Palatan accepted. Shoulders sagged soft beneath a capelet of stained horsehide, and her bowed legs, once thick with riding muscle, instead juddered soft. Sloth and corpulence had long held Chogah—daughter of Beloved Ones, Alekšu of duskLands—in their sway.

Longer yet had Chogah held sway over their tribe. Indeed, she sloughed a furious gaze back and forth, satisfied as many gave way with body and eyes. Respect, a'io. But more, apprehension. Fear.

None of the latter moved Palatan. The ones waiting sensed it, expectant.

"Have you waited long?" Chogah asked, almost courteous.

Beneath civility, the real battle was winding up.

You cannot win, cur. You wield the wildest, perhaps, of Grandmother's sacred limbs, but it matters little. Wind shall choke you, Earth smother you. And should Rain decide to enter our exchange? A chuckle. *Rain's daughter, River, has ever been able to douse your enthusiasm.*

This time Palatan let the anger come, feed the flames. *Rain quenches but cannot quell; She brings steam to banish sickness. Earth and Fire, bunged together too long, too angry, erupt into the hot-blood torrent of melted rock to sear all They touch. Wind but kindles Fire to sweep across our plains in a swath of cleansing.*

You know nothing, weakling! Chogah's not-voice hissed, a darkling dart of poison. *You fear. You fear your own Power, the destruction He carries—*

Do I? Snarl. Shield. "We have," Palatan curled his voice all too pleasant, "waited far too long for thisSun's passage."

Ai, it was not the first time Palatan a'Šaákfo had stood upon the Breaking Ground to challenge.

But it would be the last.

$$\phi \quad \phi \quad \phi$$

2
TOKELA

The talking drum fell silent, yet ša's voice refused to die.

It was, after all, drumtalk that had coaxed him here, prompted the long, tendon-burning climb of the terraces. None stayed him—better, none saw him. Boots scuffing against wood and stone, lungs heaving, thighs quivering, Tokela gained the summit.

Alone.

The drum's aftermath lingered, a second heartbeat behind his breastbone. Hanging in the dense trees like mist and breath, quivering through the massive cloudstone cliffs duskside of the Mound, pulsing outward and beyond the driftwood railing that seemed to sprout from the red rocks. Floating, across the wide, copper-ink expanse, and echoing against glimmers.

Always, River waited.

Tokela's nostrils flared: Wind brought scents of silt and wet foliage upward, then tossed his forelock into his eyes, curtaining his sight, thick and dark. A toss of head, then a shove of fingers did no good. Tokela ended up tying it back as he leaned over the railing, leather and wood talismans tangling against his callused fingers.

Not enough. He could smell and hear but not yet see, so he gave the hair-tie one last yank before snaking through the gnarled railing. One hand making firm purchase, he angled outward and over the edge. River's current was strong thisSun. It should be soon. Tokela tilted outward, sinewy knuckles straining pale, and looked downRiver, vigilant for an event foretold by the Grandfather drum.

Even outlier craft came for the festivals. And Tokela always watched them approach, like fishers perched with nets upon the coppery crags up from Naišwyrh'uq, the Great Mound-beside-River.

Shouts, first. Tokela leaned out even farther, the railing creaking in his hands. DownRiver, the mists roiled and curled—fore-drafts, it must be!—then parting. The craft heeled into view, reedweave sails set wing and wing. A big one—a true pehni chito!

Unfortunately, ša wasn't the one Tokela sought.

But no matter, for Sun gave an abrupt spill from pewter clouds, setting the craft a-gleam like dryLands silver. The combination of light and wet and wood was startling. Perfect. Tokela's breath caught and held. His fingertips itched. Twitched, longing for expression. He squirmed back through the railing, flitted a glance side to side, sighed, then smiled.

Still alone.

A quick rummage in the hide pouch slung over one shoulder produced a palmful of small bone barbs, a sheathed adze, a thin tangle of trawling gut and hooks... where was it? It should be...

There. With a satisfied huff, Tokela pulled a small roll of wabadeh hide from his pouch. Another glance—making sure—as he hunkered down by the cliff edge. A quick finger-comb through thick hair found the tiny braid that secured a hidden graphite stump, while his other hand flattened the hide scrap upon the rock between his knees.

A small piece from the inner haunch, this, scraped soft and stretched thin. Better still, it had been bleached pale as the trade grain the elders ground to make breads for Dancing Moons; the graphite needed only to define shadow and edge. Tokela's long fingers, deft by nature and quick by necessity, sketched the sweeps and curves of the approaching craft.

He also kept watch upon the terrace stair.

Such vigilance, however, soon slipped its tether to drift. River's tang of haze and brack hummed a wordless song as he worked, wrapping about him, sinking him deeper in. His breath lulled to a soft whistle, in time with the hum and the scritch-scritch-scritch of graphite against hide.

A shout. Tokela juddered, blinked through gluey eyes at the craft framed by driftwood railing. It furled its wings, heeling sideways. The shout had come from one of the Riverwalkers, swinging a bow line to catch a float anchor. Sun already nuzzled the lush treetops on River's far bank. Tokela flexed his fingers, stiff and smudged, and...

A sudden and familiar waft of herb balm touched his nostrils. A shocked catch of breath followed, with the ripple of tiny copper bells. Tokela palmed the graphite and hunched his shoulders.

He'd been caught sketching. Again.

Sliding his eyes upward, he started to explain to his aunt that he'd only meant to capture the craft in memory. Just the craft, and the light about it. It would burn holes behind his eyes until he did, and he'd not meant anything by it, none had been about to see...

Neither did Inhya seem to see him. Ebon eyes sprung wide, cheeks so ashen her pearl-inked Clan Marks were only just visible, she stared at the hide between his knees. Only those numerous copper bells spoke, a trembly shiver upon the one splash of jewel-bright she wore: hearth-chieftain's head wrap of turquoise wormweave.

Tokela's gaze followed hers, lowering to take in the sketch. Further explanations balled in his throat and choked him.

The boat *was* lovely—one of his best efforts—winged like flyingKin, rigging evocative of spinner webs damp with Sun's rising. River cradled the craft in long sweeps of shadow to support the cream and white reflections, yet...

Yet.

A face peeked out from between wings and webbing. And he'd no memory of making it.

Ša was... well, ša resembled firstPeople. Sort of. Yet the eyes were too round, too small. A long face with neck even moreso, ears set too low, nose and mouth too small, chin too pointed, skin too pale, barely touched by the graphite.

Tokela had never seen one of the outLanders close enough to guess at whether his rendition was accurate, but he'd heard stories. Ai, he'd heard too many stories.

His hearth-mother's expression told yet another. She recognised this being. Somehow.

Swift as swimmingKin, Inhya darted forwards, reaching for the sketch.

Nigh as quick, Tokela's hand grasped her wrist. "Who—?"

"Better to ask *what*." Quick, as if Inhya regretted saying that much. "Let go of me."

Tokela obeyed—and in the next heartbeat wished he hadn't. Inhya snatched up the sketch and crumpled it, shoving it out of sight in the pouch hanging from her belt. Tokela looked away, muting the questions itching upon his tongue. He didn't need them, anyway. He was fairly certain what the person... thing... was.

The one unspeakable possibility.

Sun had slipped behind a cloud, no longer fingering the boat's sides. The sails had been lowered to reveal a skeleton of bare rails, no longer winged with shadow and gossamer. He'd drawn their memory, a'io, yet had somehow added an image of something he'd never seen.

Not only outLander, but Chepiś.

Tokela scrambled to his feet.

"It's of no matter. But making likenesses is forbidden. You know this, Tokela." The diminutive intended fondness, yet Inhya's eyes narrowed into knives; Tokela sketched them, mute and unwilling, in his heart. "Why are you malingering up here? Have you forgotten?"

Forgotten. He'd forgotten something? Tokela couldn't help a slight shift, foot to foot. The wooden beads dangling from his woven hip wrap swayed and chattered, betraying the movement. Escape was impossible; Inhya blocked the stair.

It didn't bode well. But then, of late it seldom did.

Caught up with helping in the salting dens, Madoc neverthe-less heard the talking drum's message: the first of the River-walker traders had been sighted. It took a while to extricate him-self from the salting duties. No doubt his elder cousin already perched on the uppermost terrace, watching.

It made one surety amidst Tokela's curious habits. And of late, curiosity had turned to serious puzzle. Madoc liked puzzles well enough, but not in regards to Tokela. Moreover, Madoc had something to share, something surely more important than star-ing at Riverwalker vessels with faraway eyes.

Well, at least he knew where to find Tokela thisSun.

Madoc burst into the compound, skipping the daggers of light that filtered down from the cliff heights.

"Ho, chieftain-son, would you leap Sun?" a passerby teased.

Madoc didn't slow, chirped back: "To leave Him for others, old uncle!"

The good-natured laugh spread, and Madoc joined in. Hard to remain solemn during First Running. Better to let thisSun's bliss fill him. Whatever reasons the adults gathered were, after all, in-consequential. The season's first run of silvers had been spotted downRiver. It meant work, ai'o, but it also meant gathering and games and dancing and cookpots filled to brimming...

Like now. The teasing odors wafting from the cooking hearths thought to slow Madoc, but he kept going—*steadfast as the best Naisgwyr'uq hunter,* he congratulated himself—and raced upward as he reached the main stair.

By the fifth terrace, however, he'd stopped for a breather. Foiling many floods, the Great Mound also thwarted quick as-cent. The hands Madoc propped against his hide-clad knees gave little comfort: pale streaks of salt, callused every bit as hard as Tokela's, but podgy instead of quick-fingered, not yet nimble enough for the finer tasks of netting upkeep. Instead Madoc found solace in eyeing the considerable distance he'd already climbed. Not many his age could run so well and fast, after all.

Still, good to wait a little longer before resuming his climb. Nothing worse than heaving his way to the top terraces—not only from the dignity befitting a son of chieftains a'Naišwyrh, but because Madoc hoped to surprise Tokela.

More proof Madoc was strong for his age: it didn't take long to catch his breath. Tossing the thatch of Sun-tipped, unruly bronze from his face, Madoc skipped upward, counting another four and two of terraces by the dens and hollows of each level. Almost there. And not as Tokela oft teased him—heavy-footed as a herd of shaggy curvehorns—but sly, and gentle-quick.

"—you so soon forgotten?"

Madoc hesitated midstep. His dam's voice, stern and subdued, floated about the topmost terrace. A pause followed, then a low, halting response. Tokela.

Ai, and what had his cousin done now? Madoc crept back down to the hollow beneath the upper scaffolding, peering up through the wooden slats. He saw the soles of his dam's boots, then the midcalf sway of her Forest-coloured kirtles revealing the bright turquoise head wrap limned against treetops and Sky. There was no sight of Tokela, only the familiar comfort of scent— evergreen, sweat grown sharper thisHoop, and a hint of River wrack. Tokela must be over against the cliff edge railing.

He'd even less fear of heights than most, had Tokela. Would lean out into Wind from the highest branches, enough to sent Madoc's heart aflutter, but never once had Wind betrayed him.

"Tokela." Inhya's kirtles gave another sway. "Even during festival there is work to be done. First Running comes. Branches must be felled in preparation. Your uncle chose you and several others to accompany him."

Madoc frowned. Choosing the right branches and taking them to the spawning streams, receptacles for the coming harvest of tasty roe, was a task given to oških. Tracing his own hennaed Clan Marks, he frowned harder. If Tokela was old enough for the felling, then he was old enough to have his Marks replaced with indigo, to take his next path. And that meant Tokela was old enough to leave the den he shared with Madoc and the other children and remove to where the males laired. Tokela would no longer be ahlóssa, but oških.

Madoc didn't like this, not in the least.

"It is an honour." Inhya sounded... uncertain? "Why should Sarinak not include you?"

Tokela didn't answer.

"Perhaps it would help."

"Help how?" Soft, proper and respectful to one's elders. Yet. There was something... wayward underneath. Lately when Tokela spoke, his tone flirted with the boundaries of courtesy. As if he'd found a secret, one he would not tell.

"What happened is a sign, nothing more. You are too far past your changing time, that is all. Your heart longs for a place."

What had happened? And... changing? Tokela wasn't past any time. Tokela'd had the wyrh tree tattooed upon his ribs several summerings past, true, but even then he'd not gone to the oških dens like many did. Tokela hadn't so much as started to wrap his clout differently, though this past wintering had seen him grow taller, quieter, making Madoc fear the worst. But nothing had come of it, to Madoc's relief.

Tokela wasn't oških, not yet! All oških did was scuffle and preen, swagger and rut each other!

Sinking back against the stones, Madoc reached into his own memory. He himself had been possessed of three summerings when Tokela's dam and sire had been taken by River. Tokela'd had ten. Now Madoc was twelve summerings, so Tokela possessed...

Madoc's frown turned puzzled. Most took the path from ahlóssa to oških before they reached twenty summerings.

"Why should it matter?" Tokela answered, still soft. Still coiling, underground, with not-quite-resentment. "Why are you both so set upon—?"

"Why are you not? If you go to fell, then it's seen that you're starting down a proper path." More silence. "You know he won't ask again."

"Then we should both be content."

"Content? Content cannot stop the talk, growing with every return of Brother Moon!"

Talk. What talk? Madoc cocked his head to better hear.

"You've been given an honour you will not refuse. A chance to prove..." Inhya's voice trailed off.

"Prove what, my mother?"

Madoc winced. Tokela sounded more of frostKin than the affectionate brother-cousin Madoc knew.

"You misconstrue." No less adept at frost, Inhya padded nigh silent across the terrace and came to a halt directly over Madoc's hiding place. "I've every right to remove you to the oških den. Why I haven't is yet another source of speculation. But I know that you're not—"

"I know," ai, still so soft, "what I'm not."

A breath, held between then, saying nothing that Madoc could understand. Then another shiver of bells; Inhya padding closer towards Tokela.

"It remains that you are not yet oških. This is not your fault. But, now. This... this thing, this... image you've made." It wavered into a silence laden with too many things to count.

Ai, that was it. Tokela had been caught sketching. Again.

If only their father could understand. Tokela's lovely, lifelike sketches weren't Shaping! Madoc knew what Shaping was—sorcery, evil, interference with the natural ways! Like the Moonspale Chepiś giants, who had long ago Shaped parts of thisLand into unnatural Other.

"*They* let me sketch." Tokela's voice made unwilling escape.

"And you know why, Tokela. Your father came of midLands; he chose not to understand our mistrust of such things. Your dam..." Inhya's voice quavered; through the slats Madoc saw her grasp the pouch at her hip with a rustle and clink of dangling shells. The touch seemed to give her strength. "Your dam was heedless of too many things."

Again, Tokela fell silent.

"You broach dangerous paths, my son. This... thing that has shown itself to you"—another incomprehensible clutch at the pouch—"is a warning. You must cast aside anything that further threatens your place here, with your family."

"Do you think I *don't*...?" It strangled into silence. Footsteps, stumbling-quick, from the far cliff edge, and Tokela's figure lurched into view between the wooden slats of the terrace, making for the stair.

Madoc angled back farther into hiding and held his breath.

"You are a'Naišwyrh!" Inhya's voice snapped like a midLands herder's whip.

Tokela halted as his boot touched the top step. He turned, slow, and Madoc could see his face at last. Above the faded Clan Marks livid against flushed cheeks, his eyes gleamed from the coppery black shadow of his forelock; through some oddling trick of Sun they seemed more high-polished silver than indigo-and-black.

Tokela closed those eyes, ducked his head, and said, "A'io, hearth-chieftain."

So hoarse, so flat and resigned. Madoc hunched beneath the weight, miserable. It was the one thing he'd ever wanted and never received; to somehow be as deft a weaver as amongst mid-Lands folk, repair this frayed skein seeming to rip more, every Sun's passage, within his own den.

Tokela turned way, started to descend. Inhya's voice halted him midstep, soft and somehow wounded.

"Your dam was of thisLand, raised in the footsteps of her sire's People. Before her heart... changed, she welcomed me here, too. She was daughter and sister to Beloved Ones."

Tokela kept shaking his head. Madoc was unsure whether it denied Inhya, or the sudden glitter in his nigh-hidden eyes.

"This is your home. She would have wanted—"

"My dam is dead."

The shock of hearing it—so blunt, so perilous—stilled Madoc's breath against his teeth.

"And she would have told me what that"—a gesture towards Inhya—"is. Told me why."

"Tokela." A warning. "There are things that should not soil our tongues. Your dam spoke of such things, heedless, and look where it got her."

"It got her," Tokela said, deathly quiet, "with me. And that's what this is about, isn't it?"

A small, choked sound came from Inhya.

No hesitation this time; merely heavy footfalls, stumbling then strengthening, gaining. Madoc shoved back hard into the shadows of his hiding place just as Tokela came hurtling downwards.

Madoc stayed pressed there, his heart nigh lifting the tunic from his breast, the rock cool against his back. On the terrace above, Inhya's hands came to rest on the faded grey of the railing. Madoc knew those hands well, had known them since birth and even before, their slender, callused power smoothing over the belly that had sheltered him... for Madoc remembered, even though he'd been told it was impossible to know such things.

His dam held a thin-stretched and crumpled skin. It resembled the bits of hide Tokela scavenged for his sketches.

"It can't be," Inhya whispered. "I won't let it be!" Her hands clenched, and she laid her head against them, started to sob.

Madoc slid down the stone and curled his knees tightly to his chest, burying his face in the thick weave of his leggings. He didn't understand. He wasn't sure he wanted to.

The compound was crowded: people heading to the communal cooking hearths, children laughing and fretting, dogs barking, guests arriving and being settled. Then, voices, rising in surprise; hands making as if to grasp Tokela as he darted, twisted, and slipped through.

None of it mattered. By the time he gained the stair to Talking Bluff, Tokela was running.

He clambered up the drum heights three strides at a time, refusing to look back or so much as cast a glance at the shining, massive ribbon of water that fascinated... repelled... dominated him. From the moment She had taken his parents, River had been both succour and terror.

Now, it was the latter. He fled Her. Fled Naišwyrh'uq.

The drumKeeper, lounging by the great talking drums and smoking a pipe with an acquaintance, gave a small yip of query. Perhaps they wondered at his haste. Perhaps it had nothing to do with him.

No matter—he kept going.

Away. Outward. Over stony crags, through a clearing of scattered logs and stumps recently harvested for Fire's feeding, into a meadow. Tall new grass bent in the wake of his passage, swaying with lastdark's wet. A clump of grazingKin spooked in his wake.

Tokela wanted trees to take him in, bracken and moss to muffle and hide his passing, hidden pools still enough to be silent and clear enough to wash bone-deep apprehensions. His shadow flitted beside him in an unending race, then flickered and disappeared as he ran from field into Forest. The going slowed him, but only a little. Tokela's feet had eyes; his body tensed keen with running-memory, his nostrils flared to scent his way, his eyes gleamed with the darksight gifted to all kin—footed, furred, feathered, and hoofed—by the Grandmother who bore them upon Her belly.

Over rotting stumps and under low-hanging, mossy branches of standingKin; here a twist, there a leap. One of hedgeKin puffed up to twice ša's bulk and growled from a burrow entry as Tokela trod too close; a tree-lounging wildcat twitched ša's tail, beryl eyes watching avidly for a half-breath then slitting, disinterested.

Finally, quivering limbs and burning lungs enforced a floundering halt. Tokela propped palms on thighs. His eyes stung, his tunic clung to the small of his back, the thin ahlóssa braid wrapped slick and serpentine about his throat.

Truth more and more seemed the ultimate pursuer, and him Dancing it from childish whisper to ripe reproach.

You are a'Naišwyrh!

Hard to believe, when she didn't.

Wind had fallen. The only sound was Tokela's lungs labouring against the cool, damp air. Forest lay sparser here, Sun loosing gilt arrows through the treetops, and...

Tokela stiffened.

He'd never seen such a thing before. Never wandered into this particular edge of wild. Yet he'd no doubt what it was.

Šilombiš'okpulo. The forbidden place.

And an extraordinary, outLand thing guarded it.

Tokela crept closer, every sense twitching. The arch seemed of rare, long-polished stone; it reached into the ancient canopy and also tunneled deep. A guardian like—yet unlike—the tight-woven trees that led into the Great Mound. And tall, ai, it reached taller than five of Tokela standing atop himself, glowing ebon-smooth as the obsidian point to a MedicineKeeper's knife. On either side as far as Tokela could see, the forbidden place lay choked by a tangle of brier. Coiled unnaturally tight, as if even a stray bough didn't dare to grow sideways, and the scattered bits of sun that filtered through lent no light. The thing seemed to suck them up, swallow them. Nothing reflected.

As if from far away, a small Riverling could be heard, making Her way through the thicket, gleaming and glittering through briar. She was unafraid of this thing. So must he be.

Nevertheless, fear and fascination did battle within his breast. Fingers twitching with the urge to sketch it, capture it, Tokela drew closer, step by wary step.

Got a mere five paces away before he realised what he was doing. He halted. Crouched. Contemplated.

None here could say him nay. None would even know. It would be a challenge, to see if he could capture the beauty and terror of such a thing in a mere sketch. Perhaps even carry the memory of it with him...

Take the image of something Shaped back into his home? The thought prompted a shudder, bone-deep. Why would he ever think of such a thing?

Perhaps the thing had the power to turn his heart. He could feel the draw of it, an oddling, silent, thrum mimicking his heart-beat. All the taleKeepers warned how there was a arch of unnatural stone and briar that guarded an evil place—a place where Chepiś sorcery had festered and gone mad.

He should go back. Leave this forbidden place behind and never think upon it again.

Deliberately, Tokela rose, eyed the thing, then turned away.

A sharp *crack!* made him whirl back towards it, hand to knife.

The gate... entryway... whatever-it-was spoke again, with another *crack* then a deep drone. Shards of what looked like SkyFire chased across its surface—only this flared blue-white, not gold, amidst pitch. Tokela froze beneath the burst of light and sound, staring, transfixed, whilst all the while the thing flashed and leapt, speaking... n'da, it was a Dance. It moved and sparked akin to the rare Star metal he'd occasionally seen in trader hands, or the shimmer-melt writhe of copper in a consecrated forge.

It seemed full of intention. It seemed... alive.

Perhaps it was. If something Danced, his dam's dam had once said, then ša wasn't *it*, wasn't a thing. Ša had a place on Grandmother's belly, and a name.

So Tokela jerked his chin upward, answered with the outLand name used by taleKeepers. "You are *t'rešalt*."

Another spackle of light and sound, as if in acknowledgement.

Names had power. His own, never spoken even amidst his family, had meanings coiled like serpentKin beneath: Tohwakeli-fitčiluka. Eyes of Stars.

Chepiś, it was said, had come from Stars. The same Stars forbidden to any save the ancestors.

Look where it got her.

It got her with me.

Had this been the same place through which his dam had passed to meet with Chepiś? Could it answer riddles?

Tokela wrapped his arms about his knees and rocked back and forth, contemplating the entry with darkened eyes and darker thoughts. The *t'rešalt* smelt of Sky gathering a storm, and emitted a strange, not-quite-croon that teased at the edges of hearing.

A question? An answer?

He lurched upward, drew the dagger from the sheath at his calf, and strode forwards.

"I tried," Inhya said, settling beside the hearth.

Sarinak said nothing, laying the meal before her with no less of the grave pride he'd shown upon their firstdark's sharing of hearth and blanket. The horseClans moieties required a spouse who could provide a good meal, a good tipo to shelter a family, and a fine string of horses. Sarinak a'Naišwyrh had, of course, possessed none of those. So in wooing Inhya a'Šaákfo, he'd learned from his granddam how to prepare more than trail food. He'd set up a scrim of colourful woollens within the dens where so many of his tribe had espoused their mates, and if the gathered mounts had been, instead of the lithe horses of her birthing-tribe, several braces of stout dogs and a small herd of curvehorns—they were enough to pull any travelling rig she would care to load.

Even Inhya's granddam had given grudging approval to "that Mound dwelling whelp's efforts."

The Hoop had spun nearly thirty winterings since Inhya had accepted Sarinak's offerings, but in this much he still insisted: upon each quartering of Brother Moon, with skills uncustomary to males a'Naišwyrh, he'd cook a meal with his own hands, upon their own hearth, in their own company.

Such times, naturally, were a perfect opportunity to speak of heart matters.

"I tried," Inhya ventured again.

Sarinak put a wide-mouthed copper drinking bowl between them and poured steaming water from a fat jar. A shrug lifted his broad shoulders. "You waste breath with that one."

"Little breath is wasted in what talk is being made."

"You worry overmuch about talk. Folk are made to jabber. It means nothing."

"I found him up Overlook." *Sketching* lay upon her tongue; she bit it back. Her birthing-tribe held symbol makers in reverence, but Naisgwyr'uq had suffered from their proximity to forbidden Shaper's places. They allowed no such tolerance. The twisted remnants of Winnowing, so long ago but lingering, had burnt hot-deep into the memory of her spouse's tribe. *Her* tribe.

Sarinak crumbled spicebark into the steaming copper basin. The heady, warm scent rose, curling about their den. Yet such comfort did little to allay concern.

"I took others to the felling duty." Sarinak sank onto the blanket beside her. "Tokela is too like his dam, heedless of honour or propriety."

And even moreso had Winnowing's memory leapt into flames when Tokela's dam, sister of Sarinak's sire, had defiantly fanned them to consort with outLanders.

Lakisa. The whisper within Inhya's heart would never pass her lips. Respect and mourning. Love... and fear. *Your son becomes lost in River's song, sees in Her what none should. Makes likenesses of Them.*

Surrendering to such things could become an initial step down an illicit path. First the lure of an Elemental, then the thrall leading to possession, and from that merely several steps more to the ultimate transgression: manipulating the Elementals.

Shaping.

It was why any transgressions amidst their own were cleansed by the Alekšu or, if necessary, purged. It was why Chepiś and their places were anathema. Chepiś honoured nothing, used frightful abilities to twist things into abomination with what Power their kind had long ago Winnowed from Grandmother's heart. The cost was high, true: those made outcast as with Sarinak's younger brother; or like to Inhya's own brother, who'd fallen possessed in adolescence. At least Palatan had been cured, and now helped others so cursed.

Her thoughts lingered upon him, fond. Palatan should arrive soon. First Running should last a quartering of Brother Moon; the councils and festivities ran for several Suns before and after. Surely they could speak of her fears for Tokela...

N'da, her brother's empathy would be tested with this. Palatan, like others, might suspect the rumours of Tokela's siring for truth, but he'd no proof. Even Sarinak refused to acknowledge any of it. Tokela lived with them, but Inhya doubted he understood the implications any more than he'd recognised the likeness still crumpled in her pouch.

Inhya had. The creature was unmistakable, and that Tokela had been able to conjure him was...

She would give the likeness to Fire, first chance. Not that any offering could purge this worst of secrets, kept to shelter the son of her oških lovemate. Her son, now.

It got her with me.

Foresworn, whichever path she took.

"Inhya?" Sarinak peered at her, a bowl extended in one hand.

Inhya took it and looked down, continued her tread of deception's anxious path. "Tokela was watching the Riverwalker craft. Again."

"The younglings always watch, particularly upon the festival of First Running. All the comings and goings and excitement." Sarinak applied himself to parcelling the spit-roasted fowl. "They fancy adventure, and what they think is freedom. They comprehend little of what it truly means to live as outlier. Outcast."

It soothed her heart to watch him. Her spouse could steady the cliffs beneath their feet if only by the deliberate economy of his motions. In the privacy of their own place, he had unwrapped the Sky-hued scarf from his head, letting thick, emmer-coloured waves tumble back from his forehead. The long twistlocks at his temples, darkened with oil and wrapped with carved-wood beads, lay flung behind his powerful shoulders, shining dark gilt against the hearth's flickering warmth.

Sarinak a'Naišwyrh, son of Beloved ones and now Moundchieftain in his own right, had come young to his status. It had not bent him but made him stronger, moulded from the copper clay of dawnLand's protective cliffs.

"D'you remember when you first came here?"

He often spoke thus when they had this time together, with just that hint of satisfaction. Always it brought forth from Inhya a fond, equally satisfied smile. A sharp breach of custom, a fem leaving her dam's tent to make a home amongst a spouse's tribe! Yet in truth, Inhya had found little hardship in trading nomadic duskLands vagaries for a settled life here in dawnLands, within the Great Mound-beside-River. Thick RainForests, dens dug deep into the cliff mound, and an everpresent River's chill regard gave reassuring boundaries to existence. Inhya had fancied Sarinak's ambition, then fancied him, then loved him as ever she had Lakisa...

Sarinak, as usual, nipped at the heels of Inhya's thoughts. "I blame the wyrhling for filling our eldest son's heart with too many tales."

Sarinak's outlier once-brother had indeed given Tokela more Stars in his eyes than he already possessed, but... "That one has been long away."

"Perhaps Tokela watches for the wyrhling's return." Another snort, disgruntled, as he portioned the tender meat into equal servings. "Perhaps we'd best weir that stream before ša floods. It could be to everyone's good, did we send Tokela away from River."

Inhya's brows quirked. "To Aylaniś? She owes hearthing trade, true enough—"

"There's enough foolishness in Tokela without trebling it running wild as hareKin with your brother's People."

Inhya raised her brows, peered at Sarinak.

"Don't cast such eyes at me, spouse, you know what I mean." He leaned forwards, glower turning to grin. Inhya had to grin back—she couldn't help it—but the expression congealed as Sarinak continued, "I thought, perhaps, to send Tokela to his sire's folk."

And who are those? she wanted to counter, and didn't.

"His sire's uncle, for one."

Inhya sniffed. "I wouldn't loan a dog I disliked to Galenu a'Hassun."

"Hunh." Sarinak offered another smile and pushed the platter within her easy reach. "True. But the time is coming when Galenu could demand sire-rights."

"You and I will fly to Everwintering Mountain first. That one! Nothing but a selfish old khatak." Inhya deliberately slurred the dawnLands word for "solitary" into insult: *withered, can't earn himself a spouse.* "He's no fit guardian. I'd little honour my lovemate's memory, did I shrug off our son's welfare so lightly."

Galenu! He'd bewitched Lakisa from Inhya's side with his forbidden tales. Worse, he'd introduced Lakisa to the forbidden places. And not so much as soiled his fingers with the consequences. While Inhya hoped—desperate, an orison to rise and set with Brother Moon and His siblings—her lovemate's son would mature more of firstPeople, less of Chepiś. A dangerous wager from its undertaking, but her heart had felt strong enough to hold it.

Then.

"Lakisa'ailiq"—Sarinak gave sharp and deliberate invocation of the dead—"may she walk lightly the Long Path, is gone. Bones picked and honoured in ashes long given to River. Yet still her son raises her Spirit in your eyes." He shook his head and took up his food. "Ai, the sooner Tokela enters the oških den, the better."

Madoc looked everywhere.

River, first; searching Her thighs in the lee of the massive Mound. A breach of manners, to stare so intently at the craft moored, bobbing gently in the current, but they were merely wyrhlings, and Madoc had to find Tokela, after all.

When there still were no signs, Madoc headed farther down-River.

He and Tokela had with their own hands built a wykupeh amongst the thick trunk branches of a weeping tree. A few leagues downRiver wasn't so far if one ran the distance, which Madoc did.

But a thorough search of both wykupeh and the sand-and-rock cove that bordered their haven garnered nothing.

Where could Tokela be?

Disconsolate, Madoc finally gave up, knowing he'd not find Tokela had Tokela truly decided to hide. Instead Madoc ran back upRiver and took his time scaling the crest of Talking Bluff. The drumKeeper—weathered by long watches in Sun and Rain to as deep a sienna as the drum resting at her side—diverted him, offering a piece of sapsweet fit to coax a smile from her chieftain's son.

Soon Madoc was not only helping the drumKeeper's ahlóssa daughter put away more of the sweet chews, but also tossing a game of bones on a brightly painted hide.

He was sure the *t'rešalt* would stay him.

Or perhaps he'd just hoped.

Caverns were home to Tokela, a comfort—but this outland thing was neither, lingering overhead, an ominous weight. Beneath his feet the ground seemed... lax, more mossy floor than any rock, yet his eyes detected nothing but more of the oddling not-stone. Any impulse to reach out quelled itself as if struck. He found himself crouched and creeping—as if it were even remotely possible that he could bump against the lofty ceiling. His shaking fingers kept touching his knife. He kept moving.

Deeper than first gathered, the *t'rešalt* lay bare of overgrowth and darker than any dark—save for the spastic lightning-shards that occasionally spread over its surface and... well, they seemed to follow him, a wake of not-Fire that pocked his eyes in blinding white shards. His nostrils, too, were overwhelmed, filled with the charged, silt-wet cloak of an approaching storm. A shivery rash of sensation washed over his skin, lifting hair from scalp to ankles. His pace dragged more and more, a scrape and *shuss* just that much too loud. Gritting his teeth, Tokela forged onward.

In truth it was only several tens of steps, with the thing sparking and snapping and crackling about him, his breaths skittering, faint but determined, amongst the cacophony. He counted them, speeding more and more as the thing pressed upon him, tight and empty and unending...

Tokela staggered past the *t'rešalt* and fell to his hands and knees, released.

Counted a brace of his own heartbeats.

Looked up, eyes ghosting with white sparks, and irising all the wider to take in the blessed normalcy of dark. His heart, conversely, tightened and twisted against his breastbone. Now he was here—in here—he wasn't sure what to do with the reality.

What that reality meant.

It was said that only Chepiś could venture past the *t'rešalt*.

But his mother had done.

Taking refuge in the thought, Tokela tossed the hair from his eyes and rose to his haunches, curious.

Not so different, after all, than the deeper woods north of Naisgwyr'uq. Trees, towering over him in muted shades of jet and downRiver malachite, their canopy so far over his head it didn't even feel as if there were any ceiling, only darkness rising and melding into forever. Moss and lichens, with old logs fallen in their own rot, making fecund nurseries for fresh shoots and fingerling plants. Wet, dripping from the dark and hanging in the air.

Only...

This place felt different, somehow. It *smelt* different.

Forbidden. Misbegotten monsters wait, eat curious ahlóssa who don't stay upon their bedshelf, who wander where they shouldn't...

Nostrils flaring, Tokela rocked to his feet. He was being foolish. Nothing had changed. Moreover, he hadn't changed. Still in his own skin, still possessed of hale limbs, with breath to fill his lungs and heart pounding, a rhythmic if agitated drum, in his breast. Still of firstPeople.

His gaze, unwilling, slid back to the *t'rešalt*, which looked much the same—only darker, those odd sparks and cracks muted, gone quiet.

Until something erupted, Stars from pitch, with the sound of wet droplets flung into Fire's embrace. Tokela jumped like hareKin. Averted his gaze.

And went deeper into Šilombiš'okpulo.

3
ANAHLI

She'd forgotten how Air was weighted, here. Ša dripped from the trees, glittering and heavy. Ša hung in her lungs, lingering there even as she exhaled. Ša puffed her long braids from oiled sleekness, and tickled her ankles as she dismounted. The fringe of her leggings made dark swathes in the damp grass as she walked forwards, scratching her mare's black-splotched face and gathering the rein. So sodden, here, that trees grew unhindered save by each other, and had to be cleared to make proper grazing.

Letting the breath escape her pursed lips, Anahli a'Šaákfo watched it vent upward like the steam escaping the winter caverns in duskLands. It wasn't even that cold.

And she'd better get used to it.

Her mare danced in place, snoring from curled nostrils, eyes on the herd grazing the other side of the clearing. Anahli grinned and slipped the rope from the mare's nose, stepped back. The mare exploded into a run, bucking and squealing and farting. The other visitors—horses, shorthorns and even a few lammoi from hillClans—responded to the mare's high spirits. Tails flagging, they lapped the clearing, once coming so close Anahli's leathers rustled with their passing.

She didn't retreat. Instead she cupped both hands to her mouth and let out a whoop.

Another answered from behind her—more a whistle, really, and then her name echoing against the trees. "Anahli!"

Another smile teasing her lip, she pretended not to hear. As if such a thing were possible when Kuli was in full voice.

"Hihlyanahli!!"

She turned about just in time for several hands of giggling, wriggling little brother to leap into her arms and try to knock her flat. Laughing, she let him, and they rolled in the damp grass.

Which just set the herd off again. Anahli's black-spotted mare in the lead, they made for the far line of trees. The cattle lumbered after, stub tails flung high, and even the phlegmatic lammoi snorted and circled the clearing with their curious, rocking gait. Watching them go, still laughing, Anahli rolled to her feet and peered down at herself: best leathers smudged with damp and green; colourful skeins and fur mussed where they'd been plaited into her braids.

"Ai, now look what you've done!" She gave a half-hearted smack at Kuli's cinnabar topknot. "How am I to make a proper impression if I look like I've been rolling in the grass with ahlóssa?"

"You have been rolling in the grass with ahlóssa." Kuli looked up at her, flat on his back in the grass with an impenitent grin. "I was watching for you from Overlook; saw you riding ahead! Where are Aška and Yeka?"

"Soon. Our dam and sire rode slowly with the elders."

Kuli's eyes—moss-coloured as their sire's—widened. "Which ones... Ai, not old Chogah! She can hardly even sit a horse any more, why is she—?"

"Show respect, little Fox." It was purposeful, pointed. "If you're going to be ugly about Chogah, I'll leave you here."

"I'll just follow you. I don't mean to be ugly. But she started it. She's ugly to Yeka and you know it."

"That's not yours to judge." Anahli knew she was puffing up like poked serpentKin, but the subject made her tired. And angry. "Our sire isn't the one who lost honour and place."

"Chogah's honour left long ago! Yeka only did what he should've done long ago, since she wouldn't step down on her own—"

"Maybe, maybe not, but you've no business, ahlóssa, prattling elders' talk when you don't understand any of it."

"I understand more than you think." Kuli's chin quivered—rebellion and hurt.

Both got to Anahli; she understood them all too well. "Come here, my little Fox," she relented. "Let's not argue when I've missed you so."

He sprang up and sailed into her, hugging her fierce. "I've missed you too! Come on, then—The Mound is bursting at the seams, all these people. And there's food!"

As first daughter, riding ahead was a breach of manners. Anahli should have remained, entered the arched and ancient entwined conifers of Naišwyrh'uq's redoubt at her dam's side. Should have, at the very least, rejoined her tribe to formally greet the hosts of First Running, and witness the honour done to the new-Broken Alekšu.

Who just happened to be her sire.

Instead Anahli took some time replaiting her mussed quartet of braids into shining, gaily-wrapped ropes that waved about her hips. She let Kuli, chattering all the while, help brush the dirt from her leathers, then followed him—not to find their parents, but to the cooking hearths.

She was noticed, no question. Instead of a decorative head-scarf, her uncovered, carmine-daubed hair part ended in long ebon braids. Instead of woven split kirtles swishing, or a rich, full tunic, her lanky thighs were clad in pale leathers with her best fringed bag adorning one hip, and her muscular arms garbed only with a spiral tattoo on her drawing bicep, with copper rings stacking up the other.

One handsome male a'Naišwyrh—another oških, from his lack of headwear—was eyeing her from several places down in line. He looked mature enough to court opposites. Anahli wasn't. "like to like" was traditional across the allied tribes, but horseClans customs weren't so strict. And males had the illicit fascination of difference.

With a dip of head and a small smile, Anahli turned away.

Kuli was already diving into a helping of fish stew.

"Your people follow?" One of the hearth tenders smiled, of-fering Anahli a steaming bowl that smelled just as glorious as Kuli's. The next poured bark-and-honey tea.

"They are." With a grateful gesture Anahli took both. The steam from the tea warmed her nostrils, the bark bowl her palms. As if in response, her arms puckered with chill.

"You're shivering, oških." A blanket was draped over her shoulders; Anahli turned to see a smiling elder, two grey twist-locks peeping from the nape of his bright scarf. "Take my blan-ket. I don't mean to conceal your beautiful finery, but just for lit-tle while? Your people are used to dry heat... N'da, no matter, I am Chukfitohya, bred for winter and wet; I will be well."

Rude to refuse such kindness, though Chukfitohya—despite his calling of winter hareKin—seemed so scrawny he likely needed his blanket. Maybe he also meant to discourage that handsome oških. Anahli paid belated heed to her sire's warning—several times over, at that—about the stricter expectations of the Great Mound-Upon-River.

Of course, most of what he had to say to her of late was "do" and "don't".

Nevertheless, courtesy demanded same. "You do me honour, old uncle. It's not the temperature so much, but—"

"The damp." Another elder nodded understanding over her own bowl of stew. She and her two companions also stood out, a trio dressed in the layered lammoi-spun thickweave of hillClans. "It's chill even for our People, used to Wind's breath upon high-Lands. Drink our hosts' good tea; it'll warm you."

Anahli tucked in. Altogether pleasant, how their hosts cooed and spoiled Kuli. One in particular—and one her own Clan would honour as holding lizardKin's Changing Spirit—wore women's garb, yet had muscular arms and a thick moustache that few out-side River favoured. She'd thought Mound law made such People outlier. Their place amongst the cookFires crept a warm and re-lieved smile across her face, particularly when ša tugged at Kuli's ahlóssa braidlock and refilled the burl bowl with stew as fast as her little Fox could shovel it in.

It was also more than pleasing to notice several fems eyeing her. Ai, maybe she'd have her pick of partners for Dance and play after all, and maybe also... She let a smirk tilt her lip. The oških male kept throwing a covert glance her way.

"Your People are third to arrive. Only the midLands folk, and those outliers." Chukfitohya's voice dipped at that last but his smile stayed with Anahli. "Not to mention the upriver cousins—they're always late, don't you know? Must be because they're so close they always think they've plenty of time."

Anahli laughed.

The old male grinned, showing a few gaps. "So, Council starts tomorrow, as well as stickball and the races, and tomorrow you will Dance, oških? A lovemate found at First Running's festival will often become oathmate over the coming turns of our Hoop."

"Aška!" Kuli sang out. His bowl and cup clanked to the ground as he shot off towards the massive wooden entry.

With a rueful smile at Chukfitohya, Anahli picked them up. As she rose, she saw, sure enough, that their People were dismount-ing just inside the entrance.

"I've heard Horsetalkers ride to the body-soil trenches," Chukfitohya mused, taking the discarded utensils and depositing them in a large open sack half-filled with same. "Tell me, is it true?"

"It depends on how far the trenches are."

The elder barked out a laugh and gave her shoulder a fond smack.

He might be old, but his arm was stout. Anahli gave due with a rub, grinning as he laughed again, satisfied.

Kuli had reached their dam; Aylaniś was swinging him around. Her mare—always besotted with her rider's youngest—was nudging in, and almost negligently, Aylaniś swung Kuli up on the broad, spotted back. Anahli's grin turned admiring. Her sire and dam seemed slight amidst the taller, broader dawnLan-ders, but it was a litheness conditioned by Grandmother's sterner gifts, glowing dark with the blessings of a fiercer Sun. Ay-laniś stood to the fore, as proper for horseClans' chieftain, her hair bronze in the muted light and unbound save by temple-plaits—lengthened with horsehair, of course. A quartet of pinion feathers gifted from raptorKin hung just above the plaits. Her leathers, like Anahli's, lay in patterns woven smooth as a water-tight grass basket, dyed in a range from clouds to grass to the dark rose of Sunset.

Tanners a'Šaákfo were the best, after all.

Having given the mare a sound hug, Kuli launched from her withers towards his sire. Palatan caught him midsail and threw him over one shoulder. Held him there, too, with just the one hand.

"Ai!" Chukfitohya snorted, admiration and chagrin. "Your bows are short, but drawing one's like trying to run River waist-deep."

More pride trickled through Anahli at the answering murmurs. Her sire's charisma was underlain with a dangerous tension; whipcord strung in minimalist efficiency. No doubt the impressive old scar tracing a finger-length down from one tattooed cheekbone helped. And the well-muscled belly between leather vest and belted leggings, over which several of the matrons hissed approval amongst themselves. A grin ticced Anahli's lip.

"Here come *our* chieftains," Chukfitohya pointed out.

Anahli hissed approval as much for the old one as Naišwyrh'uq's leaders. They made no less splendid an entrance, merely a different one. Sarinak Mound-chieftain made two of Palatan in breadth. His head was swathed in Sky-hued cloth, beads dangling, with only those few twist-locks concealing his nape. His crimson robe spilled in many folds over one massive shoulder, and one hand held a decorated spear. Just behind that spear strode little Madoc, full of himself as a strutting fowl... and well, that one wasn't so little anymore, grown a full head since Anahli had last seen him. Tokela should be there, too, but no sign. Likely off larking with some playmate; he was only a few summerings younger than herself, no doubt had his indigo by now. Anahli brushed at her own Clan Marks, dismissing the thought, more interested in who walked at Sarinak's other hand.

Inhya's chin tilted graceful-high. The very picture of a respectable chieftain and matron, numerous bells jingled and swayed, equally graceful, from her Forest-hued kirtles, and she'd a turquoise headscarf bound round the thick, black knot impeccably braided, coiled, and oiled at her nape.

Inhya was who the leatherKeeper back home had meant, in a tone Anahli was no doubt meant to hear: *Herself'll tame eldest daughter, you'll see.*

Anahli returned the borrowed blanket to Chukfitohya's thin shoulders and began creeping forwards through the gathered welcome. She should be there, her own chin raised, doing honour to their hosts as... "eldest."

Instead she halted as a hunched figure limped forwards, shrouded in a furred cloak and leaning on a staff.

As if she'd the right, part of Anahli's Spirit sniped, and the other part growled, *She has every right! She was Alekšu!*

The crowd poured from about Anahli, greeting the newcomers. Palatan was giving his sister a fierce hug, whilst Sarinak knelt next to Aylaniś, speaking to Kuli and several other children.

Inhya said something, then Palatan's voice wafted Anahli's way upon a breath of Wind, tight with all-too-familiar exasperation. "She came on ahead. Hasn't she given you proper greeting?"

Aylaniś, speaking with Sarinak and the children, let her eyes flick over the gathered crowd.

It was Chogah, shoulders twitching beneath panther pelts, whose gaze found Anahli. Her eyes, dark and knife-edged, glittered like trade beads.

Anahli backed into the gathering and disappeared.

He, Tohwakelifitčiluka a'Naišwyrh, was the first of his tribe since his dam to brave Šilombiš'okpulo.

It gave him the wherewithal to throw off the strange intimidation of the *t'rešalt*, tread the wood with eyes high, if wary. Before long, however, his belly started complaining. Easily ignored rumblings soon became overt growls—and made him realise how still the woods were. The constant pip and burble of water dribbling over soil and leaves was there, of course, and an occasional rustling that might be one of flyingKin, or a tree climber. Otherwise, Forest held an eerie, unnatural quiet.

Which meant he would go hungry for a while. Unless...

Tokela bent over one of the fallen logs, which lay twice as big around as even Uncle Nechtoun, whose meaty muscles had long softened with the privilege of age. Pulling at the rotted bark, which crumbled in his fingers, with his broad, copper knife he poked further and... Ai! Victory! Pale grubs and crawlers of all description went scattering. They looked normal enough, so Tokela tucked into the small feast. Perhaps he could find some roots as well.

A huge sickle of ebon soared past his ear with a great *whoosh!* Tokela ducked, one arm going instinctively to cover his head and the other flipping his knife from digging to defence. A sharp creak assaulted the quiet. One of the largest flyingKin he'd ever seen touched down on the log's end and folded gleaming wings. Easily the length of Tokela's torso, ša gave a cock of head as, from above, a second croak echoed. Tokela peered upward to see another three waiting, perched on a thick branch.

The first hopped closer, intent upon Tokela's meal. The strange gleam within the beady eyes made Tokela hesitate; it seemed the Star-glitter of the *t'rešalt* had been captured there, all sparks and darkness. Maybe ša wasn't Kin after all...

But there was not way to be sure. Tokela was in their territory, a guest. Pulling several of the choicest, fattest grubs from the log, he extended them upon a flattened palm to his feathered companion. A whisper, half hiss and half creak, sounded through his teeth. Some never learned the proper way of attempting animalKin's talk, but Tokela felt most Suns he communicated better in this than with his own kind.

If such things held in this place.

Both offerings were considered—gravely, it seemed—then the bird hopped closer and accepted, pecking the grubs from Tokela's palm so light he barely felt it.

The others flew down, expectant. With a soft chuckle, he broke away more bark.

Leaving his impromptu companions working away at the remainder, he went in search of water. Humus clung to his mouth, tasting of wood-rot and tannin. Thankfully, River held no places forbidden. She'd many children, and no doubt Her fingerlings ran through here.

TreeKin spoke with creaks and sighs as Wind took the uppermost branches, but Šilombiš'okpulo lay uncanny quiet. The deeper Tokela ventured, the more its presence brushed against him. Every tree, every blade of grass, every creature living alongside him held their own brand of life... but this waiting, this focus? It drifted beyond any Dance he knew: past tribe and Clan and shelter, food and survival.

That nearly decided for him: turn around, retreat, you have no business in this place.

Fear lived with Tokela every Sun in some fashion; it sharpened nerve and sinew, built one's heart strong. Panic, however, could turn one from hunter to prey on a knife's edge of acquaintance. Panic had led him here, set his feet upon a path he'd never imagined... Well.

No more panic. Instead he'd find answers. He was no ahlóssa of seven winterings on his first hunt in a darken place. He'd all he needed: four capable limbs, nose and ears and eyes. The copper weight of his skinning knife at his thigh and the lighter eating blade upon his arm. His thick hide leggings were sturdy, his boots worn close as skin. As he walked, he ensured his tunic was belted snug and, rolling the sleeves free of his sinewy forearms, he tucked up the dangling wood beads of his hip wrap. Ready.

Water quivered his nostrils before ever he saw or heard; the scent led him, unerring, to a River-child running deep and clear. Tokela halted at the edge, gauging not only the surround but, most importantly, the spoor telling of others coming here to slake their thirst.

The River-child tasted normal, sweet, and so cold as to burn upward behind his cheekbones and down into his gullet.

He remained squatting on the bank for a while, listening, smelling, watching. Then he leapt the stream and continued on, passing silent through the huge, mossy trees.

Not far after, he came upon the pathway.

No animal trail, this; wide and well tended as the trade path leading past the Great Mound and upRiver to the crossing shallows. Closer inspection revealed the tri-cloven prints of large antleredKin and, beside that, unmistakable signs of two-leggeds, only their tread was twice the size of his own. Tokela hunkered down to trace his fingers lightly over the spoor, sniffed. The tang was sharp and unfamiliar, but strides told more than scent; four two-leggeds had passed, accompanied by six of antleredKin.

Only wabadeh were so sizeable. Some firstPeople partnered with antleredKin, on the edges of frozen upLands where the animals were smaller, docile. The great ones of dawnLands' Forests had a spooky and recalcitrant nature; wabadeh wanted kinship with none but wabadeh. Unless...

Chepiś were giants. They Shaped not only flesh, but thought and intent. What if they could tame even wabadeh? What if wabadeh were... different, here?

Mindful of his exposure on the trail, Tokela rose.

But the tracks were old, perhaps two fours of Sun. Curiosity once again won out over wariness, compelling Tokela to follow, and when the trail split his next decision made itself just as easily. The smaller path held the newer prints.

He didn't have to venture far. Something large lay across the path, laced with Sun's blinding shards where they broke the canopy.

Tokela halted, hefting his skinning knife, nostrils flaring. Wind told him little, but nothing smelled right in this place, and the unexpected twists of Sun and shadow made vision even chancier. Tokela snuffed again, but only the pungent rot of disturbed humus and the whiff of bruised conifer answered him... with perhaps a telltale tang of musk? Likely male, then. Hand upon his knife, Tokela crept towards the beast, merely to hesitate as the furred bulk gave a sudden expansion, letting out a large, moisture-laden sigh.

No antlers, not wabadeh. Living.

No trepidation, now, but pity sharp as the blade at his fingertips drove Tokela forwards once more. To be trapped in such a fashion, with no help in sight? He scuffed his feet so as not to startle the... creature, beast... whatever it was, it seemed nothing of Grandmother's making, so Tokela felt uncomfortable calling it Kin.

Splayed belly-up in a tangle-trap, neck twisted at an impossible angle, the creature made three of any predator Tokela knew. It had to be Shaped, more like to some improbable cross between pantherKin and wolfKin. Signs of a mighty struggle marked the path, and odd streaks of blue-black clotted the creature's huge, foam-flecked jaws and brindled fur.

All this flitted through Tokela's consciousness swift as a sharp breath. The creature gave another quavering wheeze, and its sideways-flung leg jerked and quivered. Perhaps its spine was injured; surely it wouldn't just lie there? Tokela uttered a soothing grunt, placing a firm, cautious foot against the hinge of the creature's formidable jaw as he reached for the obsidian blade upon his right arm. Thin and sharp, it would give swift mercy.

The creature gave into a small panic as Tokela bent over, knives in hand. Heaving and scrambling, it nearly jerked from both pinning foot and the trap—

Tokela froze.

The trap. It wasn't one. A loose tangle of tree limbs curved and broken, it wouldn't have held Tokela, much less this creature.

Tokela stomped hard on the broad head, pinning it. He turned just in time to see a three more of the creatures melt from the nearest thicket.

With a snarl, the one in front pounced.

It bowled Tokela over even as he struck out with both knives. The obsidian gave a shrill crack and shattered against tough hide; the copper knife met only air as the creature tumbled over and past. It snarled, shrill and cheated. Clearly it had overestimated his size.

Tokela took the chance, rolling to his feet, grip still firm on the skinning knife. An oddling sight sent the blood chill in his veins: the trapped creature pulling free from its snare, not unlike one of his tribe shimmying free of a fishing net.

The hesitation cost him. A massive weight rammed into him, driving a harsh cry from his chest and slamming him against a thick bow tree. Heat, and hair, and foul, fetid breath battered Tokela as he shoved, kicked, tried to wrestle his knife hand upward. The trapped creature, bait to lure the prey—only now Tokela was the prey. The only thing keeping those huge, slavering jaws from closing on his windpipe was a desperate grip, torqued hard as outLand *eirn* about the creature's throat.

Pain blazed in his thigh then in his bicep, claws ripping and teeth tearing—or trying to. Somehow Tokela kept his stranglehold on the creature and freed his knife hand. With a harsh grunt, he shoved the knife upward and wrenched sideways. The creature gave a strangely normal *ki-yi* and convulsed—a last, violent tear of teeth and claws—then fell at Tokela's feet. Impulse, to kick it away, but he might as well kick at stone. Instead, gaze fixing on the remaining creatures, he began a slow, sideways creep.

They were supine; no doubt expecting their companion to handily dispatch the puny two-legged. As their prey proved instead resourceful, the creatures rose, snarling.

The one in front stood high as Tokela's chin.

Tokela snarled a hoarse answer that steamed into the air. He kept his back to the bow tree, and his knife ready. Its copper surface, too, steamed, stained with the creature's... it must be blood. Even if it whiffed of nothing he'd ever experienced, and even if in Sun's faint dapples it looked more like to the indigo that, if these things had their way, he might not survive to Mark upon his own cheeks.

The largest creature stilled, and Tokela sucked in a quick breath, crouched-ready. Instead the creature sprang at its fellow, the "bait". Little chance for bewilderment, though; the remaining creature leapt for Tokela. He lashed out, let the momentum spin him past the brunt of the charge. Giving an eerie cry, it's lunge fell short, its jaws snapping a frantic but bloodless rent in the fringed cloth of Tokela's hip wrap.

It fell back, a penetrative—unsettling—calculation in their eyes. Still, it limped; Tokela'd done damage, at least. Yet the creature seemed confused, eyeing first him, then the grey-brindled leader, who still had the smaller one pinned to the ground. Punishment, for spoiling what should have been an easy kill?

With a last growl, the grey-brindled leader released the youngling and turned. Again that unsettling calculation, as the leader eyed Tokela up and down, lips curling back over its canines. Tokela returned the favour. To show throat, here and now, surely meant death.

"Ai, this prey has teeth." Tokela grated out, letting his senses cast about. Were there others? Would he know? For only in closer quarters did the creatures reek of fetid sweat and breath; they'd disguised their scent. The concept was no more out-Landish than the way their eyes glittered in shards of white. Akin to the *t'rešalt*. Who knew what unnatural abilities these things possessed?

N'da, he couldn't think that way. Shaped or no, they were predators. It remained: if he moved, they would strike, and if he didn't move, they would still strike.

If he stayed here, he would die.

Keeping his eyes upon the leader, Tokela slid from his boots, one then the other. Gripping the ground with long, bare toes, he snaked his free hand behind the small of his back, palm surveying the tough bark.

The chastised youngster's ears flattened; the two pacing went still. The leader's head lowered.

Tokela spun, digging feet, fingers, and knife into the bow tree. Almost in the same breath, the creatures leapt to the attack.

Tokela wasn't there. As the creatures piled against the trunk, he scrabbled higher into the bow tree. The huge leader leapt after. Stinking breath heated Tokela's backside, fangs stabbing sharp as the creature grabbed his calf. Only the thick hide leggings gave protection from a bone-deep bite; unfortunately they allowed the creature better hold. Shaking its massive head, it flung Tokela against the bow tree as if he were an ill-tied door flap. Sparks popped behind his eyes; he stayed up only by virtue of the panicked grip on his deep-dug copper blade.

Growling, the leader set itself to finding some purchase against the trunk, braced, pulled. Tokela's arm tendons stretched nigh to ripping, but he managed to hang on, gave a vicious, desperate kick with his free leg. It was enough. The creature's long claws suited more dog than any cat, and it fell with a tearing of leather and flesh. A muffled scream bursting from his throat, Tokela hauled himself upward, even as the creature hit the ground with a *crack!* that would have broken any normal creature's spine.

The others clawed and scrabbled, trying to follow. The bow tree shuddered and rocked beneath the onslaught. Tokela's slender build for once proved boon instead of bane. He kept climbing, husking faint orisons to the tree from which his People made some of the finest bows in thisLand. The creatures kept venting their fury against his haven.

Persistent. But he'd climbed enough to be safe. With a shaky groan, Tokela leaned hard against the trunk. Only then did the hot blood of fight and flight drain away, leaving him shivering like the branches. His fingers wouldn't let loose of his knife. His arm and leg flashed pain of bite and strain of ligament with every little movement. The scratches the creatures' claws had left on his thighs, shoulders, and abdomen expanded from mere sting, to sullen and angry.

If the creatures' spittle was poisonous...

Then none of it mattered. What did matter, now, was his leg. The blood smell would draw every predator around—it was driving Tokela nigh mad, a thick, nauseated scorch in the back of his throat. Not to mention there'd be little need for poison if he bled out and fainted.

The tree stopped swaying. Tokela peered down with bleary eyes. The creatures had abandoned their punishment of the tree, instead circling it with thwarted clucks and rumbles. The grey-brindled leader sat on its haunches, peering upward. The eerie cognisance in its gaze filled Tokela's heart with ice and sickness.

Was that what Inhya saw—n'da, felt?—when she looked into his eyes? Tokela had taken her recent inability to hold his stare as a shameful and sorry triumph; now it hurt him, wondering.

Breaking the creature's gaze with a small shudder, Tokela decided the stouter limb just an arm's length away might make a safer perch, and tried to shove upright. It was a miserable failure. To move, after being still, was agony. It took every fibre of will Tokela possessed to merely crawl across the limb. Forever, it seemed—with the creatures following every wobble, every shift.

Finally, he lowered himself against the thick branch, panting and grateful.

The leg looked worse than it was; bleeding, a'io, but not spurting. Untying his hip wrap proved difficult; easing out of it, more agony. Again, forever, and once Tokela had the thing free he had to lean back, wait until his heart stopped pounding and his limbs stopped jerking. Only then could he even think of wielding his knife in what should have been an easy task: ripping the triangle of spun seed-pod fibre in two. No doubt he'd catch his fair share of misery from Inhya for ruining new finery.

Assuming he made it back.

He had to prise his hands from his slimed knife, fingers sticky with the creature's... it had to be blood. Yet it was unnatural. Clotting slow and hued, not with the normal crimson of a sullen Sun's rising over River, but like...

Like indigo.

One corner of his mouth gave a sudden tip upwards. With his middle fingers, Tokela scooped the blood from his blade then made two smears across his left cheek. Smile widening—a gleam of teeth that made the creatures below him bristle—Tokela did the other cheek then looked down. Growled back.

"I'll have a new fur for my bedshelf and teeth to string for a necklace." Mere bravado. Yet the voicing of it soothed, almost as much as the prickle and draw of the oddling blood on his cheeks.

The brindled leader settled onto his haunches. He looked set to wait forever.

"We'll see who can wait," Tokela muttered under his breath.

It was as if the creature understood. Teeth showed and the pale eyes gleamed, eerie and white as Starlight.

Wind picked up and began to sway the tree branches, soft and sap-heavy, across Tokela's sweat-streaked face. He tied the torn hip wrap snug about his wounded calf and let Wind ply what comforts They could. There would be little enough of those from here on out. He'd come away with not so much as a strip of dried meat, a handful of nuts, or fruit. A clutch of small amber berries lay well within reach. Unfortunately, an overabundance of those would merely make him piss his water away all the faster.

Instead Tokela turned his attention to wrapping the lesser mauling on his right bicep, then set himself to cleaning his knife with peels of bark and what remained of his hip wrap. He'd begun a painstaking attention to the wrapped hilt when everything sidled abruptly sideways, skimming the hilt and his hands into a blur.

The fuzzy vision retreated with several good blinks and a rub against his tunic sleeve. Likely a splash of sweat or a flake of blood in his eyes. He began cleaning again.

Below, several of his captors had started to pace. The leader stood and began a strange, guttural... it was like to a howl, wavering upwards and tapering down.

This meant something.

Only Tokela wasn't quite sure what it meant. He should know, certainly, but possibilities kept drifting, just past any reach. And the odd scum—sweat or blood—returned. Tokela gave a fierce rub of his eyes, nearly dropped his knife. Catching it just before it would have fallen, he clutched it tight. Sweat rashed over him, prompting a wave of shivers. Dully, Tokela contemplated this, came to a just as leaden conclusion. The bites. Poisoned.

The lead creature kept yowling. Tokela snarled back, but it wavered, threaded with fear. The creatures knew. Had likely known all along what would happen, its timing and its end.

The rest took up the noise—not anywhere near as melodious as the pack-call of wolfKin, so Tokela refused to designate it a true howl. For all the good it did him. Soon or late, he was going to drop out of this tree, easy meat...

N'da. Tokela began unwrapping the bandages from his leg and arm, revealing an unhealthy, black and yellow tinge to the bites like aged bruises. The sick-sweet reek of it made him gag.

It also cleared his head.

Gritting his teeth, Tokela sheathed his dagger and began binding himself to his perch with the soiled bandages. If he had to die, it was not going to be as meat for those things. Ai, something would have him in the end, but the pack would have to wait for whatever dropped from the scavenges of flyingKin.

If they were indeed flyingKin, not Shaped into obscenity like the twisted whatever-they-weres below.

Hard—*so hard*—to focus. It shouldn't be. Tokela had used these wraps and knots since his fingers had grown limber enough to rig weirs and mend nets. The creatures' caterwauling didn't help; increasing in pitch, a maddening hum behind his ears that he couldn't quite hear, only feel.

And answers, faint but unmistakable. Others approached. Tokela tried to squint through the trees, but his vision kept fading into blurry shadows. His hands, too, were traitorous, twitching as he worked. His teeth chattered; he gritted them, entreating whatever Spirits would listen that the fabric should not give when he finally did fall.

Lashed to the tree like a wyrhling ship's sails during Wind's anger, Tokela growled down at the crooning creatures again.

The leader paid no attention; he'd fallen silent, alert. As quiet spread through the remaining creatures, Tokela also heard it. Different, this, a high-pitched drone hanging in the treetops. Disturbing, too; akin to the lamentations that would echo up and down River when She received ash and bone on Longest Dark.

The leader whined, thin and hoarse. The others resumed their aimless self-circles. Dark clouds kept skimming Tokela's gaze, sloe flecked with shards of blue-white.

Like the skin of the *t'rešalt*.

Tokela listed sideways, stayed in the tree only by virtue of his self-made fetters. Tried once more to blink away the lingering sparks.

But n'da, even the creatures below were plagued with the things. The leader's brindled fur seemed alive with pale flicker-flies. Tokela found himself staring, hanging limp with bark scraping his face and neck. Beneath his refuge the predators squirmed, swerved, bit at their haunches.

The strange drone came closer, filling his chest; contrarily, it hoisted Tokela back into his own senses. Clearly a voice this time, a deep drone hinged in an unmusical fashion that nevertheless suggested talk being made, But even Matwau, the tall ones who traversed Sea to trade with People, didn't speak so harsh.

Harsh or no, it held a Power akin to taleKeepers singing over solstice Fires. It buzzed at the base of Tokela's neck and spine, an itch impossible to scratch.

The predators fled. One heartbeat they were there, and the next, vanished.

Save, of course, the dead one.

Silence hung in the canopy. The undergrowth gave a rustle. A voice boomed through the silence.

Tokela tried to move, draw his knife... something! Yet he could only loll against the branch, a hide and grass doll blinking scum from his eyes as this new unseen danger stalked him.

Oddly enough, he found himself clinging to the strange new voice. Even if he didn't understand a thing it said.

The thicket shivered, parted. Tokela blinked rapidly, finally beheld a scrawny, colourful figure progressing on absurdly long legs. It seemed unfinished—or perhaps unfed. Tokela couldn't see the two-legged's face, but a pale mane squatted in tight curls atop its head, unbound and unadorned. And...

And it must be the poison, cloaking his thoughts so they refused to stay with his body; wandering, justifying, nattering like little Kuli about inconsequentials whilst the poisonous ebon haze heeled him.

The figure came to a halt below Tokela's refuge and looked up, and the breath knocked within Tokela's chest.

The face he'd drawn... or enough like it as not to matter. His own fears, mirrored in an alien gaze. Shapers. Ghost-eyes.

Chepiś.

Its skin had the same Sky-sand hue as Brother Moon's face. Its eyes were only a shade darker, with no normal spark of darksight even in dim shadows.

How did they *see*?

"Be eased, little one."

Either he was starting to imagine things, or the Chepiś was making a mangled attempt at Commingling-talk.

"I shan't eat you, though you were wise to not give these predators such trust." The Chepiś gave a nudge with its foot to the slain creature, nodded upward. When Tokela merely hung there, blinking, the Chepiś made an expression with its face. It seemed a smile, though it could have been a snarl.

Tokela wasn't sure how to respond. Or if he could.

The Chepiś laid a hand on the bow tree, gestured again. Again, it seemed friendly, almost earnest. "Come, little *ghoteh*. You're safe enough now. Yes?"

Go-tay? Yas? Nothing in Tokela tempted him to obey what talk he did understand. That it kept calling him "little" wasn't encouraging.

And he was going to be *sick*.

He tried to rise, could not. Tried to slide back, could not. His free arm fell from the branch—and surely it did so slowly enough for him to halt it, but all Tokela could do was watch it fall, recoil, then hang, swinging limp and nerveless as a dead thing. He blinked down. The visage of the Chepiś seemed to float and waft below him, like the palest of Brother's Moon's siblings...

Then it slipped and folded itself into the ebon cloak, taking the light and Tokela with it.

$$\phi \quad \phi \quad \phi$$

4
MADOC

"I almost didn't recognise you, sister-son! Eh, you've decided you won't be waiting for your changing to grow tall?" Palatan's greeting teased, yet all the while his eyes scanned the gathering; from Madoc's eager face and over the Mound-People, then lingering with a frown upon Chogah, then to Aylaniś herself, questioning. *Where is Anahli?*

Of late Aylaniś had no good answer. She tilted her head, making a quick scan of the Bowl within the Great Mound. No horizon here—and treeKin could disguise many things.

Madoc was laughing, a delighted response peppered with breathless questions fit to outdo Kuli, who kept trying to interrupt. But Madoc kept his composure in one fashion—his manners—and pitched his queries in polite talk a'Šaákfo.

Madoc's father had a quizzical frown upon his face; a middle-aged male a'Naišwyrh had sidled up to murmur in his ear. A message of some import, from Sarinak's reaction.

"N'da, horse-chieftain, I've not yet seen Anahli." Inhya's decorum showed where Madoc's had been patterned. Yet Aylaniś had never seen Madoc's exuberance reflected in Inhya; even as ahlóssa had her Spirit tended grave. Dark eyes narrowing, Inhya furthered, "My other son, Tokela, is absent as well."

"Trouble travels in pairs, like Brother Moon's siblings," Aylaniś offered. "Perhaps our two have found each other and are comparing possibilities."

Hopefully that was all they were comparing, what with Anahli's unseemly interest in the few things disallowed oških. Across Grandmother's belly, with the rich variance of tribes and customs, some things were often agreed upon: for one, the right to court opposites had to be earned.

Another burst of laughter from Madoc. The set of Inhya's mouth turned from forbidding to fond.

Aylaniś spoke to that; much easier. "Palatan is right: how Madoc has grown! He will have his indigo soon."

"Too soon, a'io?" Inhya's dark eyes met Aylaniś', who took the offered opening and touched her spouse-sister's arm. They'd little enough in common, but a dam's heart-longings made for easier agreement.

"He will be the only get of your body." Chogah slipped into their conversation like grease upon water.

Aylaniś didn't dignify it with so much as a glance. Inhya stiffened, towering over Chogah's hunched form. Flawlessly polite, Inhya gave an upward tip of chin to acknowledge a guest, if not that guest's talk, then spoke to Aylaniś. "I myself shall take your mounts to the grazing fields." Taking first the rein of Aylaniś's mare then Palatan's, her eyes lingered upon her brother, fond, as she turned away with the horses. "We welcome you and your People, Aylaniś horse-chieftain."

Sarinak repeated the words then, with a rough muss to Madoc's hair, made polite excuse and strode away with the male who'd first beckoned—some host business to attend.

"And yet you banish your eldest to these." Chogah gave a sneer after Inhya's retreat. And ai, it had been that—albeit with head held high.

"You are part of that reason, old viper," Aylaniś gritted through bared teeth. "Your base cruelty does none of us credit."

"Is it cruel to remind one so set upon ignoring the ripples in one's wake? Inhya abandoned her own tribe, after all."

"You would deny her the choice? Such talk is hardly respectful."

"Hunh! Hardly respectful is the way she treats that hearthling son of hers. Tokela, they call him here, when his mother called his Tohwakeli. As if even his name is forbidden!" Chogah pulled her shawl tighter. "Hunh! As Inhya ruined the mother, she'll ruin the son! And now, our Anahli... still, you insist upon abandoning your eldest to such foolishness?"

Pointless to dignify such talk, yet Aylaniś had to respond, still through her teeth, "Kuli thrives here."

As if he'd heard his name, Kuli looked her way and grinned. Skipping over, he wrapped freckled arms about his dam, hugging close to her belly. "Aška, I've missed you."

Aylaniś smoothed her fingers through the tangled hair that had given him his child-name. "I've missed you, my little Fox."

Chogah made a disagreeable sound.

Palatan had been watching them, a slight frown twitching at his new-scarred brow. He started to make his way closer despite being submerged beneath a joyous wave of ahlóssa chatter. Madoc was taking full advantage of Kuli's absence.

Kuli, in the meantime, had fixed an unflinching gaze upon Chogah. "Are you hungry, Aunt? There's food over there." He jerked his chin towards the cooking hearths.

"Cheeky brat!" Chogah sniped back, yet she refrained from further invective. It had been so since she'd first laid eyes upon the baby sitting naked in the Breaking Ground, playing in the cinnabar dust as if Alekšu weren't parsing his fate.

Perhaps, in that moment, she had done. Palatan often claimed it as explanation for Chogah's wariness of their youngest—but then, Palatan had no gift for prescience and, as one male in both Spirit and flesh, sparser connexion to such things.

I've no need. You are the one who Walks my future, he would say to Aylaniś, softened after loving. *You and our children.*

"...and Kuli is going back with you, isn't he?" Madoc was saying. "Once Councils are done?"

"If he wants to." Palatan's eyes were full of mischief as he meandered over.

Madoc followed, face falling. "Only if he wants to?"

Aylaniś answered glint with grin, even as Kuli shifted against her hip and hissed in the back of his throat. It wasn't approving. Madoc's nostrils curled in reply.

"Anahli was at the cookFires when you arrived, Aška," Kuli tossed his head at Madoc and turned pointedly to Aylaniś. "D'you want me to go find her?"

Palatan's eyes were still teasing, but also questioning as he gave a fond tug to Madoc's ahlóssa braid. "I suppose we should all go and find th..."

A shrill whistle made him trail away and peer towards the massive cliff frontis. Teasing gave way to disbelief, then elation.

Aylaniś felt it herself, bubbling up into a smile. "He's made it!"

"Who's made what?" Madoc asked, looking back and forth, plainly puzzled.

The piercing whistle sounded again, details soaring over the cliff frontis from River: trilling thrice, skidding into a lower register then up again shrill as raptorKin. Aylaniś read them, plain: *A long, slow journey, but I'm here! Are you?*

Palatan turned and answered in kind, beginning shrill then dropping low. *We're here! We're coming!*

Aylaniś laughed and gave Palatan's shoulder a gentle push. "Go. Greet him."

His face lit up, a shaft of sun in cavern depths. Grasping her hand to his cheek, he loosed it to tangle fingers in Kuli's hair and tug Madoc's braid. "Kuli. Go find your sister and show her where we've made camp. Will you help him, Madoc? We must go."

Madoc still seemed confused. "Go where?"

"Off with you." Aylaniś gave Palatan another nudge. "I'll be right after."

Still grinning, Palatan loped away. Aylaniś turned her attention to the two children. "Go, ahlóssa. Find Anahli."

Kuli tilted his chin in acknowledgement and sped away like his sire, but in the opposite direction. Madoc remained.

"Will you not help him, Madoc?"

"He knows where you're to stay." As stolid—and as adamant— as ever were his parents, but Madoc's composure breached easily as any youngling's. "Don't make me tag along with him again?

Please? Where is Uncle Palatan going? Wasn't that a wyrhling's whistle?"

Aylaniś chose the swiftest route—Palatan was eager, but so was she. "Indeed it was, and I'm sure you remember your Uncle Našobok. He just let us know his ship has anchored midRiver."

Madoc's face closed. "I have no uncle of that name."

Aylaniś should have expected it; nevertheless, it hit her like a blow. She answered in kind, sharp with a hint of teeth, "Madoc'enbeh a'Naišwyrh! You forget your manners, and traditions older than all of us. All leaders of the People are welcomed to First Running, whatever Clan they possess... or do not."

His face flamed; but to do him credit, he didn't lower his eyes. "And he is of *my* Clan, oathbrother to my spouse and to me, regardless of his status here. He is my tribe's guest, if not yours."

Those eyebrows, dark over wide bronze, squinched together. "I'm sorry, Aunt."

Aylaniś smiled, tugging at his ahlóssa braid. "Well enough, then."

Madoc laid his temple against her arm for a half-breath, then raced away. Aylaniś watched him go, then turned away, her smile broadening, and her steps skipping into a run.

Našobok was here!

◊　◊　◊

The galley was one of the biggest to ride River, laying-to all broad and low with cargo, mast snagging the bits of fog still drifting from the bottoms. Just close enough to be sheltered by Mound-upon-River's crescent-shaped cove, but not so close as to risk running aground. The rigs were nigh bare, save for a tiny jib set forwards—perhaps some security, set against the small Wind teasing at Anahli's cheeks. Several crew were still up and aft, tying off the furled sails. She envied them, for reasons inarticulate even to herself. After all, much better to ride horseKin than River. River had stolen...

Rough, cheerful asides carried across the water upon the breeze. Damp and brisk, it made Anahli glad for the blanket over her shoulders. The elder had insisted she keep it; he'd several more and the gift would do him honour. That memory, and the crew clambering like birds upon the spars whilst swapping cheerful insults, returned the smile that had fled.

Ilhukaia was the ship's name. Commingling-talk for "Surrender". Her smile faded again. What had the ship's master ever given up, after all? *Ilhukaia* was nothing akin to any surrender. More like escape. Insurgence. Defiance, winged and afloat.

Her fingers clenched upon the gifted blanket.

"What are you doing up here?"

Madoc's sudden appearance echoed Anahli's own inner question.

You heard the whistle, a snide, inward Anahli informed her. *You want to see him, too.*

N'da, I really don't, she retorted.

"Anahli. They're looking for you, you know." Madoc might have grown taller, but his voice was still ahlóssa—particularly when it tilted upward into whinging. "Even the Spawn."

Anahli had four younger siblings. She knew exactly what tone to take with a whinge. Propping one buttock against Overlook's driftwood railing, she crossed her arms and raised one eyebrow. "Do you even know what Spawn really means?"

Madoc rolled his eyes.

"It's not a nice term, where I come from. It suggests that someone is a thing, an 'it'. Not wholly of People. That one was Shaped, made Other."

Madoc looked uncomfortable.

"Like things in the forbidden places—"

"All right, all right!" Madoc's cheeks had paled beneath his faded Marks. "I won't. But he's so—"

"Annoying? Like you're annoying me, now, ahlóssa?"

A flush, this time. He was going to be quite a looker, when he grew up and stopped with this pretend-stone-face nonsense. Though, considering his parents...

"I'm here same as you. As these others"—Anahli gestured along Overlook where, indeed, people were gathering—"looking at the new arrivals."

"I've no interest in outcasts." Madoc's sniff returned him straightaway into self-righteousness. "I'm looking for Tokela."

They refuse to say the name we gave him. Another memory/reminder surfaced in Chogah's voice. *His dam came to us—it was her right, to come to her own grandmother's People and ask for the Naming—but still those hidebound dawnLanders consider that forbidden, too!*

Anahli let out a soft growl. She was going to smother, here.

And likely it was just what her dam had in mind.

Madoc peered at her—not tall enough to meet her gaze, though he was trying—then glanced down the walkway as if Tokela might be stowed away somewhere and she'd a hand in it.

"That's him!" The hissed accusation intruded into Anahli's reverie. Sliding her gaze sideways, she saw others crowding the best of the lookout perches. "There, in the canoe! He was own brother to Mound-chieftain, that one!"

"Was?"

"He's Riverwalker. Wyrhling."

Several mutters, one sounding above the rest, "Brother no more, then."

The small group, from their Marks and garb, came of neighbouring Forestlodge.

"Old Nechtoun himself had to publicly disown his own second-born: outlier, clanless and"—down to a whisper—"River-claimed!"

Despite scorn, Madoc's gaze went wide and fixed over the railing, towards *Ilhukaia*.

A long, husky scrape of wood against gravel and sand accompanied the whisper, drawing Anahli's own gaze. River reflected Sky in a mix of bright and overcast, hazing not only the larger vessels at anchor, but a bark-lined canoe rocking in the shallows, bearing two figures. It lurched further as the frontmost one laid his oar into the canoe's keel and uncurled from the prow. A Riverwalker's oiled-hide longcoat fluttered in Wind's breath, with quilled and beaded crimson glinting across broad shoulders. A thick mane of sleek bistre had been tailed back to hang from collar to midcalf hem. Barelegged and barefoot, pale leggings and boots tucked into the crook of one powerful arm, the wyrhling disembarked. River-claimed, indeed, for She seemed loath to let go, pulling heavy against long-legged strides as Her own sloshed for shore.

Našobok shouted a wonderful and giddy melange of tongues: Wyrh-talk, some a'Naišwyrh, mostly a'Šaákfo. He was laughing.

The canoe set off again. Back to the boat, errand accomplished.

As Našobok reached shore, a black-haired figure ran up and literally smacked into him. Boots and leggings were dropped onto the strand as, still laughing, Našobok lifted Palatan up into a fierce embrace. Anahli's eyebrows lifted; she had supposed any memories of Našobok's forelock scraping Sky were ahlóssa fancies.

Obviously not. Though it had been that long since he'd graced them with his presence.

Nevertheless, Anahli's mouth tucked into a small grin as Našobok swung Palatan around easily as if *he* were ahlóssa. The grin broadened as Palatan smacked Našobok in the back of the head, only to slightly falter as the hand lingered, softening into a caress as Našobok relented and let him down.

The busy-talkers a length away, however, were not amused. "That is—"

"Unseemly, it is, consorting so with outliers."

More were gathering, also looking as if they'd tasted sour fruit. Anahli wondered if their tongues would wag so free if she didn't have the blanket covering her head and arms. No question, with River in one's nose it was difficult to tell by smell even if, here and there, a waft of charred fern and copperwood lingered. Different from her own Clan's scent; dryer, touched with sage and needlecreeper oil.

"You don't like the wyrhling, do you?" Madoc had left off gawking to peer at Anahli instead. His voice was soft, wondering.

She didn't answer.

"Šaákfo!" A snort from the other end of Overlook. "Who can make sensible talk with those?"

"Not only a'Šaákfo, but Šilombiš'okpulo." Spoken with a hint of scandal. "And who can make sensible talk with those?"

"That is Alekšu? He looks to be no sizeable warrior—see how the wyrhling towers over him," a younger fem scoffed. "What's so fearful about this Alekšu?"

She was shushed with hisses, and glances around.

Madoc was—blessings to him!—puffing up like poked serpentKin. Anahli put a staying hand upon his shoulder. She wanted to hear.

"The MedicineKeepers a'Šaákfo have Power!" one of them retorted. "They dare to walk with those possessed."

A good thing, Anahli groused, silent, since you dawnLanders fear to so much as look upon the ones you cast aside.

Sure enough, more hisses, complete with warding gestures.

"I've little doubt of it. The one who was Alekšu before? A witch, no question."

"Yet Mound-chieftain allows her here, to Council!"

"Her fangs have finally been pulled," another murmured.

"So you say. Yet for many turnings of Hoop none could defeat her in that odd ritual they have, challenge and combat. A fem her age against hardened hunters! That is Power, nothing but."

"A'io, and if Palatan a'Šaákfo has defeated her, then he has taken her Power. I'd not try to tell him anything."

Silence fell beneath the chancy subject. But not for long.

"Eh, but none should trust a wyrhling at their back." A growling return to the original subject—obviously wyrhling were safer to denigrate than MedicineKeepers.

Amusement floated up from the strand with laughter, then an arc through the air with boot fringe flying. Aylaniś was being greeted in much the same way as her spouse, her full, delightful giggle, weaving in and out of Palatan's deep, husky chuckle and Našobok's bark of laughter. Anahli remembered the latter; it encouraged others to join in.

"There's few'll cross that wyrhling." The busy-talkers had wound up again. "Fewer still challenge him without blood spilt. He killed the chieftain before him, painted the deck in blood and hung his head on the masts as warning."

Madoc clearly hadn't heard this one; he shot another glance towards *Ilhukaia*. Disbelief slid into respect as he espied the skull hanging from the mainmast, a bony clatter when Wind touched it.

An oversized skull, not of firstPeople. Anahli knew that, like she knew a different truth from stories told long into wintering darks as a child: *Ilhukaia* had never known any master but the one she now carried, and it had been a Matwau slave trader whose head Našobok had taken.

"I think it shameful a chieftain's son would choose such a path."

"He's never taken a proper path in his life, that one. Wild and treacherous as floodwater he's been, from the Sun his dam birthed him. Hearken his name: River-mad Wolf."

Just as Kulahiši meant Little Fox Fur, just as Hihlyanahli meant Graceful Dancer. But only with an outlier's name would those busy-talkers scorn Commingling-talk with such familiarity—and disregard.

And it wasn't River-*mad*, merely River Wolf.

"*I've* heard he's a blood pact with River, in exchange for safe passages. That's too close to Shaping for any comfort."

"Your talk is nonsense. Outcasts are dangerous, but Shaping? Hunh! Stories to frighten ahlóssa. There are no more Shapers, except for the evil tall ones. Our people cast such things out long ago. Now there are only those who allow possession, who are too weak of Spirit to want healing."

Well, and Anahli'd just about had enough of this.

"—refuses to espouse anyone. I've heard possessed ones don't espouse—"

"Then how would they get their curse on, foolish mouth?"

"Nothing to do with witchery there, he's *outlier*! What dam would let her own consider an outcast? What sire would not punish an outcast if he so much as raised eyes to a cherished daughter?"

A snort. "That's not why the wyrhling's not espoused. He's more danger to a dam's *sons*. Never showed any interest in females, even after outgrowing oških fancies. Not that such a one could earn any spouse!"

"If none will tell Alekšu, well, his chieftain should. *She* should know better."

"Or at least not be so obvious."

"Obvious about what?" Anahli shrugged the blanket from her shoulders and tucked her chin, eyeing them. "That they care for each other?"

The busy-talkers turned like sand in one's hands, shifting and slipping away into stammered, forced mannerisms of apology. With their notice of the horseClans daughter came another: their own chieftains' son, glaring across his broad nose at them.

Meanwhile, down on the strand and still wrapped about each other, Palatan, Aylaniś, and Našobok climbed the steep stair and disappeared into the gated tunnel into the Mound.

More from being deprived of a target than, Anahli was sure, any shame for their sharp tongues, the watchers also dispersed.

"I'm sorry. They were rude. Some were a'Naišwyrh, so I apologise to you on their behalf."

It was very prettily done. Anahli tilted her chin in acceptance. "You haven't seen Tokela, then."

"You," Anahli retorted, a grin once more trying its way with her lip, "are a single-minded ahlóssa."

Madoc's grin slid impenitent as he recovered the shrugged-aside blanket, handing it over. "And if they ask me if I found you?"

"Are you offering to hide me under your blanket?"

"Mm. Looks as if you've one already."

She snorted, taking the blanket.

Madoc's grin widened. "Will you let me ride your horse?"

"Can you ride, dawnLander?" Anahli started down the stone-carved steps.

He followed. "Of course I can! So can Tokela. My dam still rides—she was of horseClans, you know."

"I know. She's my sire's sister, remember?"

Madoc was peering at her braids, fascinated and a little bit disapproving. "We'll have to find you a proper headwrap." Then, before she could protest, furthered, "Ebon-streaked copper with a hint of gold. To match your eyes."

Anahli halted, her foot midair above the second terrace's downward slope. "How many Summerings have you, again?"

"Ten." Another grin. A'io, he was going to be more than handsome when he was grown.

"Spawn," she murmured, and kept going.

"I thought that wasn't very nice."

"Really? I'd no idea."

Madoc blinked. Then grinned again. "I think you're going to be ever so much more interesting than Kuli."

Anahli snorted again, and kept on descending.

"Once, long ago—not so long ago that divingKin hadn't found Grandmother beneath Sea's expanse, but after that and long enough, ai, long enough—there was but one Moon. One Moon, and He was lonely."

Other than the lone, sure voice and an accompanying finger-flick of rhythm against drums palmed whisper silent, the valley compound was silent. Not even Wind spoke. Yet within the centre of First Running's opening circle, Fire made a cheerful Dance, lighting the storyKeeper's mood and her listeners' faces.

"Sister Sun was not enough for Him. Rarely did they meet; rarely did they Dance. So Brother Moon asked the People; a'io, He asked the newest siblings born of Grandmother's clutch, asked if they could find company for Him."

Indeed, as if conjured, a mist-shrouded Moon and siblings chased Sun into the horizon. The ahlóssa gasped. One infant trilled, delighted, and his dam hugged him close with a laugh.

No conjurings here, n'da—Anahli recognised the gleaming-stones as the taleKeeper struck and hung them in their metal weirs, setting shadows to dance against the surrounding cliffs and make talk with River's bottom mists.

"Hunh. Only in dawnLands." Barely audible, misting Anahli's ear. "Only here would storyKeepers cull all reference of which People Brother Moon truly asked."

Anahli didn't turn, instead shivered into the elder's gifted blanket still over her shoulders. She was grateful for the body heat of the gathering, too, all of them leaning close to listen.

Chogah wasn't deterred. "Yet your dam would leave you. Here."

"It's my right, to be hearthed with kin," Anahli murmured back.

"Hsst!" a nearby elder censured.

"And when the Beloved One, first amongst equals, led the call—"

"The Beloved One, first of the Alekšuáhoklawyhahín." Chogah growled the correction into her robes, tugging them closer.

"—what answered was neither what she nor Brother Moon expected. Sometime, wandering solitary is goodness, but it also can attract trouble..." The storyKeeper's voice trailed to a hum. The drums followed, still whisper silent.

Another tug to Anahli's blanket, this one fierce. She started to shift out of Chogah's reach, turned.

But Chogah was gone. Instead Madoc stood next to her, still tugging.

Have you yet seen Tokela? he signed. *He's not been here all thisSun.*

Anahli tucked her chin sideways in negation. As Madoc's mouth opened as if to protest; Anahli laid two fingers there and pursed her lips towards the storyKeeper.

Sure enough, the drums began to speak deeper, sonorous warning.

"Ai!" The storyKeeper's exclamation started low, throbbed up into a raptor's cry, wavered away. "Ai," she said again, soft, echoed by many throats. "Ai, my People, and with that answer came Other. With the coming of Brother Moon's longed-for company came Other. With the birthing and Fire came Sa's siblings. And with them..." She waited.

"Came Other!" It drifted like a sigh through her listeners. Anahli closed her eyes beneath the power of it.

Chogah was right. It wasn't told this way in duskLands' caverns. But neither did it have to be, no more than Anahli's heart had to agree with Chogah's. Or her dam's. Or her sire's.

"You know of what I speak, my People. We remember. We shall always remember and never forget. When Stars answered the Beloved One's call, they brought forth not just one, but two small companions for our Brother's loneliness. And in the doing, Stars also brought the tall ones. Not the tall ones from across Sea, not Matwau, who are unlike yet like to us save in their hearts, which covet Grandmother's bounty. Remember and never forget the outland ones unlike any we'd ever seen or known: milk-grey, their hides; sparked pale as polished silver, their eyes. All the hues of Other. Ones that, it is said, looked nothing like to any beings even on Grandmother's belly. Remember! They came with our Moon's siblings and, once stranded, Shaped themselves to swarm over our Land, to twist Her and make Her theirs. Remember, my People, and never forget."

"We remember!" an elder called, and it was echoed by many throats against the shadow-laced cliffs, as the storyKeeper's eyes blazed.

"They came into our Land." She stood, spun in a whirl of bright-hued skirts and scarves and finery, in a thunder of drums. "We made the Dance. We drove them away."

Drove them away because we could. Then. Anahli's thoughts etched like Fire against Dark. *Because we were Grandmother's children, with Her, able to defend Her. We truly were Alekšu'ín. Not reduced to a few charlatans whose only service is to hide in shadows and purge their own.*

"We Danced. We chased the Shapers into the forbidden places, held them to a truce. Held our own to account for what our Grandmother suffered beneath the Winnowing brought to Her."

Across the gathering, Anahla saw Inhya. Her eyes gleamed, darksight flickers from shadows and...

Something else. Something... culpable?

What blame could hearth-chieftain a'Naisgwyr lay upon herself?

Just as Inhya met her gaze, Anahli looked away, found Madoc still beside her, swaying and caught up in the storyKeeper's spell. The drums, winding up as their storyKeeper spun and sang, stopped as she halted, holding up a fist.

She opened it. A handful of stonetree berries fell, bouncing and rolling across the ground.

"Ahhh," the gathering answered, including Madoc, and Inhya—though the latter seemed more rote than real. Aylaniś had moved to stand beside her, speaking low. Palatan was not there—likely away with Našobok, Anahli thought with a roll of eyes. Then Aylaniś found Anahli, gaze narrowing.

Where have you been, first daughter?

I'm here now. Anahli looked away.

"And as did stonetree standingKin scatter ša's berries upon Wind and Earth, so did we. Some of our People wandered far and wide, with only the Broken Stave and our animalKin to guide us. Some of us stayed put, to better guard our ways and places, while others wandered so far as to nevermore gather in First Running. We honour those with us, and those away from us. All of our People, scattered seeds across Grandmother's belly, to grow and protect Her as She grows and protects us."

The storyKeeper dropped her arms. The drums started again, booming against the cliffs.

"Dance, my People! Dance dreams, Dance memory, Dance all the tomorrows, in this Land of Dawn's first glance!"

Silence after she had finished, then voices lifting joyously into the dark: open and noisy appreciation for the storyKeeper's art, all making welcome to the festival of First Running.

"Kammalo has the finest stories!" A whoop from Madoc made Anahli jump; she'd forgotten he was there.

"She is a fine storyKeeper indeed."

An impromptu gambol was starting around the drums: children skipping, others circling, open dancing for all upon thisdark.

"I bet you won't dance with me. You're oških." Madoc spun the last word out, altogether close to mocking.

"If ever I would, the way you ask ensures I won't."

"Tokela would dance with me."

"Ahlóssa of one idea, aren't you?"

"Hah?" Madoc's eyebrows did their own gambol.

"Tokela, Tokela." Anahli pitched her voice high as Madoc's, and a'io, with that distinct whinge along its edge. "Surely Tokela's oških himself, above dancing with whingy ahlóssa."

"Take that back! I tell you he's not!"

Blinking at the overreaction, Anahli held up her hands and started to turn away.

"Anahli. I missed greeting you earlier." A hint of reproof slid through Inhya's voice; enough to halt Anahli and turn her.

Just beyond Inhya stood Aylaniś, expressionless, her powerful arms crossed.

"Ah." Inhya placed a light hand on Anahli's arm, stroked the gifted blanket's nap. "I see someone has made welcome for you already. Then let me have the honour of taking you to your new den. See, even now the other oških retire to their places."

True enough. First Running's firstdark catered to little ones and elders; for oških it meant time to share tales, gain new playmates, polish and preen finery for the upcoming games and Dances. Anahli slid her eyes to her dam.

"I will see you nextSun," Aylaniś said, quiet. "Našobok is here."

"Of course," Anahli replied, just as soft. *No matter that he thinks of you—of all of us!—as less than nothing, ones to be left behind... yet you and Dada both jump like beckoned fleethounds when he does bother to appear!*

Aylaniś seemed to ken the thought as if spoken, started to protest. Instead she swallowed the breath and turned away.

And for half a heartbeat, Anahli wanted to follow. Cling to her dam as if she were still ahlóssa. Go with her, see...

"Come along." Inhya's tone brooked no nonsense. It was easy to obey, take the extended hand and meet her hearther's eyes with a nod.

"Aška?" Madoc was still there, still the ahlóssa of one idea. "Tokela's nowhere to be found."

That hint of strange and culpable... ai, it was altogether close to grief, which trembled the strong hand in Anahli's and lingered in Inhya's bodytalk.

"No doubt he'll return by Sun's rising. Until then?" Inhya slid her chin towards the drums and the other children.

Madoc might be game for many challenges, but not this one. He gave a dramatic sigh and sauntered away.

So much better, that Anahli would be taking the Spawn's place.

The drums still spoke to the dark and what elders remained, telling soft tales about Fire's lingering grace. The ahlóssa had been herded some time ago to the sleeping dens.

Yet Madoc lay wakeful therein, trying not to look at Tokela's very empty bedshelf. Trying, and failing. The light of Brother Moon and His siblings angled down from the high window near to the curved ceiling, and set full relief across where Tokela usually slept, spilling over the rest of the slumbering inhabitants of the ahlóssa den.

The Spawn's place was also empty—and for other reasons than normal. In this much Madoc had cause to celebrate; he wasn't on the bedshelf edge with the Spawn's toes nigh in his tail-split. For even when he shoved back, the Spawn would just end up there again. Even if Madoc complained to his dam, she would smirk and shrug and tell him he was perfectly capable of moving to another place. To remember his cousin was little, and from duskLands where families slept together in wide and well-bedded hollows.

For thisdark at least, Madoc's shelf was his own again, and the Spawn with his family. Fine, it was an ugly name, so Madoc wouldn't use it aloud. At least, not to Anahli, who was much more interesting than her Spawn-y little brother.

Madoc craned his neck to eye Tokela's bedshelf yet again, as if its occupant might have snuck in whilst none was looking, then tried to calculate how long before the next adult passed by. Likely a while, since when Inhya had last come in, everyone had been asleep. Except Madoc, who had just pretended.

His dam's eyes had glowed, faint, as they'd swept the den then lingered upon Tokela's bedshelf. Then she'd sighed, dropped the hide back across the doorway, and retreated down the hallway tunnel.

Perhaps, Madoc considered, he should go hunt for Tokela. Or... since he was the eldest here, in this heartbeat, perhaps he should take his rights and seat himself in the window ledge. Look for Tokela that way. Always a challenge amongst the eldest of them, to shinny the wall and find the tiniest of footholds in the smooth stones, to sit triumphant and watch Moons and Stars skim across Sky... or, more often, clouds scudder and spill Rain across Grandmother's ever-changing skin.

Some say Grandmother was first amongst ones to walk both Earth and Sea, and we are her young, laid upon every beach...

How many times had Tokela sat up there and told stories? Forbidden to sketch, what talk he'd rather express with graphite stub and nimble fingers instead crowded on his tongue, filled him with stories gleaned from the storyKeepers. And all the while his fingers would twitch, as if they longed to visualise what Danced behind his eyes.

Madoc rose and padded over to the wall, started to climb. It was not easy, but neither was it impossible. Madoc took longer than he liked, but finally settled into the curved stone with a triumphant prop of feet opposite.

His entire world lay at his feet: inner compound spreading out, a little valley bearing lodges and paths, the latter which disappeared into the upwards curves and bluffs. That swell of stone and thatch dawnward led to the tribal cooking pits. Several dogs slept along the well-swept pathways, one with several fowl roosted on ša's hindquarters. The council den entrance, where the gnarled and ancient wyrh tree twins stood sentinel, culminating the path begun at the great entry facing River. Farther back, half settled into the curve and just past the stair leading up to Talking Bluff, hunched the den for the oških males. It might as well have been on little bronze Moon's darker face for all Madoc was allowed to know—which merely made it all the more fascinating.

Everyone had their own place, but the oških dens were their own world.

The oških fems had their own den, of course—on the other side of the compound—but Madoc spared little more than a fleeting thought for them. They'd nothing to do with him, other than several who did their duties by the cookFires and liked to make his favourites: fish sides charred crisp, and fried sourberry cakes with thick cream. He'd plenty of ahlóssa companions who were fem, of course, but they turned into something else, somehow, when they went into the oških dens. Something powerful, and somewhat chancy. Fems didn't have to hunt the fullness of their Changing; Grandmother had long ago bestowed life in them, to shed and gather in their own being. Whilst males had to track their Journey, chase and wrest the Changing into life.

Or so his dam always said.

Maybe Anahli would explain it to him. She didn't seem so mysterious, after all. Less fem and more male, as if she were one of those who were of Changing Spirit. And much less the cipher than Tokela, who grew more puzzling with every Sun's rising.

Madoc glared at the oških den, wishing with all his heart Tokela wouldn't go there, not yet, just stay with Madoc for a while longer. Then maybe, just maybe, if Madoc gave avid chase, he could wrest his own Changing into being. Catch up, so he and Tokela could walk their path and enter, together, that hostile place of separation, of *change*.

Madoc rested his head against the curved sill, looked up to the crown of Talking Bluff. Perhaps he would see Tokela return.

If he returned by that path.

If he returned thisdark.

◊ ◊ ◊

5
INTO OUTLANDS

"**G**o on!"
"Another, Tokela! Another!"
"There is nothing more to tell thisSun."
A collective groan from the small clutch of ahlóssa.
"But, Tokela—stories never end!"
"Grandmother! Tell us of Grandmother!"
"Surely you all know who Grandmother is," Tokela says, half tease and half chide.
"We want to hear it again!"
"Well. Grandmother. She is dam to all who traverse Sky and Sea, Earth and Flame and Spirit. We are her young, laid upon every beach. This is why we are, every tribe, every Clan, a'Khoweh'skaanumeki, Her firstPeople. This-Land is Her, from her rump to her strong jaw; from one toe in marshLands to the opposite in iceLand mountains. Her bones and Spirit make us, body and blood..."

Blood.
His own, and that of something else... *touching* him, rank-smelling, and cold, and... large?
Consciousness took Tokela with a sickening crash of senses. Sick-sweet upon his nostrils. Bark abrading his cheek. A hum, and a shadow crouched on the tree limb above him, bent with knife in hand...
Tokela exploded into action. He twisted, kicked out. His foot impacted with something soft; he twisted again, clutched at tree bark, then air.
Dropped like a stone.
He hit, rolled, landed sprawled on his back and whacked his head against gnarled roots. It took a few attempts to breathe, let alone chase the sparks and shadows from his gaze.
It was then he saw the Chepiś, still perched in the bow tree. The Chepiś had, it seemed, climbed to cut him free.

Instinct demanded Tokela bolt up. *Flee.* His body, however, flat refused the order, limp and heavy as a weir full of water and sodden pulpwood. Even Wind denied his lungs full service, leaving only an emptiness thumping, painful, beneath his sternum.

The Chepiś swung down from the bow tree; the same distance that had flattened Tokela was, for it, a mere hop. Worse, the Chepiś was holding Tokela's copper knife.

Tokela tried to lurch sideways. Tried to lever up to his elbows, to scoot backwards, anything.

Failed miserably, again.

Instead Wind filled his lungs in a sick-making, sudden rush. Tokela could finally move—and that merely to roll over just in time to vomit up everything not in his stomach.

For some time he lay there, heaving and shuddering and mostly *not* there, and long enough for anything to have killed him thrice over and perhaps skinned him as well. Once he stopped heaving, he once more felt those chill, oversize hands pawing at him, pulling...

Pulling him upright?

A coppery glint beckoned from the corner of blurry notice. He fixed on it: his knife, placed next to him, and the only security in a world gone suddenly maddened as the Chepiś tried to pick him up. Tokela couldn't stop shaking. He managed to drag his feet beneath him as the Chepiś started to turn him about. It knelt as it held him, its small, round eyes tinged with what might have been concern but seemed more consideration. Tokela refused to wonder; instead he wrested sideways, nearly toppled but at the last saved it, and snatched up his knife, backing away.

Speaking its gibberish, the Chepiś reached for him. Tokela struck out, felt the knife make contact, didn't wait to see if he'd done damage but turned to run.

Instead he went face-first into an immovable tower of cloth and something burning-hard.

Tokela hissed, shoved back to find his eyes level with a filigreed metal clasp and a hide belt cinched about a blood-coloured tunic. Swallowing hard, he followed the line of tunic downward, to knee-high boots big enough to swim in. With another, nauseated swallow, he ran his eyes back up that fancy tunic. And *up.*

It was one thing to know Chepiś were too tall. It was another entirely to be faced off against it.

The second Chepiś raised its hands, thin fingers splayed. It might have meant it was weaponless, or surprised. Either way, Tokela was not about to assume it meant him no harm. Hide pallid as the first one, this one's hair was dark, tied into a tail of tight, crisp waves. It made more of the unintelligible, flat talk. Tokela raised his knife, kept backing.

A large grip enveloped his own, yanked his knife hand upward and held Tokela nigh onto his bare toes. And there was absolutely nothing he could do about it.

Meanwhile the first Chepiś was speaking again, in the awkward way that Tokela could somewhat decipher. "It but scratched me. Moreover, the tunic is old. I wondered what could escape a pack of *shigala*—and would dare to stand them down, it would seem. But the little one is damaged, and those beasts have been too patient for their meal. See to it, Vox, since we have taken their catch."

The Chepiś standing before Tokela looked down at him with cool, flat eyes as another figure stepped into view. Broader, more muscular, a dusky shadow amidst the moon-pale Chepiś. Slowly, the Matwau drew a long knife.

What nerve normally ran obsidian along his veins thoroughly deserted Tokela, leaving nothing more than the names with which that Matwau would dismiss their kind: little grubby animal, primitive, *sgralka*, painted dwarfling. *Savage.*

Tokela's eyes rolled up into his head, and the poisoned dark once more enveloped him, toppled him into its embrace.

> Shards.
> Bright-hot in darkness, flashes spreading, reaching; tendrils of light sparking within his skull, behind his eyes and down to his heart.
> They are warmth. Breath. Life.
> Connexion.
> Power.
> Awash in it, afloat, a deep-soft drone teasing, tickling, making promises with a tongue he does not understand, but knows.
> Somehow.
> Clicking within him, piece by piece, answer by answer, and he twitches beneath, whimpers purling in his throat merely to be swallowed by the vast surround of something he has no name for.
> And names can sway Power, so he calls it: *neverending*.
> As if with that, things begin to shift. The impossible, incomprehensible shards smooth into pinpricks of light—still unreachable and untouchable, still recognisable.
> Stars. Some of them Ancestors lighting lamps brilliant and almost painful; many more of them Other, invaders, unfriendly. Why does he long for the contact, even should he burn fingers upon the impossible?
> Small rustles, murmurs he cannot comprehend. Wind tossing the topmost leaves, breathing

more gently near the woodLand floor, fingering damp hair over his brow, touching...

Ai, something touching him, holding to him, keeping him pinioned to ground when all he wants is to soar into that glittering dark. He squirms beneath the hold; it merely presses tighter. A presence hovering. Strange. Familiar.

Something within his vision... gives, and beneath the Dreaming a memory coalesces. It has to be memory, for this cannot be. It can never be again, for she is dead, part of those Stars, perhaps.

But still, he whispers: *Aška?*

Pressed to Earth and heavy-sodden, he tries to open his eyes, deny the Dreaming as she bends over him, answers. *Peace. Be still, my son, and soon it will be over.*

A drag of cloth over his face, cool and strange-smelling and cloying, and while something within him begs for it, something else screams and bolts upright...

Something impacted with his hand, went sailing in a dark, liquid arc. There was a sharp cry—dismay? anger?—and before he was even halfway up, Tokela grabbed for his knife.

No luck there, only white-hot trails spangling across his vision, tiny sparks like Stars.

Blinking, Tokela shook his head. Growled, low and menacing, as the sparks smeared into blurry figures, hovering. Too narrow, too tall, shrouded by tree shadows and dying spears of Sun's light.

"Easy, now," said one of the figures, its deep voice speaking... dawnLands Talk? Ai, if a poor, broken version. "Done be done. You be safe."

And Tokela remembered.

He had been poisoned by Shaped creatures.

He was surrounded by Chepiś and Matwau.

He wasn't safe.

His body wasn't so quick as his thoughts. What should have been a sideways lurch ended up in a sprawl, limbs useless, against a wide pool of sticky-thick indigo sinking into Grandmother's skin.

Indigo? But indigo was not hued so until it sat, stained.

Several voices, now, rising in unrecognisable, unmusical talk. One in particular penetrated; menace lay beneath it, thrilling Tokela's muscles to action. Once again he tried to lurch upward.

Once again he went sprawling, facedown in the dirt.

Hands laid upon him and shoved him onto his back. The touch

seared into nerve and bone, as if outLand *eirn* had been laid to skin; it brought Tokela further into his body. He lay stripped to clout, wet warmth puckering and cooling on his chest, arm and leg throbbing hot. Rain pattered all around. Damp moss pillowed his head, roots curving against his spine, giving off strange, white-dark sparks that tingled against his skin. As if the roots had been Shaped to cradle him...

Shaped. He was in Šilombiš'okpulo, with Chepiś Shapers.

Tokela twisted, snarled defiance and fear upward at the Chepiś holding him down.

The Chepiś rocked back, but it didn't loosen its grip. Three others moved in, the failing light silhouetting them against the vast tree canopy. The tree beneath Tokela... moved. Too quick to be Wind, or anything natural, it curled and stretched outwards with tiny, oddling sparks and shifts, leaves moving, rustling, sheltering from Rain.

"Lie still." The talk—too deliberate—came from the Moon-haired one that had cut him loose. "We're trying to help you. The *shigala* poisoned you, and we're helping. Can you understand?"

Another growl purling deep in his throat, Tokela hesitated. He wasn't sure he did understand. He didn't think the Chepiś lied, but then his own senses were sideways; poison, he remembered, bits and fragments beginning to piece together.

The Chepiś's breathing was loud in the stillness—indeed, all of them seemed to be panting—but Tokela couldn't fathom any scent save the sick-sweet. *Like the Shaped creatures*, he thought with a chill in his gut, and only one heart's drum he could feel or hear.

Perhaps they didn't have hearts.

Matwau did, however. The one standing amidst the Chepiś had a heartbeat that echoed deep as the talking drums, steady-sure and unconcerned. Its face was distinctive—familiar—darker than even dryLands people in summering's midst, displaying lines of both life and living, with an expression that seemed... curious, no more or less. A hunter's face, used to the control of her own bodytalk... Ai, it was a fem, smoky telltale layering atop a Matwau's strange odour.

Another Chepiś spoke—it was the one Tokela had run into, with a voice and bodytalk that betrayed anger. Yet the Moon-haired one didn't so much as blink, its gaze holding to Tokela's, a courtesy he'd not expected any Chepiś to know. There was silver in the round eyes—indeed in all their eyes. As if the pale gleam of Brother Moon had been captured, and slurried by Starlight...

With a shudder, Tokela broke the gaze. He couldn't help a flinch, humiliating as it was, as the third of the Chepiś knelt beside Moon Hair..

The Chepiś made more of the strange sounds, its voice warbling soft and light, less menacing than the dark-voiced one beside it.

"It's a *ghoteh*, Rann," Moon Hair replied. "Try not to frighten it, and be good enough to speak in a tongue it can understand."

"It doesn't seem to understand even this savage tongue," Dark Voice muttered.

Savage? Ai, that was a word Tokela knew, well enough. Savage was the way these outLanders were rending talk so ancient and rich! Lacking the sort of ears that would pin, Tokela had to settle for sliding a narrow glare towards Dark Voice.

"Is it young, then?" The soft-voiced Chepiś—was it called Raahn?—kept staring at Tokela with its strange, stony eyes. It spoke his talk even worse than Moon Hair. "It is so tiny."

"I daresay it's young, but they are all small, these," Moon Hair answered. "Even the elders."

Indignation was swiftly elbowing aside trepidation. FirstPeople were not tiny; it was outLanders who were giants, too big to fit in a proper lodging! Tokela tried to angle forwards, was prevented by not only the grip on his shoulders, but the strange, sideways lassitude.

His slight shift was misinterpreted.

"We shan't hurt you," Moon-Hair repeated. "We're trying to help. You've been poisoned."

He was aware of that, well enough. Frankly he hadn't expected to wake again. If they had helped him, he owed them for that much at least.

But why had they helped him?

"What unusual markings it has." Rann started to reach out, undoubtedly towards the hennaed Marks upon Tokela's cheekbones. Indignation burbled away as Tokela abruptly felt very tiny indeed. It took every scrap of courage he possessed to hold still, and even then his hand crept to where his skinning knife should be. Of course it wasn't there—he could see it, piled with the rest of his garb at Dark Voice's feet.

"I wouldn't touch it, Rann. It could well bite, with those fangs." Dark Voice's arms were crossed in a gesture reminiscent of Tokela's own folk. In fact, all of them had bodytalk not unlike his own. "Look at it! It might be young, but it's as wild a brute as the *shigala* it killed. Like the serpents south of this wretched forest, the young even more poisonous than the parents." Then, to Moon Hair, "You should have let it die. We aren't allowed to interfere like this."

A frown gathered Moon Hair's too-pale brow, but not once did it take its eyes from Tokela. It was the Matwau who did something so incomprehensible—so *normal*—that Tokela's eyes nearly bugged from his head.

The Matwau smacked a broad palm against the back of Dark Voice's head akin to chastising an errant cub. "Quite a manner, you have, Vox, for not frightening the little one."

Vohks? It was a ridiculous name; Tokela preferred Dark Voice.

"Perhaps it doesn't understand us," Rann put in.

Tokela had often heard his elders make talk past him, but he figured none of his tribe had been "talked over" quite like this. It was more withering than even a scornful glance from Sarinak could inspire.

"It doesn't seem terribly afraid," Rann continued.

I'm only as afraid as I need be, Tokela thought. *And you're the ones who have taken my knives from me.*

The Matwau's eyes met his and held. The colour of good amber, and quite canny. As if she'd heard his thought, a smirk touched her mouth. "He understands, all right."

That he could be so easily read by Matwau was not at all reassuring.

Moon Hair was peering at Vox; the latter shrugged and retreated, coming to a halt before... Ai, it was the bow tree where Tokela had taken refuge. The Shaped creature still lay dead at the bow tree's roots. A... *shigala,* Moon Hair had called it.

Returning its gaze to the Matwau fem, Moon Hair lingered there for several heartbeats. There was an intimacy in the shared glance, unspoken but plain; one more odd reassurance amidst all the unknown.

These creatures had friends, not merely companions. Close friends, from the bodytalk of those two—and subordinates, from the exchange between Moon Hair and Vox. That one bristled like a challenged oških, while the one known as Rann seemed young, openly curious as any ahlóssa.

"You know," Rann was still peering at Tokela, curious as if he had sprouted from the rock mould, "I've never seen a *ghoteh* before. You know the most of us, Sivan. Is it very like to its people?"

Sih-van? Moon Hair's name?

While all of them—save the Matwau, oddly enough—kept calling Tokela "it". Well, then, all right, Tokela was doing the same, so taking offence was certainly questionable at this point. His nose told him nothing—again, save with the Matwau—but it seemed these Chepiś weren't unlike Matwau, if decidedly unlike his own People...

Yet they weren't so different as the taleKeepers would paint. They didn't have four legs, or wings, or many eyes like spiderKin sometimes had. Perhaps they were like serpentKin, and hid their sex.

Perhaps they were neither. And if so...

A shiver ran down his nape. If so, could Chepiś sire a half-breed child?

"My brother knows more than any of us, save my father." Sivan was eyeing Tokela, twitched narrow shoulders in what must be a shrug. "I'd dare to doubt the little one has ever seen such as us, either."

They had brothers. Fathers. So they had young. Disheartening, the confirmation, full of too many possibilities.

"It is rather slender," Rann offered. "And not quite as dark as our Maloh." A sweeping arm gesture, though unfamiliar, made it plain: the Matwau was Mah-loh. The naming rang more pleasant in contrast with the others' names, hard and angular as dead standingKin. Rann continued, "I'd heard *ghoteh* painted themselves blue, but that their hides, too, were dark as dried *kypros* berries. Their bodies solid as stones."

A glint of metal sparked Tokela's attention. Vox stood by the bow tree, leaning over the felled creature, drawing a slender, shining knife. Tokela couldn't help a small recoil of distaste; out-Landers seemed to take inordinate pride over their Shaping of the metal they raped from Grandmother's womb and called *eirn*.

Surely if these Chepiś were hunters, they would know predators made tough eating... wait. This Vox looked as if he were about to break and parcel Tokela's own kill. Tokela leaned forwards in protest, but Rann reached for him, startling him into another recoil.

"Perhaps they paint themselves not only blue, but brown?"

Sivan and Maloh exchanged patient looks. Tokela's own trepidation was swiftly fading, running the length of huffy insult to—admit it—wry amusement. Did all Chepiś truly have that same sickly pallor to their hides? Could they not imagine a Skybow's wealth of hue? He was of Forest and River, after all, not a Sun-blessed Horsetalker!

"Perhaps it hasn't been thoroughly painted." This time Rann actually touched Tokela, fingers rubbing at his cheek as if to wipe the faded Marks away. Those fingers were cool, feathery, not overly unpleasant. But the searching touch lingered, followed by an unnerving tingle. Tokela ducked out from beneath, and when Rann started forwards again, Tokela gave her a warning look.

"Stop trying to pet him, Rann," the Matwau fem drawled, wry. "The *sgralka*'s little, but he might indeed bite, and I'm not sure I'd blame him."

Tokela bristled. *Sgralka* was even more insulting than *ghoteh*! Over by the tree, Vox had looped some kind of rope about the—shee-galah?—tying it in a manner suggesting he was indeed about to butcher it.

This had all gone far enough.

"I'm no *sgralka*!" Tokela burst out. "Nor *ghoteh*! I'm a'Kowe-hoklaánutekasha, firstPeople. And I've never seen your kind, but I know what you are! And that"—he flung his unwounded arm towards where Vox was putting a knife to the creature Tokela had slain—"is my kill. Matwau are known to take what's not theirs; are Chepiś also?"

A quartet of round eyes riveted to his. Tokela refused to totter back beneath them. He did, however, swallow hard as the silence pounded like his heartbeats, one into the other.

A sudden, clear peal of laughter rang and echoed beneath the thick canopy. Sivan began, joined softly by Rann, a snort from Maloh, and a roll of eyes from Vox. Sivan rocked from kneeling to sit beside Tokela, still chuckling.

"Well said, young... kho-way-oka!" At least Sivan was trying to pronounce it correctly. "'Twas rude of us to talk about you as though you were not present. And we would not rob you of your prize, though—"

"Though we have little time for primitive foolishness," Vox snapped, still hovering over the dead creature. "Unless, little animal, you prefer dying to what scant life you do possess."

Tokela's lip quivered with the beginnings of a snarl. Sivan turned and snapped something in their flat talk. It seemed exasperation was exasperation in any Land as Vox rolled pale eyes in answer.

"We mean no disrespect." This from Maloh in her good dawn-Lands talk. "The bite of a *shigala* is evil if left untended, and we had to use what means we could."

Tokela frowned.

"When you struggled"—Sivan motioned to the upended bowl—"you spilt the blood we were using. We'll have to draw more. If we can." Sivan looked concerned. "Even with altered creatures, blood coagulates after death."

"Ka-hagoo...?" Tokela mouthed the odd word. And the only altars he knew of were frowned upon in dawnLands, though his own sire had kept one in midLands tradition, with several spirit-Dancers balanced upon carven stone bases.

"Thickens," Maloh put in.

Ai, that Tokela understood.

Sivan gave a small, curious smile and continued, "The creature does not look long dead, but better to move swiftly. If you will allow Vox, we can see to your leg. And your arm." Again, pale brows furrowed. "We might need Rann's services after all."

Vox let out a torrent of the flat talk—clearly protest. Rann answered in kind, this time. Muttering, Vox bent back to the dead creature and Rann came forwards, threading something resembling a shiny, rectangular waterskin on a thong from over her head. "Are you thirsty?"

Tokela was, but eyed the skin-that-was-not warily. It looked to be made of *eirn*. Perhaps that explained the odd feelings as Rann had touched him. "I cannot drink that."

"It's merely water, little one." Rann extended the water closer. Tokela angled backward.

Sivan was watching with a frown, then reached out and stayed Rann's hand. "Take your burl bowl, go to the stream and fill it."

"Sivan, but surely..." Rann peered at first Sivan, then Tokela, eyes widening. "Are the stories true after all? Is it possible forged iron truly burns these little folk?"

"It has a knife of copper," Vox corrected from over by the *shigala*. Its belly opened, Vox was transferring greenish-blue meat—organs, likely—into a large bowl.

"Copper is not forged steel, and many things are possible," Maloh said. "I'll come with you. This forest can be treacherous to one who knows it not."

Still big-eyed, Rann followed Maloh's retreat into the forest.

"You are not the only one who has found themselves in an odd encounter," Sivan explained. "Rann never quite believed my brother's stories of meeting with Gho... firstPeople"—the correction was quick—"though she liked to hear them."

She. "It... the young one... Rann. Rann is a she?" Tokela blurted before he could halt it.

"She is." Sivan's smile broadened. "Save Vox, all of us here choose that guise. We are not so unalike, your kind and mine."

Guise? It made no sense. It implied a path beyond garb, moiety, or society; a Shaping beyond anything he'd imagined possible. Tokela's gut gave a sharp twist: confusion, and dread.

What if they hadn't sired him? What if they'd... Shaped him?

"The claw marks aren't dangerous, if cleaned properly. Only the bites contain poison." Sivan leaned closer, inspecting Tokela's injuries. Following her gaze, Tokela saw they were indeed smeared with indigo-hued blood, and seemed less like rotting flesh than before. Sivan asked, "Are we timely, Vox?"

Vox replied in the flat talk; a look from Sivan, however, forced him to translate. "It is too long dead. But its organs should suffice. We can but hope your little animal responds to treatment." Despite the dismissive tone, Vox quickly rose and approached with bowl in hand, hands smeared blue-black. It did not look appetizing in any fashion; in fact it looked to be more poison. Tokela couldn't help a recoil.

Once again, Vox muttered something to Sivan. Tokela didn't need translation to hear the dismissal: *superstitious primitive.* Looking Vox in the eye, Tokela made a silent vow: *that* one would not again see him succumb to so much as a twitch.

"I imagine your people have also found poisons growing beside cures," Sivan said. "The *shigala*'s blood seems to follow that rule. I'm sure a bio-shaper could explain, but for now we'll just go with what works."

Bye-oh...Shaper?. Tokela refused—*refused*—to react, instead offering, "When someone is bitten by a poison serpent in the Dry-Lands, they will use organs to draw the venom."

Kneeling, Vox raised his eyebrows at Sivan, then offered, "This will sting."

"Worse than the bite?" Tokela retorted, and had to tuck a

smirk behind his teeth when Vox blinked. Even with the small eyes and too-pale lids, the expression was familiar—as was the frown that replaced it. Without another word, the Chepiś began slicing and layering bits of what looked like a heart onto Tokela's leg.

And if that was what a Chepiś considered a sting?

"It will leave a nasty scar. I imagine such holds no distress for you, considering that." Vox nodded towards the carmine wyrh tree tattooed across Tokela's ribs, received by all a'Naišwyrh when their voice first broke or their breasts began to bud.

I imagine you haven't much, Tokela retorted—silent, of course. *Imagination, that is.* Instead he revisited the smirk. The new scars would indeed be worth showing off when he removed to the oških den.

If he made it back.

"Do you—?"And it was nigh the same time as Sivan asked her own question:

"What are you called?"

Vox grumbled something that for a half heartbeat seemed intelligible. "—brother kept pets, and now you would do likewise. Your father would—"

Tokela frowned as Vox's talk gibbered off into nonsense once again. Sivan's response was terse. It drove Vox to his feet. He looked angry.

"Go wash," Sivan told him.

Vox tilted his head. It might have been courtesy, or it mightn't, but he went. He passed Rann and Maloh as they returned, shaking his head when Rann would have stopped, spoken.

"Forgive him," Sivan said. "Sometimes we are quite"—she thought upon it, shook her head then continued—"*temporal?*" When Tokela frowned, she tried again, "In this place? With our reactions. And how would it be otherwise, when we have become so like your kind?"

Tokela blinked at her. Some of her talk he didn't comprehend, some sounded insulting, and the rest simply confused. The meat upon his thighs oozed, prickling his skin. The whiff of decay made him all the more woozy.

"If it's beginning to rot," Tokela asked, "does that mean it doesn't work?"

Sivan frowned, peering down at him. "It hasn't begun to rot."

"Can"—surely his tongue hadn't been this thick even four heartbeats previous—"smell it."

"Sivan!" The name, then a string of their talk as Rann hurried over.

Sivan's answer scaled upward as she knelt, her hand gripping Tokela's chin, hard. There wasn't a thing he could do about it, either; no protest, not even an evasion as his head fell back, his neck limp as a newborn's.

And somehow Grandmother opened up beneath him, took him into Her silent womb-darkness. *Not yet*, She hummed, cradling him close. *You will be mine, but not yet...*

Voices, sharp and tense and somehow fearful. He is pulled from Earth's embrace, limp and small. He doesn't want to leave, fights...

Instead something stinging-feathery-cool spreads across his breastbone and sinks down—sinks in—as if he has been cut open for fingers to grab hold of his heart. Ice filling his veins. Pain, yet also abrupt pleasure, melting into a rush of warmth as his heart starts to quiver within caging fingers. As if he is a vessel left dry for too long, cracking along the rim from the sudden flood of this whatever-it-is, this... neverending.

A jolt strains his muscles, brings the taste of blood to his tongue as those icy fingers upon his ribs—within his ribs—force his heart back to beating. His protest is hoarse and emptied of breath. His eyes are open, yet all he sees are Stars. Wind swirls about his open mouth then floods his chest, as the ice-chill fingers give another insistent... twist, and as voices flood behind his eyes to set Stars to Dance, and as Sky opens up to...

Swallow him...

By the Bonds of Atvan...

A whisper, but not, floating astonished in the Deeps, then another, echoing beneath:

Who are you, Tohwakelifitčiluka? Who are you, Eyes of Stars?

They know his blessing-name, somehow, and dare to speak it aloud, twisted free and Power-Full. It skims the surface of panic, and the sound of it—his, Spirit breath and body—returns to him one instinct never long absent:

Fight.

And with every sense he has Tokela twists, kicks out—not only body but heart and Spirit-will. There is a cry—dismay? horror? surprise!—as his defiance takes form in the void-called-neverending, a shield of obsidian to repel, a flood of copper waters carrying him away on a swift current, safe...

Tokela kicked free from the Matwau's firm hold, fell, and hit rolling. Coming to a crouch, he hunched there, fingers reaching for a knife but instead clawing at skin: his weapon still wasn't there.

Rann had fallen back, her small eyes wheeling-white. Sivan too was staring at him. Maloh was cursing—in the flat talk, yet of its foulness there was little doubt—and holding her side.

The situation was so absurd, so implausible—three of them stood down before a weaponless not-yet-oških—that Tokela choked back a sudden urge to laugh.

"I think," Maloh said, her eyes flickering from her companions to Tokela and then back again, "he is no longer poisoned."

$$\phi \quad \phi \quad \phi$$

6
HEARTH

By the time Vox returned, the Moons had begun to peek through the branches of the canopy. Maloh had started a Fire and hung meat over it for warming. Not the *shigala*'s, Tokela was glad to see; it smelt like normal meat. Indeed, Maloh showed a good grasp of common manners by inviting Tokela to be the first to be seated at Fire's circle.

She also returned his knife to him.

He took it, watching her all the while. Maloh merely sat next to him, motioned for him to be seated. "We do not offer harm to a guest at our hearth," she told him. "Be easy. You have startled my oathsister, that is all."

Tokela peered over to where Sivan and Rann had been in soft conversation for some time, now joined by Vox. "You... have... oathsisters?"

"I do. We do." The Matwau smiled and peered at Sivan across the small, cheering blaze. "She is as near to as I will ever claim."

It was, again, such a normal sentiment that Tokela accepted not only the seat, but the first helping of their meal.

They ate in silence—Tokela would have termed it companionable had he not been sitting, a questionably welcome guest of Chepiś, in the middle of Šilombiš'okpulo, at what Fire a Matwau had brought forth.

Inwardly, he felt no such silence. Instead he felt... exposed. Sore, as if he'd been dragged over rocks. The silence... roared, almost; as if with Wind's hoarse breath. StandingKin pressed about him, lurking like shadowlings. He could hear River-children burbling, and Fire's heat tongued his cheeks, popping and hissing as if Ša would speak a tongue Tokela might fathom, did he listen.

Instead Tokela focused on the roast meat and the Chepiś's hushed voices, wondering what had happened.

For something had happened.

"Do they have young?" It was the only question he could form upon his tongue.

Maloh didn't take offence. "They do. Like my people"—her

eyes slid to meet his—"and yours. You have the markings of a young one, yourself."

He met her gaze.

"And now you're wondering how I know so much of your people. I have known some of them in my time, you see." Maloh took a bite of the meat with oddly blunt, strong teeth.

I have known some of them.

Again, questions crowded his brain, thankfully drowning out the strength of the woodland's presence. Yet Tokela feared speaking even one.

"There is an old *sgral*—" the dark eyes flickered to him as Maloh replaced the word with barely a beat "—one of firstPeople who claims to be chieftain over one of your tribes. But he is a charmer, that one, and tells stories for the fun of it." She seemed to be speaking more of lies than any deeper storied truth; nevertheless she took note of what must be scrawling itself over Tokela's face. "I wrong him. He is a good soul, if more—uh, how would you say it?—*trickster* than any his age should allow. We call him Little Fish, for he always seems to wriggle off any hook and back into water when landed."

A smile quirked Tokela's mouth. It melted into a troubled frown at what this Matwau was saying. Chepiś wandered into their Land even now, despite the ancient truce? Wandered in, and had... acquaintances? Of his People?

His attention swiveled, sharp—too sharp?—as the others approached, slow, the impromptu hearth.

Maloh paid no heed. "What is your name, young one?"

"He is called—" Sivan began, but Tokela finished it, swift:

"Tokela. I am called Tokela a'Naišwyrh." He looked up at Sivan, thought, *I've not given you leave to the sounds of my blessing-name.*

Sivan's pale eyebrows rose, then she nodded.

Tokela dropped the piece of meat he was holding. Lowering his gaze, he busied himself with recovering it. So the rumours were true: Chepiś could sift one's inner voice, hear and speak it.

Vox came slowly over and sat down, stony eyes dismissing Tokela; behind him, Rann no longer seemed unsteady. Her eyes—unlike Vox's—held little mistrust. It seemed perhaps... compassion?

"Was it your mother who gave your name to you?"

Maloh's question came unexpected; had she somehow heard, too? Whilst the three Chepiś seemed... puzzled? Disapproving?

"Your father, mayhap?" Maloh offered. She was trying to be friendly, but her eyes kept flickering from Tokela to Sivan.

Father. Sharp, stinging, this time with the poison of doubt. *If they know. Perhaps they do know.*

Tokela's hands tremored against the bowl. Perhaps Chepiś could bring this into some shape as well, like Rann had neutralised the *shigala*'s poison. Yet...

What if they did know?

What would it mean?

Tokela had never thought, faced with the possibility of any truth, to find such abject terror in it.

Instead he focused on the question without its treacherous undercurrents. "Tokela is what I'm called by my family. Any other namings we might have are given by elders who walk closer to Grandmother's path."

A snort from Vox, followed by a quick, albeit heated, exchange of flatTalk. Not Sivan, this time, but Rann.

"What was your dam's name, Tokela?" Voiced very distant and formal, as if Sivan somehow knew it was a chancy thing, to voice the names of the dead. Nevertheless the pale gaze was a demand.

"Lakisa... 'ailiq." It was a relief to speak, even with the whispered honorific attached: *I mean no disturbance to you, mother-Spirit, only remembrance and honour.*

Maloh was peering at Sivan, her dark brows twisted in a frown. Sivan didn't respond, by glance or return frown; in fact, her face seemed more stone than flesh as she asked, very soft, "Is she still alive?"

"N'da." Tokela swallowed hard, then said, low, "Did you know her?"

Maloh kept peering at Sivan, frowning. Vox uttered a fierce and unintelligible commentary; he was displeased, no question.

Sivan held up a silencing hand, her eyes meeting Tokela's. "And if we did? Why would it matter to you? Your people are afraid of mine, and mine, I believe, fear yours for reasons even they do not understand."

"Sivan, you must—" Rann started towards Sivan, desisting as Vox's hand gripped her arm and Sivan flicked what was surely a warning glance.

Silence. It lingered too long, crawling up Tokela's nape; for a scant half heartbeat he wanted to clap his hands over his ears as though they were shouting. Instead he kept his eyes upon Sivan, narrowed into the fading light.

Did you know my dam? He couldn't speak it aloud, but no doubt they all heard. Somehow.

"We mean you no harm, Tokela," Sivan finally said, though she did not meet his eyes. "Eat. We will uphold the truce, even as you must. We will take you back to the guardian threshold and return you to your place."

Quite final, it throttled any remaining speech Tokela might possess.

He was so... small, Sivan considered.

Yet fierce. *Savage!* Vox had growled, and while that might be likely, there was also a... well, a dignity that seemed strange in one so young, and an undeniable strength of will.

The last had proven itself when Tokela had made them wait while he'd removed the claws from the *shigala*—and that done quicker and neater than any of their own hunters, Sivan had reflected as the boy sniffed the razored claws, grimaced then secreted them in his clothing.

Trophies! Vox had scoffed.

Maloh had merely pointed out that any being Tokela's size who could take down a *shigala* deserved any reminder he wanted.

Sivan said nothing; her thoughts were complex enough.

They saw Tokela to the threshold. Maloh offered to take him through. The charged shield made an accounting of every passage, tallied it and sent it to the Arrogate; if Maloh accompanied the little one, it would be noted as no more than a lesser transgression with planetary natives, likely overlooked.

And Maloh well knew how to cope with the shield should the boy have difficulty.

He didn't. It jangled alarms in Sivan's brain, fitted another piece to a too-complex puzzle, another suspicion barely fathomed.

It was impossible, what she was thinking.

Wasn't it?

The threshold sparked and snapped as the two breached the exit. Through the haze of energy, Sivan could see Maloh shudder off the lingering pressure of the guardian, then kneel to converse with the boy, quite serious. She rose again, making a gesture; it seemed familiar to the boy, for he returned it. With a last glance towards the portal, he retreated across the meadow.

"Sivan." It was Rann, insistent.

Sivan did not break her silence, watching as the boy ran across the grassland then slid, smooth as water, into the trees.

They were all like that, Sivan's own people would claim; more animal than anything. A fine way to justify taking a planet, Maloh often scoffed, pretending the inhabitants are less, somehow. Creatures to be tamed—or held in their own little habitat whilst the conquerors scrutinise them.

Maloh's own people had made their choice long ago: assimilation.

Sivan's brother preferred classifying the little natives as "belonging to their world". Whatever it meant, it was a quality Sivan's own kind had alternately shunned and, though not openly admitted, envied.

This world, after all, had set itself against them from the beginning.

"Sivan."

Turning, Sivan peered at her companion. Rann's breath hung, misting damp, and her eyes were filled with starlit shadows, turned toward the little one's departure.

"Sivan," she insisted, "we cannot just... let him go. Not with what happened. We must do something."

"You know our hands are tied in this, Rann," Vox answered instead. "Sivan has done what she could. More than she should."

Yet Sivan felt she had not done enough. Moreover, she could still sense the boy's... *presence*, dwindling into the mortal rot of the ancient forest's supremacy.

A presence that had changed before their eyes. From the moment Rann had reached inward and between, taken the weight of the world away from him, to siphon the poison from his system.

"It wasn't just that," Rann murmured, following Sivan's thoughts. "I didn't change anything except the poison. The change was already there. He... helped, Sivan. He reached back, Between." Laying her head against Sivan's shoulder, she furthered, "I thought their psionics lost. Bred out, long ago. Is he some sort of throwback?"

"I don't know."

Rann parsed the lie with a frown. "What do you know, then?"

"Blood and star-iron," Vox growled, "what *is* it about these little natives? First your brother, then—"

"Enough, Vox!" Sivan snapped.

Rann's eyes were large as the Lost Station, considering it all as Maloh returned, breaching the threshold's shimmer with a shake and stagger. A further reminder: she was more hampered by the portal's disorienting effects than the native boy.

The native boy. The lost one's son.

Maloh padded over, frowning. "Now. Are you going to tell me what you were on about?"

Sivan shivered as Maloh put a hand to her cheek and trailed it down to rest on her shoulder, peat against glacier snow. "Your hands are cold, Maloh."

"Mm. I can't abide that thing."

"I wonder," Sivan whispered. "Were his hands cold? When you touched him just now?"

Maloh frowned, harder. "Our little Shadow, you mean?"

"Shadow?" This from Vox, frowning.

Maloh slanted her gaze after the native boy's path. Her smile, sudden, also quirked fond. "If the old sgral—the old kowehokla— is Little Fish, then that young one is Little Shadow. First he's here, then... ssst!" She flicked her fingers. "Gone! But to answer you, Siv, his hands were warm as a good hearth."

"Warm." Rann's words were hesitant, heavy. Pondering. "He's not of our people, yet the portal has no effect upon him. What does it mean, Sivan?"

Sivan was afraid she knew. Maloh, too, for her grip turned into a caress.

"Sivan," Rann persisted, "whoever this boy is... whatever he is—"

"It's something we should never have interfered with, is all it is!" Vox intercepted.

"But we have, haven't we?" Rann shot back. "We have, and it's formed... I formed it..." She trailed off as Vox shook his head; where such a rebuttal usually swayed her, instead she stiffened, turned to Sivan and said, flat, "It was already there. But it has awakened. We cannot just let it lie unravelled. It's *wrong*."

"I know!" Sudden, vehement, Sivan shook off Maloh's caress. "I know. But I also know there has been interference enough. I dare do nothing more until I have spoken to my brother. And"— with a heavy frown—"my father."

As the *t'rešalt* lingered to a distant shadow within the massive hedge, Tokela expected—hoped—his overburdened senses would dull.

If anything, they heightened.

Amber light fingered across the darkness, giving plenty of light... too much. Tokela staggered down the hillock, came to the next copse of trees and stumbled to a halt, leaning against one of them. His hands rose, of their own accord, to press behind his ears... and that was where he felt it the most, a strange, hot, tight-stretched sensation of not-sound, of... pressure. Tighter. Harder. *Pain...*

"N'da." Until he heard it, Tokela hadn't realised he'd spoken aloud, and he nearly laughed... as if he could stop such a thing with a small, quavering voice?

But.

It stopped.

As if he'd finally pulled from River's depths a too-full weir, with all the water pouring from the netting to leave trapped swimmingKin, glittering and gasping...

His own breath came just as thick and rasping. Any predator walking or flying would hear, take advantage. Tokela swallowed, clenched his fists. One step, unsure but steady. Then another. Several more. Each one grew stronger. Each one made the strange pressure/pain ebb. By the twentieth step, Tokela was able to walk with eyes high, hands once again swinging his strides.

But those hands were clenched, and it was not his normal, ground-eating tread. He couldn't fully replace hesitancy, couldn't fight the surety:

Things were *different*.

Every sound resonated, every shadow loomed large. Moss and bracken wafted up where he trod, an invasion of bruised green-wet. The surround cupped itself close and lingered, uncanny. Earth and Sky made Their Dance ever closer, pressing against his heart to set it wildly thumping, and They uttered sounds like... like... *whispers*.

Was this what his dam had felt? Was this what had taken her Spirit?

Tokela forced his heart calm, his gait steady. Again, to totter like a wounded buck—alone—was asking for more than a loss of Spirit. It was no more than the aura of the forbidden places, the Chepiś's interference. It was what they did, twist Grandmother's children into beasts. Like the beasts whose talons now lay in his pouch.

The latter trickled satisfaction through his being, and his senses, given something to do—namely avoid darkling predators and stay alive—set themselves to just that.

Tokela stopped at a small pond to wash away the oddling blood as best he could. It nevertheless hung in his nostrils past all reason. He avoided a pack of wolfKin by just knowing, somehow, where they were before he'd so much as noticed their passage; the same with a huge, dusky wildcat that crossed his trail and kept going. The predators knew, somehow: he was no longer so easy.

And so he passed, from deep woods into scattered settlements and small clearings, toward the glow that lit Sky above River.

Ai, how could he have forgotten? It was Silver Roe Moon, and his People were setting the greeting Fires of First Running in the Mound's wide stone bowl. He'd likely been missed.

Growling to himself, Tokela slipped into the newer copse edging the crest of Talking Bluff. Sure enough, voices raised in song reached upward from the great bowl, underlain with the purling beat of the great drums. Fire lit thisdark all copper against pitch, crackling with the sweet-spice scent of gifted wood from other Lands, and hovering higher as Tokela approached the drumheights, larger sibling to the blaze flickering, small and cheerful, in the drumKeeper's small kiln.

Thisdark's drumKeeper was thankfully dozing, an elder with gnarled hands laced across his chest.

Tokela slung his discarded leggings and boots over his injured shoulder. It no longer gave pain, just a slight sting of reminder that he veered from. As he crept past the drums, bare feet silent against the cool, carven stones, he passed his fingers in quick, mute blessing over the glowing embers...

Jumped in his own skin as Fire leapt upward and licked, soft heat, at his palm.

Tokela scooted for the stair, descending it headlong to slip into the shadows of the outer bowl. Best that he avoid any festivities thisdark, take the back tunnels and head downRiver, stay in the wykhupeh 'til dawn.

The outlying places were dark, uninhabited, save for one where voices carried upon the mists. Only partially hewn into the cliff, remainder constructed of bark and withies, clay and living roof, the longhouse's round windows betrayed the warming light of gleaming-stones. This particular common space was set apart, large enough to contain a literal pack of males, residents and guests alike.

Of course, the oških would have left after the stories, to prepare for the upcoming Suns and their own games, their own Dances.

It wasn't the only time Tokela had passed the males' den in his Moonslit wanderings, or paused to take in the flickers through the woven scrims. Particularly after the first time, when he'd received the wyrh tree, was tested—and failed. But it was the first time all the sounds tingled across his nerves like busy fingers: snores wafting outward as well as muted laughter and voices.

Perhaps his hearth-mother was right in this much: he should be here, regardless of what bodytalk he didn't yet have, because of what whispered in his heart.

Perhaps the doing would undermine the tiny and strange voice that kept telling him: *Wait, not yet. Not yet.*

Another, very different voice registered—a mewl, almost. Tokela alerted, then smirked as he saw several figures huddling in the shadows of the overhanging trees next to the longholm. Ai, there was always that at festivals, too. Mere good manners to turn your eyes from partners rutting each other—whether adults in a family den or, like now, oških playing.

There were not merely two, but three of them, a tangle of dusky shadows, skin against skin beneath Moonslight. Tokela often passed by such things, aloof and unmoved more often than not. But thisnow, thisdark...

Thisdark, awareness blossomed into abundance. As if every groan and judder probed deep, scraping a just-this-side-of-raw pleasure along his nerves, making heated promises he wanted to see kept. Heat from their breath and bodies made vapour trails upward into the dark; it teased at Tokela's nostrils, made him shift and quiver and tighten his grip on the limb until bark creaked.

There might not be anyone Tokela fancied as playmate, but his too-tight clout was no longer so fussy.

"What are you doing here, ehšehklan?"

The ugly midLands sneer—*half-breed, not wholly of People*—growled rough from behind him, and rougher hands shoved him, hard.

It would have been nice, Tokela considered as he ate dirt, if his hyperaware senses had warned him of this.

Mordeleg a'Hassun was a distant cousin from midLands. And he'd expressed an inexplicable hatred for Tokela since his arrival three Moons previous.

Lithe as stoatKin, Tokela rolled away as the other oških bent to grab him, nearly escaped.

Nearly. Mordeleg caught hold of the leggings over Tokela's

shoulder, yanked. Tokela winced, expecting pain—when there was nothing he twisted and grabbed belatedly for his leggings. It did little good. Mordeleg backed away, clutching his prize. For someone so stout and formidable, in truth he was a clumsy fighter. Nevertheless, he could pin Tokela to the ground for a sound beating. Had done, once.

"Give me my garb!" Tokela hissed. He didn't want to be caught out again. He particularly didn't want the entirety of the oških den to know he'd been gawping at a tangle, or nosing in their place.

"You want them"—Mordeleg hefted the leathers with a smile—"then take them."

The smile wasn't pleasant, and Tokela wasn't fooled. Yet surely he could dart in, take his things, and twist away before Mordeleg could so much as blink.

Surely not. Mordeleg waited until Tokela came into range, then flung the leathers against his face. As Tokela recoiled from the slap, Mordeleg grabbed him, yanked him off balance then twisted his injured arm up behind him. Hard.

Again, it stung, but not as it should.

The oških rutting each other in the corner didn't so much as look up.

"What are you doing here?" Mordeleg hissed in his ear. "You've no rights wandering here, ahlóssa." And before Tokela could so much as try to struggle, Mordeleg was pushing him forwards.

Towards the oških den.

"Let me go!" Tokela growled, digging his heels in. "I'll say nothing if you just—"

Mordeleg gave a derogatory snort, yanked Tokela's arm farther between his shoulder blades and propelled him forwards. Mordeleg was twice Tokela's size, so choices were presently limited.

Still, the tangling oških paid no heed.

Tokela envied them.

And ate dirt for the second time thisdark as Mordeleg yanked back the hide covering the door of the oških den and shoved Tokela through it.

"Look what I found, sneaking about."

Mordeleg sounded triumphant—and looked it too, Tokela considered, sloughing a dark glance towards his tormentor.

A heavy silence answered. Tokela rocked up to his hands and knees, curious despite himself. He'd never actually been in here. The den was little different from any other—larger and more cluttered, certainly, but with Fire stoked low in Sa's pit at the central place of honour, gleaming-stones to light dark corners, rumpled blankets, woven mats, and rows of bedshelves carved into sandy stone towards the back cavern.

The inhabitants themselves made the difference—a threatening one, at that. In various states of undress, the small semicircuit stood, crouched, were seated. In the shadowy den they resembled more a pack of wolves than anything.

Yet Tokela had just faced down a pack of unnatural creatures in Šilombiš'okpulo. He'd the claws of one tucked in his pouch to prove it. Lowering his chin, Tokela glared beneath his forelock at those silent, Fire-flicked faces.

None of them would dare beat ahlóssa with impunity—despite Mordeleg's tendencies. Though there were tales about what youthful trespassers had, in the past, been made to suffer for going where they shouldn't.

"He was spying on us!" Mordeleg threw Tokela's leggings and boots down beside him, then gnarled his fingers into Tokela's forelock and yanked his face up. With that grip, and a harsher one on one of Tokela's arms, Mordeleg hauled him roughly to his feet.

Almost as one, the surrounding oških lurched forwards. "That's enough!" one oških barked, rising from the Fireside.

"You presume much with that 'us', midLander," another growled the threat. "Leave him be. Or is ahlóssa all you can manage to challenge and best?"

Mordeleg's glared at Tokela, who answered with a snarl and yank of arm, freeing himself from the harsh grip. Mordeleg gave a threatening lurch, and Tokela backed, reaching for his knife.

"No live edges in-den!" Another older oških smacked Tokela's hand away from his weapon, not unkind but firm. Tokela peered up at him—ai, another towering a'Naišwyrh; he was surely tired of looking upward thisSun—and it was indeed a glare, one he couldn't halt had he wanted to.

A smirk tugged at the oških's lips. Keeping narrowed eyes on Tokela, the oških addressed Mordeleg with barely concealed scorn. "Hunh! This ahlóssa has more edge to his blade than you could ever wish for, midLander!"

Laughter all around.

An ugly flush flaring from neck to cheek, Mordeleg turned on one heel and stalked to the back of the room.

"Was he the one who blooded you?"

A small thrill of trepidation—they'd smelt it, after all—but a hand merely placed itself on Tokela's shoulder, turned him further into the light of the gleaming-stones. Another set of disapproving hisses bounced off the curved den walls as the gathered oških viewed the scratches on bare arms and legs. Tokela shook his head, looked closer at his unlikely benefactor. The oških had a half-shaven head with twistlocks hanging unbound, bespeaking the pledge to achieve his own den, his own property and rights to full adulthood—including, likely, espousing a fem he'd set his sights upon. He was tall and muscular, motions economical and sure in himself—little wonder he seemed to be leader here.

"Or did you just tangle with a too-tall tree, little one?"

"Little one" had been difficult enough coming from Chepiś. Tokela nearly blurted out what exactly he had been doing this-dark, stoppered it just as quick. Stay silent, be thankful his wounds had so quickly healed, that uncertain light disguised any unnatural remnants. Darksight had its own limitations.

Another oških came forwards. He was chuckling, broad figure blocking Fire's light and arms crossed over his chest. "A'io, you're not long away from joining us, I'd say. You've stones enough for it, even if they've not dropped yet." He grinned, sudden. "Or maybe they have, a'io?"

"Either way," the leader shrugged, "you've not yet claimed your indigo. We'll say nothing to hearth-chieftain of thisdark, and you've no bond to us for that word, but you've no rights to be here and you know it. Any more than *that* one"—he jerked his head at Mordeleg's hunched silhouette—"has rights to make rough with ahlóssa. In any fashion. Go on."

Tokela grabbed up his clothing. Mordeleg's furious gaze heated his spine as he slid out from the shadowy, heat-dank oških den and into dark's embrace.

"There are empty places over there."

The oških tipped her head in a demonstration her hands, busy with stitching a leathern belt, couldn't make. Several dark strands escaped her head wrap and fell into her eyes; she blew at them, exasperated. Another oških leaned forwards and tucked the loose hair behind the first one's ear.

"Ai, poor Saltha can't tie her own hair without a playmate's help!" another crooned, then squawked as the second oških merely lifted a foot and calmly booted the mocking one off her stool. The others seated at the banked-down hearth—about two fours of oških busy with like tasks—laughed.

Anahli watched it all, bemused. The second oških eyed her up then bent down to whisper something into the first one's ear, garnering a return flush of cheek.

"Any empty place?" Anahli asked, thankful Inhya had been called away as she'd deposited Anahli on the top doorstep of the communal dwelling—some emergency in the cooking dens, it would seem. The fem oških den a'Naisgwyr hollowed deep and cozy, nearly half into the far side of the great Bowl; Anahli could hear River running through the open front windows, and see the Bowl spreading out beyond the back wooden decking.

"Depends on whether those rumours about dawnLanders are true." The first oških—Saltha—grinned.

"Which rumours are those?" Anahli grinned back.

"At least give her time to settle her things before you tease her into play!" an older fem with a bright ochre headscarf scolded, snagging Anahli's rucksack and swinging it over one shoulder.

Saltha, grin still tilting her lip, went back to her belt-mending. Clearly disappointed the entertainment had come to an end, the other fems bent to their own tasks; mostly Dance finery, Anahli saw, glad she'd tended her own before they'd set off towards dawn. Several also polished the long, curved wooden staff used for stickball. She'd forgotten to bring her own, squander it! It took time to break in a good stick.

"This way, friend," the ochre-coiffed fem gestured. "I was told to hold a bedshelf for you, as you're staying on even after First Running. A good thing, too, as there's not much space what with all the guests. You're to replace the little brother, aren't you? Your sire—wait, your tribe holds to damline, a'io, and your dam is espoused to hearth-chieftain's brother, isn't she?"

Anahli tilted her head in affirmation.

"Then be welcome..." the fem hesitated.

"I'm called Anahli."

"I'm called Čayku."

Čayku led on and inward, past several tunnels burrowed deep into the stone. The noise from the hearthside quickly deadened as the rocks narrowed into a passage then another den, better for sleeping. There were some occupants doing just that. There were gleaming-stones set here and there in pots, radiating warmth. The space was just enough akin to the winter caverns where Anahli's own tribe stayed, save here they'd bedshelves carved into the walls instead of round, well-padded sleeping pits within the flooring. Most of the shelves were adorned with bedding or clothing, personal possessions, or charms that hung from the ceiling or sides. The one Čayku gestured to—an upper one in a back corner—was bare and hadn't been used in some time, but it had been dusted, and piled with fresh rushes.

"We made it ready for you."

Anahli answered with a polite gesture known from dusk to dawn: fingertips from forehead to heart. Čayku returned it and smiled—and ai, but was she lovely when she smiled. Of all the possible picks from this den, Čayku seemed the least silly-giddy at the prospect of a new denmate. Which intrigued.

Another burst of laughter sounded from the oških at the hearth.

"I'm sleeping, here!" came a growl from a bedshelf across from Anahli's.

"Stop drinking that midLands horse piss and you'll not need to sleep so much!" someone else retorted.

Čayku snickered as the sleeper growled a little louder and once again disappeared beneath the furs. Čayku tossed Anahli's rucksack onto the bedshelf. "I'll leave you to it. If you need anything"—again, that lovely smile and a'io, it was an invitation—"come find me." The smile quirked. "A long time since I've enjoyed a new Dance partner."

Anahli watched her go; Čayku would have been right at home in a duskLands courting Dance; her skirts promised the graceful sway she would impart to fringes and fans. Tempting, to follow, but Anahli merely felt tired and dispirited. The bedshelf, however novel, however graciously prepared, seemed in retrospect a cold and lonely hollow when compared to the sleeping pits a'Šaákfo: the comfort of family all together, or the more-impassioned companionship of the oških wintering caverns, with the hot springs and several playmates.

Putting toes and fingers to the small carved-out footholds, she clambered in. In compensation for having no floor space, the upper shelves had more headroom, and larger hollows for possessions besides. With an agile twist, Anahli landed on her back and stared at the ceiling.

It wasn't for forever. Or so she had to keep telling herself.

◊ ◊ ◊

7
OUTLIER

"I still can't get used to it," Našobok said around a mouthful of fried nutcake. Crumbs sprayed and he snorted, sending even more in a dense shower.

Aylaniś had a solution for his loss; offering up more. And wrinkled her nose at the mess.

She'd always been the tidy sort, Našobok considered around a smiling mouthful of the nut-sweet delicacy. In truth he'd been smiling since he'd whistled into the moist dawnLands air and heard the answer: *I am here, lovemate.* And would keep that smile as long as the three of them could tangle in their own tipo, with their own small Fire crafted just outside the doorflap, smouldering as happily as they were.

What can't you get used to?" Palatan asked.

With a beringed middle finger Našobok reached out and traced, without touching, the newest Mark scarified and stained, ebon and white and golden, upon Palatan's forehead. "This."

That brow twisted, ever so slightly. "I'm not sure I'm used to it, either."

"But a long time coming."

Their eyes met. "It was."

Silence, turgid with more things than could be easily counted. Comfortable, and not.

"But to *this*"—tossing back a stray lock of bistre that had come loose, Našobok offered their hearth a generous portion of his nutcake—"I would gladly be accustomed. Are you sure you won't part with your recipe? Or at the very least, come and cook for me?"

"Not likely," Aylaniś retorted. "I've seen that tiny den where you and your wyrhmates keep your cooking hearth."

They'd set up camp in a favoured place: a small, quiet ravine well set back from the busy festivities within the great bowl. Of course, Inhya had offered the hospitality of her own dens despite knowing the answer: for People a'Šaákfo, caverns were for winter shelter. Summers were for wandering beneath Sky.

Even if, in dawnLands, the thick arms of standingKin only

sometimes let Sky pass unhindered. Even now, the last of Sun's light merely filtered through, turning their surroundings into the colour of Sea and storms. A clutch of twisted, persistent trees were rooted into the rock on either side of the ravine, set opposite each other yet with branches reaching across.

How very apropos, Našobok thought, peering up then tendering that fond look upon his companions.

He had been too long away.

"And you know perfectly well all she can cook is nutcake." Palatan—beautiful, quietly dangerous, and lazy—had his own mouth stuffed with said delicacy.

Aylaniś gave him a mock scowl; Palatan smirked and reached for another piece. She smacked his hand and pointedly offered the basket to Našobok.

"Ai!" Našobok suddenly leaned back, dusted crumbs from his hands and accepted the drinking skin from Palatan, taking a hearty gulp. Tulapaiś, a ferment of šinc'teh and mare's milk, drank smooth as Seawater poured over oiled planking, with a heady kick at the end; it was another thing not easily obtained even on a ship as wide travelled as his. "I wish I could have been there to see the old she-viper have her rudder twisted!"

This time, Aylaniś and Palatan exchanged glances. Našobok noted it, his mouth twisting in puzzlement as he chewed. "Don't tell me you feel sorry for that one."

"N'da!" It was almost angry. Palatan shrugged, repeated, quieter, "N'da. I have little enough sorrow in my heart for Chogah. She deserved what she got and more."

"More, indeed. You should have killed her," Aylaniś said, low. "You'll have to, one Sun."

"That Sun is not upon us, nor was it then."

There was a flash in Aylaniś's dark eyes, one Našobok wouldn't have faced down for all the rutting followed by nutcake. "For the good of our Clan, for the tribes a'Šaákfo, you should have—"

"My chieftain." Soft, but edged. Unyielding. "You know I will say no more to this."

Našobok focused on the overarching branches. On this matter he sided with Aylaniś. Chogah had sown her poison deep into one she should have held as equal, had clutched the horns of Alekšu nigh to ruin; merely the beginnings of why she held a place close atop Našobok's own "better dead" tally. More than she deserved, to be sent to Stars and Fire, and better still to scatter her ashes to Wind, a bargain to ensure her foul Spirit couldn't whistle up further damage than she already had done.

Yet Palatan Saw things few could. Save, again, Chogah. Spit her over coals. Našobok had learned along a hard and circumspect path that Palatan was right more than wrong about such things.

It didn't make it any easier to swallow.

"You will stay in our tipo through First Running?"

Našobok started, looked up to see Aylaniś, her eyes suspiciously bright, offering him the basket again. Ai, Palatan was made of sterner stuff. Našobok felt squishy just contemplating the possibility of Aylaniś all teary-eyed.

"Of course he will." Palatan grabbed another nutcake and flashed the brilliant smile that could still weaken Našobok's knees. "Where else?"

Where else? Not only the smile, but the talk teased at soft, misted memory; another lifetime surely. Curled up in a bedhollow at the heart of the caverns a'Šaákfo, feeling the heat radiate up from the caldera's cavernous foundations, wrapped about his lovemates with bairns curled like pups to head and foot. For one who had set his face against currents of caste and Clan, who had gotten all too used to walking an outlier's path and occupying a solitary hammock on a lone voyage, the tactile, close scent and sense of Clan had almost been enough to sink Našobok's heart into Earth and Fire.

Almost.

Fire had tried to claim him, had scorched his heart long ago, but he was River's—had always been River's. And the only part of Her touching the plains and hills a'Šaákfo was a cold, fingerling of Her mighty flow. The only craft small enough to ride Her was a skin-and-sinew kaik Našobok had learned to make from ice-Lands folk. No soundings dark and deep, no fierce-salt Wind to fill hair and sails, no wide horizon to chase...

Life was not life when your heart was hacked into small, ragged pieces.

There had been comfort with his lovemates and in their places; the peace and intimacy of close Kin: caressing Palatan's Dreamings from him, Aylaniś's melange of softness and flint, reedy voices calling him "Uncle" and a'io, admit it, even those scary-cold ahlóssa toes against his haunches mid-dark. Yet... not enough. Often more than he could bear. Never truly a'Naišwyrh, a mastiff content to lair in stone, nor a hareKin trickster; he was instead one of the huge wolves who hunted and swam River. She had never stopped haunting him, the horizon had never ceased taunting him; finally he'd made the only choice he could.

For some time now Našobok had been in his own place, with his heart in his body, and if that heart still bled and twisted on occasions... well, it was only to be expected. Most darks were indigo-black and true, River bearing him into Wind unhampered. Solitary. *Free.*

But there was also no denying some were ice-white, long and lonely, leaving Našobok to yearn for the sounds of the only in-Land family he still could claim, all of them breathing beside him in the stillness.

"No babes thisdark, though."

Našobok looked up to find Palatan's Forest-hued eyes upon him, reading every thought like a sounding chart. "They grow fast, a'io? Kuli means to den with his little friends, and of course Anahli has oških obligations."

Našobok snorted. "Have you been espoused so long as to make rutting an *obligation*?"

Aylaniś returned his snort, grinning.

Palatan laughed, lifted up the skin of tulapaiś and leaned back, stretching out his legs. "Ai, to be oških again!—and a good rut my only pressing obligation!" He leaned forwards, drank then passed it to Aylaniś. "But true, thisdark the bedding will be ours alone."

"Though I'll wager Kuli will soon enough come creeping into our tent," Aylaniś added, taking a drink and offering it in turn. "Likely early dawning. So you'll have his feet on your tail after all. He adores his Uncle Našobok."

"Just like old times." Našobok accepted the skin.

Arrow came trotting from a stand of trees, damp from a wander. Too polite to beg for titbits, he greeted Palatan first, then Aylaniś and Našobok, then curled up beside his person, between Palatan and Fire's heat.

Palatan produced a treat nonetheless, gaze sobering as he eyed the old fleethound. "The mastiffs still refuse to tangle with him, at least. I hesitated to bring him this time. He grows old, and stiff. One Sun those great dogs will humiliate him."

"He'll be more humiliated should you leave him behind," Aylaniś said. "Perhaps it's time to find a younger fleethound, maybe two. They would bear him company and help him when you cannot."

And when Našobok reached out and stroked his lovemate's knee, comfort, Palatan shrugged. "Ai, it's the way of things. Drink up, wyrh-chieftain! Perhaps you can sit at my side for Dancing." Palatan nudged him. "On my blanket, I hope."

Aylaniś smirked. "Are you just trying to annoy your relations?"

"Why not? My sister has my love, but her opinion holds no fear for me."

Našobok waved a hunk of nutcake. "You do remember what sharing a blanket means here in dawnLands?"

"Probably less than it does in duskLands," Palatan pointed out, unperturbed. "And no less than the truth."

"He's here."

Dawn spilled into the great, deep-hewn den. Sarinak paused in the doorway, tying back the woven door curtain and sliding off his boots. A brace of mastiffs milled just outside; one started inward, changed ša's mind the next breath as Sarinak growled, "Out!"

On the far side of the great circle, Inhya kept seeing to Council's final preparations. "He wouldn't come, unless"—she flipped out a blanket from the well-filled basket at her feet—"he wants something."

"Surely he means only to see Palatan and Aylaniś," Sarinak mused softly. "For there is nothing in the entirety of Naišwyrh'uq that the one who was my brother would admit to wanting."

Amidst placing another blanket, Inhya blinked. "N'da, not Na... the wyrhling. I mean Galenu a'Hassun. He arrived lastdark."

Sarinak cocked his head, setting the beads and copper upon his Sky-hued head-wrap dancing.

"He stayed with Nechtoun."

"Well, of course."

"Your sire should know better."

"Inhya. My sire has loved Galenu since their time as oških. Playmates often grow into lifelong companions—look to your brother's preferences."

"Preferences!" Inhya snorted, moved to another place and unfolded another blanket. "My brother acts oških when it comes to the wyrhling. He is Alekšu now, and also should know better. Aylaniś merely encourages them both."

"One of Horsetalker ways that I'm glad you've rejected." Sarinak's grin flashed just before he turned away and put curled fingers to his lips in a shrill, short whistle.

"You are enough for my bedshelf, Sarinak Mound-chieftain. Though"—a wry moue—"no doubt your father still wishes you would take a second spouse."

This was greeted with a snort. "Despite never doing so himself."

Inhya pretended to consider, not for the first time. "It would make less work for me, at that."

Sarinak eyed her. "N'da, spouse, you're quite enough for my bedshelf. And my den."

Inhya smirked and turned away, exchanging her emptied basket for another filled with jerked fish and dried fruit. Open Council could be long.

The results of the whistle—a quartet of nigh-grown oških—trouped in, discarding footwear and tendering polite greetings. The lot of them nevertheless sounded like a herd of rowdy draught animals. Inhya's smirk broadened.

"Take the empty baskets to the stores," Sarinak ordered his helpers. "Return for the rest before the drums call Council."

Another rumbling of unshod feet, accompanied by a teasing, if muted, commentary amidst themselves as they departed, hung with emptied baskets.

"We have overmuch to look forwards to with our own sons." Sarinak ambled over and traced his fingers at Inhya's shoulder.

Inhya nuzzled them, sighed. "I fear it's our eldest where Galenu has interest."

"Has he approached you?"

"I saw Nechtoun upon thisSun's rising. He informed me Galenu intends to broach the matter in Council."

"And your answer?"

"You know my heart in this."

"A'io. And you know Galenu can claim sire rights," Sarinak reminded. "His sister's son was Tokela's sire."

"Sire rights! A foolish custom."

"Spouse, sometimes you still speak like your dam's People."

Inhya clucked mock disapproval and said, satisfied, "Well, Galenu can have no sire rights while Tokela is still ahlóssa."

Sarinak bent to take a blanket from her basket, flipped it into a place beside the long, low board. "Truly, it shouldn't be so. It's... unnatural. Tokela's well past the usual age of indigo, yet he's not so much as changed his clout-wrap or looked to another. Then there's what happened after he was given the wyrh tree. His voice and height... those have changed, but nothing else shows." He paused, musing. "Its as if those foolish rumours had some merit."

Inhya looked down, held her tongue behind her teeth. It was not the first time she had wished herself forsworn; this oath grew heavier with each Sun's rising.

"Hunh. Tokela mightn't have the maturity," Sarinak ventured, "but he does have enough ripe wilfulness for any oških. If Galenu desires sire rights—if, for despite Nechtoun's support, I'm not sure the old midLander will make any claim—I think fear isn't the emotion you should have, my heart. Merely relief."

"Sarinak—"

"I speak without consideration." Both his voice and face echoed his quick regret. "There'll be nothing more said thisSun." He grasped her hand again, brought it to his breast then leaned forwards and nuzzled her temple. "We've many things to think of. Better ones. Our youngest, for one."

"Who sounds more a herd of draught animals than your oških mob all combined." Inhya's lip curled into a teasing, proud smile. "Madoc is indeed and altogether a'Naišwyrh."

Sarinak's laughter boomed into the Council den, inviting hers to join in.

As much as Palatan loved his life and how it had centred upon tribe and Clan and family, a sharing cherished past almost anything in his heart... well. At times a surge of unattainable longings took him, regardless: *run away, far away where none can find us, just to follow Sky and Stars, heed nothing but our hearts and horizon's call...*

But Aylaniś understood. As Našobok understood.

Hearts changed, but never forgot.

Sun trickled down through the conifers, dappling shadows across their bodies. Some sleep, mostly talk, a bit of loving. And now Palatan rested his head upon Našobok's shoulder, fingers running a light ripple over Našobok's breastbone, then down to trace the tattoo over his belly. Aylaniś, always up with Sun, had departed, not only to help her spouse's sister with host duties, but also to give her lovemates their own time.

"Later," Palatan mused. "After Council."

"After Council is Dance," Našobok murmured against the numerous, coppery-black braids at Palatan's temple. "You promised me a seat, remember?"

"On my blanket." Palatan smirked. "We'll watch all of Dance, make our own after... squander it, I nearly forgot. After Dance is chieftains' Council."

"And that one they won't let me into, not even as Alekšu's oathbrother."

Palatan gave a muted growl against Našobok's chest. "I have to go. And then a pipe and more talk, talk, talk."

"The price of respectability."

"Shut it, you." Palatan curled it into another, louder growl and smirked again as Našobok shivered. "After that, then."

"After that you'll be half-crazed from what Power they'll unknowingly raise and fling about—"

Palatan's fingers moved up to Našobok's mouth, pressed for silence.

"Well," Našobok mumbled against those fingers, "it's true. And none here to hear a whisper. D'you think I don't know the edge you'll be riding after all the prattling and posturing?"

Palatan pressed firmer. "Hsst, before your mouth stretches greater than even your heart." He softened, then, and stroked at Našobok's lower lip. "You know me too well, fellow outlier."

"By happy chance, I do."

Happy chance wasn't exactly how Palatan would term that long-ago expedition into Dead Plain. There were only several such places festering on their Land—the Šilombiš'okpulo here, the place amidst dryLands where the very ground would swallow one up, the icy, twisted waste that led to Everwintering Mountain from snow-packed upLands—but those were enough. Upon that plain up from the territory a'Šaákfo, something had tried to take Palatan's power—and nearly succeeded. Only Našobok had anchored him to sanity.

Našobok had always known what Palatan was. But he'd never let on he knew until they'd nearly not escaped the Dead Plain.

"I've spent enough time in solitude," Palatan huffed. "After I took the horns from Chogah, I had to; it's the way of any Journey. And the way of any return, to be battered by what waits. Many voices, wanting to be heard."

"Too many." Našobok nuzzled the callused fingertips. "So you'll need me, after, in truth. Or Aylaniś. Or both of us, depending on how high Fire is blazing behind your eyes."

"I don't want to wait so long," Palatan purred against Našobok's chest, then raised his head. "I need you *now*." Fire... Ai, there was plenty behind his eyes; he could see them in Našobok's, overcast Sky mirroring Forest gilt. "It's been nearly three turnings of Hoop. *Three*. Can you not know how much I've missed you?"

Našobok didn't answer, just cupped Palatan's face in his hands and ran them back through his hair, fingers teasing his nape, tracing a soft breath from forehead to chin.

How much I've missed you.

How long it's been.

How they could give each other everything—except the thing they each needed the most.

Almost painful, this; conjuring too many ghosts, too many memories.

Palatan broke it with a nip to his lovemate's nose. "So. What's the point of waiting?"

"Never any point to waiting for anything," Našobok chuckled. "See? I told you it was useless for me to put on leggings this-dawn."

"Hunh." Palatan was making his way down Našobok's chest, a brush of breath and dart of tongue and ai, teeth there, right there; Našobok gave a small, shivery jerk. "As I recall," Palatan murmured, tonguing where his teeth had grazed, "you can drop your leggings and clout in the time it takes me to count a four of heartbeats."

"And I can strip you from yours even faster—"

"Promises, prom—Yai!" Palatan gave a yip as Našobok grabbed the back of his clout and tugged.

"Threats, Horsetalker. I'm Riverwalker, wyrh-chieftain *a'Il-hukaia*. I don't promise, I threaten—"

"Rotten fish entrails! Another several heartbeats and you'll be rutting like *oških*. Will you never grow up?"

Palatan whipped about with a snarl on his lips—he knew the voice as well as Palatan. More.

Sure enough, Nechtoun a'Naisgwyr strode closer, broad arms crossed over his even broader chest, a mighty frown on his face. Worse yet, behind Nechtoun was Galenu a'Hassun. The latter bore a distinctly self-important smirk, groomed impeccable—and inappropriate, considering the damp chill of dawnLands—in colourful midLand sandals and flowing lightweave garb. Even his ivory hair had been slicked back into a perfect trebled knot.

Palatan refused to be impressed. "You're not giving us what consideration you'd give oških," he gritted between his teeth.

"And standing there with his old playmate," Našobok murmured against Palatan's ear. "Eh, but they stopped rutting long ago, so there's the difference, no doubt."

"No doubt." A soft return grumble.

"Because you're not oških anymore!" Nechtoun persisted, gruff. "Or maybe you are. Hunh. Council will be called soon."

"But not yet." Icily courteous.

"That's my lovemate," Našobok whispered, hiding a grin. "Heel him."

Palatan considered kicking him. Unfortunately, such energy drained into another attempt as Palatan met Našobok's gaze— that of trying not to laugh.

Galenu was aware of it, using an annoying midLands pastiche upon manners; pretending he wasn't looking even though he surely was.

Nechtoun had never been known for his sense of humour— particularly when facing the one who'd once been his youngest son. His lip quivered over his canines. "So. As new-made Alekšu, you'd rather give due to an outlier than attend Council with the Tribes he's scorned?"

That did it. Palatan started to rise; Našobok grabbed his wrists, murmured, "Don't."

Palatan blinked at him.

"If you get up you'll drop your clout."

Another blink; Palatan couldn't help it. A smirk ticced at Našobok's lip. "I told you I could strip you faster than you could breathe."

Palatan peered at him. Raised an eyebrow.

Then dropped his forehead to Našobok's chest and let out a huge snort of laughter.

Nechtoun growled, "What's so funny?"

And that set Našobok off. Which, in turn, made Palatan laugh all the harder. Nechtoun was glowering at them as if they were indeed oških begging a good hiding, but there was, sudden-faint, a grin lurking behind.

Galenu openly laughed.

"All of you are past ridiculous," Nechtoun growled when they finally subsided. "Surely the wyrhling doesn't want to be late for what Council he is allowed to attend."

"Usually I'm absent," Našobok's riposte was blithe. "Would late be so different?"

"Hunh. I suppose I should be grateful you keep decent company when you are allowed here."

Palatan gave a brief tilt of chin, tacit apology accepted.

"We've done what we can," Nechtoun grumbled, jerking his chin past Galenu. "I'm heading back."

Galenu's smile had lessened only a bit. He gave a courteous gesture, not only to Palatan, but Našobok.

A'io, there was simply no telling, with Galenu a'Hassun.

Našobok returned the gesture politely enough, but wary. And no blame for that—he'd often claimed Galenu a likeable old scoundrel, but trust him? No farther than he could throw him. Less, actually. Galenu's dam was sister to Palatan's, and Galenu took after her: slight, shortened with age. Našobok could probably throw him a good distance if he tried.

Palatan hid a smirk in one hand.

Galenu's smile broadened as he turned, ostensibly to leave. Instead, once Nechtoun melted into the trees, he spoke. "Wyrh-chieftain, I've a shipment. Interested?"

Ai, so that was it.

"I'm always interested in good trade." Still wary, Našobok pushed back onto his haunches.

"Could be perilous." Galenu's grin widened, as if he knew he'd thrown proper bait.

And he had. Palatan knew it, too, giving a light, indulgent snort whilst propping his chin in one hand, waiting for it.

Našobok leaned forwards. "Peril can make salt sweet or lave it into a wound. Where to?"

"We'll make talk later. After, of course," Galenu lifted both eyebrows, peered at Palatan, "you've... uhn... finished with this youngling."

Palatan's lip curled, but he flicked a glance to Našobok, stayed quiet.

"Youngling. I've three winterings more than you, and that old khatak calls me *youngling*."

"I love it when you make rough Rivertalk at me."

Palatan merely threw back a glare, kept walking. And fuming.

Našobok seriously considered finding Galenu and smacking him upside his flawless hair knot. If the interruption hadn't already scuttled a perfect opportunity, condescending remarks had definitely sunk it.

Ai, well. Never good anyway, to rush through a rut. They'd waited, as Palatan had said, three turnings of Hoop. One more Sun would make the next all the better for anticipation.

Lots of anticipation. Našobok had surely had his share of rutting in those past summerings, but none of those were Palatan. None of them were pissing-mad, all-puffed-up Palatan.

It would be easier to walk with a very large tree branch stuffed down his clout.

"I thought you showed considerable restraint." Našobok made it light.

"Difficult, to answer insult with your clout around your ankles." Palatan, too, was starting to grin. "I only hope you and I can grow so old together."

"I hope we're still... rutting like oških, was it?"

Palatan laughed. "That, too. Ai, it's well to forgive any edges an elder would wield. Wisdom often outweighs any slight." His mirth turned insubordinate. "But not all. Make sure old Galenu tenders his trade in advance if he hires you."

"No worries there, believe me."

"But your sire..." Palatan's grin slid into a snarl. "I can't easily forgive the way he treats you. I despise it."

"Not half as much as *he* does."

"I can't imagine disowning one of my children for *anything*. He loved your dam past all reason."

"He never forgave me for hurting her."

"You'd no choice."

"More of one than some."

Palatan flicked a glance at him that lingered, musing. They wended the pathway approaching the main lodgings, silent amidst the murmurs and stirrings of the great lodge.

Našobok finally ventured, quiet, "You are Alekšu, now. You don't have to attend beside me. In fact, it might do you many favours if—"

"Don't let such talk soil your tongue!" Palatan snapped. "I'll never speak to you with half the contempt your own blood does, and you do us no honour to even think I would."

"I don't think you would," Našobok pointed out, still calm. "That's the point. You wouldn't hurt me, and it could only help ease your path—"

"It would hurt *me*." Unspoken was: *and you. You know it would.*

Try as Našobok might, he couldn't help the flutter of gratification. Still. "It might help convince Galenu—and those like him—that you're no youngling playing oških games."

Silence. Then, "Oathbrother. As you say, I am Alekšu. My spouse is chieftain of horseClan. I have four offspring in my tipo, twenty-four clean-limbed mares grazing 'round, and two stallions to keep them healthy and in foal. I have claimed tribute against uncountable challengers. I have *you*." A smile curving his lips, Palatan gave a light slap to Našobok's cheek. "I do not crave the regard of Galenu a'Hassun."

And there was nothing for Našobok to make in reply, except take that hand and bring it to his cheek.

8
BIRTH

Things were always better after a swim. Even this time, with everything... *there.*

River took him in, and where Tokela likely should have been shivering-sick with the sensation of Her—so close, so present—instead She gave comfort. She cradled him, enveloped him in a soft, thick hum that blocked away everything else.

He could have hung there, weightless underwater, forever. He waited, smiling and slowly twirling, until the red-black began to beat behind his eyes and his lungs, bereft of breath, began to seize and beg.

But he kept waiting. Finally, he surfaced akin to one of the air-breathing water-horses, with a blow and heave into starved lungs. Thrice after he submerged, sinking to the bottom of the secluded cove; thrice he came up, and on the last one his Spirit lay quiescent, clear.

Sane.

The coming of dawn found Tokela high in the weeping tree wykupeh he and Madoc had built with their own hands. Sun peeked through the trees to finger his eyes open and warm his cheeks, sending healing slats of roseate and gold over his battered body.

He hadn't slept. First he'd spent some time tracing, in the dust of the wykupeh's wooden flooring, his memory of the *t'rešalt.* Then, with shaking fingers, he'd sketched the faces one at a time, lingering upon Sivan's.

Once finished, though, the lines had reminded him of the sketch Inhya had taken.

The sketch that had begun all this.

He'd obliterated the drawings in a single, vehement swipe and collapsed onto his back. He lay there through the remainder of Moons-passage, the sounds and smells of First Running's first-dark gathering faint echoes off the great Mound and into the woods, with a dart here and there until they faded, mute.

All the while, Wind fingered the weeping tree branches and nuzzled Tokela's hair, whilst River sang Her unending song below.

It eased his heart, somehow, even as it roused him no less than watching those oških tangle in the shadows. River had always sung to him, but normal: a wordless hiss against the shoreline; a drag of foamy, copper-blue skirts to dress the craft skimming Her; a soft and utter stillness on a Windless Sun's passage to bely what burgeoned beneath. Normal. When he was young, Tokela had imagined his parents' voices in River's every crest and ripple. She had soothed him—or tricked him, he still was not sure which—and claimed him when no one else would.

But now it seemed She, like a tiny ahlóssa learning to make talk, was trying to tell him something important.

More like he was the babe, not understanding what She needed to say.

Talk. Elementals... talking. To him. Forbidden, to hear such things. *Not* normal, not at all.

Had it ever been?

The light warmed his skin. Tokela squinted against Sun's rising until his eyes saw nothing but white burn, then rolled over and contemplated the ghosted tracings against his eyelids. He'd rewrapped his clout snug, to ensure what was beneath it would behave for once. Not that it seemed to help. Even light seemed raw and rousing upon his skin. He contemplated donning his tunic, turned Sun-spackled eyes to where it, with his boots and leggings, were flung aside.

Not that it would help. Sun soaked through anything, eventually, be it leathers or clouds heavy with wet.

Or maybe it wasn't Sun, but his injuries. They were healing, still too quickly.

All of it, running swift along his nerves; not only the Chepiś's healing power but his own heart's drum. If he had dreaded going before his hearthmother so physically marked, he now truly dreaded going before any of his people, because... because...

What had Chepiś *done* to him?

For they had done, must have. Had Shaped something in him just as they'd Shaped that tree to cover them from Rain's fierceness. Had opened him in some fashion and claimed him—*ihšehklana, half-breed*—yet in the end had refused the claim. Had tossed him—*little fish, of course!*—back to his People with this... this whatever-it-was. This thing that had seduced his dam, taken her Spirit, and... made him.

Shards seemed to light behind his eyes, edged brilliant-keen, hot as SkyFire following heavy storms, and Tokela curled up on the hard wooden poles of the wykupeh flooring, palms hard against his temples. He gritted his teeth, nose to knees, gave a strangled-silent orison to Wind and River to make it stop, just *make it stop.*

He didn't expect an answer. Yet something deep within him responded, gave silent, strange-familiar command: *Not thisnow. Not yet.*

And the shards sheathed themselves into darkness.

"There you are! Finally!"

For a half breath, Tokela wasn't sure who—or what—had spoken. With a shudder, then a lurch and heave forwards with a prop of both hands against the flooring, Tokela peered over the ledge.

Only the grassy cove, the rocks, trees bending over River... but a scent unmistakable, and familiar.

"Where have you been?" Madoc's voice confirmed from below. "I've been... everyone's been... looking..." Punctuated with small grunts of effort, climbing the rope.

Tokela fell back, a small groan escaping his chest. He'd intended to be gone before Madoc came. He needed time: to compose himself, to figure out a way to hide what surely must be stippled upon his skin like the inked-thorn pricks of permanent Marks.

Too late. Rubbing at his eyes, Tokela sucked in a deep breath of mist-laden air, looked about him. There was nothing remarkable in the furs pulled from the corners, or his clothes strewn across the flooring... his tunic and leggings! Rinsed free of blood stains—his own and the blue-black ichor of the *shigala*—yet they still might betray him. Tokela gave them a panicky kick into a dark corner. And sent another orison to whoever would listen that he did not look as changed as he felt.

Wind breathed on his cheeks, and below River purled, *satisfied*.

A thatch of umber rose against tree boughs and Sky, framed in the open front of the wykupeh. Madoc's unruly mane always welcomed summering's return by streaking tawny. It refused to heed either oil or confinement, rippling wild about his Marked cheeks and making good attempts to escape the tight-wrapped ahlóssa braidlock.

With a grunt Madoc swung sideways, found the burl-and-branch front stoop of their hideaway. Bare toes grabbed, leather leggings creaked. Madoc's tunic, the hue of grass and splashed with Sky tones, caught on the burl. Freeing it carefully, Madoc clambered up the rest of the way. Two steps in, he halted, eyeing Tokela.

"You look dreadful."

"And may the Moons light your path as well, little brother." Tokela rubbed the heel of his hand over his face, pulled his knees towards his chest, and laced his forearms around them. Slid a swift glance Madoc-wards.

Of course, not even wry affection swayed Madoc on a mission. Eyebrows twisting up into his forelock, arms crossed, he fairly radiated disapproval. Tokela rolled his eyes, started to growl how he was not of a mind to tolerate yet another lecture from Mound-chieftain's Son.

Instead, those razored shards scraped against Tokela's skull, sparking behind his eyes like to the flickers of the *t'rešalt*, as if Madoc's ire curled about Tokela's nape like intimate, intrusive fingers...

Tokela buried his face against his knees and clenched his fists against his shins, hard. One fingernail gave an unintentional scrape to a still-healing gash; the sting of it wrested him from oddling fugue.

"I was sleeping," he muttered against his knees. "Trying to, anyway."

Silence, then a quick thump of feet over to where he sat. Callused hands gripped at his own, gave an insistent tug.

Tokela took in a deep breath, then slowly raised his eyes. Almost a dare—*can you see? is there anything to see?*—but Madoc's gaze, glinting slightly in the faint illumination of the wykupeh, reflected nothing of recoil. Of Shaping. Of *Other*.

"If you didn't want me to find you, then you came to the wrong place."

Tokela gave a soft snort. "Is it my fault I slept too long?"

"Granddam Giltha'ailiq always used to say we end up taking the path meant, whether we want to admit it or not."

"So now I wanted you to bellow like a herdbeast and wake me."

It was Madoc's turn to snort. "I waited for you. Where were you lastdark?" That he would ask yet again unless answered, Tokela had little doubt.

"I went hunting." The feint came easily; Tokela was well used to them by now.

"Ahlóssa aren't supposed to hunt alone after Sun-goes-down."

"So you keep telling me."

"First Running has started, you know."

"I know."

"We have things to do, as hosts. Grandsire was looking for you lastSun. Aška looks for you thisSun."

Tokela dreaded facing Inhya. Would she know by looking? Could she tell what Chepiś had done, even if he wasn't sure exactly what had happened? She'd seen it before, after all, with Lakisa.

Those Chepiś had known his dam. The Matwau had known her name. They'd—

"Even the Spawn came after me, looking for you. See how popular you are?" Madoc folded his legs and settled down next to Tokela, leaned against him as if he were a favourite cushion.

Kuli just got up Madoc's nose, and that was all there was to it. Usually Tokela tolerated the expletive. But thisnow, with all that had happened?

It wasn't funny.

Tokela noticed Madoc was giving him a surreptitious on-ceover, and held his breath.

"Tokela, you look like you lost a battle with a prickly hedge."

Tokela let the breath out. "In darkness such things happen."

"Where do you go?"

Tokela shrugged. "I've nothing more to say."

Madoc didn't like to honour that prerogative; but this time he did, onto fresh game. "Anahli came lastSun, with Aunt Aylaniś and Uncle Palatan. I heard she's to stay, and the Sp—" Madoc snuck a look Tokela's direction, seemed to ken the word wasn't welcome "—*Kuli's* supposed to be going back home."

"Maybe he'll stay here instead, with his sister," Tokela teased.

"Maybe he'll stow in the wyrhling's hold and leave that way."

Tokela jerked upright. "Našobok's here?"

Madoc treated him to another disapproving tilt of nose. "What do you care? He's outlier."

"You make talk like your father."

"*Our* father"—very pointed—"is Mound-chieftain. How else should we be? It's the way, Tokela. The wyrhling—"

"Našobok." Just as pointed, with ire flickering deep in Tokela's chest. Even if he wasn't sure why he was angry, save for the faded memory of a nigh-grown ośkih bothering to sit with an ahlóssa after River had taken Tokela's parents. Našobok had sought him out. Had sat with him, quiet and unassuming.

Had been rendered outlier not long after.

Yet, every First Running he was here, he still sought Tokela out.

"Uncle Palatan and Aunt Aylaniś acted like they were over-joyed to see him. Like he's Clan."

"Maybe he is."

"He can't be. He's outlier. It's the way."

"Except when it isn't, Madoc. DuskLands have their own ways. Every tribe does."

Madoc grumbled acceptance of this, but kept shaking his head. "Everyone made too much talk about it. I don't think Anahli liked it, either."

Tokela grinned. "I think you fancy Anahli."

A stammer, and a flush. "She's ośkih! She's fem!"

"A'io, out of your league. Best stay with your own, little brother." Light, teasing...

Manipulative.

But it made Madoc laugh and lean against him again. "I am with my own. And not your 'little' brother for much longer, I think."

True enough. Plump solidity was beginning to angle lanky and unfinished. Already Madoc's nose brushed Tokela's chin when they stood together. Of course, Tokela's growth had been—

Stunted? Prevented, somehow? Disallowed, until...?

Whatever the cause, it wouldn't be long before Madoc would pass him up.

"See. I *have* grown more than you."

Tokela answered Madoc's self-important smirk by smirking right back and darting a quick hand outward. Madoc gave a yip and rubbed his cuffed skull.

"Hunh, see? You're not so big I can't pound you."

"You wait." Madoc kept rubbing. "Soon I'll be grown enough to put your face in the dirt and hold you there!"

"N'da," Tokela replied, serene, "you won't."

"Will."

"Not likely."

"Very likely."

"Big trees fall the hardest, Madoc chieftain-son."

Madoc made a half-hearted pass at him, somewhat hampered by the close surroundings. Tokela easily ducked.

"And move slowly."

Still grinning, Madoc laid his head against Tokela's shoulder. Tokela smiled, rubbed his knuckles against the bright tangles. This was more like it: normal, comforting, quieting the hollow, breathless buzz in the pit of his belly.

Nevertheless, his eyes slid back to take in River.

"Kuli was looking for you," Madoc said. "He wanted you to give him a story. I told him you'd likely be off doing errands again for grandsire Nechtoun. So. You owe me."

"Do I?"

"Mm-hunh. He and three other little ahlóssa would be trying to crawl in your lap just now if I hadn't deflected them."

"So instead I have one huge ahlóssa in my lap."

"Mm-hunh." Madoc was either unaware of the sarcasm, or chose to ignore it. "I'm glad Kuli is leaving. I'm tired of him in our den."

Tokela chuckled. "At least he doesn't crawl into your bed-shelf."

"He does when you aren't around." Madoc bared his teeth and wrinkled his nose. "And he kicks like an unbroken colt."

"Not too long ago you were doing the same thing."

"Kicking?"

Tokela gave a soft snort and nudged Madoc. "You still do that. N'da, crawling into my bedshelf."

"When you're there."

When on the scent, Madoc was difficult to shift. But Tokela had no limit of practice. "Why are *you* here? Aška will have at you for hiding away."

"They're all off to Council. Didn't you hear the drums calling Council?"

Tokela shrugged.

"You didn't hear, did you?" Madoc eyed him, long-suffering in his tone.

Tokela shrugged again.

"Some things are *important*, Tokela. Like this. It's open Council! Even the Yakhling leader is invited, and the wyrhling—"

"Your Uncle Našobok."

"When I say that, Aška always corrects me. She says my sire has no brother."

A cool, close fury lit behind Tokela's gaze. He quickly flattened his gaze, peered out over River's glittering surface before Madoc could ken any disturbance.

He'd heard it before, after all. Why should it bother him now?

"I was hoping you would come with me."

"With you? Where?"

"To Council." Madoc nudged Tokela's shoulder. "You know all the best places to sneak and hide, all over."

"Why?" Tokela slid his gaze towards Madoc, raised an eyebrow. "Council is only ever elders blowing smoke and making talk about too many things."

"But if we're the sons of Mound-chieftain, then perhaps we need to know those many things."

Tokela peered sidelong at Madoc, one eyebrow rising.

"Ai, brother, I really, really would like to go. And I know *you* know the best ways to sneak in."

"You seem so certain, little brother."

Madoc sat very tall, looked down his broad, Sun-burnt nose at Tokela. "Hunh. And how else did you find out about Kuli's hearthing here, before me?"

Both Tokela's eyebrows rose.

"Or that Anahli was sneaking about with a oških from deep-ForestClan last time she was here?"

Little trickster. "I shouldn't have let that slip from between my teeth. And you shouldn't have done, either."

"It was an accident!"

"Your loose tongue will be the death of you. Or me." Tokela didn't go out of his way to glean gossip—quite the opposite, in fact. Most times he barely processed what he heard and saw. But the places Tokela had found to get about unobserved often attracted those who... well, wished to be unobserved.

"You didn't mind telling me how Uncle Našobok"—deliberate, with an endearing grin—"was allowed back in the compound after he rescued Grandsire Nechtoun in that bad storm five winterings ago."

Tokela held up his hands in capitulation, chuckling.

"So we'll go?"

"We'll go, we'll go. But it's likely to bore the spit from your mouth."

"I can take it."

Tokela shrugged again, gave him a shove. Madoc scooted over, allowing Tokela to uncurl from his perch.

"Do you think they'll talk about me? Us?" Madoc quickly corrected.

"Ai, very important Council business, that," Tokela drawled.

"It might be. You don't know."

$$\phi \quad \phi \quad \phi$$

"Here. May I?"

Horsetalkers seldom let a stranger touch their hair, but Čayku asked so politely, with the light in her eyes so admiring, that Anahli tilted her chin and relinquished the long, burnished braid she was plaiting.

Čayku knelt, humming a soft tune beneath her breath. Her fingers proved quick and nimble and, at the last, dipped into the oil pot at Anahli's knee—she'd been watching. Anahli thought on that, fancying the sensation. It was the only time those fingers faltered, unfamiliar with this sort of hair dressing. But after, but with another dip of oil, Čayku left a glistening trail from Anahli's knee to midthigh, and paused.

"We use oil for other things, in dawnLands," she said, eyes fastening to Anahli's. "Would you Dance with me?"

"Now?" Anahli leaned back on her hands and pressed her thigh into Čayku's palm. "Or later?"

"Both." A smile darted across Čayku's mouth like burrowKin beneath an overhead shadow. "We must ready ourselves soon enough, and later, of course, there will be competition."

"Of course."

"Dancers a'Naišwyrh are fierce."

"My People are fierce in all they do."

"So I've heard." The smile came back and lingered, as Čayku slid her hand upward. "I hoped you would show me."

$$\phi \quad \phi \quad \phi$$

"Watch yourself!"

Madoc was out of sight, had run on ahead through the trees. Tokela gave a quick twist, managed to avoid running his old uncle over, calculated then commenced a new route.

Instead a strong hand grabbed his braidlock. "To where are you away, sister-son?"

Not for nothing was a ahlóssa topknot called a "handle". Tokela gave up any hope of swift flight. Nechtoun had quite the grip, liked to boast that his body had softened, and remained strong as an old sap-sweet tree.

"I'm hungry, Uncle."

Nechtoun wasn't alone, either. His companion was an elder, much slighter and shorter—and somehow familiar. Obviously of some importance, even if peculiar. Where Nechtoun wore a quilled and beaded leather jerkin over his woven woollen tunic, with narrow, hide leggings tucked into tall, fur-lined boots, the newcomer wore a high-necked, sleeveless tunic and full leggings of brightly coloured wormweave. He also wore gaily decorated sandals—fancy, and woefully unfit for damp woodland going. And where Nechtoun's hair was properly wrapped with a few silver twistlocks trailing through the cloth and at his nape, his companion's had been sleeked back, trebled, and secured with what looked like a wristlet of pale, saffron-beaded leather.

"Do you not have Clan-greeting for our guest, sister-son?" Nechtoun chided. "This is Galenu a'Hassun."

Ai, now Tokela remembered. Finding his voice, he made the requisite polite gesture. "Galenu stone-chieftain, my father's uncle."

"Tohwakeli a'Naišwyrh, my nephew's son."

"He is Tokela, here." Nechtoun admonished, then furthered, "Galenu doesn't visit often, yet he is my oldest, dearest, and most contrary friend."

"Oldest, a'io, but which of us is more contrary?" Galenu's eyes were coloured a mix of Earth and Sky, they smiled when his mouth did. He spoke to Tokela, a clipped talk that also seemed familiar, then mirrored Tokela's frown. "Do you not have your father's talk, nephew?"

Spoken slower, the syllables began to untangle and make some sense.

"I... I do," Tokela replied, deliberate. "I mean no offence, my uncle. It has only been long since I've made it."

"Hunh." Still irritated, though Galenu's eyes softened. "Long indeed! At least five summerings since last we saw each other. I barely recognised you."

Tokela's smile flashed, genuine and pleased.

"Galenu is like to you, Tokela." Nechtoun reached out, gave a fond bump to Tokela's jaw with one knuckle. "He spins tales fine as any learned storyKeeper. Sketches curst likenesses, though thankfully you've learned better."

Tokela's fingers twitched, remembering the dusty smears upon the wykupeh flooring.

"The only curse upon a likeness"—Galenu's tone was mild, remarkably unthreatened"—is in your relentless denial of their wonder, you old stoat."

The insult curled fond, obviously one of long standing; Tokela discarded it as the rest of Nechtoun's statement penetrated. He blinked, peered at Galenu with new interest.

"Tokela?" Madoc's voice echoed, close. "Tokela, you let me pull ahead ag—!" Bursting through the foliage, he stuttered to a halt, voice and body. "Uncle Nechtoun!"

Some Sun, Tokela sighed, Madoc might learn how not to give a game away.

Sure enough, Nechtoun smelled trouble. "And what are you

up to now, Madoc chieftain-son? Thinking to sneak into the cooking dens while we're at Council?"

Madoc's eyes flashed to Tokela, who gave a tiny nod.

"A'io, Uncle!" Madoc agreed, all too eagerly.

Tokela rolled his eyes.

Nechtoun leaned in, even more suspicious. "Is that so?"

"You tell stories, eh? Perhaps you've a few to share with me." The voice was soft, making Tokela start; he'd forgotten Galenu. The midLander's eyes were lit with humour.

"I'm one of several storyKeepers amongst my own People, nephew." No chariness in the talk. Tokela knew the sound of that all too well.

"Take care, sister-son." Nechtoun growled at Tokela even as he tugged Madoc closer by—of course—his braidlock. "Galenu is a mid-Lands layabout of questionable influence. Makes trade with out-Landers. Even keeps company with that feckless wyrhling I sired."

Madoc, squirming under Nechtoun's hold, shrugged as Tokela shot him a questioning glance.

"Come now, old stoat, 'that wyrhling' has a name." Galenu was grinning. "Your Clan makes trade with wyrhling and yakhling, who in turn trade with outLanders. What's the difference? It's good business to keep all options open."

"You think overmuch on business. And I dislike what name the old one bespoke upon the wyrhling." Nechtoun grimaced, then mumbled further, "How like him, to flaunt it."

"Didn't Tohwakeli used to follow Našobok about?" Galenu spoke both names deliberately. "Rather like Madoc in his turn. May sweet water and shade follow your path, Madoc chieftain-son, as well as you follow your older cousin."

Madoc reciprocated the greeting as much as he could with Nechtoun's fingers still holding his braidlock.

"Shall we take these ahlóssa to find food before we—"

"I'm not ahlóssa!" Surely Tokela hadn't intended to growl so; neither could he bite it off. Nor could he lower his gaze; it met Nechtoun's, held.

Nechtoun blinked at Tokela for several heartbeats. A frown quivered between his greyed brows. More, his mouth tugged, small and sideways, and kept on tugging until it became a smirk.

A fond cuff from Nechtoun was normal. Nechtoun growling at him was normal. Nechtoun smirking at him was not even somewhat bearable.

Tokela's cheeks heated. He was aware of Galenu watching, which just made it worse.

"A'io, then," Nechtoun released Madoc, but directed his talk to Tokela. "Stay or go, your choice."

It was only after Nechtoun turned away and ambled into the tree cover that Tokela realised the smirk had not been ridicule, but grudging respect.

"What was that about?" Madoc wondered, rubbing at his pate.

"I'll be here for a few Sunrises yet," Galenu offered, soft, to Tokela, before he followed Nechtoun into the trees.

If the old one is a little Fish, that one is a little Shadow, here then— sst!—gone!

Sivan had thought of little else on the journey home, spent a sleepless night beside Maloh and rose early to spend the morning pondering. Now, feet and arms bare, settled in a shaft of sunlight upon the wide entry stair, she waited, hardly noticing the beauty around her, thinking of shadows.

Indeed, that beauty was deliberate as everything else in their surround. The stair beneath her curled from clay-tamped path, to cobbles, to the high, living walls, sculptured from wood that nevertheless glittered, a silvery craquelure wherever sunlight struck. Yet even the Temple disappeared, here and there, into poisonously green tangles and creepers. The jungle always encroached, creeping across the bounds despite any engineering to the contrary.

Sivan could no longer remember when her father's fiefdom had been named the Temple, after the buildings where the ephemerals prayed to whatever gods were fashionable at the time. Well, the ephemerals of the first-landing continent, at any rate.

Little Shadow, here then—sst!—gone!

And like shadows, so many of the ephemerals' temples were crumbling, their builders' short attention spans frittering to some other deity or purpose. Her father's palace stood, tenacious and triumphant not through misguided worship of nonexistent hopes, but the realities of a biotechnology that had remained substantial.

Even despite a world's uncanny insurgence.

Sivan heard her kin riding down the north road before she saw them, the wake of their passage ringing against the Temple then muting amidst the surrounding jungle. Mists rose, fore and aft, in mote-filled streams, concealing then revealing in a splay of light the riders. Sunlight gleamed against the delicate tines of the foremost riding cervines and reflected against metal: swords and hauberks, finely wrought cloak clasps, and of course, the fine-hammered filet upon the foremost rider's brow, peeping from beneath a cowl.

The leader halted, gave his mount a firm pat, and shook the cowl back from his face. Tight-curled dark hair fell loose down his back, tamed from his brow by the filet. "How fares my daughter?" he called. "Waiting for her father on the stair, barefoot and uncombed as any savage child?"

Sivan tried to smile at the old tease but found it difficult. Instead she smoothed at her long tunic as Cavodu, Commander of the Temple and therefore of the Western Islands, flipped his cloak to one side and swung down from his mount. Lamellar steel and leather rattled, sunlight and shadow both picking out the intricate stitches, and one hand rested upon an equally fine sword, slung at his hip.

Primitive weaponry, but they'd found out long ago and the hard way that other sorts were often rendered useless. But even more significant: how her people needed to arm themselves for a mere trip to the southeast estuaries.

"My sister would rather ride hunt for the table with her lover than heed any sedate pace!" Jorda, at Cavodu's left stirrup, dismounted with a quick grin.

Sivan returned it as the other riders dispersed through a gap in the ancient vines and columns. One took the reins to not only Cavodu's but his son's mount, following the others. As they passed into the green, behind them it twisted, shimmered briefly, then morphed into razored leaves and briars with finger-length thorns.

The three were left alone on the great, living stair.

A perfect time to speak. "My hunt fared even less sedate than you should believe, Father. I found a trail. One that you, Jorda, left cold but a few turns ago."

Her brother's pleasant expression faded into puzzlement. Her father, on the other hand, seemed to fathom what had been left unsaid. Lips tightening, he climbed the steps towards the vine-shrouded entry and raised one arm.

The vines shook, twined tighter for a breath then submitted, roiling and twisting in retreat. Beneath them a crystalline barrier revealed itself, shifting and refracting, small discolorations beginning to pulse more akin to blood than any creak of wood or stone. An opening limned itself, solidified and shuddered, then irised wide.

Cavodu gestured, sharp, as he disappeared through the gate. Jorda and Sivan exchanged glances and followed.

"Are we to just let this stand?"

They spoke the tongue of the South Island's ephemerals. Maloh's first tongue. Not many of their own bothered to learn such things, and this conversation was one they'd rather not disclose. It was the same reason they kept to vocal speech; it was altogether too easy for thoughts, if Sent and Shared with more than one mind, to stray.

"It isn't yours to decide what shall stand and what shall not." Cavodu had exchanged travelling mail for gauzy loose robes, and road-dusted boots for sandals. The latter gleamed no less than the burnished stone tiles. "Your sister acted heedlessly."

Jorda had not bothered to shed his riding clothes, though he was replaiting his dark hair. "Was she just to let the little creature die of poison?"

"If such was its fate, yes!"

"And you're sure that was, indeed, its fate." Sivan leaned against one of the wooden pillars in her father's solar, fingers idling upon the smooth surface, eyes tracing the fingerlings of light through the roof of green leaves and crystalline tiles. She and Jorda had shared the same womb, but it took no twin- or psi-bond to know what he was feeling.

"Sivan. Daughter. If you and Maloh felt the need to interfere, it should have been with more caution. Considering."

"Perhaps, Father, I was considering that most of all."

"You both know a decision made with care and craft cannot be set aside simply because it is inconvenient!"

"Inconvenient?" Jorda repeated, dubious.

"We have interfered enough with those little ones—you, Jorda, in particular have done! The decision was made long ago, by ones with more command-right than I: the native creatures are to be left alone. Protected, even."

"Like insects beneath a glass."

"Poisonous ones," Cavodu said, sharp. "They fought us, once. It was decided to leave them to their strange myths and dreams. The latter in particular seem to have some hold over this place, and there is not a one of us who has forgotten the consequences."

"Consequences, indeed!" Sivan interrupted. "It was not a myth or dream I met in the Deeps. This boy's very existence is Jorda's responsibility. Whether we wish it or not."

"But does such a kindling truly run through him?" Jorda asked. "Could it possibly have caught light?"

Cavodu crossed his arms, eyebrows drawing together.

"More than you could imagine, my brother. I witnessed it myself, as did my companions." Sivan turned once more to her sire. "Maloh has, of course, encountered the little ones before, but Rann and Vox had never seen one. Rann was open with her curiosity, and—"

"Which is why we should not interfere."

"That is exactly my point, Father! Rann *couldn't* interfere. She tried to set herself within the little one's mind, but he made parry with her! He responded, repelled her easily. As if her Sounding was an invasion he would not permit!"

Cavodu's eyes, shimmering-pale with anger, stilled and darkened, narrowing.

"They will, one and all, corroborate what happened if you doubt me. I'm sure Vox would be happy to; he did not approve."

"Vox did well to disapprove." Cavodu's words were slow. "And I do not doubt you, daughter."

"What native youth could deny an empath of Rann's calibre," Jorda mused, "if he were not somehow privy to the Matrices?"

Cavodu kept silence. Sivan slid a glance towards Jorda; he returned it and spoke guardedly—not to her.

"You are willing to involve yourself with the natives of the southern and eastern continents, Father! Even when, as now, they make war upon our places!"

"That in itself is enough to make the little ones of this continent of little importance!" Cavodu retorted. "We've enough trouble with ephemerals: the Cove Islands overrun, the harbour roads infected with brigands who capture our people and try to wrest what tech we have remaining... as if they could use it, did they have it! Savages, all of them, and we still have people held hostage we cannot retrieve!" He shook his head. "I understand, more and more, why the Domina extols the dangers of contamination. I never thought a day would come when I would curse a species' evolution."

"And what of Maloh?" Sivan protested. "She isn't contamination! She's been one of us since she first came to our borders."

"Nor is she alone," Jorda added. "Maloh and ones like her are nothing like those savages who took the Islands. Many seek us in curiosity and peace instead of conflict. And the *ghoteh* might be primitive, but the ones we've encountered are truly innocents, artless as any of the wild animals they hunt and live beside."

"Encountered. Despite the Compact forbidding it. I've heard the argument before, my son, and from your lips. You, of all of us, know what happens when boundaries are broached."

Jorda looked away, frowning.

"What has already happened," Sivan pointed out, curt.

Hands behind his back, Cavodu stepped over to the open balcony, looking out over the tangle of green. "I find it more likely this native boy has been bred from his own kind."

"It's been centuries since his kind has possessed any usable psi abilities."

"True." Cavodu shrugged. "Yet rumours persist, hints that betray this much: the little ones might still hold this planet's powers close and secret." He turned, eyed his son and daughter. "You were born here; you did not experience Landing. And it is true that there is something about this continent in particular. A force seems to... guard it. Somehow. Perhaps it is merely the continent's nature. Perhaps it is something more secret, and practiced."

Sivan frowned. "Something that can pass, unaffected, through a threshold matrix?"

Silent for long moments, Cavodu let his gaze wander back to the open balcony and beyond. "That is troubling, yes."

"Also," Sivan said, lower, "the boy informed me his people find '*ghoteh*' insulting." As her father's nostrils flared, she admitted, "I cannot pronounce the full name. But he said I might call them"—a pause, to curl the word properly upon her tongue—"*kowehokla*. First people."

"They have strange names, many of them. All twists and clicks, stops and slurs of tongue," Jorda muttered. "It seems but a breath ago. Merely twenty cycles of a world around its star. Two heartbeats, nothing more."

"To them, twenty cycles is nigh to a fifth of their entire existence," Cavodu inserted, stern. "If they survive to age, with the lives they lead."

"What is he like?" Jorda's voice was soft, almost wondering; he leaned into the wooden post, nearly whispering to Sivan. "Do you know, I called his mother Brena because of the fire in her hair and the embers from it, all over and even darker than her skin. She called them 'freckles'."

A slight smile quirked at Sivan's mouth. "Well, the child of your little lost firebird has freckles as well. He stands barely here," she cut a line across her ribs, "small and quick as a mouse. His hair is black as yours, but sleek and straight, with muted fire erupting beneath the sun's gleaning. He has the animal eyes that gleam in the dark. And his soul is keen as starstone. But," her voice hardened, "that soul is breaking. Jorda. It is your power that has wakened in him, not that of any throwback ephemeral. I would swear to it."

Jorda looked down, lips tightening. Sivan turned from him and walked over to Cavodu, hands open and beseeching. "Father. When the Domina speaks of contamination, you always speak of responsibility. Our people have set this in motion through action, unmeant or not, and now this little one will suffer because of what we have left undone!"

"Is your charge of nonintervention with these *gho*... these *khowehokla* so made of star-metal and fire that we cannot answer a call to which we gave voice?" Jorda followed his sister, steps measured. "We cannot hold out our hand to aid in a circumstance *we made*?"

Cavodu did not turn to them, but his eyes shifted, spinning with flecks of light, echoing the tangled jungle and ever-moving waters far below.

φ φ φ

9
COUNCIL

He and Palatan weren't late, after all.

Just outside the entry to the Council dens, the chieftains waited. A full assemblage, this time, of the allied tribes and moieties, with myriad Clan- and tribe-markings, their ceremonial attire comparable to Skybow's arch through light and wet. Conversation, just as multihued, rose up into the massive, overarching branches of the ancient ones guarding the entry to the council den: a pair of grandfather wyrh trees, thick and gnarled, intertwined as the veins tracing a ropeKeeper's forearms.

Našobok had possessed scarcely four-and-one summerings the first time he'd climbed those wyrh trees... and received two Suns' of ostracism for his insolence. There were few severe punishments meted to ahlóssa; Našobok had in his youth encountered them all.

As they came closer, the talk dipped into murmurs, then whispers, then ceased altogether as they noted first Našobok, then Palatan walking beside as if they were equals.

Nevertheless, greetings were tendered: full honours for Alekšu, bare nods for the wyrhling. None moved forwards or offered to include them.

"I gave you warning," Našobok murmured towards Palatan. "You should have come in from behind."

"My favourite thing, that," Palatan quipped, and Našobok gave a groan, retorted:

"I'll say, considering how many offspring you've sired. It must be true, how you always claim any good stallion drives his herd before him."

Another grin. "So now you're one of my mares, wyrh-chieftain?"

"Ai," Našobok drawled, "and *that's* likely."

Palatan laughed outright. A few eyes cut their way, just as swiftly turned aside. The great wooden door bordered by the wyrh trees gave a thick, powerful rumble and conversation ceased once more, this time expectant. The door was flung open and Darhinu, elder a'Naišwyrh and Inhya's helpmate, stepped through, followed by Inhya herself.

Despite his problematic relationship with Inhya—though she would have said they had none—Našobok had to admit a grudging admiration for his brother's spouse. The only sound Inhya made as she trod towards them was the slight jingle of bells hemming her colourful woven layers of hipscarves and kirtles. She'd the grace of the spear fishers a'Naišwyrh, and her Earth-hued eyes, matched by tawny threads running through her turquoise headwrap, missed nothing. Including beside whom her younger brother stood. An irate spark leapt to life in those eyes; as she tucked her chin, the beads decorating her headscarf batted at a jaw clenching tense.

Našobok crossed his arms, returned her glare with a tiny cock of head and a ghost of a smirk. Inhya might be deaf and blind to what Power had won her brother Alekšu's sacred horns, but her heart was solid as Earth. Inhya loved the boundaries of custom, hated with a passion anything to challenge it. Even now, she could scarce believe Našobok was staring her down.

A hard elbow to the ribs nearly made Našobok yip; it did make him drop his eyes. "Yuškammanukfila ikšo!" Palatan hissed into his ear, hard fingers sliding up to grip at the base of Našobok's skull. "You take entirely too much pleasure in baiting my sister."

Denying it was pointless. Našobok did, however, point out, "I'm not too much a thickwit to rut you. Thwarted, a'io. But you're going to get more than you bargained for if you insist on clutching my nape." He slid his eyes to meet Palatan's. "In front of that same sister, I might add."

Palatan gave Našobok's nape-hairs a sharp tug. "K'šo," was his correction, removing the "rut" but keeping—albeit shortened—the "thickwit". To deny the grin quirking at his lips was also pointless; instead Palatan leaned closer, whispered, "Better at your neck than where I'd rather have my hands about now."

"You have never played fair."

Našobok felt, rather than saw, Palatan's shrug. "Then keep your talk at the back of your tongue and save that tongue for something better." A slight push. "Go, cheeky outlier. Don't make old Grass Weaver enter alone."

Indeed, the yakhling chieftain was approaching Inhya. She moved with some deliberation, clad in her brightest with all her wealth displayed: bangles of copper and silver around her throat, ankles, and feet; dried grasses further lengthening a headful of white braids.

First in/last out was the unspoken rule for those who held low—or no—status. A group of the lower-ranking leaders milled, new-come to their duties and therefore keen to appear conscientious. They were not, however, so impatient as to make the mistake of going before any outcast.

"I'm looking forward to your revenge," Palatan furthered, leaning into Našobok one more time then stepping away to greet another chieftain. As if he'd just mentioned Sun's rising and not what he was hoping Našobok would do to him when they got against each other and naked.

Našobok took a very deep breath, held it as he walked forwards, let it out as he greeted the two females with hand to heart, head and outward. "Yakh-chieftain. Hearth-chieftain."

Inhya's return greeting was composed, formal. Našobok offered Grass Weaver his outstretched arm, which she accepted with a wordless nod.

She waited to speak until he'd escorted her through the entry and into the long tunnel leading to the great dens. "You've a good heart, Našobok."

"You're wise to not say so before my once-brother's spouse."

Grass Weaver's lined face stretched into a wide smile. "I'm wise enough to take a supportive hand when it's offered—and to know honour when I see it."

"Hunh. Don't say that too loudly; you'll sink my reputation."

"And better these mastiffs a'Naišwyrh shouldn't realise this old doe is weak in her right hind." The slight limp was all the more noticeable as he held her arm.

"The blood swelling again?"

"A kindly Matwau called it by some name sounding more of spat phlegm than any truename of what plagues me. He tried to foist all sorts of advice and outLand potions on me, but I know my body better than any Round Eyes. I ate too many sweets at the last gathering, is all. Everything has a price, wyrh-chieftain."

How well they both knew.

"Those tight-bound to Land and Law will be glad of what other talk I gleaned from the Matwau," Grass Weaver continued. "Open Council hasn't come too soon."

"Hunh. I too have outLand information to share."

The clay floor cushioning their steps was well swept, covered here and there with mats of sedge, many of those laden with food and drink. Extra blankets lay, here and there, in neat folds, though most chieftains would wear their own, extra finery mixed with practicality. Fire burned in the midst of this circle, in Ša's great cob-clay hearth where Ša was well respected, never allowed to die. All had a place near the cleansing flames thisSun; none would have the chance to feel slighted by pride of place or have a chance to complain they'd been seated where they couldn't be heard. Even the light ochre and cream wash upon the sandstone walls bid the light reflect, bring any dark feelings into illumination.

Aylaniś knelt at the hearth, settling a few more logs.

"Meddler," Našobok fondly accused.

"I hear that from my spouse enough, lovemate." Her tone changed from light chide to respectful concern, "I've extra blankets there for you, grandmother."

"If that is meddling, then I accept," Grass Weaver remarked.

"Things are different in duskLands." Aylaniś slid her eyes over to Našobok. "We lie down with all sorts, there."

"Not enough of late." Našobok let out a heavy sigh.

"And whose fault is that, outlier?"

Grass Weaver chuckled. "You'd sooner hamstring Wind, horsetalker."

"Hamstrung he's of little use." Aylaniś shrugged. "But an occasional thorn in his foot might nail that foot to one place for more than a small brace of Suns."

"I keep offering," Našobok riposted, "for you to come with me, lovely one."

"Me, or my nutcakes? Still your tongue and settle. If I know you, and I do, you'll want to watch the show."

Našobok blew across his fingers in Aylaniś's direction and did as bidden. He knew her assistance in opening Council was truly meant; a genuine desire to aid her spouse's sister. Yet there was another reason, akin to his own: the amusement of watching varied Importances arrive, Skybow-hued woodcocks strutting and preening—and shrieking, no doubt, by the end of it.

He knew Aylaniś remembered how Palatan had once been one of those woodcocks, with more bitter-deep reasons to strut and swagger than a daughter and granddaughter to chieftains a'Šaákfo could at first comprehend. A younger Aylaniś might have, at the first, been impressed with the raids and prowess of her aunt's youngest tyah, but she'd also been quite contemptuous of Palatan's raw temper and artless ways. In return Palatan had been manifestly unimpressed by Aylaniś's supposed pedigree, and openly derisive of his own dam's efforts to forward the suitability of such a match.

Našobok, at the time fostered with his granddam's horsetalker relatives, had been little better at hiding his scorn; he'd never shown much interest in anything possessing teats and tucked-away plumbing. Neither was he about to share the love of his life with any nose-in-Sky *fem*.

Twenty summerings ago, it had been, when Palatan and Aylaniś had been chosen to call the Hunt together. Palatan had come from the rituals of the Breaking Ground with an altogether different Fire beginning to light his eyes, focused upon a desire and path he'd not, until that time of blood conjuring, realised he possessed.

A recipe for heartbreak and disaster. The latter had been courted, the former inevitable, yet...

Here they were.

Našobok smiled at his lovemate. As the remainder of the tribal leaders began entry, Aylaniś passed by and gave a discreet tuck of the blanket about Našobok's shoulders. The blanket was Palatan's; it still smelled of spicewood and horse, as well as the needlecreeper balm Aylaniś used on her hands. The latter in particular wafted about Našobok as Aylaniś retreated, graceful and straight-backed, to her place.

She would wait alone for a while, for Palatan had his own pride of place, well towards the end. He'd learned. But then, in the past summerings, they'd all learned many things.

The den was full: of finery, of people wearing all that finery and sitting in a loose semicircle, of low talk, of Smoke's haze, hanging in curves of wall and ceiling as the greeting pipe was passed.

"Good, we haven't missed anyt—!" Madoc's speech, quiet though it was, muted further as Tokela's hand clapped over his mouth. In the next breath Tokela had rolled Madoc over, hand still firm over his mouth, the other forming several sharp signs. *Hunting-talk. Only!*

Madoc tucked his chin, swift acquiescence. Tokela nevertheless gave him another warning shake before loosing him.

They'd missed little, mostly the statements and orisons preceding any gathering. Their hiding place overlooked the den; a small high passage with an entry tunnel behind them, and one of many throughout the Great Mound that gave airflow to the deepmost passages. The height of it, a precaution against floods, meant they would likely remain unseen.

If Madoc could keep his mouth shut. Tokela shook his head and rested his chin upon his hands, unable to quell a tiny smirk. Madoc's audacity remained as endearing as it was exasperating.

Snatches of soft conversation upon many subjects—fishing, trade, hunting, crops—were passed back and forth with the welcoming pipe. Smoke also wafted upward—a mistake, Tokela was beginning to realise. He'd not planned on Smoke having such a fondness for this particular hidey-hole; he'd little tolerance, active wariness, in fact, for the way it made him feel.

It should be one of the things to look forward to when he claimed his indigo, a pleasure finally allowed: Smoke, sweat, and the going inward to find his Spirit's name and purpose.

Instead it reminded him of the strange, transparent dread the *t'rešalt* had engendered in his heart. The Shaped boughs denying Rain, the poison that had sent him within, the Chepiś that had brought him out.

And brought other things with it.

Smoke also sought to reminded him: until now, he'd been content enough to leave untouched what-had-been and what-could-be. It reminded him further of what would happen when he didn't.

First, when he'd lain with the lung-sick after Sarinak had

dragged him from beneath his parents' wykhupeh, wet and shivering and mud-caked in the wake of their deaths. Not that he remembered; Inhya had told him. And then, five summerings ago when Tokela's voice had deepened and he'd been Marked with the blood-hued wyrh tree on his ribs. They had given him the same fingerleaf tea they gave everyone after the ordeal, but in Tokela the draught had called dark's Mare to toss and trample him.

The herbKeeper had tsked, said a closed place lay within Tokela's Spirit. The rite had been cancelled, and he'd been given no name to take to the oških dens.

Smoke crept over his skin, curled at his nostrils, promised Seeing and Sensing; no delight, this. Too much, or too little, there seemed now to be no balance—only a heated, tactile weight upon his senses. Tokela could, suddenly, hear River even though many lengths of Earth separated him from Her, an echo timed with the thick drum of his heart.

The den of his Spirit lay no longer closed. Tokela gritted his teeth against his fists, squinted his eyes shut and whispered, silent and desperate:

N'da. Not yet. Please, not here...

And impossibly, River's echo subsided. Smoke curled away from him and wafted lazily sideways. Toward Madoc, who lifted his head for a good sniff, sly enjoyment of a pleasure forbidden his age. Madoc would, when he was Broken to oških, no doubt announce himself with a broad smack to the pointed noses of whatever shadowlings might lay in wait.

Madoc's time, however, lay some turnings hence. Tokela's had seemingly crept up and bitten his tail.

Tokela looked out over the Council and did not see it.

If only he could retreat a bare passage of Suns and never step foot inside that rotted *t'rešalt*, never let the indigo venom of Shaped creatures sting his blood, never let the touch of Chepiś pierce him, expose him, *change* him.

Madoc's hand pinched, hard, and Tokela started, found Madoc's curious gaze upon him, gleaming like polished copper in the dim. Tokela realised he was sweating.

Are you... here? Madoc signed, concern written in the twist of brow.

Comfort, somewhat, that Madoc would ask. But there was immeasurable comfort in how he didn't truly understand the reality beneath the asking.

And security, of a kind, for Tokela to answer *I'm here.*

Good. You need to pay attention to this. Madoc's mouth jutted sideways, a mutinous tilt.

"—those are our requests of hearthing. The first, Gweh a'Katasu, oških of dryLands, is keen to learn our woodKeeper's ways."

Inhya was speaking, standing next to Sarinak. The wood-Keeper had risen, his massive arms crossed over his chest, respectful. His craft was familiar to everyone there; Tokela had many times gone upRiver to the squat, dusty wykupeh. He'd also often wondered why the woodKeeper's intricate, towering sculptures weren't considered as forbidden as sketches.

Tokela slid Madoc a curious look. *What does this have to do with anything?*

Madoc scowled. *Wait.*

"—to let it be known to all that I gladly extend dryLands' offer of hearthing without trade," the woodKeeper was saying. "My own offspring, save my youngest daughter, are gone from my lodging, all espoused in trades of good faith or heart-longing. I've many things to share with a hard-working oških."

The dryLands oških stood by the door, a blanket over one arm. At his side waited a tall fem, likely an aunt. Tokela had done the same after his parents were taken by River, standing in the Council's entry with his eldest aunt—Giltha'ailiq, Nechtoun's spouse, now given to Fire and River. There had been talk of hearthing Tokela in duskLands; his dam's granddam had, after all, been a'Šaákfo. Instead Inhya claimed hearthing-right; she'd been Larissa's oških playmate, then lovemate and oathsister.

The oških embraced his aunt, then walked slowly around the circle. The blanket he folded open at the woodKeeper's feet, to kneel upon. In turn the woodKeeper rested a hand on the oških's skull for a length of silent breaths. Then the woodKeeper helped his new-made son up, took the blanket from the floor, folded it over his own thick arm. They both exited, to satisfied murmurs all around.

Sarinak raised the chieftain's staff, requesting silence, and Inhya spoke again, grave and formal.

"Another request has been tendered to me only thisSun's rising, through once-chieftain Nechtoun. Galenu a'Hassun, stone-chieftain, you have offered to open your midLands lodging to my son, Tokela."

Tokela sucked in a sharp, baffled breath. Galenu? Why? It must not be settled business, or else Inhya would have brought Tokela himself into Council. Tokela considered Galenu with narrowed eyes as the elder rose, arms across his chest.

"I do offer. It's Nechtoun's opinion that your son is of an age to know his sire's people."

To midLands? Galenu a'Hassun meant to offer a hearthing-place? Truly? Tokela's eyes flickered to where his old uncle was seated, nodding. Inhya also glanced at Nechtoun, then Sarinak. Sarinak was peering at Galenu. He didn't seem to be surprised.

Inhya, on the other hand, seemed less than pleased. "Of an age, you say. Tokela is ahlóssa."

"I saw Tokela, as you call him, only thisSun, and I'd warrant"—

a smile that didn't seem altogether friendly—"he won't long be that. So he has the right to know his sire's people," Galenu persisted.

It had been long since Tokela had heard even that part of his blessing-name spoken, and it echoed strangely in the den.

"And it's my right to welcome him to my lodging, where he can experience that knowledge. Though," Galenu's smile broadened—amity, a'io, but barbed and layered with brine, "your hesitancy is understandable, Inhya hearth-chieftain. Admirable. A mother always wishes to keep her little ones at her kirtles."

Tokela let out a slow breath. He'd never heard anyone speak so to Inhya. Not and walk away unscathed, anyway.

"You speak with all the knowledge you possess, Galenu stone-chieftain." Edged as an obsidian dagger, Inhya held to her dignity as host. Even through clenched teeth. "I will give your request what consideration it deserves."

"Aška doesn't like him one bit, does she?" Madoc mouthed against Tokela's ear.

Tokela itched to know why.

"Here, before witnesses of Council," Galenu continued, clipped, "I claim my right—and those rights Tokela may claim as my nephew's son. I expect you, hearth-chieftain a'Naišwyrh, to cede them when Tokela's old enough."

Inhya stared him down, but finally gave a tilt of head: acknowledgement, if not surrender.

I am old enough. My right. Tokela's spontaneous inner protest came from his heart, belying the faded henna on his cheeks. *I could find a new place, with new ways. Prove myself away from a mother's fears, escape and still belong to my People, in a place where rumours cannot follow.*

Rumours. Galenu surely hadn't heard the rumours... but perhaps Mordeleg would tell him. Mordeleg had pounced upon the hints of Tokela's heritage like raptorKin. Mordeleg was Galenu's cousin, after all, with more rights to Galenu's lodging-welcome than any... ehšehklan.

A familiar hand wormed its way into Tokela's own, and he slid his gaze to Madoc, found his cousin's face pale-taut.

Madoc, he signed, *what—?*

Don't go with him. Madoc's hand gripped tighter. *Please, brother. Don't go so far away from me.*

Hope withered, cold and heavy, twisting at Tokela's heart. He turned from Madoc to the gathering below and in particular the two... antagonists. For a'io, they were that and had obviously been for some time: Inhya, eyes glittering all angry, and Galenu, chin tilted, obdurate.

Madoc worried for nothing. Inhya would not let go. Would hold to Tokela from love and yearning and, yes, fear—would keep him penned and hemmed at every opportunity, unwilling to even let him draw a deep breath that was not scrutinised or under suffrage.

Should he bleed himself pale on Overlook's stair, they would somehow still find a way to keep him *here*.

"As I made plain, we will consider your offer, stone-chieftain." Inhya's voice broke into Tokela's thoughts. "I can promise nothing more, since the time has *not* come."

Tokela slid back slightly and turned over, peering at the stony ceiling barely an arm's reach overhead.

Madoc's face, upside down, entered into Tokela's field of vision. Stabs and tingles shot through his fingertips; Madoc's hand still clenched his, hard.

You don't want to go, do you? Madoc signed with his other hand.

Tokela averted his gaze, gave the easiest answer. *You know they won't let me go.*

But do you want to?

Nothing Tokela could say to that. Nothing to offer, in this heartbeat and many others, that wouldn't hurt his cousin.

Particularly the truth.

Madoc possessed only a few summerings more than Tokela himself had when River had taken his parents. It was an age with little understanding of whys and hows, no room for subtleties. Only the realisation: when someone went away, it *hurt*.

So many things already filled Tokela's heart that Madoc would never understand, should never have to know.

Only this. I am here. Tokela disentangled his hand to grip the curls at Madoc's temple. *I am here, thisSun.*

And nextSun? Or another?

A tug, sharp but slight. *Little brother, all we ever have is thisnow.*
But Tokela—

Excited voices rose, echoing upwards. Mostly male, arguing back and forth, then another voice: fem, clear and dry with sarcasm. Sarinak's powerful voice rose, overriding them all.

Until one deep voice curled wit into a whip. "Only fools believe that painting our cheeks and puffing our chests will solve such things!"

Madoc craned his neck, curious once more, scooting closer to the edge. Tokela felt as if he'd swerved from his own edge, one treacherous and deep. Neither could he muster up any remorse at his relief.

It's the yakhling elder! She is making very strong talk. At least Madoc's focus had shifted... for now. *Yeka is annoyed.*

This made Tokela scoot forwards and peer over the edge. The usual way he beheld Sarinak's annoyance was in receipt.

The yakhling—Grass Weaver, Tokela recollected; their folk didn't hold to the protection of Commingling-talk for their names—was a chieftain in her own right, and seemed eldest of all those present. She held her staff firm; her wrinkled face remained composed, daring any to oppose her right to speak in open Council.

"I mean no disrespect to your hospitality, Mound-chieftain, but I cannot sit by and hear *these*"—she jerked her head sideways, indicating two males with the close-cropped temples of desert-Clan—"young cockerels fart with their mouths!"

What do they make talk about now? Tokela signed to Madoc, who shrugged.

I think it was something about outLands.

"This is open Council," Sarinak agreed, curt, "and thisSun the rights are given for all to speak. Including outliers."

Tokela smothered a burst of irritation, wondering how exactly Sarinak could bend over with that spear haft he always seemed to have stuck up his tail split. Naturally, this wasn't anything repeatable in Madoc's hearing. Instead Tokela watched Grass Weaver. The medicine bag tied at the head of her staff betrayed her reliance upon the latter by quivering, albeit slight.

"All must speak, a'io. Truth, not foolish rumour." Grass Weaver made a sharp gesture; the staff slipped from her grasp. A broad, dark hand snatched it before it hit the ground. Našobok rose, proffering the staff even as he cupped a hand at Grass Weaver's elbow. Courtesy, nothing more, but Tokela saw the old yakhling lean against Našobok as she accepted her staff. More, Tokela caught himself leaning forwards, tense and observant, as Grass Weaver murmured something to Našobok. In return Našobok gave the old yakh-chieftain a slow, brilliant smile.

It made Tokela's heart give a huge, ungainly flop against his breastbone.

Madoc, shifting perilously close to the edge, gave Tokela the jolt of reality he needed. Reaching out and yanking his brother back, Tokela glared Madoc's burgeoning protest into silence.

If you fall in and fetch us into trouble, I will end you!

Madoc twisted his brows and signed apology. *It's just...* He hesitated, then grinned. *You know, everyone looks very fancy.*

Tokela again found his gaze sliding to Našobok.

More than fancy. Both Našobok and Grass Weaver were no casual vagabonds of tales or even memory. She'd enough layers and finery to outshine any a'Naišwyrh, with plenty of beads and metal twisted in tens of long, silver locks braided small and tight. Našobok was even finer, though: a softweave tunic wrapped loose beneath his longcoat, exact match for the longcoat's trim of vermilion beads and copper discs. Even his tall boots were trimmed with the colour of bright, new-spilled blood. A wealth of copper and silver bands adorned his fingers and wrists, valuable cowries tangled in that unbound mane of hair, his forelock pulled over and braided at one temple with three Sea-raptor feathers, those bound with leather and costly turquoise.

Shifting his hips against the stone, Tokela gritted his teeth. *Why now?* he asked, silent. As if there could ever be an answer.

But there was. River's soft hum reached for him, through sandstone and bedding rock, to trickle along his nerves. The abrupt sound/scent/taste of Her were currents, filling his heart and rising his body.

N'da, he tried to conjure, *not yet.* After all, it had worked before.

Impossibly, it did again.

But even that wasn't as impossible as the sudden yearning within his heart: that he could attract Našobok's notice, and not as the peculiar younger cousin who used to follow him around, pesky as Madoc at his worst or little Kuli at his best. N'da, Tokela would have to puff his chest and daub his entire body with oških indigo like flyingKin in full mating plumage, assuming he possessed the cheek to actually strut up to Našobok and utter *I beg your pardon, you probably don't even remember me, and I'm so pissing ignorant about this entire business I'm not even sure how to ask, but... Will you?*

Even thinking about the possibility made Tokela's breath catch in his chest, his heart pound behind his ears, and a soft whisper from River, rising him...

"—encroach farther than they've yet been!" This from Forestlodge's chieftain. "We have seen Chepiś outside their own places. Even those cursed beasts they've Shaped have been ignoring the bounds."

Tokela frowned, snared from ache to apprehension beneath mere utterance of that name.

"Disregarding what territories our ancestors set long ago would mean breach of truce." Palatan's voice resounded, firm. "That can be dealt with, if you're sure you've seen more than a few together."

Several voices rose at once, all in protest but none of them definite.

"SwimmingKin are late this year!" Nechtoun's voice carried, muting the others into grumbles. "Every summering, the changes have come. Unnatural ones, and our Land cries out while we sit, doing nothing! The Chepiś are not so idle, I promise you, whether they breach truce-laid bounds or no!"

"You blame Chepiś for a Sun-drenched day when you wish for Rain's touch, old friend." Galenu sat beside Nechtoun, but in this they were clearly not in accord.

"Who knows what they're Shaping in their cold dens?" Nechtoun retorted.

"Everyone knows they want our places, to make and Shape into their own abominations!" another elder snapped. "They'd have our people as slaves!"

"Chepiś don't take slaves," Galenu retorted. "Those are

ahlóssa tales, nothing more, meant to frighten. I can't listen to such ignorance."

"It is well known that stoneClan takes slaves." Another chieftain, from dryLands by her regalia. "So naturally, that Clan's chieftain would—"

Several hisses.

Galenu stiffened. "We do not keep slaves!"

"Surely your—what do you call them? Boundlings?—would dispute the distinction—"

"Enough!" Sarinak's staff rose and came down with a crack upon the wooden board. Cups rattled, contents sloshing. "We were speaking of Chepiś and their predations, not midLands customs!"

Boundlings were outliers, of a kind; miscreants and lawbreakers, or so Tokela had heard—and thusly not allowed a Clan. Still, Tokela wondered at the anger making the accusation—and Galenu's equal ire at the voicing of it.

For, despite the enforced change of topic, Galenu's voice shook. "There are Chepiś that take what isn't theirs, just as with our own People. Not all of them are our enemy. We would do well to remember that—"

"We would do well"—this time Nechtoun interrupted in anger—"to remember what they did to our Land!"

"Long ago."

"Not long enough!" Inhya snapped, and a host of voices rose in agreement.

"We still suffer from their predations!"

"Just look at the despoiled places—"

"A'io, like Šilombiš'okpulo!"

"I have made trade with Chepiś," Galenu protested. "Have called some friend!"

Galenu not only made stories, and sketches, but was friends with Chepiś? Tokela frowned, tilted his head to better hear.

Sarinak gave a disagreeable snort. "And so, you tread where you shouldn't, stone-chieftain."

"I wasn't aware that Mound-chieftain had the authority to tell not only dawnLands, but midLands, where to tread."

Sarinak refused to be baited into anything resembling indignation. "I should think an elder of any Land would have sense to see trouble when it openly stalks him."

"Trouble?" Galenu countered. "How is it trouble to welcome wisdom from another People?"

"But they aren't," Nechtoun inserted, "People!"

"Come now, you can't mark them all with the same hue. Just as our own agreements, tribe to tribe, are crafted to allow a Skybow's wealth of ways and colours and customs." Quite pointed. "If some Chepiś make overtures of friendship, is it sensible to meet those with fear or superstition?"

"You drag all of us in your wake, yet still refuse to perceive the folly of your actions," Inhya said, flat. "We a'Naišwyrh are still dealing with the consequences of your 'friendship' with outLanders."

Tokela found himself hunching like hareKin beneath a winged predator's shadow. Ai, and he'd teased Madoc about the egocentricity of wanting concerns aired in open Council, never dreaming his own would be fair game.

Almost angrily he pulled his shoulders straight, snuck a glance at Madoc.

Madoc wasn't paying attention. Done with worrying over Tokela's possible hearthing claim, or ogling the fancy dress of the adults, he'd dug a thick spinning thread from his belt pouch, winding a game of spiderKin about nimble, grubby fingers.

"—Hoop turns different, of late." Sarinak's admittance seemed reluctant. "It is worrisome."

"But have Chepiś broken the truce?" Palatan stood abruptly, and it seemed for a half breath that Fire's reflection glinted, copper-cobalt, behind his Forest-hued eyes. "I hear talk, talk, talk about sightings and speculations. If they have broken truce, if they have come into our Land in disallowed ways, then we will act. *If.*"

Silence.

"Let us offer orison," Inhya's voice drifted soft and heavy as a winter blanket, "that it need never come to that."

"Yet our own history," Galenu had mastered his own ire, determined to make his point, "sets forth what can happen when we refuse to deal with outLanders."

"Then," one of the desertClan males pointed out, and Galenu rolled his eyes.

"It seems to me," a chieftain ventured, from fenClan by her garb, "dealings are not wise, period."

More murmurs, mostly in agreement.

"I have seen them," fenClan's leader added. "Not in numbers, n'da. But they do take fishKin from our estuaries without asking, without reverence. They trade overmuch with Riverwalkers, but we have nothing to do with them."

Tokela was now the one creeping to the edge, ears straining.

"Is there such a thing," Našobok drawled, "as overmuch trade?"

"If it brings outLand menace, a'io!" the fen-chieftain snapped. "I would not expect such as *you* to understand."

Tokela's snarl was silent, but heart-meant.

Below, Našobok merely shrugged. "Yet I see you wear the fruits of Riverwalker trade upon your shawl fringe, and fancy work hanging upon your nose and ears. Or has fenClan suddenly found a source of Matwau-mined milkrock in the bogs?"

She stiffened, looked as if she would retort, then turned away, those ear dangles bouncing.

Nechtoun shifted in his chair. "Surely, Galenu, you cannot be so lost to reason as to welcome Matwau in your lodge."

Matwau? Tokela thought they'd been speaking of Chepiś.

"How would they fit?" A lesser chieftain from dryLands frowned. "A'io, we see them, sometimes. They're sturdier than Chepiś, but similar enough. Too big for any proper dwelling. And the smell of them!"

"They do smell strange," Galenu admitted. "But perhaps we smell and look strange to them."

"What matter what they think? All that matters is where Chepiś think to venture, their Matwau pets roam. And Matwau aren't constrained by truce." This from one of deerClans. "All tall ones are dangerous. Matwau routed People like to us from over-Sea, long ago; as many of us are descendants of those who escaped here as we are of People who've lived here since Grandmother birthed us all. The tall ones would take thisLand if they could, yet there are those of us who trade with them? Have we learned nothing?"

"Matwau have come before, from upLands. We put aside our own differences, banded together to rout the invaders and sent them back to their own places." Inhya's voice was quiet, but carried nonetheless. "This very den was burrowed so our alliance could meet. All who sit to this Council are descendants of that alliance, and nearly all of us have traded, hearthed and espoused beneath the wings of our cooperative. Together we drove Matwau from our Lands, and together we will again, should there be need. Matwau are unkempt cowards. It is the Chepiś sorcery and Shaping we should worry about."

Tokela winced. Shaping. Chepiś sorcery.

"—does not kill as many as Matwau *eirn!*" challenged Grass Weaver.

There was a small buzz of murmurs, some obviously taken aback by not only her bold talk, but to whom it had been directed.

Curious, to see the struggle—respect for her age versus the fact of her outcast status. Yet open Council meant all could plainly speak.

Madoc gave Tokela a sudden nudge. Tokela did his best not to startle, wasn't sure he succeeded as Madoc gave him a piercing look and signed, *Should we go? This is boring.*

I told you. Tokela wasn't bored. In any fashion, unfortunately. *Go if you want. Quietly.*

You're not?

Tokela shrugged, kept listening. Madoc gave a sigh, more with his body than his voice, but stayed. He bent once again to winding the thread about his fingertips.

"The secret of metal-that-burns was given to Matwau by Chepiś sorcery," Inhya answered, hard and even.

"Metal working is no sorcery, hearth-chieftain," Galenu spoke up. "A skill, nothing more. A *science.*"

A strange, harsh word, and one Tokela had not yet heard; he leaned forwards, hoping someone would speak it again.

"Hunh!" This from Nechtoun. "You make too free with talk about this *šai'ens* of tall ones." He didn't stumble over the strange word, but it sounded different upon his tongue. "We have our own ways, more accurate than any outLand sorceries. Matwau or Chepiś, we have seen enough doings of tall ones here, and none of them good!"

Again, Tokela felt the sear and backlash as Nechtoun continued.

"Galenu. I love you. We were once playmates, will ever be oathbrothers, but I will never agree with you on this. We shouldn't even be trading with ones arrogant enough to manipulate the sacred Elementals! Big water-bronzes or fancy forge work are not worth the corruption such things bring! So much of their work is torn by force from Grandmother. It burns not only our skin, but our Spirits! It is unfit for us to even look upon!"

"Father." Sarinak's voice had changed, from inflexible to soft and placatory.

Tokela's own nerves crawled uneasy. Beside him, Madoc's fingers stilled, his breath gone shallow. They both knew the signs. Nechtoun bided unwell, some Suns. It was why he no longer held Mound-chieftain's staff.

"Nechtoun, what's gotten into you?" Galenu didn't seem to see what was happening. "You sound hidebound as your sire at his worst!"

It wasn't naming the dead, not exactly, but close enough that several including Nechtoun made the quick, placatory gesture before he retorted, "You say hidebound? I say tradition! If we have no tradition, we have nothing, and deserve to be overrun by Shapers!"

Tokela knew he was watching Našobok overmuch. But it was puzzling how Našobok's hands, large-jointed and relaxed where they were resting upon crossed knees, began clenching into slow fists. His eyes, gleaming from where the hair had fallen into his face, slid over to where Aylaniś and Palatan sat.

Aylaniś returned Našobok's glance. She seemed sad, concerned. Palatan's expression alone gave no purchase whatsoever into his thoughts, slick and unyielding as wet rock.

Not that Tokela truly had any idea of what thoughts Našobok and Aylaniś were exchanging, either.

"Do you suggest if we just latch our doors and put our heads into the body-soil trenches"—Galenu's voice had begun to rise—"nothing will happen in thisLand just because we don't *want* it to?"

"While you suggest we invite it in?" Nechtoun half rose.

"Yeka." Sarinak again, gentle. The den's murmurs had subsided, everyone peering at Nechtoun with varying shades of pity and disquiet.

"I will *not* be silenced on this!" Nechtoun retorted. "I am... was... Mound-chieftain! Galenu, you mightn't hold in your heart the love you once bore for our Lands, but—"

"Nechtoun, there's much my heart holds to in thisLand. I've never said there wasn't. But there is *more* than thisLand, and I well know because I've seen it!"

Madoc had crept closer to Tokela, snuggling close, curving along his back as if wanting every fibre of touch-comfort to permeate them both. Tokela reached back, tangled fingers in Madoc's hair, and silently implored under his breath: *Galenu, please. You don't understand. If you were oathbrothers once, surely you must see what is happening.*

But Galenu didn't stop. "I've walked the stony outcrop past the Omrikasten and seen ša's Fire. I've witnessed wonders past imaginings in Chepiś glitter and ebon *glašg*."

Aum-ree-khas'n? Another word Tokela had never heard, but he recognised *glašg*: the smooth, shining and translucent not-metal made far downRiver in Matwau holts. Like, but unlike, the *t'rešalt* with its reflections of dark and Stars.

More, a strange, wild enchantment—a recognition—rose at Galenu's talk. It sang in Tokela's ears like River's soft melody, drowning apprehension.

"I've also seen horrors, in strange villages reeking of Matwau, their valleys tamed past bearing and smoke hanging thick over clear-cut Forests. Warnings, as sure as the beauty. For the more we think thisLand is the only place in existence, the more our comfort will be overcome by plain reality: we are not the only people here."

"We are the only ones who *belong* here!" It thundered into sudden silence. Nechtoun's face had gone blood-dark; his fists clenched. "I want nothing of them, *nothing*! And I want nothing coming here to change our home!"

"Change isn't *coming*." Našobok spoke from the shadowy end of the den, flat-calm amidst the stiff froth of feral currents. The sound altered Nechtoun's focus, turning him towards where his disowned youngest half crouched, as if he would rise but dared not.

"Change," Našobok continued, very soft, "is already here."

And within the time it took for Tokela to draw another breath, Palatan had also moved from the shadows quiet as huntingKin. He knelt beside Nechtoun, reached out and put a hand against Nechtoun's temple.

"Peace, grandfather," he murmured, voice soft and soothing. "Be at peace. It's done."

Tokela wondered what Palatan thought he could do, then remembered. Alekšu. *Alekšu.* Tokela's gaze slid to Inhya. What did she think of this? Palatan was her brother, after all.

Inhya didn't seem disturbed.

Sarinak, on the other hand, did.

As Nechtoun fell silent, eyes clouding, Madoc's arms stole about Tokela's waist. Tokela ran comforting, albeit absent, fingers through the bright hair, watching as Palatan shot a narrowed glance at Galenu. Galenu blinked and took a sharp breath, as if to protest. Then, eyes narrowing upon Nechtoun, he sat back and gave way.

Perhaps Galenu had simply forgotten Nechtoun's uncertain state. What must it be like to watch someone—one you'd loved for a long time, considering—and watch that one deteriorate while you stayed reasonably whole, and aware.

A sudden stab of pity quivered Tokela. Not only for Nechtoun, but also Galenu.

"Wyrh-chieftain speaks truth," Aylaniś said, her quiet voice directed around the circle. "The very Earth beneath our feet is shifting, changing. Moreover, if we try to keep things contrived, unchanging, then how are we different than Chepiś? They keep their places in some altered and untimely state. They once sought to turn all thisLand so. To have no change? *That* is unnatural."

"It's as our ancestors say," Palatan added, his hand still upon Nechtoun's shoulder. "If we turn aside from Grandmother, She will merely roll and submerge us in the Deep."

"Indeed, horse-chieftain. Alekšu." Grass Weaver, both hands crossed respectfully at her heart, gave a brief nod. "You remind us of wisdom. And Našobok wyrh-chieftain makes talk that none other than outliers choose to hear. And stone-chieftain? It is... interesting, how you make the talk of outliers."

This was met with shocked murmurs, but also satisfied ones. Galenu, it seemed, had some antagonists.

"But stone-chieftain, *I* say you've not earned rights to wander. You have taken them, and given nothing in trade."

Earned. Tokela found himself unintentionally charmed by the sound of it, the possibilities.

"I disagree with your assessment, yakh-chieftain." Galenu's tone was firm, yet held more respect than most others would give an outlier.

"Hunh," the old fem grunted, unconvinced. "Taken. Even as Matwau take. Even as Chepiś take. Consider this: things cannot *be* taken without some damage. What have you let outLands take, stone-chieftain, without earning any protections?"

The ominous ring of it silenced even Galenu.

Madoc tugged at Tokela's braidlock. The motion slight and slow, Tokela angled his head to peer at Madoc.

What are they talking about? Is Grandsire... here?

Madoc realised what he'd implied only after he had brought it forth, and shot Tokela an apologetic look. *I didn't mean it in the same way as with yo—*

I'll explain later was all Tokela could trust himself to reply, turning away. A small choking noise sounded from behind him, but he didn't turn. His eyes stung a betrayal no less than Madoc's thoughtless talk.

"While Chepiś remain on our borders, Matwau daren't intrude too far," Grass Weaver continued, implacable. "Many of Matwau bide even more fearful of Other than dawnLanders."

"You forget yourself!" Sarinak growled.

"N'da. I never forget what I am. Often you do, when we have something useful for you. But we never forget. We cannot afford to." Grass Weaver gave a sharp, decisive jerk of her chin. "Your talk is straight as arrowflight, Inhya hearth-chieftain. Chepiś are dangerous. Their abominable Shaping has bent Grandmother's shell nigh to breaking. They have never belonged here, and they know it. More and more they lose themselves to their own madness. Take refuge, like the old tales of Tsin'oe, in Stars- and Moons' light."

Tsin'oe, who'd climbed Everwintering Mountain to reach those Stars, but instead had fallen to his ruin, entombed in rock. An outlier story; Tokela remembered Našobok sharing it.

"Why, who knows? They cannot eat those things, cannot drink them or take them as mates. But Chepiś numbers thin, while Matwau have learnt their masters' ways too well. They flourish in the abandoned places, circling the carcasses of Chepiś settlements like scavengerKin. The tall ones are, *all* of them, partners in desecration."

Again, silence, as if submerged in the wake of Grass Weaver's speech.

Then Našobok stood, walked forwards with a powerful, quiet tread to stand beside the old chieftain, and Tokela felt it as a blow, wiping every other coherent thought from his heart.

"Yakhling and wyrhling speak with one tongue in this Council. You could do worse than listen to ones who haven't your pride of place. Some truths only outcasts dare to see. I too have seen, with my own eyes and those of my people: the Chepiś are on the move."

"Moving, but not inward," Palatan murmured. "Not breaking truce."

"Yet." Aylaniś said. "Where do they go, wyrh-chieftain?"

"The tribes hold such places forbidden. But outliers don't fear the same things." He crossed his arms over his chest, gave a slow, lazy smile towards Sarinak—who still refused to acknowledge it. "This is why we're sometimes useful to each other, a'io?"

Sharp white canines flashing in that crooked smile, tall as a grandfather oak, broad-shouldered, cords of vein and muscle flexing beneath Sun-dark skin. Those callused hands, so quick to catch the old yakhling's staff, were surely skilled with other weaponry, privy to *other* secrets.

Tokela groaned, nigh silent, and rocked back to bury his face against his doubled-up knees, trying to escape his own skin, trying to still the blood-rhythm into something around which he could, indeed, hear.. Not that it helped. This was worse than Smoke. It quivered in him like the sweet tongue-melt of honey raided from the hot stings of bees. Breath-stirring. Lovely. *Dangerous.*

This was an awakening for which he'd not been prepared. This was an ache he could not still with his own touch.

He wanted more.

Tokela stayed there, huddled into his knees, as silence once again broke beneath his hiding place. A rush of excited voices, all vying to prominence. It took Council almost as long to come to order as it took Tokela to bring his own senses into some veneer of stability.

When he could, he purposefully turned from Council—and Našobok—to face Madoc.

Only Madoc was gone.

IO
INDIGO

A strange place to seek answers, this lair of chill shadows and heavy stillness. Beneath the upper shapings and wooden façades the caverns lay, burrowed by silted water or the molten electrum of past eruptions, winding wormholes leading from a geologic event horizon.

This cavern was small, almost unremarkable, save for what inhabited it.

The dark walls of the volcanic cistern merely emphasised the leached pallor of what once had been vital flesh. Clad in robes of polished ash, one with her stone couch, the statuesque, seated figure remained motionless... save for a minute spark in staring, filmed-over eyes. One tiny light, roiling with the minutiae of seismic shifts. One Sounding held deep to quell even the least of burgeoning catastrophes. Focus, utter and eternal, to bid a jungle kingdom quiescent.

"Ranlaia." Sivan made slow approach, knelt and laid her head to chill, chalk-pale knees. "Mother. I..."

Wish you were here. With me. Even though I shouldn't.

Her voice echoed, drifting against rock and equally stony consciousness.

"Why come here, Siv?"

Sivan started. But no such voice would ever come from the stone couch and its occupant. Nay, this was alive, beloved. Sivan turned from cold, androgynous Purpose to its antithesis. Mortal, unquestionably fem, Maloh glided amidst the shadows; one with them, born to them. Well-camouflaged, whilst Sivan stood apart as surely as the stone figure that had once been her mother, both of them pale as the blue-metal gleam of the marooned ships, cast into orbit kloms above these very caverns.

Ill-camouflaged. Easy target.

Alien.

Sivan and her brother Jorda had been born here nearly a century after the Stranding. Yet they didn't quite belong here, perhaps never had.

And Sivan had never managed to not want the belonging.

"Is your mother even there, anymore?" Maloh continued softly. "Ah, Siv, why do you keep coming?"

"Why does Jorda ask you to follow me?" Sivan riposted.

"He's your twin."

"Who keeps sending my lover to find me instead of coming for himself." Sivan shivered. It seemed the chill of what remained of she who'd borne them had crept into her soul.

"Perhaps he knows there are no answers here for either of you." Maloh stepped slowly closer, laid a hand to Sivan's cheek. Her fingers were so *warm*. "Perhaps," Maloh continued, gentle, "Jorda is more accepting of this one's soul-flight than you."

"And you?"

"Mm." Maloh looked up into Ranlaia's blank visage. "I'd rather be dead than rendered into nothing more than a fault line detector."

"She is Synced into the Matrices. She's at peace."

"Is she? Or is she just... not?"

"There is peace in that," Sivan retorted. "Her work is sanctified."

Maloh shrugged—no doubt she heard the desperation of it. "Keep telling yourself so. But come back upward, Siv, stay in the sunlight. There are no answers for you here."

"She would have known what to do."

Maloh nuzzled closer and kissed Sivan's brow; more warmth, more fingerlings of heated reality. "Maybe. Maybe not. Ranlaia has abdicated any say over the mortal world, but you cannot. I know you; you will not."

"I may have no choice."

A frown.

"My father departed this morning."

"I know."

"He's headed for HQ."

"The Grotto?" The dismay in Maloh's black eyes leapt forward, unfeigned.

Sivan felt it herself, to be sure. The Domina was... unpredictable.

"Why would he involve *Her*? Over a Sgr... a native boy?"

"A native boy whose genetic code has been altered by one of *us*."

"But isn't that a minor thing, easily dealt with? Why would Cavodu make a journey of seven sols through dangerous territory, just to bring this to *Her* attention?" Maloh never mentioned the Domina by name. Ever.

"He's taking the fastest stream-slip and gliding up the coast."

"With pirates lying in wait in every cove."

"They won't catch a stream-slip as long as the crew avoids the vortices."

Maloh grumbled beneath her breath. "Why doesn't he just... *think* it at her?"

Sivan laughed, bitter-tinged. "If he uses any of the matrices to communicate, it won't stay secret for long."

"If it's so secret, then wouldn't it be better to take care of it ourselves? I mean, after all, Jorda made him. Surely that counts for something."

"I'd rather that. But it's out of our hands."

Maloh's teeth gleamed in the murk, more snarl than any smile. Abruptly, she grasped Sivan's hand. "Come away, then. Let's go for a ride. Something."

As they departed, Sivan glanced once more over her shoulder, seeking the figure upon its couch. It seemed that the stone-slick eyes glimmered, followed her for several split timeparts. Breath in her throat, Sivan hesitated.

The eyes flattened, filmed over. Sivan sighed, turned and followed Maloh back up into the light.

"Yeka!"

Palatan gave a grunt as several stone of excited ahlóssa smacked into his thighs, grabbed his woven belt and started to climb him not unlike a tree.

"You stayed in Council ever so long"—Kuli kept climbing—"and so did Aška, and... *Uncle!!*"

Palatan let out another grunt as Kuli launched from his hip to fly at Našobok, who snagged Kuli midair then promptly tucked him beneath one arm, baggage for the road.

Kuli's yip of protest quickly collapsed into giggles. Somewhat truncated, true, since he was nearly folded in half over Našobok's forearm.

Palatan smirked. "You have a way."

"Crude but efficient, that's me," Našobok quipped back, and hefted the wriggling Kuli slightly higher. "I hope there's food nearby; all that yap-yap-yap works up an appetite. And I mean real food: stew and good flatbread, washed down with your tulapaiś."

"Ooh... Ai...!" Kuli kept protesting—and giggling. "Let... me... up!"

"He did say up?" Našobok asked, and Palatan smirked again, shrugged.

"Several times, by my counting."

Kuli shrieked as Našobok swung him around once and tossed him into the air, caught him and set him up on one shoulder. More passersby than not were adding their own laughter to Kuli's—and those who tried to quell their response to an outlier's antics seemed hard-pressed to decide how they should respond, considering whom that outlier walked beside.

Not that it mattered. Kuli rocked sideways, barely holding on, convulsed with giggles. Palatan laughed his own content.

The drums had changed their message from background rhythm to open invitation. Shouts issued from the valley clearing—the first of many stickball games—and Dancing would start, soon, on the wide adjacent field up past the Drum-heights. The smell of roasting meats, thick šinc'teh stew, and assorted breads wafted across the Bowl, enough to edge any hunger. Including Našobok's; his stomach let out a loud growl.

This, of course, sent Kuli into further hilarity.

"We'd better feed you, or at this rate you'll disrupt the drums." Palatan stretched up to tug at his son's coppery braid-lock, then let his hand fall to Našobok's shoulder. "Aylaniś is with Inhya. She told me—and I bring talk straight from her tongue—whilst they have their hen gather I'm to make sure you're decently fed before we begin our cock gather. Says you'll need your strength to ogle the dancers."

"Cock gather." Našobok slid dancing, storm-hued eyes towards Palatan. "Our lovemate knows me too well."

"I want to be in on the cock gather!" Kuli announced.

Palatan's chuckle turned to a snort.

"Your son," Našobok pointed out with a wide grin.

"What's so funny?" Kuli demanded, settling down upon Našobok's broad shoulders. "Can I have Madoc come along? I was looking for him. You're so tall, Uncle, and I can see so well from up here, I'm sure I'll find him... *Madoc!*" he suddenly bellowed. "Over here!"

Našobok winced, put a finger in the ear closest to Kuli and wiggled it. "Upon the Sunrise this one's voice breaks, I'll blood myself in gratitude."

Palatan wanted nothing more than to hug Našobok senseless—just on the strength of how much Našobok could make him laugh.

It hadn't exactly been a summering to encourage good humour. He had wrested Alekšu's horns from Chogah, but new fetters always fused such triumphs with as much rue as honey. The far-flung wandering of grazing time gave some recompense; there, he could be merely his spouse's mate, tyah and raid leader. And thisnow, this heartbeat, shared in tandem with one who knew so intimately the sound of that heart, where and why and how...

"I've missed you, oathbrother," he said, sharp-soft as an arrow tickled to string, and Našobok flushed—*flushed!*—and slid another look Palatan's way, half mast and explicit as his own.

"Madoc!" Kuli shrilled again. This time they both winced.

Madoc was heading their way, but as Kuli summoned him, he seemed to hesitate. Palatan didn't give him the chance, striding over and laying one arm about his shoulders. Disarmed, Madoc grinned and let himself be pulled closer.

"He'll be taller than I am before long, Ai, Našobok?"

"He will. You'll be a great, proud a'Naišwyrh like your sire, Madoc. I can't believe the size of you—has it been so long?" Našobok reached out, gave a rough tousle to Madoc's curls. The ahlóssa stiffened, but flashed a smile as Palatan snugged him closer.

"Are you hungry, nephew? Come, share your meal with us."

"I'm so very hungry," Kuli announced, shifting as if there were crawlers in his clout. "Maybe we'll find Anahli at the cooking dens. Or Tokela. He eats more than even Madoc does."

Našobok winced again—the result, no doubt, of those narrow butt bones digging into his shoulder.

"Not more than you, greedy gut," Madoc riposted. "I don't know where you put it."

"I have a hollow leg," Kuli replied with a wave of one hand. "Aunt Inhya says."

With a guffaw, Našobok treated Madoc to a wink and smirk. Madoc nearly returned it; instead the ahlóssa flushed and looked away. Našobok seemed to shrug it off, but Palatan slid Madoc a taut, thoughtful gaze.

"Speaking of Tokela, could you believe the cheek of Galenu? As if your sister would even consider..." Našobok trailed off as Palatan gave a barely perceptible jerk of chin towards the youngsters.

There is much to consider, and not only Galenu, Palatan signed, with quick fingers, out of sight. *Though the old khatak is clever and quick enough to find advantage in any uproar.*

Clever is not going to stop a rotted thing, Našobok answered.

Speaking of clever—Madoc was eyeing them a little too close for circumspect talk. Palatan started to speak, but Našobok beat him to it.

"I would like to see Anahli." Sudden uncertainty quivered Našobok's deep voice; Palatan heard it, thin as well-spun thread. Since she had become oških, Anahli had spurned the uncle she had once adored. None of them could get to the meaning of it. Palatan had his own suspicions, ending and beginning with Chogah.

"No doubts she's with her own," Našobok continued, "having a grand First Running. No use for male company, eh? But Tokela—" He grimaced as Kuli shifted again, shrugged, then swung Kuli to hang upside down. Kuli gave a shriek of pretend dismay; Našobok continued with hardly a hitch, "I figured he would surely be with you, Madoc."

Within the circle of Palatan's arm, Madoc peered, stolid, at Našobok. When Našobok merely peered back, Madoc flushed again. It seemed almost... angry.

It seemed like his sire.

"He's always walking along River," Kuli put in, still giggling despite the strain of his heels being higher than his head. "Sometimes he lets us walk with him. He tells the best stories, Yeka! I'll bet if we should go out the compound we'd find him... Uncle! Let me back up and I'll look for him."

"Then keep your bony haunches *still*," Palatan advised. "Squirmy ahlóssa will end up thrown—and who can blame the horse?"

Našobok chuckled and swung Kuli back up—on the opposite shoulder, this time. "Your sire is determined I'm part horse."

A fine, sturdy, bronze-bay stallion with eyes like a wintering storm, Palatan signed with a grin. *I've always heard it's water-horses who have the largest—*

Našobok grabbed Palatan's hand, made his own talk tickle promise against his palm. *Tease.*

"You're a fine horse, Uncle Našobok!" Kuli enthused. "But I guess you'd be a River horse."

"A'io," Palatan warned, "one of the *puquhiś*, the legendary ones who coax you to back them, then toss you to drown."

"Not true!" Našobok pretended to pout.

Palatan laughed, soft. Madoc shot him a puzzled look, and Palatan gave a fond ruffle at Madoc's hair. All ombre and gold beneath Sun, braided here and there with turquoise thread and carved wood beads, it curled unruly as his sire's. Madoc responded to the affection with another huge grin.

"But I *like* riding my horse in water," Kuli was protesting. "I like River. Tokela does, too. You know, Tokela and I are going to travel River together. When I'm old enough, that is."

Madoc puffed up like a fantail in mating plumage. "If Tokela went anywhere, which he is *not*, it wouldn't be with *you*."

"Well, it won't be with *you*," Kuli countered. "You don't like going on boats. You get sick."

"Once. I was sick *once*, you *Spawn*—Yai!"

This as Palatan flipped a sharp smack to the back of Madoc's head.

Kuli gave a satisfied snort; Madoc rubbed at his skull and eyed Palatan, wounded.

Palatan shrugged. "Then mind your tongue, ahlóssa."

"Sounds familiar." Našobok arched an eyebrow towards Palatan. "Except for the 'once', of course. And here I thought only pretty horsetalkers found River uncertain."

Palatan rolled his eyes.

Madoc, left off rubbing his head to attend one of the hem lacings to his leggings, untied and flapping loose.

"Tokela loves boats," Kuli informed them. "*He* doesn't get sick. He takes me in the dugouts all the time. Maybe Tokela and I'll travel River with you, Uncle Našobok."

"Maybe." Našobok swung Kuli down. "For now, run with your own feet, Little Fox."

Kuli beamed at the intimacy, grabbed Našobok's hand and

half ran, half walked between them. Našobok kept grinning, a tiny curl of satisfaction. Palatan saw the bodytalk of that in a heartbeat.

"You are not," he informed Našobok, "stealing my chieftain's only son away to your oversized canoe."

"Ship. You know perfectly well *Ilhukaia* is a ship," Našobok parried, then addressed Kuli once more. "But your yeka's right, Little Fox. You have to grow tall and strong before you can make such choices. Perhaps after nextSun's rising I can arrange a ride for you and Tokela and Madoc, if..." He looked back, trailed off.

Madoc had disappeared. Palatan slid puzzled eyes to Našobok.

Našobok's satisfaction had flattened; he gave Palatan a small shrug, signed, *I should have known.*

"Yeka! Uncle Našobok!" Kuli gave a tug. "I nearly forgot, I promised I'd eat with Laocha, so I'd better run."

And he was gone, bare feet speeding over the grass and towards the trees. There was indeed a group of ahlóssa waiting there; Kuli burst into their midst like a spark from a hearth, and a young fem about his age—likely the aforementioned Laocha—grabbed his arm and dragged him away. The rest followed, carrying on with high voices, exuberant leaps and darts.

Našobok chuckled. "Ai, to have all that energy."

Palatan didn't answer. Instead he watched Našobok's back, straight and broad beneath the leather longcoat, watched the blood-hued beading glimmer as Našobok crossed his arms. "You should have known?" Palatan prompted, quiet.

Again the beads glimmered, betrayal of the barely perceptible tremor beneath. "Madoc."

Palatan's brows twisted in sudden understanding.

Našobok gave another shrug. "He's of an age where 'shoulds' outweigh too many things. Just as well. If he was already wilful, he'd just end up like I did."

Palatan put a hand to his shoulder. "Is that so bad, wyrh-chieftain?"

"For me, n'da. I'd no choice. But would you want an outlier's lot for any of your children?"

"What sort of outlier do you mean?" A fine spark of bitterness kindled beneath. Palatan didn't bother to conceal it; he knew Našobok understood.

Našobok nodded and sighed. "I suppose neither of us has an easy answer. Entirely too complicated."

"Particularly given what you said in Council."

"What I said?"

Palatan's thoughts were all too lengthy, too complex to easily parse. Instead he snugged Našobok's arm in his, to the plain dismay of a trio of elder males—*Alekšu seems entirely too familiar with that outlier!*—and started walking again. He kept his voice low, quiet as hunting-talk. "You said: 'Change is coming. Change is here'." His fingers twitched upon Našobok's sleeve. "Fire lay beneath your words."

"Gah! Fire?" Našobok's light attempt fell flat. "From a wyrhling?"

"A'io. That, too."

"Hunh. 'That, too.' Which means none of them will listen." Našobok shook his head, sending a stray lock of bistre over his eyes.

"I'm listening." Palatan reached forwards, pushed it back. "I will always listen."

"You always were a stubborn clot."

"Hunh. Like who else?"

They started walking again, joining the crowd about the Firepits. Several gave hasty way—trepidation or scorn—but neither Našobok nor Palatan gave notice.

Until Našobok, accepting stew and bread from a fem who gave him a friendly enough smile, looked about and shrugged again. "I did think I would have at least seen Tokela."

Palatan peered at him, unsure of what to say. There truly was no talk for such things—but bodytalk said more than any vocal promise. He leaned his temple against Našobok's shoulder, regret and understanding.

"Hunh." Našobok shrugged. "It is what it is. This wyrhling should well be used to ahlóssa running from him by now."

The drums, until then a comforting background, ramped up into sudden booms. Sharp and penetrating, they echoed against the rocks; were answered by several cries from Overlook

"Come on!" Našobok grabbed Palatan's arm. "That sounds like a big one!"

Indeed, a big one, but no ship, not this time. A runner had come from downriver, with news of a great, boiling mass of bloodfins making their early run. All fishKin runs provided, but this first one brought everyone together. Vital trade, fresh food source, preserved meat against hard times—and that for everyone, every tribe gathered beneath the alliance meeting within the Great Mound.

So everyone responded.

In the aftermath of the drum-talk, Song arose, filling the reverberating air of Forest's valleys. The main tributaries—the little River-sisters—churned with industry above and below, as every tribal member or relative or guest gave proper greeting to the mass of swimmingKin roiling upRiver. This Running was early—earlier, the old ones said, than in memory. Did it matter? Perhaps it was even a gift, Grandmother's acknowledgement that all the allied tribes, from duskLands to dawn, were gathered to honour River's bounty. Naisgwyr'uq sat upon the front entry to several tributaries and hatching grounds, so food and livelihood came swimming—for standingKin to the winged ones, to the four- and two-leggeds—and all gleaning a shining harvest, singing after their own fashion. The bloodfins would be heavy with toothsome eggs, or hoping to claim those eggs as their own, ready to fight for the chance.

More, certainly, than even all the gathered tribes could take and use; they would net what they needed and still leave plenty to spawn farther up.

Inhya's voice rose and fell, one with her chosen People's, fitting—and carrying—accompaniment to the drums echoing against the cliffs. She didn't stop singing as she strode the shore, overseeing the nets as they were dragged from storage by eager ahlóssa and adults alike. Her words were not only joy, but long-honoured instruction; everyone sang with her as the nets were deployed. Some were handheld dippers of only a handspan. Others were long, flawlessly woven. All were carried to the various upstream waterfalls.

Sarinak's powerful voice boomed along the opposite side, a drum of directions carrying even above River's voice. Amidst directing the dip nets, Inhya caught sight of Tokela, who'd reappeared in response to the drum message, Madoc in tow.

Something had to be done about that, and soon. Tokela might exist beneath the fiction of being too young to wander; Madoc *was* too young, in every fashion. Ahlóssa and oških didn't make the best of cohorts—their paths were too diverse. And for all the things Tokela did well, he did just as many in a fashion Inhya would not have her youngest emulate.

A sight of beauty: all gathered, elders to ahlóssa, stripped down to dive and slosh River's children, setting nets and ensuring they spanned Her with grace, untangled. Anahli and another oških—Čayku, wasn't it?—played nets from bank into River. A mere stone's throw downstream, a sopping Madoc laughed with the other ahlóssa, even Kuli, whom Madoc professed—too frequently, Inhya thought with a grin—to loathe. Stronger swimmers were out in the deep water. The wyrhling in particular seemed one with River—of course, he would, wouldn't he?—but still working alongside his former People, ensuring the nets didn't snag on rocks and were played out deep enough. Aylaniś and Palatan exchanged snatches of banter with him from the shore, but it didn't stop their helping with the nets. Tokela also swam amongst the deep waters, quiet and efficient; known as one of the best swimmers they had, he was reliable in this at least.

They would speak about where he'd been, and perhaps a few other things. But not thisSun. ThisSun, there was a living to be made.

◊ ◊ ◊

The drums echoed his heart, pounding fierce-glad with the work. Or so Tokela thought.

He didn't realise his excitement had another cause. Didn't realise that he was looking until he saw him. Or, more accurately, saw *them*.

His granddam had once said it: *All paths lead to the one you truly intend, whether you pay attention or not...*

Našobok let out a yelp of laughter, sending Tokela's heart further a-thrum and his stomach lurching: recognition, and something else he didn't ken. Tokela cocked his head to espy Kuli's dam and sire on the far bank. Aylaniś and Palatan hauled nets with little finesse but much enthusiasm. Even dripping and stripped of much of her finery, Aylaniś too made Tokela's stomach clench; a remembrance of graceful authority that merely made her more accessible, more... lovely. Palatan, on the other hand, seemed less Alekšu and more the trickster his tribe revered; he'd tangled a foot in the netting. A mishap any ahlóssa wouldn't make, but the mistake was, no doubt, what had prompted that familiar yelp of laughter.

A tiny ahlóssa threw a net tail Tokela's way; he snatched it midair then dove with it across the tributary and to a waiting elder. The old fem had hunkered down as much from laughter as to take the net. She tilted her head towards the antics upstream, chuckled "Horsetalkers!" as she took the net tail from Tokela. It made a prime opportunity to swim closer, not only to unsnag the net's drag, but also remove a low-drooping branch from it—and Tokela's line of sight.

The two horsetalkers might be ungainly with the nets, but their wyrhling companion was not. He'd tied his long hair back, a wet tail that hung between bare, dark shoulders. The latter quivered with laughter as Našobok played out the tangled net. Carefully, ostensibly so Palatan didn't end up dragged into River, though in the next breath Našobok tightened it, shook it with mock threat. Aylaniś yipped warning, and Palatan threw his assailant a look half panic and all promise: *If you do I'll end you!*

Našobok wrapped the net around one sinewy, broad-knuckled hand and tugged again. His eyebrows arched their own promise; his teeth gleamed. Aylaniś splashed at him. Našobok merely wrapped the net once more about his hand. Palatan tossed him a gesture Tokela had seen amongst the Riverwalkers, then hauled back. Leaner, smaller, yet those bronze-wet arms were corded taut from the bow. Našobok lurched forwards, landing face-first with a huge splash.

Aylaniś doubled over, stumbling with laughter.

Others were getting into the spirit of it, shouting encouragement to both sides of the playful struggle. Palatan's own laughter yipped upward as Našobok rose from the shallow, climbing the net upward. Tens of summerings of net-hauling made a match for a duskLands bowarm... and Palatan hadn't let go. He went sailing.

Cheers from up and down the banks greeted this.

Fortuitously—or by design?—Aylaniš had released the net. One arm wrapped about her ribs; she was laughing herself into hiccups.

Palatan rose, sputtering, shaking his head and hands. Tokela had to laugh—Palatan resembled a midLands wildcat gone for an unplanned ducking. Našobok trod forward, water curling and foaming, and scooped Palatan from the water with one arm. Setting him upright, Našobok gave a fond tug to his companion's sopping temple plaits. To this liberty, Palatan responded with a laugh and a cup of his palm at Našobok's nape.

More yelps of encouragement greeted this.

"Give him a ducking, Alekšu!"

"The bloodfins are spawning, not you!"

And a snort from the elder playing out Tokela's net. "Too old to indulge in that sort of play! But what to expect from an outlier and a horsetalker!"

Tokela barely heard. His notice had riveted to the cling of Našobok's hairtail, like a trail of ink down his well-muscled back and dipping into the cleft of buttocks outlined by his clout. Or the slick-lithe, *knowing* language of Palatan's back, arching for just that much too long beneath Našobok's embrace, fingers clenching at Našobok's nape, pulling the thick, black tail of hair to glide along Našobok's back then swing sideways. The glint of Palatan's teeth could have been snarl or smile, but Našobok didn't take offence. Instead he gave a cheeky grin, one that made Tokela dizzily wonder how bees had taken sudden residence in his belly. That fascinating tail of hair flipped over one shoulder and snagged on Našobok's left nipple—actually, a silver ring piercing that nipple—for a heartbeat.

Perhaps more, for Tokela's heart hammered, sudden-quick and so loud he swore it was audible. As Našobok released Palatan at the bank, Tokela kenned the reason he was getting dizzy. He'd forgotten to breathe. He sucked in a huge gasp, and as if in answer River swirled about him, a quick eddy that nearly pulled him from his feet, a caress that rippled up his thighs and tongued his belly.

Našobok stiffened. Palatan asked a question too low to be heard, and Našobok shook his head. But as Palatan turned away, Našobok darted a quick gaze about, a frown quirking his brow.

Tokela hunkered down in the water, tearing his gaze away.

It was then the whisper tickled at Tokela's nape, not just sound, but making talk:

He is mine. You are mine. My own.

Sucking in a harsh breath, Tokela slid beneath the tree limb and sloshed from the water. By the time he reached the banks, he'd started to run.

◊　◊　◊

Anahli saw him, tearing away from the tributary as if fleethounds were on his heels.

Strangely comforting, to see that she wasn't the only one who found the playful wrangle of wyrhling, Alekšu and horse-chieftain upsetting. Somehow.

Why would Tokela be upset? Why would she be herself? Even if part of her wanted to laugh, join in.

"Inappropriate." The soft, bitter voice merely encouraged more acrimony. "Like foolish oških, those three, with eyes only for the long-lost lovemate."

Anahli refused the bait. "I'm oških. And people laugh to see their joy."

"The joy will sour, as soon as those here remember that Alekšu openly courted an outlier." For all her bulk, Chogah could move with grace and speed. She gained Anahli's side with barely a pebble disturbed underfoot. "Why aren't you with your own playmate, oških, instead of eyeing outliers and fools?"

Of course she knew Anahli had a new playmate. Chogah seemed to ferret everything, one way or another.

"I'm resting, Aunt. Even here, they allow time for rest."

"You are too bold. Defiance gains little without the proper stealth for success." Head tilting, Chogah moved closer. "I tried to change your dam's mind. You know you don't belong here, any more than that one"—her chin jerked the way Tokela had fled—"does."

N'da, I don't know. I know nothing about you, and sometimes too much...

"But I am Alekšu tuk, in power no longer, and now your dam gives me only what respect she must. Instead the respect I earned goes to her spouse—a male, nothing more—who stole my place."

"He stole nothing."

"Stole my place, and my rights!" Chogah spat. "And if you do not stay with your People, take your place, then how will we overcome what has been taken from us?"

"It's time I proved my place, aunt. What if I just want to be what I choose, not what you keep saying I must be? You, with your secrets and suggestions. Are you any different, truly, than my mother or my father, who also try to say what I must be?"

Chogah was smiling, in her charming, pitying, oh-my-heart sort of way. "Oških will challenge. It's their way and their right, eh?" The smile slid into a sneer. "So we have a new Alekšu who hasn't even the wherewithal to shun a wyrhling as he should. As he must, if he is to keep his place amongst firstPeople." A sigh. "I only wish your parents could see what fools they are made. Thankfully you are not so easily played, Cousin. You saw the wyrhling for what he was, from the beginning."

N'da, only from the time a second father had abandoned his family, let his River quench Fire.

And played by whom? The thought had come to Anahli, more and more. She was no longer the ahlóssa that had hung upon every web a powerful and supposedly-infallible Alekšu had once spun.

Anahli kept her thoughts her own, and her ebony eyes upon Chogah, gauging. Uncertain.

Festivities had been postponed until nextSun's rising, when the successful harvest of bloodfins would be given their due honour. Shifts of preparation had begun, of course, and would continue over the coming Suns to ensure none missed more than their share of First Running. For now, many guests and residents rested, tired and satisfied with thisSun's work, eager for a large meal and good sleep.

Tokela had no wish for the latter. And after a quick stop by the ahlóssa den for his pouch, his nose led him to the former, tantalised by the peppery scent of fat dripping onto Fire's tongues. Already a sizeable line had formed, patient, where a group of elder females ladled, from enormous pots, šinc'teh stew over fresh-poached bloodfin meat.

Glad to be nothing more than one in a hungry crowd, Tokela fell in. When his turn came, he tendered a grateful smile for Darhinu's generosity. She always insisted he was just skin over bones, remained intent upon feeding him up. Filling his skin with fruit water, Tokela skirted the crowd and found himself making his way up Overlook.

For the first in a long while, he didn't head for the driftwood railing—not even a longing glance where River lapped at the watercraft and Her sand-and-stone shore. Instead Tokela settled his back against the sienna stone wall and heeded his meal.

The stew was rich with fat and redolent of spices, thick with last summering's dried šinc'teh and this summering's early greens. The bloodfin fell from the bones—tender, and hot. Not minding singed fingers, he just dug in, sucking air to cool it until he'd finished every bite and scraped the bowl with his flatbread. Giving a satisfied sigh, he leaned back against the stone and closed his eyes.

So quiet, above. River pushed gently at the edges of his notice; Tokela set his teeth and instead focused on the echoes of gathering wafting upward from the Bowl; the happiness of everyone sated from work, willing to wait for play. Part of him wanted to return, join in. Sit with his family, *belong*...

Everything had changed.

N'da, not everything. *He* had changed.

The *t'rešalt*, the Chepiś, had changed him. He had gone into the forbidden places, all tossing mane and snort of defiance. Had taken a path he shouldn't have done, hoping... denying... daring the blood that without doubt surged his veins.

You are a'Naišwyrh!

He was his mother's son. None could take that from him. But if his sire was of those scorned, feared...

Shunned. Not only outlier, but not of People.

Tokela had walked his own changing journey when he'd gone through the *t'rešalt*. Been Broken with benefit of blood, smoke blessing, and guide. Only not in a way he'd ever expected.

And now, in the aftermath of Breaking...

River spoke to him. Made talk. To him.

Claimed him.

He is mine. You are mine. My own.

Tokela sat there for a long time, fingers idly tracing the well-swept stones. A loud *Yip!* from the great Bowl made him jump and snatch his hand sideways—instinctively, to brush away the sketches—then halted. This time, a curious smile touched his lip at what his fingers had conjured from dust and damp. Eyeing the stair once again, Tokela relented. No graphite, no traces left in the wake of a forbidden talent. Instead he licked his fingers and deliberately sketched more figures upon the pavings—*Ilhukaia* rocking and bobbing gently in a swell with trade weavings flying; Aylaniś's laugh upon the banks, Palatan and Našobok's embrace in the Riverlet—then ran a careful touch along the first sketch:

Ilhukaia's chieftain, eyes upon Sun and Wind in his hair.

Tokela threaded the pouch over his head and reached in, took out one of the objects he'd gathered from his basket in the ahlóssa den. The Seashell fitted in his palms as if formed there, and when he raised it to his ear, it whispered his name.

Našobok had given the shell to him, nine summerings previous. More, Našobok had believed when Tokela had told him:

That's Sea's voice you hear, cousin. More powerful than River, even.

Does She whisper your name, too?

Sometimes... sometimes, I think She does.

I want to go there. I want to hear for myself.

Then one Sun, little Riverwalker, when you're old enough, I'll take you.

At the time, he hadn't understood what it truly meant. 'Riverwalker' hadn't been the insult others would make, but a fond, close-spun camaraderie offered to placate a lonely ahlóssa. Merely a kind exaggeration or evasion, not unlike the ones Tokela used to distract Madoc.

Had Našobok found, even as Tokela was finding, how kindnesses could turn, how fair intentions could noose and love's intensity smother?

Why else would he bend over the shell?—whisper *I'm here, now. I am.*

Why should he think the shell would agree?—breathing soft-faint into his ear.

Because I want this. Not to be Other. I want my people, my place... Here. I want to belong here, be in my body if only for thisSun, this heartbeat, if...

Perhaps he can show me how.

He hears you, he said as much, Tokela informed the shell. Then slowly, inexorably, his eyes slid upwards, cast over River. *He's yours, after all, and if he hears you then, perhaps...*

Perhaps this was not...not... of Them. Of Other. Perhaps this was what it meant to be wyrhling?

And from behind his eyes She rose, pounding the blood at his temples and neck, surging in the back of his throat with a tang of brack and copper silt. He shuddered, sucked in a gasp, flinched away.

Dropped the shell.

His booted toes thankfully broke the fall; a heartbeat later he had snatched it up, head pounding, and hunched over it.

Stayed there, for long breaths, as Wind riffled Tokela's hair to sting his hot, hennaed cheeks. His heart pounded, the surge of blood overtaking River's insistent voice.

Only the drums, and the sound of his pulse.

He was his mother's son. He would admit nothing else. He was normal.

Normal.

And he would make this decision before it made him.

It wasn't the way. There would be no one to Smoke and Mark him, none to see him safe upon his oških journey... but hadn't he already made it? Already wandered into the wild and come back in different form... changed.

N'da, not changed, not like that. Broken, they called it in duskLands, when the change came to ahlóssa. In the end, weren't all such journeys made alone? If he was to belong, then he would ensure that belonging in the only way he knew.

The Moons peeped through the new leaves of the weeping tree wykupeh, ghosting shadows down where Tokela scooped out a small pit in the sand and gravel to kindle Fire's breath from berrywood and spicetree. Beside that he smoothed his blanket, well within range of Smoke's breath. On the blanket he'd settled a pouch, a clean burl bowl, the shell, and a pair of tiny, corked pots—all with some care. Upending the pouch, he separated the contents with nimble fingers. A strand of beads and amber tailed with charms of carven wood, a small assortment of copper bands for hair and fingers, a wristband decorated with quills and amber. A pair of thin, fine armlets, silver inlaid with turquoise. A thick ear spiral of pale horn, cunningly shaped like serpentKin; it had been his dam's. A necklace of teeth; the River lion had tried to take several ovines as they drank, and Tokela and his father—well, mostly his father, Tokela then possessed of a mere six winterings—had taken the lion down.

The claws taken from the *shigala* creature were shoved back into the pouch, deep-hidden.

Unplaiting the cloth-and-bead lanyards already in his hair, he put his palms against his doubled knees, contemplating his wealth. Not much, gathered all together, but they were things of quality. And after thisSun, after he made his Marks and Danced, Tokela would be able to claim more.

He hoped his treasures were... Ai, what did he hope? Suitable? Appealing?

It felt odd, to care so much about his appearance.

Yet he had to care. Tokela was under no illusions he could physically outshine the other oških who would Dance beside him, but he knew the steps from watching and imitating them his entire life. He had some grace, was nimble on his feet. He was also nimble with his wits, which was a good thing. He'd surely have to outwit Našobok. Trick him, somehow, mask what he was and once had been. For Tokela knew—*knew*—if he didn't? Našobok would only see the little cousin he'd carried on his broad shoulders, the ahlóssa who'd pestered him for Sea tales, who'd followed him, eager and determined, in long walks on River's thighs.

He did not want Našobok to see that ahlóssa. Not anymore.

The next was tricky. But a bath was necessary. He rose, taking hesitant steps into the shallow Riverlet, then clenched his teeth and dove in. Breath escaped him at the shock of Her, bubbles glistening bronze and pinkish-green, rising to catch in his hair. Buoyant, drifting, closing about him, touching him, yet...

She filled him with nothing but peace, and the sound of Her made soft accompaniment to the drumming of his heart.

Tokela waded out, bending over to shudder away the wet. Wind nipped at his damp skin—affectionately, it would seem. Black-chestnut hair gleamed with wet and dusk's shadows, clung to him as he shook... save the braidlock snugged to his skull, slapping at his cheek.

He had forgotten it. Forgotten, and suddenly he couldn't wait to be freed of it. Fingers shaking in their eagerness, Tokela raked the unbraided locks sideways and held the braid taut. His new obsidian knife was just as sharp as the old one shattered upon the Shaped beast; it made a ripping sound as he cut the braid a handspan from his scalp. Tiny prickles of chill raised the scant fur on his thighs, groin, and belly. His scalp tingled as he loosed the remainder of the braid to drift across his face—forelock, not braidlock, no longer.

Plait end in one hand and his knife in the other, he knelt and passed both above the remaining honour: Fire. Cleansed by River, severed by Earth, set free upon Wind and now, the visible Power of Their commingling—Smoke—wafted over him. Tokela sniffed gingerly and held the wisp within his lungs, disallowing the luxury of a cough, then bent over his finery and exhaled the misted breath in a faint orison.

Warmth rashed over him, dispersing any chill. He took that as a good omen, and poured from the first pot a grainy, loose powder the colour of conifer needles. Setting the bowl into Fire he took up the second vial, poured the oil. As it runnelled and beaded over the dry matter, he began folding it together with a peeled stick, adding small amounts of steaming water—another commingling, this. Another Dance.

His fingers faltered. What if even indigo made no difference? What if he made his Marks, and Danced, and still Našobok only saw an unremarkable younger cousin?

There had to be a way. Something. Somehow.

If only he could *be* invisible. Or a true skin-changer, like the ancient tales of Šaákfo...

He couldn't believe he was even thinking such a thing. But for perhaps the first time in his life, Tokela did not want to be thought of as unremarkable.

All the while he rolled the shorn braidlock on one thigh, watching as the oiled powder lifted then thickened, altering with River's coppery Power, shifting like a Dance mask...

A Dance mask.

Tokela smiled. Testing the mix with his smallest finger, he took the pot from Fire's palms and paced over to squat in the shallows. Then, using the Moons-bright River as mirror, he dipped the twisted skein of hair into the indigo and began to trace across his cheekbones.

$$\phi \quad \phi \quad \phi$$

II
DANCER

The mask called him, pure and simple. Perhaps it was his blood—his dam had been over half of horseClan, after all. The fur-trimmed, grass-woven half mask of Hare seemed to speak his name, make promise:

We are alike, you and I. We are creatures of speed and thought, guile and skill. Be one with me, Tohwakelifitčiluka. Be the clever one, the one who hides in plain sight, the one whose heart can outwit and outspeed almost anyone.

Tokela stood leaning against the whitewood stave of his spear, eyeing the mask where ša hung, amidst many others. The other oških males milled around him, murmuring, making their own choices. Torchlight flickered over their bodies and glinted along the points of their spears: bone and sinew and obsidian. Ceremonial Fire had been captured in torches to illuminate the oških in all their finery; the torches smoked the tall ceiling of the weapons den, cast shadows along the clean-swept expanse of testing ground, as well as the long, smooth walls where weaponry both ancient and new hung.

The masks were displayed in exceptional prominence: animalKin, all. It was acceptable—sought after, even—to emulate the raw, highly prized senses of their wilder brethren. The Elemental Powers were sacrosanct, forbidden to the skills of Grandmother's mortal children, but these...

After all, Šaákfo šaself had been mate to Forest Spirits, get of hareKin.

Be one with my skin. The hareKin half-mask flickered, seemed to speak. *Taunt him to the chase. And if he can catch you? Dance him giddy.*

Skills. Senses. Thisnow seemed to deny the alien latency biding within his Spirit. His heart pounding to match the bass pulse of the drums. The songs lifting, voices rising and falling, over and under the beat, carrying sharp towards Sun and Sky. For every denial there remained a pleasure, with every warp woven into his senses, a woof snugged it to him, *his.*

No vocalisation was adequate. Tokela peered at the masks, his fingers twitching with longing. Only forbidden arts, it seemed, could describe the truly indescribable.

Tokela walked forwards, gently pushing through the group. They gave courteous way, as they had done to every other who had so obviously made his choice. And if there was a whisper or two?—well, Tokela was used to that. He took down the hareKin mask and peered into the eye sockets. Unremarkable, empty. Yet as he tilted the mask to the torchlight, the hollow orbs glittered, a trick of shadows that was not.

Enemy, Hare suddenly whispered.

Tokela shivered, blinked. A voice sounded from behind him and he whirled, hand going to the knife sheathed at his pectoral.

Mordeleg stood with arms akimbo. "Look to how you have changed our game." Too close, broad and encroaching, truly more alien than any presence trying to surface in Tokela's Spirit. Eyes dark as his heart, talk pitched to Tokela's ears alone. The others, intent upon their own doings and choices, paid little heed.

How had stoneClan birthed the gentle strength of Tokela's father, yet also this?

"Finally, your Uncle has done his duty," Mordeleg murmured. "Made of you oških."

Tokela, already too conscious of the indigo paste still on his cheeks, felt even more the dry pucker and flake. Mordeleg's eyes scaled him, starting with Tokela's cheeks then up and down his body like slimy feet.

Tokela gave the only answer he knew: with a steady, flat-eyed glare he walked away from both Mordeleg and the mask wall. He'd little hope it would help.

Mordeleg snatched up a mask with such indifference that several oških, also pondering a choice, barked protest. Mordeleg ignored them. Clutching the bearKin mask in his thick fingers, he shadowed Tokela. Tokela made a seemingly casual path towards where the group of Dancers had gathered within the den's heart. With Mordeleg, there was safety in numbers—even if those who'd defend ahlóssa would likely pay little heed to another oških who should be perfectly capable of defending himself.

The oških were laughing and scuffling, preening, flexing both muscles and authority. All the while, they pretended not to see each others' choice of masks. Several were oiling their skin in preparation for the upcoming contest. One was tying a gaily beaded ribbon to his spear haft, another tying back his forelock with finery of beads and fur. Tokela leaned on the wall not too far from them. He knew many of them, of course, but thisDance would include others from far-flung tribes and moieties. Not to mention that ahlóssa did little mixing with oških. Many of the painted faces seemed unfamiliar.

And Mordeleg kept shadowing him. "But Sarinak has been in

Council constantly. And you have not been gone long enough to make any Journey. How is such a thing possible?"

Tokela flicked a scornful gaze. There was an oddling *something* in Mordeleg's eyes; it scraped uneasy against Tokela's hyperactive senses.

N'da. He was normal. This would prove it, as Inhya always said.

"Perhaps you were enough of your own heart to make them yourself, as we do in midLands."

As ill-aimed shots went, this flew too square for Tokela's liking.

"Did you make them for someone?" Mordeleg smirked and shifted, heavy on his feet but no less a threat. "Did you make them for me?"

A derisive snort escaped Tokela. "I make nothing for you!"

Mordeleg's face darkened. Tokela answered by taking a whetstone from his pouch. He began to sharpen his obsidian spear point. Growled, soft, "One thing, then. A keen edge to my bla—"

"Eh, hold up, newcomer!" An oških, his Clan Marks of neighbouring lowForest, sauntered over. He looked, from well-muscled maturity to wealth of finery, well along his way to earning his adult Journey. "N'da, not you, midLander." He shoved Mordeleg aside with careless arrogance.

Tokela's mouth twitched in bleak humour.

Mordeleg puffed up and angled forwards, a threat.

Within a heartbeat several other oških moved forwards, ringing their companion. The lowForest oških gave a slight smile, rocked on the balls of his feet and lifted one hand, palm up. *Come, then.*

Mordeleg snarled, threw first the gathered oških then Tokela a venomous look. The debate was clear: pride or wisdom? The latter won. Mordeleg turned on one heel in swift retreat.

Tokela couldn't help another tucked-away smile, though he well knew he would have to doubly watch his back after this. In response, his hand once more started a draw of whetstone against spear point.

The lowForest oških made a grab for Tokela's spear. In pure reflex, Tokela snatched it away, and the oških grinned, unoffended. "You're a quick one! Good! But stop whetting your spear. Blades are dulled for Dance, sharpened for hunting."

Tokela coloured, looked down.

"It is well." The oških gave Tokela a friendly clout on the upper arm and pursed his lip after Mordeleg's retreat. "With *that* tracking you, I don't blame you baring your teeth. Your indigo is new? Hunh, I thought so." He looked closer. "But I've seen you before, haven't I? You're a'Naisgwyr?"

Tokela stiffened as the small group peered at him, recognition setting in. He said it before they could. "I'm hearth-chieftain's son."

"The half-breed," one of the oških muttered, and another hissed "Spawn!"—unwisely, for he was given a clout. Both retreated into sullen silence.

The lowForest oških shot the others a quelling frown, returned his attention to Tokela. "You're the one whose parents were taken by River?"

Tokela nodded, resigned.

The lowForest oških made a gesture—reverence and regret—then directed another frown to those about them. He made a shooing gesture, which was obeyed, not without a few more circumspect looks in Tokela's direction. "Don't mind them," the oških said. "Naisgwyr'uq has strange ideas sometimes. Only our dams matter—they choose who sires us, a'io?"

This didn't ease anything, but it was, at least, not censure.

The oških leaned on his spear and extended his hand to Tokela; cradled in it was a pot of grease. "Here. You'll be glad of this in Dance. I'm called Akumeh."

"I'm called Tokela."

Akumeh grinned. "I remember you from the silver run last-Sun. The ahlóssa who swam like otterKin! No longer ahlóssa, though—your Change has graced you well. I almost didn't recognise you."

Tokela blinked, surprised.

"One who swims like otterKin"—Akumeh nudged Tokela with the blunt end of his spear, then gave a negligent tap to the Otter mask hanging at his own hip—"would surely be lithe in other ways." He gave a sudden, charming smile, juddering Tokela all the way to his bare toes. "Maybe we'll make a Dance, you and I. It'd be an honour, to be your first. I could teach you a few things. I've been told I'm skilled." He leaned closer. "You want better than that overfed midLander. Or a bunch of superstitious k'šo."

"I... you do me honour." Tokela, heart suddenly racing, couldn't help but smile through his newly loosened forelock. Akumeh's dark eyes widened; his lips moved as if about to say something.

A sharp whistle sounded through the weapons cache.

"There'll be time, soon enough." Akumeh shrugged and grinned. "For now, we go." He jerked his head to the exit as the other oških began milling there. "Time to give over our spears. Dance well, Tokela."

Tokela watched him saunter away, bemused, then followed. He kept his distance behind the others, felt his heart sink as he saw Sarinak waiting in the gathering dusk of the doorway. And Sarinak spent time in letting the young males through, making sure each was eligible to participate and had a proper weapon.

Tokela bit his lip, hesitated, then tucked his chin. This was his right. Even Sarinak would not gainsay that.

Surely he couldn't?

Nevertheless, Tokela pulled the mask over his face before he reached the door.

He should have known better than to even try. Sarinak might seem ponderous, but in truth he missed very little. He grasped Tokela's spear then paused, holding it between them, eyes narrowing. Tokela's own gaze flattened into indigo stone; his lips quivered with the slightest suggestion of a snarl. This, of course, did not deter Sarinak. He reached out, tilted up the mask. His eyebrows climbed upward to the charms upon his headwrap as he saw the new Marks on his hearthson's cheekbones.

"Hunh," he said, then shrugged and snapped the mask back down. Adding the spear to the ones he already held, he jerked his head towards the door and the circuit beyond.

Tokela didn't hesitate. Hardly believing what had just happened, he darted out the door. Did mere indigo make this much difference?

He could only hope Našobok thought so.

"Ai, but I adore Spear Dance."

Našobok was just settling into comfort on Palatan's wide, ivory-and-indigo blanket as the drums changed. The River-quadrant circle had begun a deep, growling rhythm recognised by every male whelped a'Naišwyrh. Added to the gathering dusk, a full belly, a beloved companion—as well as the skin of tulapaiś he and that companion were steadily depleting? All was well.

More than well. The wide, grassy clearing was lit by Sun's last rays, and the tongues of Fire that leapt merrily in Ša's place of honour, raked bare and sown with ash by many such festivals. A group of masked dancers were infiltrating the dancing space, herding the previous revellers outside the circuit's boundaries. Clad in clouts and all their finery, hair unbound to fall behind their half masks, they had already started dancing: all male, all unespoused, mostly oških.

Palatan, already seated comfortably beside him, chuckled and took a drink. "You just like watching the Spear Dancers."

"Very much so." Našobok grinned. "Better yet to Dance one, but if the mangy old outlier were to dare step a toe in the circuit?—the scandal!" His grin went wide. "Might be worth it. And if it came to the looking, I don't see you covering *your* eyes, oathbrother."

"Mm." A glint of canines, grimace and grin both, then Palatan took another swig from the skin. "Unfortunately, the time comes when I'll have to look more for my daughters' interests than my own."

Našobok gave a yelp of laughter. "Now *that* would put a twist in their clouts, did Yeka steal away with a budding playmate... Yai!" This as Palatan cuffed him, hard.

"K'šo!"

The closest of their fellow watchers chuckled; it was hard to be offended by even unlikely companions during First Running. Though several had earlier expressed displeasure over an outlier seated in such a coveted spot.

Našobok rubbed at his head and told Palatan, mocking-meek, "I suppose I should count myself lucky, after all, how one as exalted as you allows me to share his blanket."

Palatan snorted and shook his head, setting the beads in his braided sidelock to chatter, then passed the tulapaiś.

Našobok took a long, noisy gulp and wiped his mouth with a sigh. "No whinging, now. You're the one sired all those bairns."

"Or so my spouse assures me. I love my offspring," Palatan added, if less than convincing.

Našobok snickered. "Aylaniś is intent you get them, anyway."

"K'šo," Palatan accused again, grinning. "Watch the oških and contemplate poking one of them for a change."

"I can poke more than the one. I'm never averse to a tangle."

"Ai, promises! Already I'm thwarted past reason and here you think I can take more than one of you?"

"There is only one of me," Našobok boasted. "It's just as well there's only one bendy horsetalker who invited me to sit on his blanket. And who, by the by, introduced *me* to tangling at a tender age."

Palatan laughed. "Behave, you! I'll have our lovely Hawk join us here and then you will be in the middle of more than you bargained for."

"My favourite place, between you and Aylaniś." Našobok's couldn't help his wistful tone as he peered sideways at Palatan. "You're not the only one being thwarted, you know."

"There is always a place for you on my blanket," Palatan murmured, eyes casting down until his lashes were another smoked smudge upon his tattooed cheekbones. "Getting you to stay there longer than three heartbeats is the problem."

"I'm here thisnow," Našobok said, also soft. "Do you truly think this unNamed one came merely to watch oških Dance?"

Palatan slid his gaze upward and tilted his head.

A shrill whistle made them both start and look up. On the Dancing Ground the milling oških parted, giving respectful way for a figure resplendent in Forest-coloured tunic and leather leggings. He wore Mound-chieftain's turquoise head wrap, and a wide, woven sash in jewelled tones girded his waist.

"Here we go," Našobok murmured, and tossed his hair from his face. "I tell you, you'll rue giving me this place of honour."

Palatan's response was to simply move closer, a heated, guarding presence. Našobok tucked a smile against one cheek.

Sarinak's bare, muscular arms cradled a large collection of spears. His gaze, dark as oiled Smoke, swept the watchers, taking meticulous note of everyone, everything. Sure enough, it narrowed as he beheld his outcast once-brother seated in such prominence. Našobok peered back, unresponsive. But a grin threatened his lips as, beside him, Palatan gave a small growl and tensed.

It never failed. Palatan would go all wild-eyed horsetalker and then Našobok would get… distracted.

Sarinak scowled. He didn't show any throat, but his eyes flickered sideways. It lasted scarcely a heartbeat, and no doubt Sarinak could claim his own distraction: the sudden, loud cries from watchers and dancers both, persuasion for Dance to begin.

Našobok cocked his head, peered at Palatan whose hackles were still raised. Ai, but the slighter ones were most dangerous, little question. "When again," Našobok murmured, "will you have a chance to work out some of that aggression on my very willing body?"

Palatan turned twisted brows upon Našobok, incredulous. Then laughed, hard.

The dancers kept their distance from each other, all the while watching Mound-chieftain and eagerly pacing, circling. Any breath now, the signal would be given, and they'd run to snatch up their spears, all decorated with gifts from a relative, or a playmate's favour, or—for those who had earned them—beribboned tokens signifying their skill at games or the hunt.

"Here we go, then," Našobok said again, but eager. A good tussle was guaranteed in Spear Dance, whether a oških took a spear not his own, by accident or a-purpose, or had his flung aside in the same fashion.

Palatan was watching him. "You miss it."

"Perhaps" Našobok shrugged. "Occasionally. You?"

"I still have my chances." Palatan elbowed him. "Those of duskLands never shrug off the sparring-play. We've not River to sustain us; we can't afford to allow *our* adults to soften."

An old spar in itself, that, which Našobok answered with a rude gesture. Palatan gave a soft laugh and leaned his chin on Našobok's shoulder.

Surrounded by the waiting oških, Sarinak laid the spears on the ground, backed from the hardened circuit and lifted his arms.

Silence.

"Not that you're soft," Palatan murmured with a grin. "Probably not anywhere, considering how close you watch."

Našobok grinned.

Sarinak dropped his arms.

Shouts rose up the walls of the Bowl. The dancers dove for their weapons. A mere smattering of heartbeats later, the first scuffle had broken out.

A tall, skinny oških wearing a silver's fishKin mask, so dark he seemed a shadow against the waning light, rammed up against another wearing a mask of beaverKin. The latter shoved back, but the fish-masked oških's oiled hide was Beaver's undoing; he literally slid off and went skidding into another. This, of course, meant another scrap. Silver snatched his spear to a good-natured cry from the audience—him being first was an omen fitting to lastSun's good work. Hefting it with a long, victorious cry, he leapt and spun, landing in a crouch. First capture meant first preference in partners, and every dancer coveted a wide choice.

Others were quickly grabbing up their spears, tussling and sparring for preferred places.

"I do so love Spear Dance, have I mentioned it?" Našobok sighed, and Palatan grinned against his shoulder.

"Several times. I take it back, you *are* soft."

"Hunh! What's soft about fancying the sight of well-oiled males? If you think... hunh! *That* one's not from here." Našobok broke from happy lechery. "Speaking of *soft*..."

The oških Našobok indicated stood burly enough to match his mask of bearKin, but indeed bore a paunchy, unfit look. He stepped well enough, albeit slow; he possessed more flesh than muscle, and wielded the two spears with more bravado than any true skill.

"MidLander, I'll wager," Našobok said, "They don't know one end from the next of any weapon longer than a knife—ai'ye, this should be good."

Another dancer, much slighter and wearing the mask of hareKin, stalked up to the bear-masked dancer and grabbed for what was obviously his spear. Bear puffed up and held on.

"I'll wager that one's a'Šaákfo," Palatan muttered. "He even wears the honour mask. But he's Marked a'Naišwyrh."

The youth with the hareKin mask was indeed rangy as any duskLander, his dark hair shimmering copper in Fire's light... and indeed bore the vermilion wyrh tree of their hosts across his right shoulder blade and ribs.

He also knew how to handle a spear. The larger oških proved his unfamiliarity with the spear, giving one an ill-timed heave and swing. Quick as an avatar of the mask he sported, the hareKin oških loosed his hold, ducked, and recaptured the spear's haft, using it to regain his feet.

"That's the way," Našobok murmured, then leaned forwards on his arms and shouted, "Now *take* it from him!"

The other dancers clustered, vying for position and beginning to merge into groups, obscuring any view of the tussle. One oških, an older one from the look of him, spun past Našobok and Palatan and halted several lengths away, preening and brandishing his spear for an admiring group of fems.

"Hunh!" Našobok rumbled, diverted. "Isn't that Anahli with those older fems?"

Palatan looked over, scowled. "I told Aylaniś she'd do well to keep an eye on our eldest. Anahli's too precocious, and you well know things are stricter here."

A'io, Našobok knew. Yet Anahli openly flirted, encouraging the dancer.

"Give her to me," Našobok entreated. "Just a half of Brother Moon's journey. I'll tie her to *Ilhukaia's* prow on rough main; if she's anything like her sire she'll be sick in two heartbeats and that'll bend her stiff neck."

Palatan gave Našobok a sour look. Našobok hid a rather sadistic grin behind a cough as Palatan rose, bodytalk promising dire circumstances for a wayward daughter.

Anahli wasn't used to being bored at any Drum circuit. But thisnow, seated oh-so-proper beside the oških fem a'Naišwyrh? Her body craved movement, her feet twitching to the drums, the beads of her finest moccasins flashing in the last bits of Sun. She was unused to sitting for this long at a stretch.

First it had been the ahlóssa dances. Then the elders. Then the tiniest Dancers—all right, they had been adorable, all garbed in their best. But after that had come more ahlóssa, and a spouse's turn, and... when were the oških ever going to Dance?

It wasn't the way it was done in duskLands. But she wasn't of duskLands in thisnow, was she? Bound of their hearth for a summering. And while her companions certainly seemed willing to wait forever, sitting so patient and prim, Anahli was ready to chuck her finery, strip down, and go find a good, rough game of stickball. Something!

And *finally*. A low, growling beat she recognised!

Only when she leapt up, ready to join, Čayku grabbed the fringe of Anahli's leggings, as wide-eyed and insistent as the rest of their cohort of gaily garbed fems: Spear Dance was for oških, a'io, but males only.

Males only? Truly? All right then, gendered rituals held common across thisLand... but. This particular Dance was Anahli's favourite! At home, anyway.

Obediently, she sat back down, pretending a smooth at the blush-coloured blanket spread between Čayku and another who'd proven a skilled and limber playmate, Bimih.

Sarinak strode into the Circuit's midst to relinquish his armload of weaponry.

"Fems do such things in duskLands?" Čayku tilted her head.

"Of course they do," Anahli said, glum, pulling her knees to her chest.

A rash of giggles rose behind her, from the third row of oških fems. These younger ones tailed Čayku and Bimih—and thusly

Anahli—hanging on their every word and gesture like foals to a nursing dam. Anahli scowled into her knees. If the males pouring from the weapons den were strutting and preening like woodcocks, the fems had gathered together close as a bunch of broody hens. Those occupying the coveted front row in front of Anahli guarded it like hawkKin. All old enough to openly consort with opposites, they'd left off commenting on the parade of dancers to throw speculative, critical glances Anahli's way.

Čayku, however, showed no such censure. Her eyes lit with admiration, she leaned closer to Anahli. "You mean you've actually Danced the Spear?"

Another shrug; thisSun looked to be longer still if they weren't to Dance until the males were done.

"Which spear do you mean, Čayku?" This from the eldest in their row, who smiled as her talk inspired another rash of giggles from the younglings behind. Plump and pretty, dressed to display her wealth, her fancy skirts were laid out just so, her beaded boot-tips peeping out to shimmer in the slatting rays of Sun's setting. Tilting her chin towards an otter-masked oških, she lifted an eyebrow and said, "I fancy his, truth be known."

"Covered with beads?"

"Sliding belly-down along River?"

More laughter, though the eldest fem didn't seem amused.

"I fancy both spears on that one," Anahli riposted, just to hear the little ripple of dismay from the young "hens". "Tell me, have none of you Danced a weapon?"

"Of course!" Another spoke up, defensive. "But not spears. We use staves."

Well, that was something, at least.

Anahli spared a longing wish for the past Summerings, where she had been raiding with her sire during First Running, and neither of them required to attend. Only now he was Alekšu. Now they had to attend, and she'd been handed over to her aunt for... "taming".

"DuskLands' ways sound intriguing." Čayku had a sincere grin quirking her lips, which eased Anahli's heart.

But her words came clipped; she couldn't help it. "All oških who can wield a spear without accidentally stabbing someone can join duskLand's Spear Dance."

"Ai'ye," Bimih murmured, appreciative. "I think I'd rather be in duskLands."

"Not me!" another vowed.

"Nor me!"

It was echoed by most of the fems. Unfortunately.

Otter stuck his spear in the ground and leapt up to twirl around it thrice. Anahli whistled encouragement. It drew his attention—and the irritation of the eldest fem.

"Huhn! You're not old enough to be looking his way despite

your bold talk! Just because you're eldest of Aylaniś horse-chieftain, and new spice to the stew—"

Čayku hissed disapproval. The eldest turned away to flip her unbound, blunt-cut hair over one beaded shoulder, trying to regain Otter's attention. Anahli slid her eyes sidelong at Čayku and smirked.

But Otter seemed more interested in new spice than familiar wealth. He tossed his spear into the air, twirled twice and caught it, smiling at Anahli all the while. That smile niggled, as did the smoky eyes behind the otterKin half-mask. A common enough hue towards dawnLands, but combined with the smile, Anahli recognised the youth who met her eyes so boldly as she'd first arrived. She returned his smile, raised it by several whistles of appreciation as he turned to answer another male's challenge.

The fancy fem was fuming. Her playmate glared, made a gesture plain as plain: *Crawl back to your cradleboard, little horsetalker, we've real business here!*

"Anahli," Bihmi protested, "you're courting trouble."

"There are plenty of ways to Dance a spear that won't have you gravid before your time, if that's what you mean."

"I mean that it's not allowed!"

"Even a horsetalker should know that!" another warned.

Even a horsetalker. It flowered mutiny at the base of Anahli's spine. Leaning forwards, she met Otter's eyes, making silent promises as she flipped one braid over her shoulder.

"Anahli!" Čayku, this time.

Anahli should have let it go there. Instead she stood up and gave a pirouette that took her to the front of their little group, the fringes of her long tunic belling out.

Otter swung the butt end of his spear towards her. She stood firm, didn't so much as flinch. Sure enough, the spear halted just before reaching her solar plexus. His grin growing wider, Otter turned and delivered a flurry of blows to his newest attacker. The other oških gave as good as he got, but gave way, a cry of frustration escaping as his spear flew out of his hands—and out of the game.

The spear fell with a clatter and rolled, bumped Anahli's toes. She turned, eyebrows lifting suggestively at her playmates. Čayku's face was a mix of admiration and disbelief; Bimih merely the latter. The others stared in wide-eyed astonishment.

It was then Anahli saw her sire, heading her way with a mighty frown across his brow. Frustration, anger...

A'io, me too, she thought, and smiled. Though it was likely more a snarl, come to think of it.

She pirouetted again to face Otter. "Where I come from, playmates have to show they can win each other, not just show off."

Hooking her toe beneath the fallen spear, she popped it up into her hands and leapt forwards, light as Wind.

Her blessing-name, after all, was Graceful Dancer.

Našobok turned his attention back to the dancers, a triumphant hiss escaping as the crowd parted, allowing him another glimpse of Hare and Bear. The latter was still hanging onto both spears for all he was worth, but the former kept dodging and feinting, wearing him down. Bear, irritated past good sense, let go of one spear to grab at his opponent's arm. Unlike his own—another sign he was unfamiliar with Dance—Hare's arm was oiled slick. A slight twist enabled Hare's escape. Hare dropped to his haunches and darted sideways, finally taking up his spear.

The bear oških cursed and lifted his own spear. Point down, as if for the kill.

"Ai, watch him!" Našobok shouted, coming up to a crouch.

The dangerous turn to their scuffle was nearly lost amidst the mêlée, but Hare either heard the warning or sensed his danger. Diving sideways, he hit the ground rolling and regained his feet even as the spear point impacted where he had previously been. The bear oških staggered forwards, caught off balance. Hare spun in one swift, agile move with a vicious snarl, swinging his spear.

Two swift steps forwards, and spear blades clinked and hung. Another sideways jerk, and the bear oških's spear went flying.

Unweaponed meant out of the running, by any rules. The hareKin oških cocked his dark head and retreated a few steps, lowering his spear.

Bear charged.

"*Blood* him!" Našobok shouted.

"Treacherous as Matwau!" another growled. Others, seeing the byplay, echoed disapproval with sharp calls and sharper gestures.

The slighter oških leapt out of his opponent's way as if evading a bull's blind charge. And like a bull, the bearKin oških tottered to a stop and turned about, charged again.

This time, he snatched a spear from another's hands. That oških, finding his palms unceremoniously emptied, gave a shrill and outraged cry. It was echoed by Našobok and quite a few others, all becoming aware of the smaller, grim battle going on amidst the sporting one.

"If they don't know the limits they shouldn't be in Dance!" Našobok spat, furious. "Blood is one thing, to go for guts is another altogether! Where's—?"

Finally! Sarinak had taken notice. Arms upraised—*I hold no weapon, I do not Dance*—he plunged into the packed circuit. Several drums faltered. Even those dancers who hadn't seen the trouble felt the difference in the beat. They slowed, uncertain.

But there was nothing Sarinak could do, truly nothing to be done other than what the hareKin oških did next. After a startled and frozen heartbeat of shock at what was bearing down on him, Hare swung his spear upward in defence.

The two spears clapped and clattered, the greater bulk of attack almost shoving the slighter oških off his feet. If he'd braced the impact would have felled him; instead both instinct and skill kicked in, well-tutored muscles allowing a sideways spin. When the next angry swing came, he was ready.

With a tip of spear, the clumsy strike was parried, and returned with several rapid—and capable—blows. The stolen spear went flying. The bearKin oških let out a yowl as the butt end of the spear rapped his arm, then his solar plexus. When that didn't take him down, the spear butt arced again, whacking him upside his head.

Bear was flung with a heavy grunt onto his backside.

Našobok whistled approval. Even more a coup, to take someone down with no edge at all. Over half the watchers joined his approval, calling and whistling and stomping. Some of the dancers—they hadn't seen the fight—leapt higher, sure the accolades were for them. Their renewed energy alternately obscured and revealed what was going on. But it was obvious Hare wasn't wasting any opportunity. Putting a foot to his opponent's throat, he leaned over with a snarl and angled the spear, point downward, next to his foot.

Again, not by the rules, yet considering what provocation had been given? *Piss on me, will you?* Našobok thought with a grin, sorry when Sarinak moved in. After giving several orders—to no effect—Sarinak ended up grabbing the Hare oških by his thick, black-chestnut mane and hauling him backwards.

Našobok chuckled, merely to have it twist into a small oath as his view once more was blocked by dancers. Just as quickly, though, another gap opened up, revealing Sarinak looming over the hareKin oških with fierce talk and even fiercer gestures.

A roar lifted from the other side of Circuit; some other dancer, no doubt. Sarinak peered across, and the most extraordinary expression claimed his face. Hare took the opportunity to lunge at his tormentor; Sarinak snatched his arm, gave him a shake. His next gesture was just as plain: ordering the treacherous Bear from Circuit.

Bear shot a dark look towards his opponent—no less than a promise of revenge. Hare looked to be saying *Bring it, k'šo*—fists gripped tight to his spear, mouth quivering with a snarl as Sarinak repeated his command. Bear stomped off.

Sarinak's attention was still divided; with another shake of Hare's arm, he released him and strode from the field, dodging dancers as he went. Hare watched him go. A quartet of older oških moved past him as he spun his spear and disappeared from view. Našobok gave a small huff.

Another roar filled the far end of the grounds. People were

standing up, trying to see. Again, chance parted the dancers, and Našobok beheld the cause.

Anahli, who'd somehow managed to obtain a spear, pacing an astonished Otter, who kept backing away.

The poor oških didn't stand a chance. He likely more expected Anahli to bite him on the leg than enter Spear Dance and come at him. Instinct alone helped him field off the first two blows, but by the time he'd recovered, it was too late. His spear flew into the air, end over end, and landed point-down just inside the bounds.

The oških males clotted together again, intent upon the drum and their own Dances.

"Ai, Anahli," Našobok groaned, and flopped back on Palatan's blanket.

Aylaniś was going to have a conniption.

The Otter oških didn't even try to dance. Not really, and it was over too quick, his spear flying, and the eyes behind the Otter mask clouded with puzzlement.

Only then did Anahli notice the lull, small and tight about them, as if the drums had muted into distance. Caught her sire's scent just before he grabbed her arms, swung her about, and growled into her face:

"What is *wrong* with you?"

Over his shoulder, she saw Aylaniś. And Inhya.

And realised, frustration eking into dread, that she had, once again, landed herself in a basket of boiling water.

"You're a *guest* here! You owe a guest's courtesies to ways not your own!" Each gritted phrase accompanied by a shake, Palatan whirled and started to drag her from the Circuit—like a ahlóssa, like a... a babe in a cradleboard! His talk stung even more, like clay-spitting wasps, and all the more because they carried wide within that tiny, sudden mote of stillness. "Here, of all places. You've only had your indigo four summerings! You well know you've not earned the rights to openly court opposites!"

Surely humiliation urged her to snap back, more venom-and-clay. "Some would say I follow my sire's footsteps, choosing to lie where I shouldn't!"

Palatan shoved her out of the Circuit and nearly into her dam's arms... had Aylaniś's arms been open and welcoming.

They most definitely were not. Aylaniś held herself tight as stone, delivering her own barrage like a stinging slap. "Hihlyanahli. You are insolent. You humiliated that oških for no purpose."

Cornered, Anahli did the only thing she ever had: lash out. "Humiliated? If he can't best me then he can't. I am oških, trained by you, horse-chieftain, and by you, tyah a'Šaákfon! I am horsetalker, from duskLands where any proper Spear Dance is open to all who can defend their spear!"

Aylaniś smacked her hands together between them, stoppering the torrent. "You are not in your place! You're here, in dawn-Lands, by the grace of hearth-chieftain a'Naišwyrh. To *learn* new ways, not insult them."

"Chogah says any ways that would keep a fem in scarves and skirts—"

"That is a lie from one whose tongue curls and spits, and a'io, part of why you're here."

"I'm here because you've brought me to be 'tamed' by Aunt Inhya! You're hoping to drown my 'insolence' in River!"

Anger had prompted it; disappointment and, she suddenly knew, the subtle poison Chogah had given her to sip. But it was too late to take them back.

"That isn't true," Palatan whispered.

Aylaniś stared at Anahli for a long, inheld breath, then let it out. Turned her back.

"There is no danger of such insolence drowning," Inhya growled, quiet, then also turned her back and walked away.

The drums, once seeming-soft, now filled the Bowl. Behind them, Spear Dance continued as if nothing had disturbed it. Palatan's fury showed in the trembling of his fingers, in the glimmers behind his eyes. Nevertheless, he hesitated, started to speak to Anahli—in the sudden clarity of her own broken temper, she could see that.

But her dam slid him The Eye and, jaw tightening, Palatan turned away. Walked away, slow in his sister's wake.

Aylaniś followed, her back muscles roped even further with tension.

The other oških fems were still seated in their tidy rows. They hadn't so much as met her eyes, or smiled encouragement. Not even Čayku. They, too, turned away and began talking amongst themselves, as if Anahli weren't there.

Palatan returned, shaking his head when Našobok thought to question. His fingers signed *Later*, his talk soft and heavy as the tilt of his shoulders. *She's had her tail trimmed.*

"I'm sorry."

"Mm. She's too much like me. Thankfully she feels the sting of public shame more than I did. Or"—a cheeky smile—"than your vicious hareKin dancer clearly does."

This made Našobok's desire to root for the slight oških all the stronger. Yet Hare had disappeared. The treacherous Bear oških also had vanished, and Sarinak, retreated to the sidelines.

The drums were building even stronger, a fierce, body-pounding rhythm. The dancers were starting to pair off, no longer using their spears solely for combat, but for choice. Several older oških were still flirting with fems, but in the end all would follow the customs of Spear Dance and choose partners amongst their own. Našobok remembered his own Spear Dances with vivid affection: the indisputable conflict and resolution—both in circuit and, if lucky, off.

The skinny silver-masked oških had first choice by rights. He whirled through the crowd, lithe and agile, and sent his spear point-first into the ground, blocking another dancer's path. His chosen partner grinned then took it, pumping it Skyward like a trophy.

"Mound People are so... obvious," Palatan drawled.

"You always have been a torment."

"But the gaming's half the fun." Palatan leaned over and nipped Našobok's ear.

"You'll sink your reputation," Našobok warned. It didn't stop him from leaning into the caress.

"For a mangy outlier, you fret overmuch. D'you truly think I crawled and crafted and fought for my rights as Alekšu so I could lose sleep over what a lot of over-tall fishKin eaters think of my choices?"

It was Našobok's turn to laugh. Several people nearby glared at him; it merely made him laugh harder, while Palatan leaned back and radiated innocence.

Other dancers quickly began pairing up, sparring in Spear Dance's elaborate teaching and mimicry of conflict.

One tall, well-muscled oških leapt in the air in front of them, crouched down with his spear raised and gave Palatan a direct look through a stoatKin mask.

"Seems this oških likes his partners experienced as well as pretty," Našobok hissed, not at all quietly. "Maybe obvious isn't so bad, eh?"

The dancer's eyes flickered from Palatan to Našobok, then to the blanket they both sat on; with a sudden, knowing grin and a conceding gesture to Našobok, he moved away.

This time Našobok burst out laughing. "See what happens when you sit a wyrhling on your blanket? Too bad, he was definitely your type."

Palatan slid an amused gaze sideways. "K'šo. My type is seated beside me."

"But that one's prettier. Bendy and lively as stoatKin, I'll wager." Našobok waggled his eyebrows suggestively. "*Younger.*"

"That one," Palatan leaned closer, wafted a breath across Našobok's ear, "doesn't know how to make me howl between the furs."

Našobok quirked a smile, closed his eyes as hard, slender fingers stroked at his nape. "I love it when you make blanket talk."

"As much as you love the Spear Dance? I have to admit, watching all these stags click their horns can be—"

"Provoking? Frustrating?" Našobok grinned wider, turned his gaze back to the dancing. "But it's a sight to behold, eh? And soon the fems will have a Dance and you'll have twice the provocation! Quite a shame, Alekšu, how you've gone all respectable and have too many councils thisDark to even contemplate easing that frustration until nextSun's rising."

"I can contemplate entirely too much, there just isn't a lot to be done about it."

"And"—it was Našobok's turn to slide eyes Palatan's way—"sneaking away for a quick go against a tree is out of the question?"

"*Spawn.*" Palatan smacked Našobok on the head again. "Now who's the torment? We'd just get interrupted again. Watch the Dancing and quit baiting me."

"*I'm* baiting *you*?" Našobok grabbed Palatan's hand, laced their fingers tight and held them against the ground. "You're too free with those hands, my beloved, and all because I'm just getting back some of my own... Ai, look at the way *that* one moves."

Palatan followed the gaze, smirked. "Our young Šaákfo has rejoined Dance."

Našobok made the discovery at the same time, lips quirking. "Hunh. I wonder what he looks like beneath his mask." Eyes narrowing, he leaned forwards. "Mm. The rest of him is rather nice, eh?"

"A bit scrawny amidst all these Mound People," Palatan teased.

"Lithe, I'd say. Graceful. *Bendy.*" Našobok nudged Palatan. "My type, that."

A chuckle. "Keep dreaming, wyrh-chieftain."

"Hunh. I must be dreaming, all right. The oških keeps looking at me." Našobok glanced Palatan's direction. "Am I? Or is he?"

Palatan was also peering at the oških, a frown quirking his brow.

"Pal, you look as though you've seen—"

A familiar, deadly sound, between a hiss and a thump, made Našobok start back and bump into Palatan's arm propped up behind him. He looked up. Blinked. Ran his eyes from the be-ribboned spear stuck in the ground between his knees to the taut, bowed muscles of the arm still holding the spear. Then trailed his eyes upward.

Dark hair all wild about the mask, eyes glinting from shadow. A full lower lip dropped, just this side of sulky, showing a hint of teeth as the oških panted in quick rasps. The drum of his heart, throbbing amidst the cords of his neck beneath a taut, angled jaw. Upper arms and pectorals quivering, holding the spear. And the rest of that willowy body, slick with oil and sweat, thin streaks of moisture runnelling down from the freckles on his belly—freckles!—and into the sparse fur disappearing beneath his clout.

"I think the oških wants something." Palatan drawled, soft, with a nudge at Našobok.

Mask-shadowed eyes blinked, slid over to Palatan, and widened slightly. Muscles tensed further; it almost looked like retreat. Before Našobok could fully consider what he was doing, impulse had taken over. He grabbed the spear just above its feathered obsidian point.

Those gleaming eyes returned back to his, held. Našobok softened his grip on the spear, slid his fingers up and down, was rewarded as the oških actually *quivered*. His breathing caught then escaped him in a low growl.

An answering growl purled in the back of Našobok's throat. Belatedly he realised Palatan's hand was resting between his shoulder blades, giving him a slight push.

"I think you want something too," Palatan murmured. "Go on, then. Teach the oških how wyrhling Dance."

12
TRICKSTER

Tokela couldn't believe it. Couldn't believe he'd actually *done* it, actually flung the spear down and dared Našobok to take it.

Couldn't believe Našobok had taken it.

Still couldn't believe, even when those broad hands gripped the spear to let Tokela haul Našobok to his feet. Believed even less when Našobok toed off his boots and shucked from longcoat and tunic.

The surrounding watchers had fallen into murmurs and a strange, sullen hush. Tokela knew, with the sensitivity of one constantly and inexplicably going afoul of Normal, that somehow he'd done yet another unacceptable thing.

Whatever it was, he didn't care. Našobok had taken the spear. Našobok followed him—*followed!*—into the circuit.

It was a good thing Tokela hadn't paid attention to the one seated beside Našobok; he might have lost his nerve. But now he saw: Palatan watched him, intense and unnerving and... approving. Forest-hued eyes gleamed, and a slow smile lifted one corner of Palatan's mouth. It was as if, beneath that smile, the hush of disapproval from the surrounding watchers wafted into Hare-voice; soft encouragement, rhythm throbbing behind Tokela's eyes and down to his bare toes: *Dance him. Dance him giddy.*

It was the mask, but Tokela didn't care, because he'd seen the look in Našobok's eyes. First when he had approached him—a hungry *knowing* flaming sparks all along Tokela's nerves. Then when Našobok had stroked the haft of the spear with fingers just as knowing, making promises...

> Hands slide up, from spear haft to wrists, a searing touch with cool fingertips. But Hare isn't about to be won so easily, and with a twist of oiled forearms and a push with the spear haft, tiptoes aside.

Tokela didn't know enough—didn't know anything, not with this—but he didn't have to understand anything in thisnow, only shiver with pleasure as those storm-hued eyes followed him....

> Challenge answered as opponent/partner circles, stalks. Here is danger, Hare knows, danger to set heart drum dancing, for where a bistre-maned wolf had been yawning and stretching, lazy-drunk in Sun's setting, now the yawn turns fierce, grin gliding into low laugh. Hare feints with the spear left, then right and upward. But there is none where the strike would touch, only a blur of motion as a River Wolf spins, then snatches at the spear.

It was the mask. The mask, and Tokela laughed, soft, because with the mask he wasn't the Half-breed, wasn't the little ahlóssa cousin. He was oških, Hare, Swiftfoot, Ša'abo the trickster. The choices were laid before Tokela even as he'd laid indigo on his cheekbones, with Fire purling in his abdomen and a drum for a heart, chanting...

> So Hare paces, step by slow step. Remains quick, wary, for Wolf outweighs him twice again. Close enough to touch, to want to touch—
> *N'da, impatient cousin,* says Hare. *Touching is for later. Now is for testing.*

Tokela laughed out loud, heard Našobok answer with a chuckle as they circled, both holding the spear.

First Dance.

The drum rhythms slowed then sped, demanding the steps. Bare hands sharing the spear's haft, bare feet circling and pointing, pounding and shuffling. Dust rising, sifting across their ankles, coating silver bangles upon Tokela, breathing a curling, stark tattoo of emerald/black kelp upon Našobok. Laughter, and panting breaths, and hair flying, Fire glittering upon sweat as the drums quickened even more, setting the stage for struggle...

> Hare opens heart, growls as he tugs—mine, this weapon, mine!—but Wolf bares teeth back, dares: take it! Hare swings hind foot, pulls then pushes, hard; Wolf trips back, surprised... and doesn't loose the spear.

Tokela gave a yip as he was yanked down; the yip throttled into a gasp as he landed on Našobok and slid sideways, propped only by his fists clutching the horizontal spear haft.

"A little soon to have me on my back yet, eh?" Našobok twisted, yanked the spear—and Tokela—over. Pushed against the spear, pushed down with his hips as he straddled Tokela...

> Hare freezes. Quivers. Bodytalk humming—
> gasping in it, writhing/ sinking/ drowning in
> the Storm-wrack of Wolf's eyes, in the heat of
> his body, hard and growing harder. The sound
> of him.

The sound of Her.

River.

The sense of recognition nigh flattened Tokela; his heart pulsed wild then smoothed, rippled into rhythmic currents that crooned a wordless melody behind his eyes: *Come to me. He is mine. You are mine, little wyrhling...*

> Hare tries to break the spell—*not yet, not yet!*
> *Are you so little and foolish, ahlóssa heart still, to give*
> *in so easily?*

"I think this Dance is over, lovely one," Našobok breathed against Tokela's ear, then nipped it. "Want to try another?"

Tokela's back arched, the spear pressing against his throat, pushing the air from him. Wasn't sure he cared.

"Ai, I think you do." And Našobok sat up, loosened the spear, reached for the mask...

Hare leaps, shrieks, scoots for cover.

Tokela gave a quick twist, one hand shielding the mask, the other still on the spear. He twisted, wriggled, and scooted downward. Dirt scraped his buttocks, clung to his back. Našobok, taken unawares, snatched a belated grab. It slid on oiled skin, and only a swift hand propped to keep Našobok from falling on his face. Tokela kept scooting, yanked the spear haft. Našobok grunted, lurched forwards again. In another swift and desperate motion, Tokela escaped out from between Našobok's legs, yanking the spear with him and curling his knees upward into Našobok's haunches.

Našobok went flying, heels over shoulders, and smacked flat on his back with a heavy thud and a great *huff!* of lost breath...

> Free! Hare leans against his weapon and
> vaults to his feet. Shifts, hind foot to hind foot,
> watching Wolf shake his heavy mane and roll to
> one side, eyeing him. There is surprise. There
> is...
>
> Respect.
>
> It fills Hare, sleek and Power-full as the bo-
> dytalk, as the slide of skin upon skin.
>
> *Skin within skin,* croons Hare, *is even better. But*
> *make him earn it. Remember you have teeth at your*
> *throat already.*

A'io. He wanted this Wolf fangs and all. Tokela spun the spear one-handed, pulled it back over his shoulder, and rocked into a crouch. He held his free hand out, palm up, and twitched his fingers in the same sign Akumeh had given Mordeleg earlier, in the weapons cache.

Come, then.

Našobok's mouth pulled sideways in a grin as he rolled to his feet. He made a show of rubbing at one haunch, and several watchers laughed. Tokela thought he caught Palatan, lying ai-so-casually back on his blanket, rolling his eyes. But there was a smirk on his face to match Našobok's.

"Treat him gently, young Ša'abo!" Palatan suddenly called above the din. "He's old for this game!"

"Not that old!" Našobok avowed. "Never too old 'til I'm dead."

> Several dancers cut between them, intent on their own sparring; one whirled a spear so close to Tokela it sent a lock of chestnut hair wafting over his mask. He didn't so much as twitch. Watched. Waited...
>
> There is another raucous shout—outside circuit, focus in, no matter—but someone throws a spear, gives more teeth to the Wolf. Wolf catches it. Hefts it. Smiles.

Našobok took two steps forwards. Tokela also, but sideways. Then again. And once more—four steps instead of two, leading them in a tiny and twinned circuit.

"You're as pretty on your feet as on your back," Našobok purred, tossing the spear from hand to hand. He feinted sideways; at the last instant rocked forwards.

Was foiled, not by Tokela, but another dancer who stood before Našobok, motioning with his spear. The crowd greeted this with a loud surge of bloodthirsty encouragement...

N'da, growls Hare. Mine. Find another.

"Hunh" was Našobok's comment as he flicked his eyes over the new dancer. "You know you're just going to start trouble..."

> Hare moves forwards, all silence, all intent. Either the new dancer—Gull—doesn't see him coming or is too arrogant to bother watching his back. Perhaps he thinks Wolf will give warning. But Wolf watches, gaze betraying nothing, as Hare gets in the first blow—a round sweep to Gull's legs, sending him flying.
>
> But Gull is no Bear, to fall heavily or easily; he has the carmine wyrh-tree on his ribs, has spent his Hoops in the practice and the hunt. He hits the ground, rolls up to face Hare. He is smiling.
>
> Hare does not smile. He snarls. Waits.

Našobok watched, a lopsided grin tugging at his generous

mouth, and drawled, "D'you know how long it's been since I've had two males fight over me? You're quite turning my head." The grin became a laugh as he flipped the spear hand over hand. "Both of 'em."

A small part of Tokela heard him, gave an inward chuckle; outwardly he stood, lone stillness amongst the dancers, the drums throbbing in his chest and rushing through his veins like Riverlet overflow. Shards of light made a Dance behind his eyes, sparking and scattering, copper and silver brine... Rivertalk lit by the Moons.

Tokela found himself welcoming it. *Wanting* it.

> Waited, silent and still...
> Gull is unnerved by this silent determination, by the eyes-meeting-eyes of challenge. He lunges forwards, a move of desperation, and Hare sees it as if his opponent is moving through River water, slow and easily targeted. Gull is skilled, but Hare has also spent many Suns in the practice and the hunt. Gull is stronger, but Hare is lightning-swift, skimming a silent undertow.
> Spears clack and slide and clack again, and Gull shows throat, retreats from the blazing eyes behind the Hare-mask.

"You," Našobok said softly, "are quite the fancy dancer."

The talk sank Tokela even deeper into his own skin. Here. He was here, and around him the drums beat heavy, slower. Spent. Many of the dancers had already chosen. Masks were coming off, weapons were being lowered, partners had been wooed and won. Tokela looked at his chosen partner, felt their gazes lock hungry. Hung.

"Ai," Našobok breathed, "just look at you. You want me, lovely Ša'abo?" His lip quivered up over his teeth. "Do us both a favour and just come *get* me..."

> *Not yet,* Hare whimpers, not yet. *Prove yourself before he takes the mask from you, before he sees.*
> So no more silence, no more waiting. With a cry, Hare swings his spear, whirls and spins. Wolf is driven backward, surprised, unable to do much more than shake his mane and parry protest. Spears talk, arguing in clacks of hardwood and tings of folded bronze points, catch and slide. A line of crimson blossoms on Hare's breast as Wolf dodges and strikes—first blood!— and Wolf is given a return streak of scarlet along the outside of his thigh. Blood stings with sweat, grunts of effort and harsh gasps...

"Enough!" Našobok went to his knees, spear haft held up above him, offering and surrender. Tokela froze midthrust; momentum disagreed—violently—and he stumbled, went down as well.

Našobok dropped his spear, lurched forwards. He almost didn't make the catch, but an improbable twist of his torso let him grab Tokela. They both half rolled, half sprawled across the ground.

This time it was Tokela who collided atop Našobok, only to find himself stilled, held fast by gaze, by sweat-slicked muscles, heated skin, rasping breaths. Found himself willingly lost in eyes meeting eyes, in skin against skin... lost even further as a heated, hard knot pushed close against his hip, rousing undeniable reaction in Tokela's own already-tight clout.

He wished he could come up with talk as sharp as the knife on his calf, or as clever as the talk Našobok had been making. But, nothing. Našobok merely panted against Tokela's shoulder, murmured something Tokela couldn't hear over the humming behind his ears. He was dimly aware of the drums still going, the remaining dancers still sparring and stepping. Aware of the solid and thick edge of quiet spreading into the watchers closest to them. Then Našobok laid his head back on the ground, dark hair spilling behind him like kelp washed up ashore, and closed his eyes, smiled.

It was a smile to break whatever will Tokela might have left.

Našobok opened his eyes and reached up, smoothing fingers across the woven surface of the mask. The motion made Tokela more afraid than he'd ever been in his life and those strong fingers, amazingly gentle, began to push the mask upward. Tokela raised his hand out of protective instinct, forced himself still. Covering Našobok's fingers with his own, he pulled them away just as gentle. Then he tilted up to his knees—he didn't want to, just wanted to mould and melt himself into that warm, broad body—but gritted his teeth. Stood.

Našobok started to protest, then settled onto his elbows, the soft smile still on his face. This was going to be interesting.

The oških yanked the mask off with a sudden vehemence and stared down at him, the mask dangling from one hand. Dark hair fell across his face, chin tucking further, almost as if taking refuge. Then he hung the mask at his belt, tossed the hair back and, almost challenging, eyed Našobok.

It was those eyes—large and unshadowed by any mask, gleaming and reflecting Fire's light—that feathered the first, tiny thrill of recognition in Našobok. Several heartbeats, then everything set in and sunk him, and by then "interesting" was not quite the word he needed. Instead he said the first thing that came to his tongue, foul and flummoxed.

"Yuškammanukfila ikšo! Tokela?"

That forelock fell again, and the oških gave the first familiar gesture—a bothered blink, sideways tilt of head, and a tiny, self-deprecating flash of smile... and poke Našobok sideways, it *was* little Tokela. Only not little, not anymore, but grown tall and sleek and just this side of heartache-about-to-happen.

"Uhn," Našobok said, tried to push up from his elbows only to have one slip on a slick patch of grass and send him sprawling.

Tokela lurched forwards, letting his spear fall with a clatter as he reached out. Našobok gave a small flail, wondered if it was possible he could look any more ridiculous.

He grabbed Tokela's forearm, watched lean muscles clench and teeth grit together, felt a grin tugging at his face as, with a little determination and a lot of pride, Tokela hauled upward someone twice his own weight.

"*Tokela?*" Našobok repeated—inane, but he couldn't stop it any more than he could halt his helpless repeat of, "Yuškam-manukfila ikšo..."

"I really hope you aren't," Tokela said, as the half smile blossomed, sudden, into full-bore, heart-stopping intensity. "Too stupid for rutting. Because that would sort of ruin it."

It wasn't Tokela's voice, either—at least, not the one Našobok remembered; this voice belonged to the agile stranger who'd given him quite the tail-trimming with a spear. All furry and low, with a hoarse tension running beneath it, and about as subtle as a buck in rut.

Or so it seemed to Našobok's too-tight clout, anyway.

Tokela just stood there, quiet, as if waiting. They were out of the Dance, anyway, from the time Tokela had dropped his spear, but the drums still pounded for the remaining dancers. Našobok became aware, abruptly, of the strained hush in the watchers closest to them. Taken away earlier by the unfolding novelty and drama, now there were plenty who had, with the players stilled, come back to themselves. Thisnow, they remembered who—what—had entered the circuit.

Našobok's gaze went to Palatan, who jerked his chin slight and sideways, plain as Sun on water: *If I were you I'd consider making your talk somewhere else. Now.*

Našobok tried to take his hand from Tokela's arm, but his fingers seemed loath to let go. He hesitated further as dark brows, still beneath their inevitable overhang of forelock, drew together. Tokela angled back, ever so slightly, his gaze upon Našobok searching. Whatever he was looking for, it didn't please him; face clouding, he released Našobok.

Našobok's fingers still refused to do likewise. "Tokela. We should—"

"That's enough."

Sarinak's voice shouldn't have been much of a surprise to Našobok. Even more surprising was the reaction it tendered in Tokela. Suddenly the oških was gone, and if it wasn't quite the shy ahlóssa Našobok remembered, it was a strange reflection of that memory, ramped up into an apprehension surely inappropriate to the situation.

Trouble, a'io. But not enough to kill them.

"Mound-chieftain," Našobok started, respectful. "It s—"

"You. Outlier. Leave this circuit."

Not only Sarinak, but Inhya was there, glaring an entire quiver of arrows at Našobok. Not so surprising, that; what was surprising was the flat stare Tokela turned upon his dam.

Another, larger surprise, as Inhya looked aside.

Sarinak reached out, grabbed Tokela's arm. The oških stiffened as if the touch had burned, but Sarinak did not loose him. "Tokela."

Tokela rounded on his hearth-father with a snarl. "This is my right. You can't—"

"That's where you're wrong." Sarinak, of course, was implacable. "I can. I do. I put a stop to this. And your rights—which you have taken, not had bestowed upon you as is our way—such rights do not extend to bringing an outlier into Circuit. Your Dance is over."

Palatan had risen, padding without a sound to join them. There was a set to his jaw Našobok well recognised. "Perhaps there is a better place to settle such things?" The talk rang quiet, all too reasonable—definitely a new-acquired skill, that.

And one with which Našobok agreed. There'd already been one open humiliation thisSun, and despite Palatan's offhand assessment of indifference, Tokela's cheeks were blood-dark.

"There is nothing to 'settle'." Inhya's voice went low but Našobok heard it. No doubt he was meant to. "Your heart is great, but not always wise, little brother."

"You are tyah of horseClan," Sarinak stated. "You are Alekšu, to whom I must give honour. But your ways aren't ours. Do likewise honour. This isn't your concern."

Palatan met Našobok's eyes, shook his head ever so slightly. Našobok gave a slight nod and returned his attention to Tokela.

Those cheeks were still flushed, but his eyes had gone flat, impassive. Našobok tried for intention in his own gaze, loud and clear. There was no need for any of this. They shared Dance; more could be shared later. After this unpleasantness was circumvented.

"I'll go," Našobok said, quiet, keeping his eyes on Tokela's. He was quite unprepared for what he saw flicker there. Scorn... ai, perhaps not, he amended, but the truth was even worse.

Disappointment.

Yet had he not been watching, Našobok never would have

seen it. The twinge of reaction vanished as Tokela looked down and away, forelock covering any further revelation.

"We all go," Sarinak said.

They left the boundaries of the circuit. Palatan tried to meet Inyha's eyes, failed, then gave Našobok another weighted glance and returned to his place.

A short way, the walk, into the cool mist-gloom of evergreens and, thankfully, away from further scrutiny. Tokela kept darting quick glances at Našobok, as if waiting.

Waiting for what?

This was becoming more tangled with every breath.

Tokela gave a sudden twist of his arm. Sarinak lost his grip, tried to reclaim it, but the oil that had aided Tokela in Dance did more service. Silent and swift as the hareKin mask still dangling at his belt, Tokela disappeared into the trees.

"Wait!" Inhya called after him. "Tokela!"

"Ai, leave him." Sarinak growled, intemperate. "He'll come back; he always does. What was he thinking?"

"Did you really have to do that?" It was the first thing that came to Našobok's lips.

Sarinak turned to him, frowning, examining him as if he were some new species of prey. That he gave an answer was as surprising as the answer itself was not.

"Did I have to remove an outlier from openly consorting with my tribe? You, of all, should know the answer."

As things went, it was better than puffing up and refusing any talk, which no doubt Sarinak would have done in front of others. Ai, but what a tangled and perverse game two once-brothers had come to play. Našobok was owed some obligation for saving their sire's life three winterings ago—the same sire who, as Mound-chieftain, had made Našobok outcast. It was its own little Dance, truly, and one Našobok usually had few inclinations to join.

He should have left it there, walked away. But he didn't.

"You know what I mean. Did you really have to humiliate Tokela so?"

"I let you finish Dance with him, Našobok. I did so for Tokela. To expect more is expecting too much. Whatever humiliation he faced, it was of his own making."

"Sarinak—

"I am Mound-chieftain to you, outlier."

It shouldn't have stung, but it did.

"My eldest son chose a wrong path. He has done, more and more. Should there be no consequence?"

Inhya said nothing, watching the two of them. Našobok wasn't sure he liked the canny gleam in her eyes, but shook it off. Argued, "The wrong path for whom? What of Tokela's rights to choose?"

"He has that right, a'io. He does not have the right to throw our ways in our faces. Of course, that's something I don't expect *you* to understand."

Našobok clenched his teeth.

"He shouldn't have asked you to Dance at all."

"But Anahli joining Spear Dance is just fine."

"She is paying the consequence of her actions."

"And the midLands oških nearly goring Tokela with his own spear? Is that also to have consequences?"

"I removed him, you may have noticed." Sarinak tilted his chin down, dangerous-quiet. "Perhaps such things happen when we allow outliers to sit in honoured places."

Našobok didn't care; his thoughts were on another course. "And where is the midLander now?"

"Why does it matter to you?"

"I merely thought it should matter to *you*."

Sarinak rolled his eyes. "I've no more time for your talk."

"You astonish me."

"I don't know why," Sarinak growled. "I have nothing more to say to this. Come, my spouse."

"I shall. Presently." Inhya was still eyeing Našobok. He slid his gaze to her, eyed her right back.

With an irritated grunt, Sarinak marched away.

Našobok watched Inhya watch him for several heartbeats, then turned aside. The smartest action to take at this point was to let the entire thing slide off his back. Go back to *Ilhukaia*, tend his own business even as Sarinak was.

If only he didn't keep remembering the disappointment on Tokela's face.

If only he could forget the thwarted fury of the Bear oških.

If only he didn't keep remembering the inherent promise in Spear Dance.

Našobok was not one to lightly forsake a promise. Particularly since it had been taken from him with such quiet mystery.

"Našobok."

He halted, slid a curious glance towards Inhya. She rarely spoke to him if she could help it, but using his name?

"Don't go after Tokela."

Ai, and she was too canny by halves. Pity she hadn't used half that intellect with the oških she'd hearthed. Eyes narrowing, Našobok peered at her.

"Show you have some remaining sense. Don't let this thing go any further."

"What 'thing'," Našobok ventured, "is that?"

He'd seen softer eyes behind a drawn bow. "Don't play games with this, wyrhling. You know of what I speak."

Našobok crossed his arms, considered her.

"The indigo on Tokela's cheeks was not there upon thisSun's rising. He put it there himself."

Despite himself, a guffaw escaped. "Is that so? Then I'd say he's made quite a statement, hearth-chieftain."

"He made even more of one by asking a wyrhling to Dance!" she shot back.

"Sink me... I'm his cousin, Inhya. He has every right to ask an elder cousin to be his playm—"

"By your own choice, you are not."

"I never chose to disregard my blood."

"Oh, but you did, wyrhling. You walked away without a qualm."

"You know nothing of my heart, then or now."

"Without a qualm," Inhya snarled between her teeth. "I was there. You were *weak*. You let River take your Spirit, refused any help, even when Chogah offered to take it from you."

"I'd sooner have handed that n'batuweh a dagger and bared my chest."

"She was Alekšu, she could have purged the weakness from your heart. You *let* it take you! You turned your back on your Clan, on your sire's hopes, your brother's love. You pulled your dam's heart from her breast and threw it at her feet."

Upper lip curling in a snarl, Našobok took a step forwards, looming over Inhya with fists clenched.

She didn't back down; in fact leaned towards him, her own fists clenching. "Do it, then. Prove me right. Show everyone how being Riverwalker means respecting nothing."

"You have no concept of what Riverwalkers respect." It was too quiet. Dangerous. "I'm not the one who swims a tainted pool, sister." The endearment curled on his tongue, became affront. "I thought I was beneath even your notice."

She didn't miss a beat, bared her teeth. "You're not only beneath my notice, but Tokela's. You've already pulled my brother into *your* 'tainted pool'. You will not drag my son as well."

"And how is it," Našobok marveled, "that you are comfortable being Alekšu's sister?"

"As Alekšu, he's made sacred use of what abomination threatened to take him! He didn't submit—though I'm sure you would have him do so!"

"Your mouth sprouts ignorance like flies from a carcass."

"I'm ignorant? You besmirch ways which have kept our People vital and safe for generations!"

"And like anything else walking our Grandmother, there is a price to be paid. The fittest survive, and the weeding out must take place. Sarinak said it, that Tokela's path is wrong. What if it's the only choice he has? What if he belongs here no more than I did?"

Her face leached into ash. Somehow he'd struck a nerve. "You know *nothing*, outlier!"

"A'io, you're right. I don't know, not near enough. But neither do you, I'm thinking."

"I know you've been nothing but a disruptive influence every time you've deigned to show yourself in decent society. Particularly for Tokela."

"Because I gave a few snatched heartbeats of notice to a lonely little ahlóssa?" Našobok snapped back. "Because I answered an invitation to an oških's first Spear Dance? Perhaps you should wonder why he keeps seeking me out!"

Again, it pinked her. "And what will you do this time but confuse him more? You'll guide him as an elder cousin should? Only you are not, and all you'll 'teach' him will be the tricks and games you should have outgrown long ago—"

"Careful, you're parroting my sire, now."

"—and then leave him to chase after a forbidden Spirit. You'll abandon my son, just like you did your Clan and my brother."

"That," Našobok grated out, "is something I refuse to speak to with you. What talk you spout!—your brother, your son. Not everything is about you."

"Of course this isn't about me! Can't you underst—"

"I think you're the one who doesn't understand."

"Tokela is the one who doesn't understand!" The raw plea in Inyha's voice startled him. "He doesn't ken what he's doing! He's like his dam, reaching for Fire even if Ša burns, and you've no right to encourage him!"

Ai, there. Truth, dripping blood.

"You have no right," Našobok growled suddenly, softly, "to cloak him with the memories of the dead. Even to protect him."

He should have expected the slap. Perhaps he even deserved it. But he was not prepared for the glitter of tears in Inhya's eyes as, breathing hard, she shook her head and backed away.

"We have nothing more to say to each other."

But as Našobok watched her turn and go, he imagined before this was over they'd have a lot more.

Tokela should have expected it. Should have known he never made the right choices even when he tried. Instead it all... twisted, somehow.

Twisted. Maybe he couldn't. Couldn't make appropriate choices, couldn't be normal, couldn't belong. He was half-breed to Other. It didn't matter that all he wanted was to be one with his Clan, because he wasn't. It didn't matter that he didn't want to spend First Running in constant upheaval against almost everyone that mattered.

Inhya. Sarinak. Nechtoun and his odd friend Galenu. Mordeleg—not that he mattered—and then, Našobok.

"Tokela?"

Of course. Only Madoc was left.

Tokela didn't stop walking, didn't hesitate at all and he wasn't sure why.

I fought for you! The small wail built, silent, behind his chest. *Why didn't you fight for…?*

His hearth-mother would say he'd indeed sunken low, to hope an outlier would speak for him. Fight for him.

"Tokela!"

Even that wasn't truly his, merely a naming given in denial of the inevitable.

Tohwakeli. Tohwakelifitčiluka. *Eyes of Stars.*

Another call, and the sound of approaching feet, running to catch up.

Always, Madoc tried to catch him up. Always, Tokela couldn't help but leave him behind. And still Madoc kept running after, ardent and determined, and Tokela hadn't the heart to stop him. No one else bothered.

"Tokela!"

"What?" He rounded, quick and fierce.

Madoc just barely managed to not run head-on into him, and backed so swift, Tokela found himself wondering what Madoc saw in his expression. Maybe he needed to cultivate it more.

Then he saw the wide-wary eyes, the tension quivering along the half-grown frame. Seeing such disquiet, such wariness—and in Madoc, whom he'd never wanted to see with that look…

It broke something in Tokela. There was a crack, then a shiver, then it all went shattering into friable, uncountable, irretrievable pieces.

"Why do you keep following me?" Tokela snapped.

"Because you keep running!" Madoc shot back. Then, with a small quaver in his voice, "You never used to run from *me.*"

Too much hurt had piled itself atop Tokela; he was not inclined to remorse or mercy. Not thisnow. He peered at Madoc with flattened eyes, silent.

Waiting.

Madoc had never been good at the wait. He shifted, back and forth. "I didn't mean what I said. When you're not… Here. It's not the same as what Grandsire does."

You meant it, Tokela wanted to say, and then, *What if it is like? What if it's…*

Worse?

He remained silent, forelock falling into his face.

Madoc only lasted a breath longer. "You… you made your indigo."

Tokela turned his head, still said nothing.

"You never said anything, never…" Madoc faltered, tried to re-gather his indignation, like a bellows against Fire. "I didn't think it mattered. I mean, you were taller, but so was I. Your voice changed, but it didn't seem to matter either. Even when Yeka… when he spoke to you of you taking your oških Journey, you wouldn't talk about it. I heard. To him, or Aška. You never speak of *anything* important."

"Maybe I don't want to."

Maybe he couldn't.

"You've always made a Dance with me, with all the ahlóssa. Instead you made your Marks and a Dance with that wyrhling!"

"*That wyrhling* is your Uncle Našobok!"

"You're the only one who says that!" Madoc challenged. "Even he knows what he is! What makes you so special as to ignore what's right?"

"What makes you so special as to *say* what's right?" Tokela blurted out. Talk, so often slippery and unwieldy, suddenly wouldn't be silent. "Shunning people because they're different, that's right? Rendering someone outlier because they do something, hear something, feel something the people around them either can't or won't admit to? That's right?" Thick, salty heat filled Tokela's eyes, as uncontrollable as the sudden flow of talk. "Is that the sort of leader you want to be? If it is, and that's 'here', then I don't want to be here!"

"But you're my brother! My cousin! I love you!"

"Našobok is my cousin. Your uncle."

Madoc's lips quivered and he looked down.

Still, no mercy. Tokela had to know. "Tell me this, Madoc. If I was... gone. A lot. Like Nechtoun."

Madoc's face twitched and Tokela felt his will begin to fragment: too close, too possible.

"N'da, if I was to go away, go to River, be outlier—wyrhling—what would you do then? Would you love me then?"

"That isn't fair!"

"Answer the question, Madoc."

For once, Madoc seemed bereft of anything resembling speech. He stared at Tokela, fists clenched, and his mouth opened several times, yet nothing came out. Finally, with a strangled groan, he whirled and sped away.

Tokela watched him go. He knew he should be feeling something. Anything. Instead the chaotic and nonsensical hum rose behind his eyes, heat slicking his throat and runnelling down his spine; his fingertips twitched, uncontrollable, as if they wanted—needed—to craft something. Anything.

This wasn't feeling. It couldn't be, because he was cold and stilled, as if he were game for the board hung and up and split open, entrails removed. Heart taken. Bled out, with nothing left in his veins but...

But chill Riverwater.

Tokela stumbled in the opposite direction, away from Madoc, the drums, the compound... everything.

$$\phi \quad \phi \quad \phi$$

13
BREAKING

Anahli preferred standing firm over running—she'd in truth never met anything she cared to run from. But there was no standing against that sea of hostility. She'd kept her head high, true, but her swift, angry walk had been a retreat, nothing but. Where to, she wasn't sure, but for now, away from these withering, hidebound, fish-stinking cliffs.

Her dam's ire was easily understood. Her aunt's, less so. But her sire... disapproval from him had always put salt to any wound. And it seemed since he'd taken upon Alekšu's horns, his gaze had turned, more suspicion than sympathy. As if he waited for some strange happenstance, one both feared and hoped-for.

Palatan had always concealed things . His heart and smile had never been withheld; his love for his spouse and children—indeed, for all horseClans—was there for all to see. But he cloaked his eyes any time Anahli spoke of anything concerning the Elementals they must inexplicably deny even as they revered them.

Anahli wanted to rip that cloak away. And she'd found a keen, sure weapon: talk.

You mean to give me to River, even as you gave him up to Her! You let him abandon us! Let him turn his back on caldera's Fire for cold-cruel Rivertalk, even as you would abandon me in this place where fems are barely warriors!

Anahli's feet had eyes in them, and a good thing, too. The woodland lay tangled with new growth, what paths she discerned made for short hoofedKin, not lanky horsetalkers. Nevertheless, she took the smallest, ill-travelled one she could find and kept going, both heat and wet spilling over her cheeks. A bramble slapped her, then one of treeKin clawed at her hair. Giving an angry dash of hand across her face, she looked up, ahead.

The trees had thinned, dwindling into a small meadow. Across from her hunched...

What was it? Some ancient cavern? A gate such as the mid-Lands herders used to corral their sheep? To be sure, the tangled hedge to either side seemed impenetrable.

The thing was nearly tall as the ancient trees curving around it, shining ebony and—somehow—silver. If it were indeed some kind of stone, it bore no moss or greenery. She could see now that even the close-hemmed trees and bracken hugged—but didn't touch it. Even the Riverling that had followed her had retreated from the thing. Narrower now, a mere burble and tumble beneath thick bracken and a clump of grass that waved in Wind's breath, dotted with tiny budlings and braver blossoms. The Riverling disappeared—or seemed to—beneath the cavern's entrance.

If it was a cavern.

Anahli rose to a half crouch, wiping her hands on a patch of moss thick as a horse's fur during snowMoon. Head cocked, pace measured-slow, she advanced upon it.

As if in answer to the tens of questions vibrating upon her tongue, the thing seemed to shiver. Something akin to SkyFire chased across its surface, followed by a thick *crack!* that made her start. Frowning, Anahli reversed her steps, her eyes never leaving the thing.

It was then she heard the approach. Quiet, but clumsy, at a two-footed half trot that occasionally stumbled.

And was there anything she desired less at this breath than encountering a clumsy someone?

Anahli, still keeping an eye upon the ebony cavern, slid behind a thick quartet of trees and hunkered down, silent.

Našobok knew how many hiding places there were within and without the Great Mound. He had, after all, frequented most of them—and, it seemed, for many of the same reasons Tokela had.

So. If he were a pissing-angry, hemmed-in oških again, where would he go?

Hunh. There were too many places still.

He had to narrow down to what he knew—which wasn't much, but it was something. Tokela was drawn to River. Tokela liked his own company. Tokela liked...

Two places suddenly came to the forefront in Našobok's mind. One was a place where he'd found a small ahlóssa wandering, several furlongs downRiver from the Mound. The other was an overflow, a Riverling several leagues distant, with a lovely cavern in which to make camp, and a deep pool perfect for a soothing swim. He knew it well, knew Tokela was aware of it—the last time Našobok had visited, Tokela had let slip he'd found the very place a young Našobok had once made his own.

Of course, either of those made the supposition that Tokela wanted to be found.

Well, perhaps he didn't or perhaps he did. But something in him yearned for... something. Else Tokela would have never invited a wyrhling once-cousin into Dance.

The strand first, then on to the little cove. If that wasn't it, then...

Našobok narrowly avoided being bowled over by a half-sized, Sun-haired projectile. More out of instinct than anything resembling sense, he grabbed the missile by ša's ahlóssa braid, skipped forwards a few steps until Madoc had slowed, then stopped.

Truly, Našobok wasn't prepared for the small fury that descended upon him.

"Let go of me! You have no right. *No right!*"

Shock more than anything made Našobok release his hold. "Madoc, what i—?"

"It's all your fault!" Madoc rounded on him. "Everything was fine—fine, I tell you!—until you came here and... and...!"

Then Madoc spat on the ground not a hand away from Našobok's boot, turned on one heel and marched towards the compound.

Našobok watched him go. Was it even possible that the entirety a'Naišwyrh had gone completely mad?

Ai, better he head for home, board his ship and never look back, because every time he did involve himself, even in the slightest, with some aspect of his birthing-tribe, it inevitably meant stepping in a pit of sleeping viperKin.

"I'd better go find Tokela," Našobok finally said.

Tokela ran.

Again.

His feet knew where he was going even before he did. Up and past the drum heights, through the trees along the cliffside and away from the Great Mound, towards the trebled Moons rising, peeping from behind high-hung clouds and ghosting against Sky.

The hareKin mask bumped and scraped at his hip.

Drums and voices muted in the dense green, with only an occasional call or lift of bass beat. Dance and Fire left behind, cordoned by thick woodland, only the rush and burble of the Riverling's overflow, only the rustle and hiss of leaves in Wind's breath to fill the quiet.

Tokela needed the stillness. Needed something to quiet the twitching, humming, surging *thing* lighting behind his eyes, as if burning to cinders the drum that would let him move, Dance, *breathe.*

Instead of growing, the Riverling dwindled beside him, and the trees thinned. His steps slowed, from run to stumbling half trot, and he blinked, somehow surprised at where he'd come.

Surely he'd meant to go to the wykupeh.

If you didn't want me to find you, then you came to the wrong place. The memory of Madoc's words informed him: maybe he hadn't meant to go there, after all.

But to come *here*?

Tokela approached the *t'rešalt*, one foot before the other, silent, the pit of his stomach roiling with the weight of dread and a strange, rogue tickle of... anticipation? The Riverling teased him, burbling as She disappeared into Earth, as if all things fell silent before the thing looming before him.

It too was quiet. Dark. Had he misremembered? Imagined the sparks and shards of light chasing across its surface?

But as he moved closer, the *t'rešalt* started to hum and spark. Slow at first, then faster the closer he came; as if his presence nudged it, somehow. The lights flickered soft, this time seeming more welcome than warning...

No matter. He should leave.

Instead Tokela hesitated, then crept closer and extended a cautious hand towards the thing.

Smooth, his fingers registered. Moreso than the finest-sanded wood, slick, almost, and...

Tokela yipped and yanked his hand back just as the thing lit up with tiny, feathery bits of SkyFire, all arcing towards his fingers. A jolt thumped his calf, where his knife lay in its sheath, and seemed to tingle at the copper on his collarbones. More, the flickers... followed, somehow, tiny lights sparking a connexion between stone and fingers, carried on Wind's breath.

He shook his hand, as if shaking away one of insectKin, and the light shattered into several sparks that fled back into the slick surface.

Yet, the *t'rešalt* remained, humming. Waiting.

It speaks to you, Hare said. *It knows you. As River knows you. As Wind and Earth, Fire and Sky all know you. Maybe there are answers to be found in it.*

Wind and Earth, Fire and Sky and River...

Tokela peered down at the hareKin mask, frowning. *This is forbidden.*

Yet here we are.

Silence, with only the disappearing burble of the Riverling to break it. With a tiny growl of breath, Tokela untied the mask and set ša gently on the ground, just beside the tiny stream. After a few breaths of hesitation, he also shucked away what had given him the unpleasant tingle: both his knives, the few copper ornaments. Then—slow, careful—he reached for the not-stone. His fingertips skated across the slick surface—and that, upon this closer inspection, seemed almost like the *glašg* he'd seen and touched from the traders. Belatedly he realised he was holding his breath, braced, waiting for another shock. It didn't come.

Instead the strange, furred streaks of light gathered beneath his fingertips, followed as he moved, where he moved, and left behind pale ghosts of where he'd traced. Like sketching...

A smile touched Tokela's lip and remained there. His fingers sketched a feather made of blue-white sparks, then a wing, then...

"I'd heard this place was forbidden to those a'Naišwyrh."

Tokela whirled.

Mordeleg held both of Tokela's knives, and his eyes gleamed yellow in the muted light. "This is the outLander place, isn't it? The gate to Chepiś. Do you come here often?"

There was no answer Tokela could make. It was no comfort that, from behind him, he could feel the little tickles of warmth and spun blue-white, and the *t'rešalt* humming an odd, low song that rose the hair along his nape.

Or maybe that was because Mordeleg took one step closer. "Did you enjoy Spear Dance?"

He had. He *had*.

"Did you bring the filthy outlier here, then? He must have serviced you quickly. Hardly time enough to enjoy it."

Cheeks flaming, Tokela spat, "I more enjoyed kicking your tail into the dirt!"

"You were lucky." Mordeleg bent, put the knives back onto the ground. More fool him, Tokela silently sneered—or maybe not; Mordeleg's next motion was to step over them, putting himself between them and Tokela. "But you were lucky before too many. You owe me, now."

"I owe you a deeper cut with my blade."

"I think it's time we used my blade."

"You don't have one. MidLanders are soft; they use blunt edges to dig in sand."

"Says the one who claims his sire was one of us, who lives with posturing, dull fish-eaters." Mordeleg's voice dripped scorn. "And then comes to meet his true kin in the forbidden places, just as your dam did. Don't pretend you were sired by a midLander, half-breed. Your mother took after her horsetalker grand-dam, opening her legs for any stallion who'd service her."

"I will end you!"

"Then come for me. Do it. Maybe I'll show you what blade I do have."

Tokela was tempted. Still stripped to clout from Spear Dance, Mordeleg's hands were at his sides. He hid no weapon Tokela could see. It had been relatively easy to take Mordeleg down in Dance. Surely Tokela could do the same now.

"Or are you afraid, little hareKin?"

Abruptly, Tokela was. Something quivered, deep-set and dark-clouded, in Mordeleg's voice. Tokela couldn't sound it, couldn't parse it. The oddling not-stone at his spine no longer spread warmth, instead seeming to leach the heat from him. The Riverling's burble shattered into the silence.

Enemy. The open, blank eye sockets of the set-aside hareKin mask winked warning. *Predator.*

Something scratched between Tokela's shoulder blades, a faint tease of spark and feeling.

Bring him in, Hare whispered.

The not-stone's hum increased in pitch. Tokela's eyes watered. His temples pounded. "What do you want?" he whispered back.

"Come away from that thing and I'll show you," Mordeleg answered.

"I didn't mean..." *You*, Tokela finished silent, uneasy.

"Or I can leave you here and find your little cousin. I saw him wandering off by himself earlier. He was pretty upset, not paying attention to much." A glint of teeth, more snarl than smile. "Does he really think nothing can touch him?"

Tokela rocked forwards. "You wouldn't dare."

Mordeleg shrugged. "You're sure? River took your dam and sire... if he was your sire. A wrong step on the strand, and River would take him, too. An accident, surely. So many things can happen."

So many things. The Hare-voice bade Tokela's hands twitch, led his fingers sliding in some unconscious Dance upon Air. Mist breathed chill into his lungs, not quenching, but kindling Fire in his heart.

"Why are you doing this?" he asked, low and quiet.

"I told you. You owe me." Mordeleg came forwards a few steps. "And I think I know how you'll pay."

"Or I could just go, now, and tell them what you've threatened."

To Tokela's surprise, Mordeleg laughed. "Do you think they'll believe you? You brought an outlier into Dance. And now I find you... here. At this place forbidden to everyone. Except—" he stepped a tiny bit closer "—you, perhaps? The ehšehklan, visiting his sire's home—"

"That's a lie!"

"Maybe it is. Maybe it isn't. The question is, will it matter if they find you've been visiting this place?" Another step, another smile-that-was-not. "Ehšehklan."

Tokela stood firm, though his trepidation stirred, murky and treacherous as Mordeleg's gaze. Strangely unreadable, the latter—more murk, rising about them, invisible but *there*. Until now, things had been clear: Mordeleg wanted to see Tokela beaten, wanted to be the one who did it. Whys were unimportant.

Until now.

Tokela's fingers kept stroking. Some trick of light trailed blue-white in their wake, as if Tokela had graphite and leaf, sketching... only these were symbols he didn't know.

Because they weren't. Symbols. Only a trick of light.

Are you so sure? Hare whispered.

The words quickened Tokela's heart and filled it. Like the yaiyai of the elders, singing warrior courage into being. Like the *t'rešalt* at his back, humming and sparking...

"You want me?" Tokela sneered. "Come and take me."

Mordeleg hesitated, slight but there. Tokela took the chance, feinting to his knife hand then darting opposite. Mordeleg followed the first motion, and Tokela ploughed shoulder-first into Mordeleg's knees.

Arms windmilling, Mordeleg floundered, seeking purchase against the soft loam.

Tokela struck again, a shoulder against Mordeleg's hip, then whirled with a twist and turn to dart away, snatch up his knives—

Instead a hand snarled in his hair, gave a brutal yank. It enabled Mordeleg to find his footing; he heaved himself upright, dragging Tokela with him. Tokela gave a yowl and twisted, lashing out. Mordeleg cursed as the blow landed; he grabbed Tokela's arm and twisted it behind him, propelled him against the *t'rešalt*. Another brutal shove sent Tokela face-first, bloodying his nose. With a growl Tokela twisted, nearly won free, but Mordeleg lunged forwards, slamming every bit of his considerable weight against Tokela, pinning him.

All the breath popped from Tokela's lungs in a wrenching grunt. He lurched and bucked; it made no difference. He might as well have moved the Great Mound.

"Be still." Mordeleg growled. "Don't you want me to answer your question?" One of the hands holding to Tokela suddenly softened. It trailed downwards, across the wyrh tree stippled onto his ribcage, slipped on a remaining bit of oil in the small of his back.

Tokela froze.

"You asked me why I was doing this." Mordeleg shifted, rocked his hips forwards. The end of his clout tickled at Tokela's thigh, the hard, thick knot beneath making many things altogether clear.

Hands quivering, wanting to draw, but no blade to hand, nails trying to dig into slick not-stone, teeth bared to bite at air.

Trapped. Panting Hare for real this time. Helpless.

Here.

"Now you see," Mordeleg whispered. "I don't need weapons. I choose closer means."

So, the whisper came again, *do We.* Thick, wet heat reverberated against Tokela's cheek, rising behind his eyes with convulsive flares and sparks, humming and jerking down his back, setting his heart lurching and stuttering in his breast. It nerved him, impeding any movement save an uncontrollable twitch and spasm: his hands, fingertips tracing tiny pictures against the *t'rešalt*, blue-white sparks travelling up his pinned arm.

Mordeleg tried to shove Tokela further against the thing, but instead hissed a midLand curse by Tokela's ear. It slipped from anger into panic; the grasp turned from stone to sand. Tokela thought to resist, but a... a croon, it was, deep within his breast, and it sent another odd twitch/spasm up his arms. As if something deep within had disconnected him from his body, a preparation for some reflex he hadn't known he possessed.

The sparks rose about him, lifted his hair. His fingers kept sketching. Kept...

A dull, meaty thud and a hoarse yelp broke the spell. Mordeleg fell sideways, so limp-heavy that Tokela's knees collapsed and he slithered downwards. The opportunity of freedom further broke the fugue, and he twisted, put his back to the *t'rešalt* and raised spark-filled hands, ready for the fight.

But Mordeleg remained crumpled on at his feet, insensate.

And a lanky, black-haired fem in duskLands leathers strode forwards, another stone raised and ready in her hand.

Perhaps she'd waited overlong to act. But Anahli'd no desire to interfere in the foolishness of two sparring oških. Not that is, until she'd heard the underlying venom to the exchange, and seen the heavier oških grab the slighter one, slam him against the oddling cavern and... and...

Her eyes widened, scarce believing. The punishment for this sort of aberration in duskLands was quick—and fitting. Surely dawnLands didn't allow such a thing.

Not that it mattered. She was a'Šaákfo. Gliding down the weeping tree all silent, Anahli snatched up two stones adequate to the deed.

She didn't need the second one.

Again, she saw more. The Riverling had overflowed Her banks, wet trickling down towards the unconscious oških, and...

The other oških spun about, ready for another scrap now he'd the liberty to make it. He bore the wyrh tree tattoo along his ribs, but he was lanky as a weanling colt, more a'Šaákfo than any stout-muscled a'Naišwyrh, even to the sheen of chestnut in his shoulder-length black hair. It fell, weighted with beads and copper, about a face that, again, was broad in the cheekbones and narrow in the chin like her own folk. Anahli started to make soothing talk. Instead, the spit dried in her mouth.

The first thing she noticed was that his hands were *glowing*. Roped with strange, sparking tendrils that matched and met the gleam of the oških's eyes, blue white beneath his forelock. Not Darksight, either. More like the glitter-life of an Elemental... and yet not. Anahli knew the look of the former, had seen such in those who'd come, desperate, to Alekšu. Had seen the dimming, the dying, after first Chogah then Palatan Danced the cure, killing the connexion.

The oških wrenched his gaze away. The blue-white tendrils wisped into Smoke, as if they'd never been there.

Had they? Suddenly Anahli was unsure of exactly what she'd seen. The wonder vanished all the further as the oških turned with a snarl to the figure insensate at his feet and toed him. Making sure.

Well, and Anahli approved of that.

But the Riverling was flowing close to the downed oških; even a cupful of Her could drown. Anahli strode forwards and grabbed the motionless oških and, after a small hesitation, the other bent to assist. Together they hauled him away from the cavern-thing, and deposited him beside a tree.

Anahli leaned against the bark. "Are you well?"

"A'io." Husky-soft, against a spray of leaves. "My thanks. It was a good throw."

Anahli grinned and looked back at the fallen oških. "I didn't kill him, did I?"

"Killing that one"—the slender oških looked up and threw the forelock back from his face—"wouldn't make me weep."

Recognition settled in, then. His eyes were still the give-away—too wide and not deep-set enough, more intense than pretty, dark indigo leaching odd-pale about narrow pupils flecked with small lights.

The latter still discomfited. Anahli masked it with humour. "So you're Madoc's fascination. Tokela a'Naišwyrh, it has been long. Sun light your path, cousin."

"Fascination? Me?" This with a wry smile. "I'd say he's more struck with you at present, Anahli a'Šaákfo. River sing you welcome, cousin." The smile abruptly slipped, and Tokela gave an inexplicable stagger; Anahli grabbed at him with both hands.

"Are you well?"

"I'm..." It quavered and Tokela fell silent, his gaze curious and captious, all at once. His eyes glimmered, not tears but with those tiny lights—*of course,* she reasoned, *Chogah said he had been called Eyes of Stars... but this is...*

Is it? something chided, deep and inwards. *I remember. Do you?*

Do I what? Anahli wondered. Wind tilted the trees, skirled about them and pulled tiny strands about her cheeks; strangely enough, Tokela's hair barely moved. A rash of heat prickled her palms and flared upwards through her bones—or so it seemed— to set a flashFire swirl behind her own gaze.

Remember, the something said. *Eyes meet eyes to waken Spirit. Spirit wakens our Mother's heart, and Her heart wakens. You must remember...*

Remember.

Talk/not-talk. Darkness, and echoes. Not just River, but many voices... *too* many: Wind and Earth, Fire and Stars, curling about the entry to Šilombiš'okpulo.

Eyes waken the heart, and the heart wakens silence. The pathway of silence, followed too long. *Remove the mask, O trickster. Show the way to those who are ours.*

Tokela didn't understand. He didn't want to. But as Anahli released him, leaving pale marks where her fingers had dug into his biceps, it was as if she'd tugged free some scab deep within him, taking flesh and leaving it to seep empty.

This time, he did fall to his knees.

Silence.

Then, gentle and terrible, Anahli asked, "How long has the Elemental been with you?"

The Elemental. Been with you.

Tokela didn't look up. Couldn't. "What are you talking about?"

Anahli knelt, grasped his arms again. Bent close and, nose to nose, looked into his eyes.

The *surge* again, noise but not-noise. Heat behind his eyes, in his arms where she touched him, and Tokela found himself raising one hand, fingers tracing the Marks upon Anahli's cheeks then to the growing squinch of brow. Another Mark, there, like Alekšu's horns but not, seeming made of SkyFire, unfamiliar. Yet still the blue-white light danced upon sienna and...

And Anahli... shivered. Closed her eyes, swallowed, then opened them.

Said, obdurate, "I think you know what I'm talking about."

"What is going on here?"

And ai, but yet *another* voice rent the clearing, making them both start. Tokela fell back on his haunches. Anahli bolted upright and whirled on Našobok like an enemy.

"We've done nothing! You've no right to even ask wh—"

"I've no right?" Našobok's voice jolted against hers, River and Ice. "You're the one with no rights here. Neither of you. What are you doing here? This place is forbidden to..." He paused as he glanced at Tokela, but turned back to Anahli, warmth fading. "What have you done to Tokela? What's happened to the mid-Lander ošk—"

"You've no idea what's happened here!" Anahli didn't back down. "Don't you dare assume the worst of me."

"If I assume the worst, I have cause. This game you're playing is dangerous, ehši."

"I'm not your daughter! I never have been, and I have nothing more to say to you. *Outlier!*"

Našobok's face twisted. He nearly lurched forwards but just as obviously strangled the motion, fists clenching. "You go too far." Barely audible, fury scoring icy calm. "Up, Tokela."

N'da, he didn't think so. If he did, he was going to be sick. Worse, he didn't even know why...

"Tokela?" The voice was unchanged, so why was there concern bleeding from beneath the raw anger? And Anahli... something fragile and tensile as spinner's webs harnessed Tokela to all the fury and grief she flung, like spear from atlatl, against Našobok. And trying to quiet *that?* Easier to caress lightning, hold to Wind. The oddling flickers renewed their dance against his eyelids; Tokela squeezed them tight and bit his lip, hard. The sting brought him back within himself.

"One Sun will rise, Hihlyanahli," Našobok gritted out, "when you think your own thoughts, not merely echo the poison that n'batuweh Chogah feeds you."

A long gasp, as if Anahli were about to reply.

Našobok forestalled it. "Go. Now."

Silence. Then a choke and the sound of feet, heavy and stumbling, in retreat.

"Tokela." Calmer, but no less a command. "Get up."

I can't. Don't you see, I can't.

Hands grabbed his wrists and hoisted him upright. Tokela let them and kept his eyes tight-shut, glad of the new forelock that fell into his face—*don't touch me, don't look, not now*—but couldn't wrest free.

"Tokela." No question, no demand, but the fingers taking Tokela's jaw were as merciless as gentle. Even curiosity at that last didn't impel him to open his eyes.

A forehead touching his, brief, and Našobok's breath against his cheeks. This did open Tokela's eyes, in time to see Našobok loose him and go over to inspect Mordeleg's prone form. "Just stunned." Still quiet; soothing, almost. "What are the three of you doing here, Tokela? What has hap—?"

"I tell you, nothing happened between us. Anahli did nothing." *She didn't... it was me. She saw. Knew... and then we...*

We... what happened? How does she know? What does she know?

"So tell me why you're here. At this place." Našobok gestured to the *t'rešalt*, which was, thank every spirit nameable, dark and dormant. "Have you come here..."

It trailed away, but Tokela answered, quick as a quirt, "As my mother did?"

Even Našobok, it seemed, found the subject of Lakisa uncomfortable. Instead of meeting Tokela's eyes, he frowned at the *t'rešalt*.

"How did you know I was here?" Tokela pressed, wondering how anyone had known, at that.

"I tracked you. You weren't so careful about your steps, and that one," he jerked his chin towards Mordeleg, "left a trail like a wounded buck. I feared he would come after you, and it seems he did."

"A'io." This was easier than the... Other. "He threatened Madoc, too. I nearly took him down again, but he pinned me. He tried to force me. I didn't want him!"

"That was obvious even in Dance."

The reassurance gave some ease. "Anahli saw, too. She threw the stone. I wish I'd..." Anger rose, not hot but cold. *I wish I'd done... whatever the Riverling and the Elementals and the t'rešalt would have...* It sickened him even as the thought surfaced. "Anahli did nothing, but if she had, at least she'd have given me the choice!"

Našobok peered at him, mouth quirked. "Tokela, you and Anahli have already attracted enough trouble thisSun; are you so set on flaunting tradition—"

"It seems tradition would forbid you to me as well. Is that why you didn't want me?"

Našobok's closed his eyes for a long breath. When he did speak, it was a growl. "If you didn't see that I did want you, then you weren't paying attention, cousin."

Was that condescension? "You didn't fight for me!"

"If that's true, then why am I here?"

This stopped Tokela midbreath of another angry volley.

"No doubt Anahli would say I'm here to thwart her. She and I don't exactly get along of late. But then Anahli doesn't get along with anyone of late but the n'batuweh." Našobok shrugged and stood, toed Mordeleg's haunch. "Well, as it stands, if this one weren't oških, I'd take him to River and pitch him to Her mercy. But he is, so we must do something, not just make talk about your... uh... unconventional choices in playmates."

"Anahli didn't—!"

"I meant me."

Oh. Tokela's cheeks burned. A slow smile tilted his mouth; he kept it and closed his eyes, watched the flickers fade to darkness, listened to the drum of his heart quicken into silence.

"Tokela."

He found Našobok watching him, gaze unreadable. It seemed Našobok had many things he would choose to say,; instead he merely continued, "The chieftains are in Council until the Moons touch the Duskmost trees. I certainly can't interrupt and you'd just catch more trouble did you do so. I also refuse to just let this"—he toed Mordeleg again, this time prompting a tiny groan—"wander free. Neither can I stake him down somewhere away from here." The slight smile turned wider, tipped into a snarl. "Though it might be a good thing did one of lionKin take the treacherous lout."

The image of Mordeleg trussed like hunting bait appealed mightily. Tokela couldn't help a broad smile.

Našobok, still watching, let out an odd staccato of breath before a contagious, lopsided grin returned. "I think I know what to do. I'll be back."

Heart stuttering in inexplicable panic, Tokela shot Našobok another wary look.

Another frown, then Našobok repeated, "I'll be back. If..." He hesitated, and it seemed odd upon the normal surety of his body. "If you want me to, that is."

Tokela felt his cheeks flaming, lowered his head. Gave a tight, self-conscious nod.

"But not here. We shouldn't be here, it's not safe. You shouldn't come here, Tokela, and you know why."

A knot fisted itself in Tokela's chest, half resentment and half relief.

"Where shall I find you?" Našobok's persistence was all relief.

"There's a place downriver, with a deep sink surrounded by weeping trees—"

"I know the place." There was a grin in the voice. "Meet me there."

And when next Tokela looked up, Našobok was disappearing into the mists, Mordeleg's unconscious form slung across his shoulder.

$$\phi \quad \phi \quad \phi$$

14
DAUGHTER OF WIND

Anahli flung open the door hide of her Clan's tipo, and fled inside.

The tipo was deserted, quiet. Not even her sire's elderly fleethound lay by the hearth's well-banked embers. But the wide, scooped-out hollow brimmed with furs and blankets. She dove in, rolling in the remaining warmth and scents: her sire, all spice and sharp musk, the needlecreeper balm her dam used, the ever-present and powdery smell of sweated horse blankets, the sweet-sage and grasstails offered to their temporary hearth.

No cold den with separate bed shelves. No disapproving play-mates bound in skirts and headwraps and interminable strictures about what and who and how...

She wished her sisters had come. Niše, Samke, and Vinka would pet her, comb and braid her hair, make understanding talk. Particularly Vinka, who'd also never forgiven Našobok.

The worst of it? Anahli had obeyed him, instinctive as if he hadn't long ago cast aside any rightful respect! As if she were a bare-cheeked ahlóssa! Her heart burned, her eyes seared with tears of humiliation. How was it her fault the otter-masked oških hadn't been prepared for a fight? How was it her doing that Našobok thought she and Tokela had been courting?

Anahli lurched upwards, clenching her fingers into the bedding.

Tokela, whose heart lay in his eyes when they followed Našobok—and Anahli hadn't had the chance to warn him off.

He'll tear your heart out upon the ground and turn away. He will...

Tokela, Madoc's fascination, whose eyes had flickered like Stars. Who had... pulled the sparks of light from the alien thing and set them to Dance upon Wind...

Anahli drew her knees towards her chest. The sparks had... landed upon her chest, sunk into her heart. Našobok's accusation stung, for whatever had happened, it was not so simple. She'd heard—n'da, not *heard*, a silent not-talk making questions beyond any true hearing and begged answers she couldn't supply. Still begged answers.

Her temples pounded with the pressure of memory; her heart thumped against her breast. She took in a deep, cleansing breath, hoping to quiet it to no avail.

Possession. It had to be; it was the only answer she knew. The Riverling had answered, tiny as She had been, and the strange cavern... Shaped thing or no, it obviously had some life, and responded to one with the ability to listen. An Elemental's Power had begun to ripen in Tokela, which meant...

She had to tell her sire. He was Alekšu, he could help.

Shaking her head—with a wince, as it set her pulse to pound in her temples all the harder—Anahli growled against her knees. Help? N'da. Alekšu was oathbound to take any gift away—and it was a gift, had been, would be again somehow! Palatan's existence was now predicated on eradicating such things. Foolish, to think he'd do any different with Tokela.

And it wasn't only Alekšu. If they found out, here? Surely Tokela didn't deserve that kind of punishment. The tribes upon River's thighs were adamant: purge or exile. Našobok had been a chieftain's son, but that hadn't helped him.

Yet...

Hadn't Tokela's dam been possessed? Hadn't they tried to help her, before River had taken her? Hadn't her spouse drowned as well, trying to save her?

A shadow loomed in the door. "Are you well?"

Anahli started and leapt to her feet, holding her sire's blanket against her like a raiding-shield.

Chogah came inwards, slow, head tilted. She refused to share a tipo despite the distance travelled, insisting upon her own small habitation—set apart, even if it meant an extra horse.

What is she doing here?—what spinningKin traps does she think to set? Immediately Anahli banished it as unkind, untrue. Chogah had likely seen or heard Anahli's approach.

Indeed, the ancient eyes held concern, chiding Anahli's suspicions. "What has happened, ehši, to send you running home as if huntingKin nip your heels?"

Home. These smells, this tipo... not a damp, unwelcoming, hard-hearted fish eaters' Mound upon River.

And ai, but her eyes pounded in their sockets.

Eyes meet eyes to waken Spirit...

"My heart, whatever is the matter?" Chogah knelt, wrapping her arms about Anahli, who hesitated then burrowed grateful, heat-filled eyes against her aunt's ample breasts.

Spirit wakens our Mother's heart...

Chogah stroked Anahli's braids, murmured, "Did your dam humiliate you so? But she shows kindness even so; precocious ways will earn you no friends here, ehši. You must learn restraint. Wretched outLand ways loom too close for tolerance, here. Even River takes as much as She gives."

And the ebon cavern, squatting on the edge of their territory. Reminder. Threat.

Anahli squinched her eyes shut, surrounded by comfort though her thoughts sped panicky as unfriended horses. "River. River took Tokela's dam. His dam was... possessed, wasn't she?"

This seemed to confound Chogah. She pushed Anahli back; her eyes, ebon filmed here and there with faint, approaching clouds, narrowed like knives. "I do not speak ill of those who have walked on," she finally answered. "This is all true, what I tell you. Lakisa a'iliq was possessed, a'io. Not to the Spirits of thisLand, but that of Chepiś sorceries. I could not help her."

"But they let her live here. Stay."

"They did. There was the unborn child, you see."

"Tokela."

"He was named Tohwakelifitčiluka. Eyes of Stars. They have even taken away his name, here, out of fear. No child deserves to be born outcast." Chogah frowned suddenly, as if her thoughts unsettled her. "When he was born, the possession left Lakisa'ailiq. It was an oddling thing." Then a huff. "When they could no longer prove she was possessed, they allowed her to stay. But she seemed always... fragile, after."

The possession left her. Anahli's own thoughts were just as unsettling. What if the possession went with Tokela? What if... it was his?

Chogah was watching, gaze too canny. "Why these questions, ehši?"

Anahli started to pull back; Chogah's grip snugged at her wrists, held. "What made you come back, Hihlyanahli, when your chieftain has decreed your bed shall lie in the oških dens a'Naišwyrh for at least a Hoop and one Sun? Why ask after a male oških?"

Anahli shook her head.

"You saw him, didn't you?" Chogah pulled her close, peering even closer. "Did you see something in him to make you ask questions, to form others in your heart?"

Anahli didn't have to ask how Chogah knew such things; she had been Alekšu, still clutched to what Power she could.

Why was it permitted for an ancient fem to wrap such secrets for holding—using? Why could Chogah keep hold when others had it muted, appropriated, silenced?

"Already," Chogah said, quiet, "the risk is high for him. Cause for suspicion, isn't it? And this much is true: his birthing broke not only his mother's possession, but her Spirit. Poor Talorgan, for this much is also true: he lost both son and spouse to Chepiś sorcery."

The compassion was real enough, but Anahli also saw the canny gloss behind Chogah's gaze. Alekšu-that-was, waiting. Watching.

Wind rattled the door flap, sent a small gust into the tipo. Chogah started, glanced about. She seemed... confused? The stray breeze rose prickles upon Anahli's bare arms, prompting a memory held against another set of glossed-over eyes, luminous with Stars.

Remember. Mother's heart wakens...

"Wakens what?" Surely Chogah couldn't have heard the not-voice. "What has happened, ehši?"

"Nothing. My head hurts," Anahli answered, true enough. Her temples and heart both pounded fit to burst. Chogah was too close; she smelled of mould and sour milk, of a tipo too long closed away from Sky. "I just want to sleep one more dark in my own place."

Chogah took a breath as if to say something. It escaped in a sigh; with a clucking sound, she released Anahli. "Rest, then." Rising with a grunt, Chogah made her slow way outwards. At the still-open flap she paused, seemed to speak more to the hide than Anahli. "Perhaps I shall speak with your sire. Your dam listens to him overmuch. Perhaps he can persuade her to relent from this wrong-headed course." She looked around, then back towards Anahli. Her eyes gleamed: piercing, too canny.

"Ai'o. You must come back home, my Dancer. I shall speak with Alekšu."

It's but a game, great and complex. Full of promise.

So Aylaniś had told him before they'd entered the Council dens, as much reminder as coax. So she'd told him many times before he'd been allowed in the Council of chieftains. But unlike Aylaniś, Palatan had never enjoyed this sort of game, never enjoyed the underhanded machinations that passed for interaction. Alekšu was what he was. What he had no choice in becoming—or now, being. But had he fully realised the political—or afferent—implications?

If only they didn't insist upon making everything so absurdly complicated.

"...if you drive outliers from any place in your territory, they'll just move elsewhere. To the boundaries of sandClan, perhaps, where resources are already scant. Or here beside River, where MoundChieftain has enough difficulties, even with his own blood."

"I appreciate you are trying to make a point, Seguin," Sarinak growled. "Kindly make it with less insult. I'm fully aware of my own problems."

Seguin a'Nunkáhiti, leader of Forestlodge, can be trouble, Aylaniś had informed Palatan as they'd travelled to the Mound. And he'd listened. She'd canny instincts for such things. Indeed, the several

Suns of riding Riverwards had been filled with advice and trivia. *Seguin begrudges Sarinak's wide-flung control. Seguin knows he is unable to the challenge, but resentment makes him unwilling to bend his neck, even to Mound-chieftain. You've seen his like.*

She'd smiled as she said it. Palatan had *been* his like.

But now he was Alekšu, his own honour and an important curve along Council's Hoop. He could have demurred. Certainly Chogah'd only hied herself to First Running as she pleased—and often she hadn't pleased.

Save this one, and Palatan still wondered at the perversity of that.

Just as perverse, his own understanding as to why Chogah acted as she did, including preferring a closed tipo.

The Council pipe passed a second time round. Palatan gave the gaily painted bowl a fond stroke before pulling Smoke deep into his lungs. Within the bowl, Fire flickered greeting, smaller twin of the hearth's blaze.

"...suffering because stiff-necked midLands farmers refuse to suffer a few yakhling."

"Not all midLanders are so stiff-necked," Galenu a'Hassun pointed out with a lazy smile. "As I said before, in stoneClan territory, outliers are permitted to come and go." That smile betrayed the commonality Palatan shared with Galenu; they both preferred more than a token amount of Smoke aboard to deal with Council matters.

Well, two commonalities: Galenu's dam had been great-aunt to Palatan.

Dance and sparring had their places, raids and rutting too, but Smoke truly blunted the keen emotional edge of acute disagreement. The inevitable clash of differing customs and ways of being could erupt into something more resembling the flowing Firepaths of Naišihloyeh than any reasonable Council. Smoke had a necessary place—and had the surreptitious benefit of dulling Palatan's own Senses from roar to murmur. The forces running like hot blood beneath skin were that importunate. For now, what Fire lay behind his eyes was quiet—Smoked—within. Palatan could, as Našobok would say, "keep his heart in his body" for a change.

Another reason to loathe Council: taking Palatan from a lovemate he saw far too seldom. Though Našobok no doubt was busy indulging Tokela.

And there'd always been something more to *that* one. Palatan found himself wondering, not for the first time, if Tokela had begun maturing in more ways than those of a mere rutty oških.

"—does Alekšu say to this?"

Palatan disguised his unwary start as a shift of weight, seeking Aylaniś. Her lip tilted; she knew he'd been leagues away. Inattention wouldn't be discourtesy, considering how Smoke's effect could vary, but it nevertheless pointed out the newest to wear Alekšu's horns was too wayward, more skilled at being the trickster horse raider than wielding any authority.

Well, so be it. Palatan would rather knock someone off their mount with a well-placed blow than endure this endless prattle. And what secrets he had? N'da, not bartered for any price.

He straightened, one eyebrow raised. "Say again?"

Seguin smiled—more a smirk, and one Palatan longed to wipe from him. Not in Council, of course, but later, facedown upon Grandmother's apron. "I merely state how long it's been since Alekšu has graced this Council. Since you are not your predecessor—"

"Thankfully," Inhya put in, wry.

"—surely you've opinions?" Seguin continued. "Particularly since you are known to have... uh... close relations? With outliers?"

Palatan leaned forwards with a slight snarl. Fire, in Ša's place of honour, gave a flare upward; Palatan chided his co-tenant to silent patience. Not easy, considering the challenge nigh flying about the room; Palatan could See the bodytalk with eyes closed.

Sarinak leaned forwards and tended to the hearth, muttering about dry fuel and sap pockets.

"I have opinions about many things," Palatan finally answered, soft. "And considering my... close relations, as you say, you've also already guessed at least one. Unlike Chepiś or Matwau, outliers aren't Other. They're of us."

"There has already been too much talk of Other thisSun," a chieftain from dryLands demurred.

"For good reason," Aylaniś pointed out. She kept sliding her eyes to Palatan, query and concern.

Not that he blamed her. His heart hadn't felt properly in his body since he'd stepped from the Breaking Ground with victory in his hands. Chogah had carried her birthright carelessly, but many turnings of Hoop had given her ease beneath the added weight of so many Spirits. Perhaps emerging from the dark and solitude of Awakening and diving headfirst into Council busytalk hadn't been the smartest of transitions. And since crossing into River's territory, Palatan's nerves scraped all the more raw. He wasn't sure why, either.

The chieftain from midLands—the farmer at the centre of the debate—protested, "By their actions, outliers and outcasts choose Other. They are not my people. Why should I allow them to scavenge my Lands?"

"I was not aware any portion of thisLand belonged solely to you." Palatan didn't bother to so much as look up, kept peering into Fire's eyes.

There is not enough Smoke in thisLand to shut them up—or out. Ai, my co-tenant and Spiritmate—lend me strength!

And Fire answered in Ša's not-talk, soothing warmth that coalesced into *Always, my own.*

Several disapproving hisses echoed in the chamber—nothing to do with Fire, or Palatan. Agreement.

The farming chieftain held up his hands. "I meant nothing of the kind! Seguin is not the only one to note the... ah... lenience of those a'Šaákfo."

Palatan lifted his gaze then, subtle challenge belying the mild tone. "This much is true: my People aren't as willing to discard a tunic merely because it ill fits us. We prefer to find one who can wear it easily, give it a place. Less... wasteful."

Inhya, from her place beside Sarinak, gave a warning roll of her eyes. Aylaniś hid her smirk beneath a scratch of nose.

Galenu's soft chuckle echoed through the Council den.

"Brother of my spouse," Sarinak ventured, "your heart is great. But—"

"My heart's no greater than yours, spouse of my sister," Palatan riposted. "But my confusion, perhaps, holds greater. When we've Chepiś and Matwau upon our doorsteps—a fact those outliers you so vilify have bothered to share with those of us as *have* Clanrights—I have to admit I see little wisdom in worrying over our own kind."

"They are *not!*" the farming chieftain, stubborn as wabadeh, insisted.

"Our. Own. Kind." Rolling to a half-crouch, Palatan shrugged away his blanket. Fire reached upwards to hiss covert heat behind Palatan's eyes. Inwardly quieting his co-tenant, Palatan and smiled.

It was not a pleasant expression.

"They're of us. Blood of our blood. Cousins. Sisters. *Brothers.* Anyone who'd waste energy barring thisLand against our own kind? Instead of welcoming their help and using their knowledge to dampen a wild that might well scorch us all? That one is a superstitious k'šo who not only uses outLander's talk, but deserves what ša receives of it."

Silence. Palatan slid a swift glance to Aylaniś. Her mouth quirked in wry agreement.

Still in silence, Palatan quit the den.

Quiet, too quiet. Even the oddling not-sounds that had dogged his steps since... since Chepiś... those, too, were silent. Only the Riverling sink pool, feeding from top to bottom, lapping at Her banks as Tokela climbed the weeping tree wykupeh and settled against the weeping tree's sturdy bark.

Normally, he was good at the wait.

Normally, he didn't mind being alone.

But too much spun through his Spirit. What had happened with Mordeleg? With the *t'rešalt?*

With Anahli?

Tokela stared at the hareKin mask, hung up on the doorway, willing ša to answer.

Ša didn't, but the sink pool did; beckoning and promising, if not answers, at least easement of questions. As Sun sank beyond the far trees, Tokela clambered down.

He took the mask with him, setting ša carefully on the sandy bank like a guardian, and went for a swim. Not merely a swim, though; he glided through a haze of water and thought, diving deep and coming up for breath only when he absolutely had to, and finally everything went numb and slow and chill.

Aware, this time, when he'd company. But this time the murk was clean, silt and water as opposed to treacherous slime and undertow. The Riverling seemed to encourage, press him forwards.

Tokela didn't want to fathom any more complexities, not now. Nor did he have the courage to approach. He stood, River tickling his belly, as Našobok squatted on the bank, also waiting.

"I was afraid I'd have to come looking for you again."

I was afraid you might not come looking. Again, awkward, too complex, too exposed. Talk stuck to the back of Tokela's mouth. Again. He trailed his fingers in the water, tiny sketches, then noticed what he was doing and stilled his hands.

Was Našobok just giving Tokela breath? Or had he reconsidered sharing such breath?

"What did you do with Mordeleg?"

"Hunh." Našobok shifted, foot to foot. Tokela suddenly realised: his cousin was uncertain, too. "Let's say I set some things in motion. And if none will finish those things, I will. Either way, Mordeleg won't be in a position to bother you again. Let his own people deal with him. Hopefully with a lodging pole."

The thought of Mordeleg getting clobbered with a well-peeled tree trunk tucked a grin into Tokela's cheek.

"Look at me, Tokela."

Uncertain, Tokela did so. Našobok still hunched on the bank, resting his forearms on his knees. But he had taken up the hareKin mask, was twirling ša in his fingers.

"Ai," he ventured, very soft. "In thisNow you bear a very different face than when we Danced." A frown teased at Našobok's brow as he considered the mask, almost thoughtfully.

Tokela found he'd talk for this as well; still awkward, but there. He gestured to the mask. "It was *that* face."

"Was it?" Našobok's eyes met Tokela's own, darksight glinting in the full Moons flickering through the trees. Long heartbeats spun out, heavy yet underlain with the soft soothe of the Riverling's song.

Tokela looked away. It seemed a nest of viperKin lay writhing in his belly, all coils and tiny, stinging fangs.

"Do you always run to Her?"

He didn't have to ask, he knew what Našobok meant. Forbidden, but this more sweet than rue; Našobok's voice held a low and reverent quiver, which the Riverling—and so River—somehow echoed. She lapped at Tokela's belly, soothing and startling both. He was beginning to wonder if She had always been present, outwards and inwards, even before the tides of Changing had begun flowing through him, before...

Before the *t'rešalt*. Before Chepiś.

Panic rose then flirted itself dry within him. There was nowhere left to run. And Našobok's expression held: open, accepting.

Does She speak to you, too?

Sometimes... I think She does.

Neither did Našobok turn away; he just kept squatting there, chin on forearms, arms about bent knees and toes digging into the sand. The steady regard should have been uncomfortable, a warning flare within Tokela's Spirit—*too close, too close to your secrets*. Instead, it held comfort.

Našobok was here. Even as Anahli, somehow, had been. Listening. Not judging. Not waiting with white-rimmed eyes for the half-breed to do something Other. Just... *Here*.

And it tumbled forth. Not what Tokela truly meant to speak, but nonetheless what lay within his heart. "I didn't know Mordeleg was following me. I should have... paid attention. Inhya's right about that."

Našobok seemed puzzled.

"He saw the mask's Power, too. Just as you did."

"You keep making such talk. If you mean there was nothing of you in Dance, I don't believe you."

"Then you don't understand what a mask is for."

Našobok's eyebrows went up. He reared back, ever so slightly, then rolled forwards to sit on his bent knees. The clouds veiling Sister and Brother Moons gusted aside, pooling their light downwards.

There were still smears of oil on Našobok's chest and thighs, catching light as he shifted. Tokela went weak-kneed just with the sight of him. Particularly where oil splotched a faint scrim over the tattoo on his belly, particularly where it glittered on that beringed nipple. Particularly considering he had gotten the oil from Tokela's own skin.

Wind blew across Tokela's neck, a light touch that set warmth first, then wet chill. He shivered. "You were raised here."

"I was indeed." It was wry; Našobok gently tossed the mask back onto the bank. "I understand masks better than you might think."

"Then you should believe me. Should know. It's easy to... better to... when none knows wha—*who*—you are. Even you. When you saw me, you stopped. Because it was me. You saw the mask, not me, and when... when I..." Talk started to tangle again, unwieldy and untrustworthy; Tokela repeated, "The mask."

"The mask only covered up part of you—"

"The important part, obviously."

"N'da." A sudden grin. "N'da, not really."

"You're making fun."

"Only a little."

"Is..." Tokela's throat closed up, tight; he made it work. "You wish we hadn't. You... touched me, made Dance with me, and..." The memory of that rose him again, here and now, cool Riverwater merely a support for what was kindling just beneath Her surface. "Now you pity me."

"Tokela!" It was a growl. "How can you possibly think—?"

"I know I'm... odd. I know I don't look like anyone else."

"Sink me! Of course you don't look a'Naišwyrh. You look a'Šaákfo. There's an entire tribe of firstPeople with your look, cousin. Your mother's blood came from dusk as much as dawn. How can you not know this?"

Tokela squinched his eyes against a sudden, humiliating sting.

"Have you even bothered to ask? Ai, Tokela." Našobok lurched to his feet, running hands over his face and chasing back through his hair. "Has it truly come to pass no one has told you how lovely you are?"

And Tokela didn't know what to say to that. Had little breath to make an answer even if adequate talk would glide from his tongue. Instead his chest heaved and hot, sparse trails spilled salt-wet down over his cheeks. It was only then he realised he was weeping. But silent; as silent as his throat.

An utterly foul curse from the bank, then a slosh and rush of steps surging as quickly as they could into hip-deep water.

"Ai, sink me is right, you've already sunk me too far. Just drown me this time and be done with it, leave my bones to wash up on a blighted shore." A growl and grumble, and before Tokela could turn around, Našobok's hard arms had wrapped around him and yanked him close. "I really don't think I've ever seen anyone cry as fetchingly as you."

Tokela suddenly didn't care what weakness it betrayed, what tale it told if he should submit, only that he could, that he wanted to. He set his teeth against Našobok's forearms, sucked in a breath that strained against the tight hold, then reached up and gripped back, slender, strong fingers digging into hard tendons.

"You think I saw a mask?" Našobok's whisper was almost angry. "I saw beauty and grace that made my heart leap. You were a wilding current, pulling me in your wake." Našobok bent closer still—Tokela hadn't thought it possible—and whispered against his ear, "I saw *you*, Star Eyes."

What the Chepiś had tried to call him. What he'd refused to

allow. Tokela didn't like hearing it aloud, and none seemed to like voicing it. It was a reminder, even if it was what his name meant—another mask, Commingling talk. But no one, not even Madoc, used this particular intimacy. And the way Našobok spoke, so low and soft and... and close—so close... too close... not close enough—breath teasing warm against Tokela's cheek. The scent conjured Smoke and tulapaiś, sweat and sex and brine. Tokela's heart skipped against the too-tight drumskin of his breast, thoughts running scattered, water over breaker rocks.

"And if we're having awkward, insecure confessions, I have several for you." Našobok's grip tightened, shook, sending River in rippled spirals about their close-hoved bodies. "I never thought to tread the Mound's circuit again, and I never dreamed it would be you who'd Dance me around like this. I'm River-walker and Wyrh-chieftain, but in our birthing-tribe I'm nothing. Outlier. You and I have shared many a story, but I never thought you would want to share this one."

It could have been kind lies or indeed a confession, and all Tokela wanted was to deny—*nothing, outlier?*—to affirm—*want you, want you...*

Tokela twisted in the firm embrace until he could reach Našobok's face with both hands and grip. Hard. "You," he gritted, "talk too much."

Našobok's face held no pity and no lies. "I guess I talk too much when... well, when I'm not sure what else to do. And if I talk too much, well, you don't make enough talk to tell anyone what you want for dinner, much less—" Again the mellifluous voice cracked, went rough; it weakened Tokela's knees. "Tell me, Star Eyes. Plain and pitiless. There's no reading your bodytalk now where I could only a short while ago. What do you want of me, here, in thisNow?" Not so soft anymore, it echoed the rapid drum of Tokela's heart.

Tell me. Here. In thisNow.

Were there other Nows? For River was quiet, quieter than She'd ever been since he'd returned from Šilombiš'okpulo.

Tokela reached out with trembling fingers. Angling his head forwards until his forehead rested against Našobok's chest, he grasped Našobok's hand and cupped it to his nape.

He'd seen it done, this intimate and evocative lover's gesture, and had never truly fathomed why.

Until now.

I'm speechless with want. My head is heavy, my eyes spin, my heart wants to fly. Only your heart can carry me. Only your heart can drum the truth for me.

Against Tokela's forehead, beneath the thick bone of Našobok's breast, another beat lurched and quickened. Našobok whispered Tokela's name, and the fingers at Tokela's nape twitched, slid up to tangle where a braidlock had, only that morning, hung, binding him to an existence in which he no longer belonged.

And River, silent, curled about them close as skin.

"Thisnow," Tokela breathed. "*Here.*"

Palatan didn't return to Council. Instead he returned to his tipo, merely to find Anahli nested in the heap of their blankets, asleep.

Odd.

Arrow didn't think so. Giving a low purl in his throat, the fleethound began the arduous process of curling into the blankets beside one of his People: first the circling, then the decision of location, then a fold of his sinewy body—front-first of course—before rolling onto his side against Anahli's blanket-heaped form.

She barely stirred.

Palatan tucked a smile into his cheek and knelt, regarding his eldest daughter with cocked head. A soft, curious sigh escaping pursed lips, he reached out and tucked the blankets closer, traced a light touch over Anahli's cheek.

Another oddity: she was radiating heat like a well-stoked Firepit.

Black eyes opened, blearily took him in. "Yeka?"

Palatan hesitated but a half heartbeat before lowering himself gently next to her. He'd never been one to waste a chance. "I am here, sa ehši."

Anahli lay silent for several breaths, then ventured, "I'm... not so well. I wanted to lie here. It smells like home."

Her voice quavered, vulnerable reminder of the leggy, open-hearted ahlóssa who'd shadowed Palatan both mounted and afoot. Recent memory seemed implausible; surely this wasn't the oških who'd only thisSun openly humiliated one of the Spear Dancers and defied her elders.

"I see," Palatan answered, quiet. "Is there pain?"

Anahli seemed to consider the question before answering, dull. "My eyes hurt. My temples pound..." A frown gathered at her brow and she shrugged the blankets down. She was still dressed in her Dance finery. "N'da, not just that. More like... hiveKin. Buzzing about in their Dance, filling up their little lodges with sweet and wax until they're too... small." She looked up at him, cheeks flushed dark, and Palatan froze.

Those eyes glittered, with an overlay of oddling white and turquoise.

It wasn't the normal gleam of darksight in shadowed places. Nor was it the backwash of any co-tenant he'd ever seen. It flickered like tiny lights within Dark's upended basket, like...

Stars.

This was impossible.

Sucking in a long, slow breath, Palatan gritted his teeth and reached out, put gentle fingers to his daughter's throat. Bent his head and breathed the invocation, seeking.

And heard. N'da, more *felt*, indeed as if hiveKin had taken residence in her heart. Thousands of tiny wings vibrating, a breath pouring into the back of Palatan's throat to rest there, humming. So soft, so present; surely to release them all he'd to do was just breathe...

Within him, as if teased by the current of many translucent wings, Fire expanded and lit the backs of his eyes, pure and ecstatic. Palatan had no heart to quell the response. This was his child.

And it comforted, reassured his acute senses with familiarity: *Grandmother's own. Ours.*

"Yeka?"

"Peace," he murmured, tracing a tiny sign at her throat. With it, he released his Power and opened himself to working. Though he could not remove those tiny, industrious Spirit forms, he could ease them into temporary complacency. Fire murmured consent, morphing into soft embers. Smoke, and quiet...

A hiss. Fire blazed upwards then gusted sideways, guttered. Palatan swayed and nigh lost his balance, saving himself from falling atop Anahli with a swift prop of arms.

Bracing against the sudden gust of Wind, he glanced around.

Crouched there, transfixed.

The tipo had vanished, leaving them both surrounded by nothingness...

N'da, not nothingness. He heard water. He felt Earth beneath him. But he gazed into forever. Into darkness, heavy and immense, into which, slowly, spackles of light began to appear: first one, then several, then more, and more. So many, like Sky's night basket. Uncountable, slicking faint lights upon the waters and silhouetting the mound rising beneath them. Ai'o, rising, as if he and his daughter had come from Beneath Worlds and arrived home, whilst above them hung the lost Spirits in the wide weave of Sky's basket, shining down upon Grandmother to light the waters.

Suddenly the basket shook, upended itself. And Stars began to fall.

Palatan tried to tear himself from the contact, squinching his eyes shut and gritting his teeth, hunching like hareKin beneath a predator's drift of shadow. For long breaths the Vision refused to loose him: he saw tailed Stars falling all around them, heard them hissing as they struck the waves, flinched from the burn of sparks...

Finally, the Vision released him. Palatan twisted sideways,

thudded onto his back beside Anahli and lay there, panting, for what seemed like forever.

Only when Arrow started licking his face did Palatan dare open his eyes. A familiar, homely sight met his gaze: the seasoned hides and poles of his family's tipo. No Stars. No basket up-ending them to fall upon thisLand.

No Chepiś sorcery slithering through his daughter's heart.

"Yeka?" Anahli's brow was furrowed; she'd risen to her elbows, curious. Her eyes were sleepy-dark, normal. Lit with concern but nothing more.

She had seen nothing. Fire curled in the hearth, dozy embers, and when Palatan sought silent reassurance, his co-tenant oozed complacency.

"Yeka? What's wrong?"

"All is well, my heart." His movements cautious—muscles quivering, waiting for the next blow—Palatan scooted back over beside Anahli. "I merely slipped on the furs and knocked my head."

"You must be careful," she fussed, burrowing back into the furs. "Sometimes, Yeka, you're a bit clumsy."

With a chuckle, he cupped her cheek. "I am indeed." But his thoughts whirled, still in thrall to the Vision.

Of all the Elementals, Stars were no longer of firstPeople. Not even when People walked on. They had once gone to Stars, but that way had been blocked. Few Spirits could make the journey, opting instead to sink into Grandmother's embrace.

Stars belonged to Chepiś, now. Chepiś had stolen the Kinship for their own twisted uses. Even as they longed to steal Grandmother Herself.

Arrow crept back into bed, this time folding into a furry, fawn pillow. Anahli sighed, curling one arm over the dog and ducking her face into Palatan's palm.

The pang of it was sweet and rue. "Better then, Nani?" With light purpose he used the pet name—gleaned from her own first attempts to speak it.

Another drowsy smile. "You never call me that anymore."

"I do. Just not often enough."

"Why does she hate you so?"

Palatan blinked, startled. "Who?"

"Chogah."

Palatan leaned on Arrow—who huffed content—and stroked Anahli's hair. So many answers, none of them simple... save one. "She wants what is mine. She always has."

"What is yours."

"A'io, eldest daughter of my chieftain. I have a few irreplaceable treasures. You, for one."

A frown; with firm fingertips Palatan rubbed it back into complacency. "Enough for now. Sleep. Sleep long and well, with pleasant dreamings." A tiny push, a hint of Smoked somnolence should any hiveKin linger.

Arrow grunted, shifted, and burrowed in. Anahli's fingers twitched in his fur—once, thrice—then stilled.

Palatan stayed there for some time, watching her sleep.

Found himself remembering a long, hard wintering seven years before Anahli's birth. Another defiant oških, crying for his Vision within the vast deeps beneath the cavern mound a'Šaákfo. Fire had woken, sprung from Palatan's singular torch to catch others, lighting the cavern walls. Beneath his feet the caldera had stirred, rumbling and smouldering, flowing beneath him...

Had greeted him.

Palatan would never forget the smell... the *taste*. Nor could he deny what he had become in the consequence of that Vision.

Chogah had tried to deny it. Ai, had she tried.

And now, this. Palatan hadn't experienced a Vision this strong in many summerings. And to have one here?

Here, where remained an outLand presence he'd Sensed but once before, in any children of the Alekšu'ín.

◊ ◊ ◊

15
ACCORDS

Galenu a'Hassun took his time returning to his guesting-den. Old eyes didn't pierce the dark like they once had, and admittedly, his walk came a bit unsteady. But surely it could be considered disrespectful, to refuse or waste prime Smoke. Naišwyrh'uq had enviable trading connexions; there were places downriver that produced the best leaf thisLand had ever seen.

And this First Running had produced the most entertainment Galenu had seen in some time. New information, stories and gossip to catch up on, a bit of scandal to liven the Dance circuit—who could ask for more? He and Nechtoun would have plenty to talk about over nextSun's first meal...

Nechtoun. The reminder sobered. Reaching out, Galenu touched the curved stone walls and paused to gain his bearings. While the youthful elements of Council diverted, not all of them were nonsense.

Change isn't coming. Change is here.

Sarinak always claimed the wyrhling hadn't the sense Grandmother gave a wabadeh in rut; yet the wyrhling's speech had proven exactly who knew what and how. Wayward, a'io, but Našobok was no great fool.

Galenu resumed his progress through the tunnel. A fair courtesy, to be quartered with Mound-chieftain's immediate family during the height of First Running. More from Nechtoun's influence, certainly, than any change of heart in Inhya. She'd never liked him.

A smirk touched Galenu's lip as he circumnavigated a pair of coupling oških fems, a heaving elder who'd imbibed too much, a pack of noisy ahlóssa who nigh trampled him on their way to who-knew-what, then finally found the set of switchbacked passages he sought. A small climb, with openings that allowed a view of River. The moored craft lay quiet beneath the Moons, rocking.

Ai, another reminder—he had to find Našobok come Sun's rising, make arrangements for the shipment. Perhaps charm more talk about what he and Grass Weaver had hinted about in open Council. They seemed to know more than even Galenu himself.

Granted, Galenu's own outLand connexions had dried up, or so it seemed. It had been a brace of summerings since he'd seen his acquaintances. Maloh always brought him the oddest things, as if she thought he were ahlóssa, swayed by shiny baubles. Well, all right, some baubles were a lot of fun. But after the business with Lakisa, what visits Maloh, Jorda and Sivan had always made—middark, of course, and gone like mist—had ceased. As if they felt responsible.

Galenu sighed. No one was responsible for what happened. Just as none could have stopped Lakisa once she'd made her mind up. And with such a renewal of ill will hereabouts, it would be imprudent to travel past the Threshold and seek them out.

Old Grass Weaver had been forward, to say what she had. Galenu had earned his travels, and the old fem had no rights to imply otherwise. Yet Grass Weaver was right about the encroaching outLanders. Maloh had given dark hints Galenu's way about taking care where he wandered; it seemed her own kind had expanded their horizons to include slavers and zealots.

A'io, the rest of Galenu's fellow chieftains were fools did they not heed the outliers' warnings. Even Nechtoun.

Galenu shook his head, let out a grumbling sigh. Nechtoun was, well, not himself. It was the worst insult to give any a'Naišwyrh, to be sure, but it was the truth. Galenu hadn't meant to upset him so, particularly in front of their fellows. It had seemed more like an old debate of their youth, where things had either ended in fisticuffs or a bout of rough-playful rutting. Talk was all they bandied of late, of course; he'd not meant to cause such distress in his oldest and dearest friend.

Another set of switchbacks. Galenu slowed, feeling his way.

Most surprising had been the sight of the Alekšu attending Nechtoun—and that Alekšu's identity. Of course Galenu had known about the business with Chogah; he kept up on the doings of his dam's birthing-tribe. But no question he was getting old, because he'd not fully processed its meaning.

Palatan as Alekšu? The young, wayward tyah who'd failed every attempt at wresting control from Chogah, and finally been married off to the tribe's chieftess? He'd walked out of Council, also, with such strong talk. Galenu had assumed that Chogah had long ago ground the mutiny out of *that* one.

Of course, neither was Palatan a wayward oških, no more than Galenu himself was in his prime.

Nechtoun's snores filled the corridor. Galenu followed them, flung back the doe hide that covered the den from which they emanated. An uncovered bowl of gleaming-stones both warmed and illuminated the windowless den. A thoughtful gift for thinner blood and elder eyes—Inhya might not like him, but neither would she shirk her duty as hostess. With a happy sigh, Galenu headed to the bedshelf, shrugging from his cloak.

Instead he nearly went toes over haunch across another gift.

It had been left in the middle of the den, trussed and gagged like hunting tribute.

"How am I supposed to impress upon our offspring that making games with Fire is generally frowned upon?"

"I knew it was you." Palatan didn't take his eyes off the hearth, nor did he move his hands away. Fire leapt upwards, curling about and caressing his fingers. A comfort, to test his control—and a way, curiously enough, to siphon away what quicksilver and oddling flames still ran rampant along his nerves.

Aylaniś trod over, slow and silent as hunting wolfKin. "Nor should you be in the open like this. What are you doing out here?"

Palatan pursed his lips towards the tipo behind them. "Anahli sleeps, guarded by Arrow."

"I suppose there's a good reason you didn't march her straight back to the oških dens?"

He shrugged.

"Are you and the Wolf in competition for the hardest shell and squishiest heart?"

Another shrug. There was no speaking to this, not yet. Not when he wasn't even sure what he had Seen.

With a shiver, Aylaniś pulled her fringed shawl closer and came over to kneel behind Palatan. "It smells of Rain constantly here—and feels damp as an outlying cavern. I always forget how it is. Perhaps I too grow soft, used to our caldera and the warmed caverns of our wintering." She spooned close, nipped at his ear. "I still remember the first time I came upon you doing such a thing."

"You shrieked like raptorKin. I became... distracted."

"You became *burned*."

"Not the first time with you, my Hawk." Palatan chuckled as she gave his ear another nip.

"For burning? Or distraction?"

"Mm. You obviously think much more of my control now."

"I wish control was a game you would not play." Another nip, sharper. Palatan acquiesced, sliding his fingers from Fire's grasp. "I thought you'd be well amidst another game, between the furs with Našobok. I'd hoped he'd be distracting you." Yet another nip, just as sharp, and Aylaniś nestled closer, one hand sliding around his chest and tracing down his belly.

Palatan closed his eyes, leaned back. Then with one swift motion, he twisted and pushed her back, pinning her to the ground.

"Ai'ye!" Aylaniś pummelled at his chest, mock grievance. "Beast!"

"Sss. You'll wake her."

"That wouldn't break my heart; we could have our furs back."

"When have we ever needed a soft bed, my chieftain?" He bent closer and licked her nose. "I would dearly love to have our Wolf distracting me. But he's obligation to a young lover thisdark, so I imagine you'll have to do."

In the next instant, Aylaniś had hooked her legs about Palatan, flipped him onto his back—hard—and straddled him. "Have to do?" she repeated with a sharp-toothed grin, thumbs laced over his breastbone. "Perhaps I had hopes for two stallions in my furs thisdark instead of one—so it seems you're the one who should step up his performance."

Palatan laughed. It warbled into a sigh as Aylaniś laid a hand across his mouth, rolled her hips. Said "Sss, quiet."

Sometime later, after they'd wrestled and revelled, sweated and tangled and howled—softly, to be true; they were not in their own place—they lay beside the hearth with heartbeats commingling, breath slowing.

"It will be better," Aylaniś said.

"Better might kill me," Palatan replied, drowsy and purposeful misunderstanding. He grunted as she poked his ribs—it, too, was lazy.

"My first few Councils, I thought I would die of boredom. Or fury."

Fury. Ai'o, that he well understood. His eyes flickered to where Fire crouched, sullen with the damp but waiting. Always waiting.

"Yap, yap, yap, neverending."

Palatan chuckled. "That's exactly how Našobok described it."

"Well, he's right. Saying so much, doing nothing." Aylaniś pushed up, stretched. Sleek with sweat, Fire gleamed over the curve of breasts and shoulders, caressing the soft swell of belly that had nurtured their children.

Palatan reached out, trailed fingers over her skin, always surprised how the dark glitter of it didn't smudge his fingertips like hallowed, fecund Earth. "So remind me again, why?"

"Someone has to make sensible talk. Letting anger rule your head and feet does nothing."

"I had to leave. Next time will be easier. I know what to guard against."

Aylaniś nuzzled his hand, a keen understanding worth every oath strained, long ago, when he'd been forced to reveal what he was. She and Našobok... they knew all that could be known or shared.

"There are better things to consider." Palatan smoothed his hand down between their bodies. She pulsed with heartbeat and heat, slick against his fingertips.

Aylaniś hummed pleasure into his neck. "Perhaps we should

consider leaving nothing for our ungrateful Riverwalker. Abandoning our furs to roll in another's!" Aylaniś slid her hips forwards then back against his hand, slow and thick and lovely. Fire fingered her ribs as they expanded, His light tonguing her nipples into peaks as rigid as Palatan himself was becoming—and exposed the stutter of her throat as Aylaniś threw her head back, ground down against him.

He rolled her over, pushed her down. She gave an abrupt, painful yip and kept rolling; they ended up on their sides, face to face.

"Wha—?"

Reaching beneath, her grimace turned to triumph as she brought forth one of the bone-and-feather pins she wore in her braids.

Palatan snorted, reached over and twined a fallen strand about his fingers, admiring the gleam like polished, darkest bronze. "No pointed sticks. No torture thisdark. You have my secrets."

"Most of them, anyway." Aylaniś leaned closer and ran her tongue over his lower lip, sank her teeth lightly there.

Most of them. He pulled her close, sudden and uncertain, shrugged it off by laying a trail, with lips and tongue, down the tattoo on her arm.

"Perhaps," she said, breath quickening, "a little bit of torture?"

"Ai, are you two the only ones here, then?"

Aylaniś stiffened, sighed. Palatan gave a curse, rocking up to his elbows to glare at the ahlóssa standing on the other side of their small hearth.

"Kuli chieftain-son!" Aylaniś twisted about. "Where are your manners? Can't you see we're *occupied*?"

"I surely can see that," Kuli said with a sigh. "But I'd truly hoped Uncle Našobok would be here too."

As if cued, Rain began pelting them; huge drops, gaining in momentum.

They all three ducked for the tipo, startling both Arrow and Anahli from sleep, and ended up tucked together, laughing fit to burst. Just like before, Palatan thought, as his daughter and his spouse fussed at each other over a quickly cobbled meal of trail food, whilst his son went to milk the mares.

Perhaps the Vision was merely too much Smoke, too much tulapaiś, too much... yap-yap-yap.

"He says he was viciously attacked."
"Without or with further provocation?"
Galenu paused.

"Surely," Sarinak prompted, "provocation enough existed in Dance. I told Tokela to leave it, but oških hearts beat hot. Perhaps this matter can be solved between us alone, and the humiliation of being beaten twice by a slighter opponent"—a quick, proud smile ticced his broad face, slight but there—"teach a lesson in humility to your oških."

As far as Galenu was concerned, Mordeleg likely earned that lesson. But his Clan's honour also lay at stake. "The oških has demanded arbitration, as is his right. He says Tokela promised to lie with him and instead lay in wait to kill him. In light of that, he's important evidence against Tokela that will prove his false nature."

Sarinak gave a low growl, stalking from the door where he had admitted Galenu into his den. By the hearth, Inhya continued pouring fragrant bark tea into several birchbark cups. Necessary, the stimulant; it was not yet Sun's rising.

"That's a lie!" Madoc, on the rug beside his parents' hearth, clambered to his feet. His dam stayed him with a look.

"Sit, son."

Madoc obeyed, reluctant but taking advantage: Inhya hadn't harnessed his mouth. "But it's a lie! Tokela hates Mordeleg, and he'd never—!"

Another look from Inhya, forbidding.

"Kindly forgive my son, Galenu Hassun-chieftain," Sarinak offered, even as Inhya said through her teeth, "You will excuse your rudeness, Madoc." She pulled Madoc to his feet and gave a slight push forwards.

"There's no need," Galenu said, his eyes steady upon Madoc. "I don't think he was calling me the liar—were you, chieftain-son?"

Big-boned and gawky, Madoc had the promise of his people's height and breadth, as well as the tawny hue to his hair that ran sporadically through the Mound People. Inhya gave another push, Madoc grimaced and met Galenu's gaze—ai, no midLands ahlóssa would meet an elder's eyes so boldly. Madoc's had interesting glints of carmine amidst sepia.

He would break hearts, this one. Handsome, likely a chieftain himself some Sun, Madoc a'Naišwyrh would have his pick of mates.

"Nevertheless," Inhya prompted, bringing a cup of tea over to Galenu.

He took it with a grateful nod, sipped as she went over to stand with Sarinak.

Madoc tucked his chin, firm. "I wasn't calling you false, stone-chieftain, but Mordeleg has to be lying. Tokela has every reason to take him down, but he wouldn't..." Madoc's Sun-bronzed cheeks darkened further. "Wouldn't."

Galenu took this in. "You are close with Tokela, then, ahlóssa?"

Interesting, how Madoc looked away. "He's my brother."

"My youngest," Sarinak put in with a weary air, "has been foolish and surly about his brother's doings. Unreasonable, if understandable."

Madoc flushed harder. Anger, then, not embarrassment.

"As to my other son, it would be equally as foolish to deny Tokela can be more trouble than not. But this?" Sarinak shrugged.

Inhya continued. "What your oških has confessed to you, Galenu stone-chieftain, seems unlikely."

Galenu often found much of Mordeleg's claims unlikely, but he wasn't about to admit that. Not here, not yet.

"Until lastSun, Tokela showed little sign of"—Inhya considered her talk—"interest."

"In Mordeleg?"

"In anyone," Sarinak muttered.

Inhya slid him a slight frown. Sarinak gave an almost-imperceptible shrug as she continued. "You sent Mordeleg here because he proved intractable in midLands. He's continued to be so. Restrictions anger him; not that I care, he'll follow them. But Mound-chieftain and his fellow oških are the only ones keeping him contained. They outfight him, of course."

Of course. Despite the smugness, Galenu had to agree. "I'd hoped a change of place would help. And time."

"He's been here nearly three Moons," Inhya reminded.

"The other oških detest him." Madoc was scowling. "He's weak and they know it."

"Madoc," Sarinak growled, "if you cannot keep your tongue still, I'll send you out."

Madoc slumped, aggrieved, but shut his mouth.

"What happened in Dance merely exhibited your oških's malicious nature." Inhya put hands on hips.

"Hunh. With some males, rutting can be as much struggle as satisfaction." Sarinak gave another shrug, this time with a twitch of a grin. "I'm sure Galenu remembers what I mean."

"Neither memory nor motion has thoroughly failed me yet," Galenu answered, wry, and offered his own slight jab. "I, too, saw Spear Dance. Tokela made his choice—unsuitable, perhaps, but it wasn't Mordeleg."

Sarinak's face went stony. Madoc's hadn't that self-possession—his glower could surely melt the well-swept floor. Jealousy stuck out over him like quills. Galenu had to hide a smile. This one was his dam's son, all right.

"Where is Mordeleg now?" Inhya asked.

"In my den." Galenu's turn, now, to shrug at their scepticism. "I doubt he'll stray. I told him if he wished a hearing, he needed to wait Mound-chieftain's convenience."

"I will listen," Sarinak agreed. "To him and Tokela both."

"I can find Tokela!" Madoc piped up, and Inhya, after throwing a silent question at her spouse, consented.

"After the meal," she added, making a grab for Madoc as he leapt into motion.

"Later thisSun should be convenient for arbitration," Sarinak added. "I will gather four elders, and you, Galenu, are allowed a midLands witness. Bring that witness and Mordeleg to the Council dens after midSun meal."

Galenu tilted his head to his hosts, replaced his cup next to the others by the hearth, then departed.

"You're smiling." Tokela's fingers smoothed, back and forth, across a wide, satiny scar tracing from Našobok's ribcage to his belly. He seemed fascinated.

"I'm thinking of pleasant things," Našobok told him, riffling fingers through the dusky, fur-soft forelock that would not stay out of Tokela's eyes. "And looking at you."

Such a simple—and true—compliment had altogether too much power. Yet sheathed in Tokela's innocence was an intriguing edge, a keen blade of wit and want beginning to sharpen itself.

Našobok might end up with a few more scars from it before this was all over. He smiled again. *Ai, bring it.*

They both had their toes in River, swishing companionably back and forth. There was a lambency within Tokela, one the darkling trust of newfound intimacy had explored and started to free. As if he would sprout wings and take to them, if only he hadn't been told his entire life that flying was impossible.

Našobok welcomed impossibility. He closed his eyes, sighed, and thought upon every heartbeat leading to this one pulsepoint, thisNow.

When he opened his eyes again, Tokela still watched him. Almost too closely. Restless, in the wake of Našobok's silence.

I thought you liked quiet. When did you become so anxious? The question hurt Našobok's heart. Too many questions about too many things...

Enough. Better to make more talk in a way they both comprehended. He grabbed a handful of chestnut hair to pull Tokela close—

"There you are!!"

One of Našobok's canines grazed Tokela's lip; both of them winced before rolling apart.

Kuli stood not two lengths from them, fists planted on his hips and cinnabar head cocked. "Everyone's looking for you, Tokela. You're in trouble again. And Uncle! What are you doing lying with Tokela?"

Tokela gave a slight growl, lurched upwards, belatedly seemed disconcerted by the fact he was very erect. Ai, then, so was Našobok.

So it was decided: after bedding Palatan one final time, Našobok would have to kill him so he couldn't breed any more like this stealthy, precocious little being.

Who refused to shut his yap. "I know you were dancing with him, and I know that usually leads to a lot of rubbing up against each other—"

Anger and thwarted lust had joined battle across Tokela's expression, quickly losing ground to a third combatant: sheer astonishment.

"Blood myself, I swear I will," Našobok murmured. "If only that reedy voice breaks soon."

Tokela made a sound somewhere between a chuckle and a snort. It was true: Kuli could doubtless be heard leagues down-River.

Nor was he showing any signs of stopping. "See, it's one thing for you to dance with Uncle, but you shouldn't be rutting him—"

Shouldn't? Tokela mouthed, eyes wide.

"—because he belongs to Yeka and Aška!"

Tokela turned those wide eyes to Našobok.

The only answer Našobok could make was laughter. Under its pressure, a smirk touched Tokela's mouth.

"A complicated story for another time." Grabbing for his clout, Našobok gained his feet. With a wince, he angled the sodden leather about his hips. That put the finish to it, even more than a mouthy little ahlóssa.

Našobok sighed. "So you've found us, Little Fox. What trouble, and who's looking?"

"Galenu stone-chieftain, for one," Kuli said. "Making all sorts of talk about someone dumping one of his Clan just inside his guesting-den, trussed and gagged like bait to trap lionKin."

Našobok grinned. Tokela's puzzlement was beginning to slide into gratification.

"Then I went to find Madoc only to hear Uncle Sarinak letting loose—he is not happy, I'll tell you, and said if there's trouble to be found, Tokela will find—Ai! I'm just repeating what he said, I swear!" Kuli clipped onto the end of his recital as Tokela made a threatening gesture his way.

"And you say *I* talk too much," Našobok murmured Tokela's direction, finding himself treated to a darkening of those freckled-sepia cheeks and another smile.

"Anyway, Anahli would say 'all is chaos'—only I think she rather likes it that way—but no one seems at all happy and least of all that Mordeleg. He has to stay in stone-chieftain's dens and didn't even get to break his fast—which is worse than being tied up if you ask me—and Aunt Inhya wants him out of here and kept growling as much at Uncle Sarinak, which made *him* all the more growly, and Madoc was s'posed to come looking for you, Tokela, since you're not there—obviously—but you know how Madoc is, when I found out what he was doing he didn't want me to come, and since he had something to do before he *could* come, I figured I would come find Tokela on my own. I'm not sure, though, that they knew you were off rutting Uncle Našobok."

Finally, Kuli took a breath. Našobok tried to speak.

It was in vain. "Aška thought you were supposed to be in our dens to break your fast, Uncle, but Yeka must have known you were out and about—you know, Yeka just knows things doesn't he?—and Aška was annoyed because she doesn't like it when Yeka knows things she doesn't, and she had baked extra nut-cakes but Anahli and me ate them all since you weren't there and ai, but when Yeka finds out you've been rutting Tokela when you were supposed to be breaking your fast with—"

"Kuli," Tokela broke in, low and quiet. "You won't make talk about who I was with. Or why."

Kuli shot a look Tokela's direction. The flood of talk choked off. And stayed off. Kuli's gaze held to Tokela's and, a'io, the ahlóssa seemed worried.

If Našobok hadn't seen it, he'd never have believed it.

The unnatural silence held. Našobok was almost afraid to break it. "We will come, soon enough. So, Little Fox, fly!"

Kuli tried to rally. "Foxes don't fly—"

"You will be flying if you don't go away," Tokela interrupted.

Kuli shut his mouth. And went.

Našobok watched, befuddled just as speechless, as Kuli scooted over to the trail down the cliff bank and clambered up. The last sight of him was his cinnabar hair, flying in Wind.

Meanwhile, Tokela brushed sand from his thighs as if nothing untoward had happened.

"Tohwakelifitčiluka. What Power-full weapon do you wield to shut that one's yap?"

"I once stopped giving him stories. He barely lasted four Sun-rises."

Našobok blinked, then laughed. Hard. Tokela frowned, then smiled and joined in. Našobok came over and snugged an arm about him.

"We go. I'll come as well. Since I was the one who dumped the oversized owl pellet on Galenu's floor, after all."

Tokela's smile hung on—just barely. His eyes took on that re-mote, forlorn cast that twisted at Našobok's heart. For he recog-nised it. Knew it for himself, all too well.

Našobok nuzzled Tokela's forelock. "And after this is settled? Come to *Ilhukaia*. Be with me this Moon's passage as well as last. If you want." At first a tease, but as he finished speaking Tokela's smile turned all lovely.

"You want me again? You were only obligated to one Dance once you laid hands on my spear."

"I laid hands on your spear several times lastDark—or have you already forgotten?" Našobok drawled, and counted coup as the smile blossomed full-bore. "So I think I'm rather entitled to a few more rounds as playmate. We go together, and you come to my ship when Sun begins His descent. I'll give you a proper tour of my truest love, and..." Našobok trailed off as Tokela turned to walk with him, came to a dead halt.

This time Madoc stood at the entry trail, bristled-stiff in challenge. His eyes flickered with something quite unpleasant as they detailed the arm slung across Tokela's shoulders, strafed the owner of said arm, then returned to Tokela.

Then Madoc turned on one toe and stalked away.

Našobok felt Tokela lean forwards, slight but unmistakable. From one too-swift heartbeat to the next it was subdued: muscles still quivering, jaw twitching, but impulse conquered.

It was fearsome. No oških should be so... contained.

Našobok dropped his hand to the whipcord small of Tokela's back, gave a gentle push. "Go after."

Tokela shook his head, watching as Madoc disappeared into the thick wood.

"Cousin," Našobok chided. "Life is already too filled with paths left fallow."

Still, Tokela didn't move. But his gaze turned to Našobok, unyielding. "You said consequences."

"I did. But," Našobok shrugged, "Madoc is young."

"Not too young to be another who would"—emotion blazed in those eyes, sudden-hot—"*own* me."

Not only sliding the knife home, but with a twist. Našobok closed his eyes, hung his head, then shook it and started to circle his arm about Tokela once more.

Tokela sidestepped the intended caress as if it were a brand, and there was a strange glimmer beneath his eyelids as he lowered them, averted his face. Našobok dropped his arm, peered at him, curious.

Tokela's fists were clenched, his teeth gritted tight enough for the cords to rope and flex along his jaw and neck, and one answer was suddenly clear: do not touch.

Našobok waited for several lengthy heartbeats, then said, "We should go. They will look for us."

"And why should a wyrhling care—or need—to obey?"

There was the impulse, strong and barely heeled, to grab Tokela by the hair and shake him. Instead Našobok retorted, clipped, "This wyrhling doesn't care a plague carcass what Mound-chieftain has to say to him. What this wyrhling cares about is what Mordeleg thought to do. I want that one away from here. Away from you."

Tokela's gaze met his. Surprise... and something else that lurched Našobok's heart upwards in his throat. He'd long known the "starry-eyed" one had been truly named—but not like this. Tokela's gaze flickered in the half light, not merely with ebbing traces of darksight, but something else.

But before Našobok could suss it out, Tokela turned away.

"We should go." He started walking, his forelock once again falling over his eyes.

Našobok watched him go for several breaths.

Perhaps nothing. Hints of another impossibility. A reflection of his own experience, a belief...

Unexpected, this recognition. And possibly dangerous.

This is... unexpected.

Cavodu shifted foot to foot, sandals creaking in the damp. He hated the Grotto. He always had. Dank, dripping, reeking of brine. But it was where, this centum, she had fashioned herself to reside.

They all had ways of dealing with exile. Or choosing not to deal.

Yet you come by slow and primitive means, and with news of this import!

Skimmers were hardly primitive! "I thought 'twould be better to speak in person. You know the Matrices are less... secure. Or reliable, come to that."

Very true. Even our own tech has become contaminated by this place. And now, your own children have succumbed to the lure of it. Despite the Accord.

"I fear it's inevitable, the drift," Cavodu replied. There were many reasons they had decided upon treaty and nonintercession: for scientific study, for expediency, to avoid further contamination...

And because they'd had no choice.

Drift is one thing. Choosing a savage's things over our own? That is worrisome. A flit of blue-white skin in darkness, then a swirl of bubbles loosed in a flutter of translucent membrane as the Domina floated past the clear portal.

She had always been graceful. Cavodu remembered—as few did—how she had danced with the Dominus in the Great Halls of Mount Klariyon before it had blown, coaxed by the savage powers into volcanic eruptions of fire and ash. She'd been a creature of dry land wrapped in layered veils of shilla-weave... eons ago? Or a mere hundreds of this recalcitrant world's rotations about its meagre sol?

Cavodu wasn't sure. But the Dominus had betrayed them in the end, as surely as this world had betrayed them: a trap laid in the click-tick passages of a small and powerful world's rotations, of their own bioengineered flesh grown obsessed with corporeal realities.

Adaptation had been the only answer. It wasn't one they cared for. Time—a bare philosophy flung against a distant future—was catching them up.

Time, indeed. She followed some thoughts as easily as she slipped through the salt waters of the now-extinct volcano. *Which got us into this disarray. Then. And now.*

Other thoughts Cavodu kept close. "I don't think"—*careful, go careful*—"that either of them chose this path."

Another flash of pale in the dark beyond the crystalline viewing portal; another spin and swirl of seawater. She preferred her present form and its physical expression. Cavodu had tried it once; not unlike a long-ago memory of space, and freefall, disconcerting if held too long. Full gravity had its drawbacks, but still. Preferable.

Your Sivan has chosen a native lover. Jorda chose to aid one of the little animals when he should have allowed it to whelp in its own fashion. And you—her eyes spun with the Sending—*chose to allow it.*

"They were born here."

Another choice that should not have been allowed.

"But it was, and here we are, Domina." He inclined his head, respectful. "What is your will?"

She circled once, then twice. *Already the natives gain ground against us. They've evolved with our help, and now prey on us as we travel, attack our ports, raid our places! They've taken the Far Atoll, and our own people enduring unspeakable cruelties at their hands! If the Big Island also has decided to break the Accord we made with them... if the life force that continues to thwart us is actively turned against us again—*

"Why would a native boy want to do such a thing, even if he could?"

She stopped before the portal, hanging in the brine. *Never forget, Cavodu, the seeds of our present ignominy were sown long ago by a traitor's choices! What if your foolish son has switched on some oddling genetic pattern? Triggered some default we thought long deactivated?*

A chill, nothing to do with the damp, draped Cavodu's shoulders. "Surely there's no possibility of that!"

But if there is? We once refused to believe in the sentience of this parasitical planet—and that to our ruination. If there's any possibility it could gain a final weapon against us, it likely will. The risk is too great. We're vulnerable. We must act. This creature must be found again, by any means necessary.

She didn't openly say that the native boy shouldn't have been allowed to leave their territory. But then, she didn't have to.

Your son and daughter will go and find him. She begun swimming back and forth, swift and almost nervous. *If they can. The little savages are nomads.*

"Not all of them."

Have our contacts converge on every edge. Disperse a description, offer a price they won't refuse. Not for a corpse, mind, she interrupted just as Cavodu started to protest. *If it's truly been engineered, then it could prove much more useful to us alive. Haunt the ports, the slave markets—*

"Domina, all of this is against the very Accord you speak of! It protects us as much as it does the Big Island!"

Cavodu. She flattened both hands upon the portal. *You know what's at stake here.*

He did, more the pity.

And as to the Accord? She pushed away, membranes casting a swirl of bubbles and foam. *In light of this, it can no longer matter.*

16
TRIAL & TRUST

"I weary of fish," Aylaniś tossed a tidbit to Arrow—who plainly was not tired of said meat—and stood up with a stretch. "Your mother, Madoc, has given me leave to hunt; I was hoping you'd do the honour of accompanying us? It smells of a light Rain, perfect for the stalk."

Us. Anahli grinned as her mother looked her way with a slight nod. Anahli had fully expected to be packed off to the oških dens after midSun meal. Particularly since her sire—mending a riding pad—nevertheless had been watching her since they'd woken.

"I'll stay, finish this," he said, his gaze still considering Anahli even as his fingers worked, nimble and skilled.

Madoc sat upright from the game of toss-bones they were playing, puffing his chest like a rainbow cock.

Kuli, meanwhile, leapt up and scooted about the tipo thrice. "A hunt! A hunt!"

Madoc's face was a plain giveaway, realising that "us" included Kuli.

"We will go after wabadeh," Aylaniś told him, "so you'll need your strongest bow."

Doubt fully landed, then, and Anahli could all but see Madoc's thoughts skittering.

"Aunt, I mean no... uhn... disrespect. But even the best hunters find wabadeh, uhn, difficult. They don't easily give themselves in any hunt. The old storyKeepers say they're angry, that they enjoy humbling two-leggeds who like to think themselves best."

Anahli smirked, knowing what her dam's response would be.

"All the better! Let the canniest win, two- or four-legged!"

A soft rain indeed began to fall as the quartet of hunters approached a hillock overlooking a proportional rarity in thisLand: open meadow. Creeping silent to the crest at her dam's request, Anahli peeked over to find a damp progress of dusky copper and fawn. Five young wabadeh grazed below—bucks, most having shed their antlers already. A smallish one had a broken half antler still attached.

Aylaniś crawled up to crouch on the wet ground beside her dam. The trees were shielding them, somewhat, but their braids were fuzzed with damp.

Daughter, draw with me. Aylaniś spoke hunting-talk one-handed, with the other holding her double-curved bow and three arrows. Her eyes never left the grazing wabadeh as she told the two ahlóssa behind them, *Madoc, flank my draw. Kuli, go Sunwise. Don't rise until I do.*

Kuli set off, keeping low. Anahli crouched next to Aylaniś, who tossed her a quick grin. Just behind them, Madoc hefted his own longer bow.

A snap froze them all in place. Kuli gasped. Anahli turned to see him looking down at the dried branch beneath one extended hand, both hidden by tall grass.

The wabadeh flagged their tails, whirled and fled.

"*Rot* you for a senseless, heavy-footed Spawn!" Madoc stomped over and whacked Kuli across the back of the head.

Kuli gave a snarl and, quick as thought, gained his feet to kick Madoc in the shin. Hard.

Anahli lunged forwards at the first signs of altercation. She yanked Kuli aside by his ahlóssa braid, growled at Madoc when he started forwards, and turned to her dam.

Aylaniś wasn't there. Instead she ran along the ridge, sighting down a nocked arrow. The herd had nearly made the trees; she loosed, nocked another, loosed—all in the time it took for two breaths.

One of the wabadeh stumbled, went down, and Kuli let out a tri-umphant cry. It truncated into a yip as the wabadeh rolled, stag-gered up, fell, then leapt up again and floundered into the trees.

Aylaniś cursed a string of mixed horseClans and Rivertalk.

"Aunt—"

"Aška—"

"Quiet!" Anahli snapped at the two ahlóssa, starting after Ay-laniś, who'd already leapt down the hillock. "We have to track the buck! Follow!"

Madoc hesitated, then sprang after. Kuli already was at Anahli's heels.

Over the plain Madoc was nearly left behind, but in Forest's depths he caught up. He obviously knew the terrain like the weight of his ahlóssa braid, and as he drew even with Anahli, she smiled sideways at him.

Aylaniś, a stride ahead, also saw. She echoed Anahli's smile and nodded Madoc ahead. "Track him, then."

The honour of that flushed his cheeks, but Madoc didn't let it shift him; he surged forwards, eyes quick and nostrils twitching.

Imperative, that they find the injured wabadeh quickly. Disrespectful, to leave one's quarry to suffer overlong—and Rain could wash away the blood trail more swiftly.

Anahli caught wind first, signalling to Madoc as he faltered, uncertain. The hot radiance led forwards, into a stand of tall evergreens. Then, against their ears, the crash through thick undergrowth of desperate and wounded prey.

Madoc pumped his fist and shot off like a racing pony. Aylaniś exchanged a quick, pleased glance with Anahli and followed.

They found the buck: the smallish one, lagging. Aylaniś allowed Madoc to deliver the death stroke with a well-aimed arrow.

"It would have been better with a spear," he lamented as they circumnavigated the thicket and reached the stand beside which the wabadeh had fallen.

"Ahlóssa aren't allowed to hunt with spears, only to fish off the platforms. Under supervision, mind!" Kuli piped up, albeit without his usual brilliance. Smarting, no doubt, from alerting the small herd.

"Even did I have a spear, you'd likely step on it," Madoc sneered.

"I didn't mean to! It was a mistake!"

"It was a mistake, a'io." Aylaniś was threading her strung bow over her back, convenient to hand but out of her way. She lightly cuffed first her son, then Madoc. "And it's done. Learn from it, both of you." When Madoc would have protested, Aylaniś's brows drew together, stern. "You do our four-legged brother little honour by arguing over his death."

Madoc flushed—as well he should, Anahli thought. Kuli knelt—out of reach should the wabadeh give a last kick—and stroked a small, penitent hand along the mottled nap of dusky fur. Aylaniś too knelt, one knee on the head as she leaned across and touched the animal's staring eye. No response. She gave a short, satisfied nod and closed her eyes, traced a sign upon the wabadeh's bony forehead and muttered a quick reverence.

Then she looked up, her lip twitching. "You owe your cousin a Sun's worth of grace, Little Fox. His woodlore negated your error."

Madoc gave a haughty look down his nose at Kuli.

Except Kuli didn't seem abashed, flashing a broad smile. "That's true. It'll give us more time together nextSun! Perhaps two or three Suns, for *such* a silly blunder."

Anahli laughed; she couldn't help it. The look on Madoc's face!

He scowled at her.

"One will be more than enough, son," Aylaniś chided. "Go fetch the horses. We'll need help to pack our four-legged brother. Anahli, you and I'll start to gut while Madoc keeps watch."

As Kuli obediently vanished into the green, Madoc nodded,

pleased with the duty. "If a predator comes looking for an easy meal, we'll know."

Companionable silence fell. Anahli bent to the carcass with her dam, began to work.

Like earlier times, this. Comfortable. Even Rain's patter upon rich foliage didn't disturb the sense of normalcy and peace Anahli hitherto had found only on the wide, dry plain, her horse galloping between her thighs and her weapons at her back.

Also like earlier times were her dam's next words, all soft reproof and lesson.

"Mind this, Madoc chieftain-son," Aylaniś said, quiet, as she tossed a braided hempen rope across to Anahli, who caught it easily. "To reject what's owed is not honourable. I know Kuli's love seems a burden to you, but you must remember it *is* love."

Madoc frowned. "But he hangs on me, all the while. He won't even let me breathe!"

Anahli had to fight a smirk, started to mutter how Tokela might feel the same about Madoc.

With a small shake of head that belied a tiny grin, Aylaniś touched Anahli's hand. "It's a hard lesson, little cousin," Aylaniś told Madoc, "to set free what we love. Harder for males than fems, I think. We must let our loved ones leave us before their first breath, even."

Warmth pooled in Anahli's belly—the words, and her dam's smile, turning fond upon her.

Madoc frowned. "I don't understand."

"I know." Aylaniś tilted the smile to Madoc, but her eyes remained upon Anahli. Anahli nodded, and stood. Throwing the rope across a lower branch, she tied a gathering knot and began to haul at the rope, exposing the wabadeh's pale belly. Aylaniś continued, "When a dam bears her young, she must reconcile herself to the letting go. It is a thing of Grandmother, bonds that must be severed, but never can be."

"Sometimes they are, though," Anahli found herself saying, quiet. "Sometimes people willingly sever them."

Still, the amber eyes held to hers, soft but resolute. "Loved ones are always with us. Their Spirit never leaves, even if their bodies are far away or gone. It doesn't mean they don't love us, it only means something weighty has called their heart."

Something weighty. Perhaps like her sire taking Alekšu's horns from Chogah. Or Našobok leaving his family for River.

River, who made silent talk with Tokela with such fierceness.

If River spoke to Našobok with the same fervour as She had Tokela... Anahli didn't question how she kenned such a thing; the knowledge had sunk into her heart, undeniable. And if She possessed them so utterly, took their strength, filled their hearts...

Perhaps that was love, too? And did anyone have the right to deny such things, to anyone?

"Love should be enough to keep anyone at your side!" Madoc claimed stoutly.

"Sometimes." Aylaniś inspected her knife, then bent to the carcass. "Sometimes not. There are all kinds of love, and none of them are wrong... other than they may not be right for you."

Madoc kept frowning. Anahli bent once more to the buck, thoughts tumbling.

"Madoc, when Kuli returns, we'll need your strength to help hang this wabadeh," Aylaniś deflected an ahlóssa frown with some mastery. "Between us we should be able to parcel and pack the carcass onto your horse."

"My horse?"

"A'io. My mare is young, and would prefer a treble of our People on her back than a blooded carcass."

"My dam often says that horses a'Naišwyrh are only fit for draught. Of course my sire says horses a'Šaákfo are hot-hearted silly things not practical for work..." He trailed off, only then realising it might be construed as insult.

Aylaniś laughed. "Well, I'm pleased to see Inhya keeps you riding as she can. Even a coarse draught pony. You're of my tribe through your dam, and without our four-legged Kin we are nothing."

"Aška taught us to ride, both me and Tokela," Madoc started, then subsided, his realisation obvious. Likely he and Tokela wouldn't be riding together anymore.

"Your eyes are not watching outwards, but inwards," Aylaniś chided, gentle, and as Madoc quickly minded his duty, she continued, "You'll follow Tokela's path soon enough, nephew. Never wish away what Suns you have. There's little honour—or content—in resenting the way things must be. Paths differ, others will go ahead and trail behind, and we must wish their steps be fair and firm. Otherwise our heart grows small."

"*A great heart*," Anahli abruptly sang, pulling on the carcass, "*is coaxed, like a wild horse ša is coaxed, with open eyes and Spirit.*"

"*And sweet, sweet talk,*" Aylaniś joined in.

Madoc wasn't having it. "So I'm to just let Tokela push me away? Like he pushes everyone away except *that* one, and *he'll* take Tokela away on his rotted old boat and—!" Madoc broke off, cheeks once again flushed dark.

"You'll not find me agreeing with you on Tokela's chosen playmate, my nephew. Našobok is oathbrother to me and mine."

"But he's Riverwalker! Outlier!"

Again, Aylaniś answered Madoc; again, her eyes slid to Anahli's. "I respect your tribal law, Madoc, but it's not mine. And even a chieftain-son must respect that."

"But—"

"Našobok's heart is great with love. He will be kind to Tokela, and Tokela wants him. What else should matter?"

"Tokela just likes to flout everything that matters!"

"Perhaps he does," Anahli found herself saying. "Perhaps he feels he's little choice. Or," she narrowed here eyes at Madoc, "perhaps you should ask yourself what you feel like, now, without him. I don't know Tokela as well as you, but I think he feels alone about many things."

"He wants it that way!"

Anahli shrugged, aware of her dam's eyes upon her as she continued, "There are many ways to be alone, Madoc. Some make you content. Some just make you more isolated."

Madoc subsided, chewing at his lower lip.

Aylaniś reached out with bloodied fingers and traced them, first on Anahli's cheek then across her breast.

Anahli smiled, resumed the song. Aylaniś joined in, and even Madoc hummed along.

A rustle interrupted, alerted them. After a brief cock of head, Aylaniś nodded.

"That will be Kuli with the horses."

So still. So quiet.

The space behind his ears wasn't all crowded with thick heat and not-sound; his eyes weren't filming over with sparks and indigo-ebon; his heart didn't try to spend itself in fiendish labour or slow to an alarming, bass *lump*.

He was not filled to bursting with wilding things.

Tokela leaned upon Overlook's railing, watching the clouds drift, roiling from silver to dark pewter. From them Rain fell soft as breathing, lying like fuzz upon his hair and skin. Even sound was held captive; faraway voices echoed clear, whilst near ones muted. A low growl of industry hummed in the Bowl behind him; the midSun meal. River had her own stillness as well; what voices carried from wyrhling craft were hushed, as well as any activity from Her westmost thighs where the yakhling caravans sat hunched against the wet, their draught animals tethered close. So quiet, Tokela thought he could hear the rip-click of their teeth as they grazed the grassy banks.

So. Quiet. Ever since lastdark.

Tokela smiled and traced one finger against the stones next to him. Sketched a proud, broad nose and chin, full lower lip, bistre hair blowing in Wind. Looking to the horizon.

Našobok had been better than anything he could have imagined.

Unfortunately, play was over.

Sarinak had sent for Tokela earlier—private talk, before the arbitration—and had listened, stolid and patient, as Tokela had explained what happened with Mordeleg. Sarinak had even agreed that Našobok should attend, and speak. Anahli had been sent for, but she was off hunting with Madoc, Kuli, and her dam. Tokela was glad the ahlóssa were well away from any of this, but Anahli would be another voice on his side...

Another muted sound: booted feet upon the stair. Tokela flattened his hand upon the sketch, smeared it back into mere dust.

"Inhya was waiting when we returned." Clad in hunting leathers, the blood-pardon stripes were still vivid against Anahli's lower lip and chin. "I'll be there, tell them I threw the rock. That Mordeleg didn't have your consent." She looked about, then resorted to hand-talk. *I won't say anything else.*

A breeze tickled at Tokela's damp forelock then died back, sullen beneath Rain. With a hard swallow, he turned his eyes to the caravans across River. "Anything else?"

Silence; Anahli must be trying to sign her answer. With a huff of frustration, she murmured, "You know what I mean."

"N'da. I don't."

Her hand shot out to grasp his. "This."

The contact tingled before Tokela could pull away, like heat and ice all at once, like...

Like the *t'rešalt.*

Tokela couldn't help a brief glance at his fingers, saw Anahli was rubbing her own together.

"Well enough. You don't trust me, and—"

"It isn't—"

"—and in your place, I wouldn't trust me, either." Anahli kept considering her fingers, as if she'd never seen them. "But... You gave me an... an ache. Behind my eyes."

"I seem to do that with all my kin."

Anahli let out a short laugh, looked away. "Tokela, if you hear nothing else I say, hear this much: don't trust Alekšu."

This was... strange. "Don't trust your sire?"

"And take care with the wyrhling."

Enough was enough. "Look, I don't know what you have against Našobok, but—"

"I know he's your playmate. Did you know that he once lived a'Šaákfo, one of our family?"

Tokela tipped his chin, puzzled negation.

"He has been with my sire since they were oških. They have secrets, long-held. But even that didn't stop him from leaving. He'll leave you, too. It's what he does."

"I know what he does." Tokela finally rounded on her, eye for eye. "Better than you, it seems."

Anahli sighed, leaned against the railing. "Just don't forget what I've told you. Please. But if they do find out—"

"I have nothing more to say to this."

"—don't let them take you a'Šaákfo. No matter what."

As hearthChieftain, Inhya had ultimate charge over the children either fostered or made Clan a'Naišwyrh. If they were involved in any dispute in which the elders were required to arbitrate, she was always present, seated beside Sarinak upon the small rise of stone. Rarely, however, did she speak in such cases, preferring to remain a silent, vigilant witness to her charges' welfare.

In this case, silence was not easy.

"I didn't fully ken the rules of Spear Dance. You must believe me. I meant no offence." Mordeleg certainly told his tale with all due courtesy. He had relinquished his one eating knife peaceably enough; he kept a respectful seat, rump resting on heels, before the small group of elders.

Nechtoun and Galenu and several from Galenu's tribe sat with Inhya and Sarinak. Anahli stood—compliant for once, Inyha approved—behind Palatan in Alekšu's place. Both of them stood behind Tokela who, hands upon knees, knelt at the opposite side of the hearth, following the unspoken maxim: always good to have cleansing Fire between antagonists.

Mordeleg didn't meet Sarinak's eyes as he spoke; while such rudeness could be excused as midLands custom, Inhya believed Mordeleg's downcast gaze little more than insolence and deceit. "We'd an understanding between us, Tokela and I."

As Mordeleg had been asked to speak, Tokela had turned his face aside, the recent ahlóssa braid now a forelock that curtained his eyes. One would almost think he wasn't paying attention to Mordeleg; he stared, unblinking, into nothing.

Inhya had fully intended to stand beside Tokela, but someone had taken that place.

The wyrhling had been allowed, after some deliberation and at Tokela's request. He didn't merely stand beside Tokela, either; he lounged against a wooden pillar bearing the honour of several ancient spears and atlatls. An insolent pose. But to do the wyrhling credit, the insolence was clearly inspired by anger.

He wasn't half as angry as Inhya.

Nor as Tokela. His sparse-freckled cheeks were dark. An occasional reflection of Fire, distinctly unsettling, limned his half-lidded eyes.

Mordeleg was still protesting an unlikely innocence. "It's not the first time he's refused with his mouth even though his bodytalk said otherwise."

"Interesting," drawled Našobok, "when his indigo is new-laid—"

"Silence," Sarinak warned.

"Is it my fault if ahlóssa tease?" Mordeleg protested. "Is it wrong to expect him to follow up on his promises when he is able?"

Inhya wanted to lean forwards and slap the broad, earnest face.

"He gave me every sign he was willing. He didn't push me away."

The wyrhling shoved up from the pillar. "When you're pinned with your arm twisted behind, even someone your size would have difficulty pushing!"

"By your own account, you weren't there when this transpired," Nechtoun censured. "Be silent."

"How long do we have to hear this one spew his shi—?"

"Enough!" Sarinak rose from the bench, hammering his chieftain's stave against the floor. "You will be silent, outlier, until you are given leave!"

And indeed the wyrhling subsided, mumbling several choice epithets—just soft enough for none to take notice, but there, nonetheless.

For the first in a long time, Inhya found pleasure in that one's antics. Even more in Tokela's satisfied half smile.

Sarinak would hear it all out—and it was right he should—but as for herself, Inhya had heard enough between the talk to stake Mordeleg out on a stinging-ant hill.

Mordeleg gave a supercilious sneer down his handsome nose at Našobok. "Why is that one even here? And for him to bind me hand and foot... he's no right to so much as touch me! He's nothing!"

"He's more than you!" Tokela's snarl came sudden. "You are less than nothing! Yuškammanukfila ikšo! *Coward!*"

Mordeleg lurched upwards. Galenu's hand went to his shoulder, clenched. The old khatak's sense had always been in question, Inhya mused, but a firm grip he still possessed. The lined knuckles whitened. Mordeleg's face slackened in surprise and he sank back to the blanket.

"Tokela." Sarinak's reprimand was quieter. "Your own time for talk will come, and none shall interrupt you."

Mordeleg started to open his mouth, Galenu's hand tightened and he bent down, murmured something. Mordeleg scowled. Galenu did not move, but whatever he said next had more weight. Mordeleg's scowl deepened, eyes narrowing at Tokela.

"I've more," he muttered then, louder, "I've more. But I'll wait."

Sarinak peered at him, then at Galenu, who shrugged acknowledgement. Sarinak repeated the shrug and turned to the one who had been his brother.

"Wyrhling. Tell the elders your part in this."

The wyrhling stepped forwards, clasped both hands and brought them to his breast. Respectful now, at least. Again, Inhya did have to give him this much—he'd always known how to work a crowd. "Tokela told me what transpired. I do have to apologise to one I wrongfully accused." His eyes went to Anahli's and held. "I am sorry, ehši."

And of course, he had to emphasise what relationships he had been allowed to claim in Council, brash and bare. Inyha sniffed as Anahli's expression warmed.

"As to that one, a'io, I came after he'd already been taken down. I did tie him up and dump him in Galenu's den. My apologies, Nechtoun a'Naišwyrh, that it was also your place. But considering everything, the little owl pellet is lucky I didn't leave him staked on River's thighs for wolfKin."

"Then let us hear from another who was there and saw everything. Anahli a'Šaâkfo?"

Inhya watched closely as Anahli rose from her place beside Palatan. Her chin was lifted, her eyes sharp, her dress and demeanor respectful. She exchanged a long glance with Tokela. He was the one who looked away. Inhya frowned.

"She wasn't there!" Mordeleg protested. "I didn't see her!"

"Of course you didn't. No one sees my arrows coming." Anahli smiled, honey over salt and sharp-toothed. "Or my rocks."

Several chuckles expressed the elders' appreciation. Nechtoun laughed out loud.

"She was banished from Dance, and you'll take her word?"

"You were banished from Dance, and we have to listen to yours," the wyrhling growled.

More laughter—quickly suppressed for, after all, the outlier had inspired it. Inhya couldn't help the grin that blossomed behind a quick hand.

"Be silent, outlier," Nechtoun snapped. "By all accounts, Anahli a'Šaákfo, you were there. Tell us what you were doing in such a place and why."

"More," another elder added, "tell us what you saw."

Another odd and sticky glance between Anahli and Tokela. Inhya's eyes narrowed; they were hiding something. Had it to do with that wretched place?

If only they could dismantle the thing, tear it down, burn it!

"I wandered in amidst Forest, considering my... errors." Anahli's gaze slid towards Inhya this time and lowered, an apology by any means. Sincere? Ai, but anyone's guess, that. "I wasn't paying attention, truly. Once I saw the outLand thing, I gave it a wide berth, and settled in a copse across from it."

"Why did you stay there if you knew it was forbidden?"

Anahli considered the question. "I didn't know it was forbidden, exactly. I was curious, I guess. As I said, I gave it a wide berth. Anyway, it seems to me what's more important is what happened, not *where* it happened."

Nechtoun started a protest; one of the elders leaned over and whispered something.

"I don't know why the other two were there, but I saw them

come into the clearing. First Tokela and then the midLander. There was a tussle. I ignored it at first. I mean, oških males will wrestle over anything, a'io?" Anahli's smile charmed the elders, invited them to join in—and many did. Palatan, however, was looking at her as if she'd sprouted a full rack of antlers.

"I'd thought to leave them to it, but then it started to have a vicious sound. I watched as that one"—Anahli jerked her chin at Mordeleg—"pinned Tokela and started to force him to play. It was force, no question. Tokela was unwilling. I'd throw the stone again. Harder, this time."

Mordeleg was fuming. Tokela, on the other hand, peered sideways at Anahli. His bodytalk seemed anxious. Another small glance passed between the two.

A'io. Something had happened with them.

Anahli tilted her head, slight, at Tokela; it seemed reassuring. "As to whether Mordeleg tells truth about Tokela wanting to be pinned down and poked against his will, I think that would be obvious. For me, I have nothing more to say."

One of the elders turned to Tokela. "Is it as Anahli says?"

"It is, indeed, as she says." Dark indigo eyes levelled against his accuser—Inhya had seen softer gazes aiming one of the hanging atlatls—then softened, turning to the elder. "I did not give Mordeleg leave to so much as touch me. Perhaps he thought it a game." The allowance was wooden. "I did not."

"What about the rest, then?" Mordeleg burst out. "If she saw so much, then she also saw what happened after!"

"If you keep interrupting, I will see you removed with no further—"

"Witchery! He led me to that place, then used its witchery upon me!"

The midLands word—witchery—fell into the Council den like stones in a still, deep pool, echoing into sudden silence. Inhya's heart lurched in her breast. Visceral, immediate—perhaps wrong, perhaps accurate—but always, always there.

It didn't mean she watched her wards any less carefully. Anahli stiffened, eyes narrowing. Tokela's shoulders quivered, hunched; his eyes remained straight ahead, fixed on the floor.

Palatan broke the silence, leaning forwards. "That," he spun the word out with a small click of tongue, "is a serious accusation, oških."

"And why bring up such a thing now? Why not before?" The wyrhling spoke to Palatan—well, and he would—but also just loud enough to be noticed. "Desperation, I should think." He'd moved closer to Tokela, touched his hair in open comfort. Tokela jerked as if surprised, yet didn't pull away. His fingers twitched against the floor.

Inhya could only hope he wasn't foolish enough to start sketching.

"Who are you, outlier, to question me?" Mordeleg demanded.

"Yet the outlier has a point," Sarinak allowed. "Such an accusation shouldn't be attached to a dog's wagging tail."

"I mentioned it before!" Mordeleg turned to Galenu. "Tell them. I said I'd more!"

Galenu started, resigned, to agree. He refrained, lips thinning as Mordeleg continued:

"Everyone knows Tokela's dam was a witch who consorted with Chepiś! Is it so hard to believe—" Mordeleg winced and broke off with a yip. Galenu's hand had once again slid to his neck tendons.

"That has nothing to do with thisNow," Inhya stated, flat. "You've no rights to invoke the dead so."

The elders were murmuring agreement to this. Tokela still gave no defence, body or voice, head bowed and forelock fallen to cover his eyes.

But then, Inhya told herself, her eldest preferred the protections of turtleKin: sinking inwards, lashing out only when cornered.

"Even outliers can speak from their heart," Palatan ventured, soft. "If you claim the Elementals were used, Mordeleg a'Hassun, then what face did the possession display?"

"What... face?" This clearly had Mordeleg confused.

Palatan leaned forwards, hands propped on thighs. "What Elemental answered? And if ša was no Elemental, but Šilombiš'okpulo that responded, then surely you saw..." As he trailed away, Mordeleg opened his mouth—eagerly it would seem—but Palatan held up a hand and continued, "I charge you, oških, to think before you make such talk, because it would merely prove that you tried to force Tokela. Why else would Tokela be desperate enough to openly call upon an Elemental? Not to mention"— Palatan's lip curled—"that were you in duskLands, the penalty for such violation is harsh. And appropriate."

"We aren't in duskLands!" Mordeleg's voice went a little squeaky, all the same. "I saw what I saw. His eyes... changed! They began to gleam! The Riverling overflowed Her bank! And there were sparks upon the stone!"

"River has surges," the wyrhling snorted with a roll of eyes, "even this far upwards, rolling in from the estuaries. I saw no sparks."

"You will be silent, outlier, or be excused!" Sarinak growled.

"Wyrhlings know River." Palatan slid a glance the wyrhling's way. Inhya saw the frown quirking there, puzzled. "They understand Her more than most."

The elders murmured amongst themselves, shock and consternation; the suggestion played at affront even if true—and proper, as Inhya's frown reminded them. It remained Alekšu's right—his duty, in fact—to suggest such things.

Even as Inhya's own thoughts circled: *It can't be true. Can't be...*

"The Riverling started to flood!" Mordeleg's tone crawled into desperation. "And I saw what I saw, blue-white, almost like Thunder's arrows! *She* had to see, if she saw so much!"

"Anahli?" Sarinak prompted.

At this Tokela's head did shift, albeit slight, sending some sort of quick appeal to Anahli. Unlike him, she was aware of Inhya's notice. Lowering her chin, she raised her gaze to Inhya's, her voice ringing through the den clear as a thin-stretched drumhide. "Everything coming from that one's mouth is made of venom. Lies."

"You're the liar!" Mordeleg shot back.

Anahli didn't bother to so much as turn. Instead she slid her eyes sideways, giving Mordeleg the same interest she might give a nit she'd picked from Kuli's scalp.

"Tokela?" Sarinak said, and ai, but her spouse could be as gentle as fierce. "I understand that this is a fearsome accusation, but you must speak."

Tokela started to raise his head, at the last minute seemed to change his mind. Instead he extended his hands, palms up. "I have wandered closer than was wise to the forbidden place, that is true. I often wonder why my mother went there. But this is also true; wherever I was, I didn't want Mordeleg. He tried to force me, and he threatened my brother Madoc. I do not answer his accusations, because I do not have to answer lies. I only tried to defend myself against him. If Anahli hadn't interfered, I would be the one who'd asked for arbitration. Now, I merely ask my elders for justice."

The wyrhling tugged at Tokela's hair. A smile appeared beneath the forelock, slight but genuine.

Inhya wanted to warm to it. All she could think was that Tokela hadn't truly answered. And when she slid her gaze towards Palatan, she found him peering at Tokela, a slight frown twisting his brow.

"Alekšu?" prompted Sarinak.

The frown wiped away, as if it had never been. "The matter is plain. There is no true evidence of possession at present, Mound-chieftain."

Sarinak conferred with the other elders, quiet and rapid, then nodded. "It is quite plain to me as well. Such things can get tangled up and mistaken on either side, but there's no doubt Mordeleg tried to force Tokela. It's particularly craven when you, Mordeleg, well know Tokela is new to his indigo and unskilled at such play. You have rendered not only insult, but injury, to a member of our Clan and tribe."

Satisfied murmurs from the elders. Mordeleg leaned forwards, as if to speak. Galenu once again employed his grip; Mordeleg fell back with a wince.

"Galenu Hassun-chieftain."

"A'io, Sarinak Mound-chieftain."

"You are bloodKin to this oških. As he does not have his own wealth, you will see that his sire and dam make compensation of five young and healthy ewes to the herds of Tokela's sire, kept by your People. Also, Inhya hearth-chieftain has made her will clear to me in this: Mordeleg will not stay here another Sun's rising. He is banished, from here and for a Sun's running in all directions, from the heart of the Great Mound."

"It will be as you say, Sarinak." Galenu might be irresponsible in too many ways, but he had also kept his tribe prosperous. Inhya was confident in this much; Galenu would act lawfully.

"Also, I warn all three of these oških against the Šilombiš'okpulo." Sarinak's gaze swept the room. "It is foolish, to wander nigh to such places. They confound the senses... can take our sense from us! If any of you are caught there again, there will be retribution. Do you understand?"

Tokela and Anahli. after another sideways quick glance, agreed. Mordeleg had to be prodded by Galenu, but he too capitulated.

"It will be done." The chieftain's stave was pounded, a swift four-beat upon the swept stone floor.

At Galenu's prompting, Mordeleg rose. His face was flushed in what might have been repentance but more resembled anger. Nevertheless he did his duty: first a duck of his head to the arbitration council, then over to where Tokela was rising. The wyrhling murmured a warning; Tokela looked up, wary and waiting.

Mordeleg did his duty there, as well, and as prettily as Inhya had ever seen it: a tilt of head with hands outstretched. Tokela's gaze still would have looked at home behind a nocked arrow, but he recalled his own duty. Though nowhere as obsequious as Mordeleg, he perfunctorily covered the outstretched palms with his own.

Galenu gave a lift of eyebrow to the Council, then took up Mordeleg's eating knife and herded his charge away.

Once they were gone, Tokela couldn't exit fast enough. The wyrhling followed. Inhya wasn't sure she was any happier with that last than she had been the previous Sun's setting. It could only mean more trouble.

The other elders, including Sarinak, were already exiting in the opposite direction, well rid of the entire business. Palatan was speaking with Anahli—something indeed had happened, for Anahli listened, nodding. As they departed, Palatan raised a hand to Inhya.

She knew she should follow, ask him his thoughts. Instead, she followed Tokela.

Voices in the entry tunnel gave her hesitation.

"Ai, old Galenu has him on a leash for now, to be sure, but that one's no sorrier for what he did than I believed his lies." The wyrhling's voice purled low, insistent. "Watch your tail."

A small grunt from Tokela, followed by his low, delighted laugh. Inhya hadn't heard the like in some turnings of Hoop.

"I would rather you watched it." A throaty purr of response. Disconcerting, to say the least; Tokela had so long lacked any emotion in Inhya's own presence.

It made her hesitate further.

"Mmm. Tempting. But I've business with your old uncle khatak, and you've yet to remove your things to your new den. Not to mention I need a nap. I'm no longer oških, to hunt all Sun and howl all dark. Though you do howl quite nicely."

Again the laugh, though self-conscious, and a soft, not-quite silence stretching out, inferring what occupation filled it. Inhya gave a tiny sigh, pursed her mouth sideways and decided to just leave, turning away.

"So. When both the Moons rise above River, make your way to my love, eh? You can see how you like *Ilhukaia*, or if River sings any sweeter to you there."

Inhya halted. She didn't hear Tokela's murmured answer.

If River sings any sweeter to you...

Nigh twenty summerings past, thigh-deep in a Riverling, where Lakisa had insisted upon delivering her young like some mad wyrhling.

River sings sweet to my little one...

How the blood of the birth, beneath copper-clear water, had not spread and stained River with any normal hue, but wafted downstream more like the discoloured indigo egest of one of the twisted and Shaped creatures.

Can't you hear? Lakisa had asked, in a delirium of pain and—now Inhya knew—Other. *Even now, She knows him. Do you hear Her?*

Inhya had kept her own answer silent, buried it deep in her heart: *N'da, I cannot. I will not. And neither will your son.*

And now, Mordeleg's talk of the Riverling. Of the forbidden place.

Inhya's heart twisted, settled hard. With a dip of chin, she started forwards—

Only to nearly run headlong into Tokela, returning the way he'd come.

Tokela jolted back, soft bemusement sliding away. Inhya's own trepidation overruled any pain his recoil might have given her—in fact hardened further into anger as his gaze rose, just as cross, to level into hers.

Humiliating, how he could gut her with a glance. Yet for perhaps the first time in too long, Tokela's eyes were not merely flat, aloof mirrors, coolly deflecting what might seek to touch him. Something stirred—desperate, seeking. No wild-eyed infant born in a wash of River brack and indigo ichor, but the too-small ahlóssa who had sought a foster-mother's company after they'd sent the bodies of his parents to Fire and River.

Tokela took in a shallow, shocked breath and broke the gaze, veiling it with forelock and lashes both, colour rising in his cheeks.

"Tokela?" Inhya tried, soft.

"I left my knives on the hearth." Tokela's gaze stayed downcast, hidden. And when she didn't move, he slid around her quick as a mouse.

"Tokela."

He didn't stop, seemed a bit unsteady as he kept on.

"Tokela."

"What?" It was as weary as hers was sharp.

"Hear me. Please."

He stopped halfway to the hearth. Not quite, but almost, a question.

Inhya had no answer. But she tried. "Take care. The River-walker won't mean to—or perhaps he will—but he'll hurt you."

With each word, the bony shoulders beneath Tokela's best tunic pulled, more and more, into knotted fishing line. Instead of answering, he continued, steps tottered once then twice. Each time he stiffened, as if angry, yet bulled on. Just as he reached the hearth, he stumbled hard and fell.

A startled cry truncated to a whimper within his chest, the smell of singed hair and the *whoof* of burning fabric. Face against the heat, mouth lax and eyes wide, he stared into the flames as if he couldn't believe what was happening.

Inhya fell upon him, knotting fingers in his hair and tunic, hauling him back. Tokela slammed against her and they both went sprawling, flailing, rolling to douse what Fire remained. On his back beneath her, Tokela struggled. Inhya gripped tighter and he gave a tiny, panicky moan, kicked out. His heel caught her thigh and Inhya released him with a grunt, watched in disbelief as he scuttered back on his hind end, holding his burned arm tight against his body. The ends of his forelock fell across his cheeks, a tattered and singed curtain. His breath came in a thin, wheezy pants. Again, she started for him, but he cowered like the lowest cur in a pack, retreating until he backed into the same weapons pillar against which the wyrhling had lounged.

Inhya gritted her teeth. It was not going to be pretty, but she needed to see just how severe his burns were. She scooted closer, reached out. "Tokela—"

Another wheeze, and he jerked away as if her touch burned him more than Fire had. Grim, she caught his fingers, held firm as he tried again to shrug her off, retreat.

"Tokela!" It was sharp as she yanked his arm towards her. "Let me *help* y—"

Her voice stuttered to a halt.

The tunic sleeve had burnt away half up his arm. The scorch of the woven fibres lingered in her nostrils. She could taste, acrid, the scant fur of his arm all singed. But...

No flesh had burned. His forearm was whole, unmarked. His skin was cool, with the pallor of a dead thing. And the gaze he flung against hers...

Inhya witnessed it, plain: shadowling sparks of ghost-mist, with scattered clouds and rain and jagged poles of hot silver, StarFire against indigo night.

And he kept *staring* at her: the babe she'd pulled from both his dam and River, who'd taken Wind without a sound and looked at her with dark eyes that kenned all she was, and how. And even now as then, try as Inhya might, she saw nothing of Lakisa, nothing of Talorgan who was the only father Tokela had known... nothing of *their People*.

A wail built within her chest, strangled itself into a small whimper. She scurried back on her haunches like to frightened rodentKin beneath a winged shadow.

"You have been with them!" she stammered. "With Chepiś. That is what you were doing at the forbidden place. How many times have they seen you, touched you?"

StarFire flickered, faded. "H-how?" Tokela husked, too shocked to dissemble.

"You are not the only one who has seen Other," Inhya hissed, and rolled to her feet, and fled.

17
SHELTER

"Ai, wyrh-chieftain! I thought I might find you hereabouts." So close! Just a matter of a few more strides and he'd have made it. With a gusty sigh, Našobok turned from the beckoning hide of Palatan's and Aylaniś' tipo. He knew his expression was less than pleasant; neither did he care.

But the little Kin of Skybow cock just puffed all the more. Well, Galenu had guts, Našobok had to give him that.

"I thought to find a bed, a meal, and two lovemates to share both thisdark. You, Galenu stone-chieftain, are none of those."

The Skybow cock deflated slightly—but then, Našobok knew just where to wing him. "Not all of us have more lovemates than we know what to do with—"

"Now you're just jealous."

"—or even wish to have them."

Našobok snorted and let his head fall back to contemplate the dusky Sky basket, just starting to fill with Stars. "Tell me another, old one."

"You did say you were interested in my cargo?" Galenu reminded.

Poke the old one sideways, but he was right. Našobok sighed. "How dangerous?" Despite himself, a tiny tickle of anticipation flowered in his belly. First Running had another brace of Suns, and then it would be time to depart. A break from normal trading routine would be welcome, not just for himself but his shipmates.

Instead of answering, Galenu chuckled. "The oških wearing you out, is he?"

"Is your oških the outwards cargo? I could wrap Mordeleg in a very tight bag and troll him overboard. He'd make lovely bait."

"You tempt me." Galenu shrugged. "Mordeleg is under the eyes of two of my most trusted bondlings. They've no liking for him, believe me, and they'll see he—and his message—are delivered starting nextSun."

The old khatak was quite serious. Still, Našobok couldn't resist one last jab. "Meaning you don't want to face his dam when she hears."

"Of course." Galenu's teeth gleamed. "Have you *met* Mordeleg's dam?"

Našobok's bark of laughter echoed sharp against the trees. "Well, old khatak, you mentioned danger?"

"I did." Galenu's face lost any levity. "I wasn't exaggerating, either. You're the only one I know who'll dare Serpentback and Mirror Cove."

Našobok frowned. Serpentback was a Riverling, true, but only slightly smaller than the great She who'd spawned Her and aptly named, twining treacherous through mountain passes. Many thought it easier to go the coastal route and around—except "around" held tricky currents and fierce grandfather Winds, was laced with Matwau slavers, pirates, and thieves, and for good measure dotted with places twisted and tainted by ancient Chepiś Shapings.

Mirror Cove was itself a Chepiś place.

"What could possibly be worth that journey?" Našobok queried. "What do you want so badly, old khatak?"

"An instrument common enough to Chepiŝ. But to us it could have immense value. I tried to obtain one from my friends, but they refused the first time and I've not seen them since. I had to widen my search."

"So you're buying contraband."

"I wouldn't say that."

"I would. This new source of yours is willing to trade in something others have refused. By any definition, that's contraband."

Galenu was puffing up again. Nothing more indignant than someone caught cheating. "You think to judge me, outlier?"

"I prefer to judge the accuracy of danger. My people's lives are worth more than you playing the injured innocent. Don't feed me shit and call it honey, stone-chieftain, or *Ilhukaia* won't as much as raise her sails. What. Are. We. Carrying?"

"Something your like should welcome, Riverwalker." Galenu was still indignant. "A forged eye of metal and sand, spun finer than even the downRiver *glašg* blowers can craft. A device to gauge Stars."

"Such a wonder!" Vocal sarcasm insufficient, Našobok rolled his eyes and propped hands on hips. "I know you're Land-bound and therefore ignorant, Galenu, but surely you know wyrhling already have the finest ways to gauge Stars."

"Not like this, you don't. With such an eye of metal and *glašg*, we could see the shadows on the twin Moons. We could cross the dawning Sea."

"Some of our People did just that, long ago. They came in smaller craft than mine, and found Kin already here. They needed no unhallowed metal eyes."

"But many were lost."

"Sea is dangerous." Našobok shrugged. "More so than even River. It is Her way."

"If they'd possessed these things, our far-flung cousins could have arrived here in greater numbers, safe."

"And perhaps overrun those already here. Instead the lucky ones—the strongest, the most willing to coexist—survived."

"But they could have been safer in their navigation—"

"Safe!" Našobok scoffed. "If such a thing can be had, who can afford it? What price will it demand?"

"Knowledge outweighs any price." Galenu's eyes, flecks of Sky against umber, shone with intent. "What would you do, wyrh-chieftain, to keep your crew safe? To know you could fix yourself more accurately upon Sea, to better make port?"

"I don't know what I'd do, were my people's lives handed to me on a balance scale. I'm glad such a choice isn't mine to make. But I'd hope to never take Sea's grace for granted." Našobok watched the trees sway, spiky silhouettes against Dark's breeze. "You say knowledge. I say weakness. There's no such thing as safety, and those who think there is? They're fools playing a dangerous game."

"So you refuse."

"Not necessarily." Našobok inclined his head first one side, then the other. "Ai, I need sleep. More, I'll need good trade for this journey, old khatak. There is little... uhn... *safety* in your errand."

Galenu smiled. "Which is why I came to you. Figure your price and we'll come to an agreement before I leave. I'll be here for a while yet."

"I know Nechtoun is glad of your company," Našobok said, and meant it.

Galenu smiled.

Našobok turned, nearly had the door flap in his hand as Galenu's voice sounded again, muted.

"How is Tokela?"

Našobok hesitated, slid his eyes towards Galenu. "Why?"

"Can I not ask out of courtesy?"

"You can. But generally you don't."

Galenu's expression was odd. Našobok didn't trust it, not even a little. "What are you and old Nechtoun contriving now?"

The old one's eyebrows rose. "And why should you care?"

"That should be flaming obvious. What isn't obvious is why *you* should."

"He's son to my sister's son."

"And you'd forgotten he existed, until Nechtoun told you of his sketches and his stories."

Galenu blinked. "You know of those?"

"I pay attention, Galenu."

"When you're here."

"Which means I need to pay attention," Našobok agreed. "Unless you intend to send Mordeleg away from midLands, you've no business offering a hearth to Tokela. Someone will end up hamstrung, and Tokela deserves better than owing restitution for a spoiled anki'i."

Galenu again started to puff up, opened his mouth for what surely would be a heated retort.

The smell of sweet spice and honey wafted outwards as the door flap behind Našobok was flung open. "I've held nutcakes for you long enough, lovemate."

Aylaniś looked fit for the highest of Councils. Her bronze hair was immaculately oiled and braided, her bare legs and feet touched with woad and chalk, her tunic spotless. About her shoulders was a beaded doeskin shawl pale as Brother Moon.

Rescue! Našobok wanted to laugh with relief—and with genuine amusement as Galenu's expression swerved from annoyance to surprise, then appreciation. Then came the charm.

Ai, well, if Našobok possessed even half that charisma when he gained that age...

Aylaniś let herself be beguiled, allowed Galenu to bow over her palms and even to brush one cheek against her knuckles. Then she firmly grasped Našobok's arm and began to steer him into the tipo.

"—know how it is, StoneChieftain, nutcakes are best still warm... and here's several for you. I'd invite you for some tea, but after I feed Našobok, I'm taking him to the furs for a while." Aylaniś smiled, every bit as charming as Galenu. "A long while, I've hopes. So if you will excuse us, stone-chieftain?"

Was the old khatak *blushing*?

He was! Našobok started to comment. Aylaniś reached up and shoved a piece of nutcake in his mouth.

"You never know when to leave it, do you?" Aylaniś murmured against Našobok's ear. "Next time I'll just leave you to argue yourself sideways, you stubborn k'šo."

Fine and fragrant Wind upon tall fems; Našobok didn't have to bend much to nuzzle Aylaniś's cheek, mouth full of nutcake and all. He knew a rout when he saw one.

Galenu did, too, from the hastiness of his retreat.

"But if you're too tired to have a good go in our furs even after I feed you, I will go find that oških and smack him."

Našobok allowed her to put an arm around his waist and staggered, playing along.

He didn't need the nutcakes. All it took was having a look at Palatan lounging in the furs, looking tousled and thoroughly done to—and ready to be done again.

"Are you staying, this time?" Low, vibrating into a growl.

Našobok *loved* it when Palatan growled.

Aylaniś raked Našobok's hair over one shoulder and bit his nape, making him judder like a first-rutted oških. "I think this time he'd better."

Ai, well, Moons' rising was some time away, and sleep was overrated. Našobok let Aylaniś feed him another nutcake, watched with no little appreciation as Palatan rolled to his feet and ambled over.

Arrow let out a small whine, rising from his hearthside doze. Not a breath after, there was a chirrup from outside the flap, and a familiar voice.

"Palatan?" Inhya.

Ignore her, Našobok wanted to say, but the timbre of Inhya's next words stayed him.

"Please, brother, are you there?"

Palatan heard as well. He frowned, slid a glance to his love-mates and, slinging a blanket over himself, went to the door. Arrow followed on silent feet, nudging his narrow head against Palatan's thigh as Palatan shoved the hide flap aside.

Inhya stepped in, as carefully put together as ever, save that her kirtles swung silent, devoid of bells, and her headdress also was naked of adornment. "Brother." Hoarse-soft, and a-tremble. "It's urgent. I must..." She trailed off, seeing Našobok beside Aylaniś. Her face—swollen, lined with tears both shed and burgeoning—closed. She wrapped her shawl closer, her talk clipped, formal. Almost angry. "It is a matter for family. For Alekšu."

Palatan reached out and stroked a comforting thumb to her cheek, turning to Našobok and Aylaniś with a twist of brow.

And there went another promising dark, sailing past. Našobok sighed, muttered, "I've a promise to keep by Moons' rising anyway." Squeezing Aylaniś's hand, Našobok snatched up a discarded blanket, openly gave Palatan's nape a stroke as he passed. Said, merely, "Inhya hearth-chieftain," as he bent through the door flap to let it fall behind him.

Tokela stayed in the den until he heard stirrings from the outer ways: others coming, perhaps, to prepare for additional gatherings. He took up a blanket, wrapped it close about his neck and shoulders, and slunk out the way he'd come before anyone could find him.

It was late, and wet. The talking drums began to boom out the call to supper. The traders and merchants had already started to close their stalls, with grumbles cheerful and otherwise about Rain's light and steady persistence. Tokela pulled his blanket closer, kept walking. He couldn't fight; too numb to take flight.

Or perhaps it was flight after all, though he wasn't even sure of where he was going. Other than in the opposite direction of that cursed *t'rešalt*. A surge of guests and residents closed in about him. Chatting and laughing amongst themselves, they too strode the Bowl, some moving off towards the dining dens. The traders travelled opposite, towards the tall carved entry arches: some were laden with packs and baskets, some accompanied by dogs pulling hitching poles and slings for extra goods, and a few, more well off, had an ox or pony to haul their wares. And others, like fishKin swimming upstream, were coming in.

The latter smelled of Smoke, which also hung heavy upon Wind's breath, albeit weighted by Rain and the thick trees. The latest fishing haul was still being cured. Not even for First Running did fish preparation stop.

Tokela was supposed to have been there earlier, to help repair nets.

Instead he was invisible, merely another traveller hunched against Rain's patter, heading to thisdark's shelter. And if he had no shelter and was heading nowhere, it didn't matter, not yet.

The ones ahead of Tokela all spilled onto the embankment where the overpath joined the frontis road. Heading to the wyrhcraft, or to the flat that would ferry them to those waiting caravans. Still unsure of what he was doing, or why, it wasn't until Tokela half-leapt, half-slid down the embankment that he realised.

River.

She was there. She had never left. Even when Fire had... recognised him, River had pushed back against the burning presence, importunate—yet comforting—behind his eyes.

And how appropriate that another was there, waiting upon Her flanks? Tempting, to just flit past Anahli like a shadow and disappear into the Rain and Sun's setting.

But.

He owed her. She had stood with him. Had lied for him. And he still wasn't exactly sure why.

On silent feet, Tokela walked over, took Anahli's hand and held it between his own. Silent, the vow, and much more than mere thanks as he drew it to his forehead. *Oathsister. There is a bond between us, from thisSun onwards.*

Anahli's brow twisted, as if unsure. A smile appeared, if trembly in the corners, as she performed the same service for him. Closed her eyes as his fingers brushed her brow.

As they both heard the not-voice:

Eyes meet eyes to waken Spirit;
Spirit wakens our Mother's heart...

"Are you..." He quavered silent, unwilling to so much as voice the possibility.

"I only hear the... voice... when you touch me," Anahli answered, quiet. "It's you."

"It can't be. I don't want—"

"How can you not want it? It's a gift, Tokela."

"A gift? Chepiś gave me a curse!"

Her brow furrowed. "Are you saying you believe what people say? That Chepiś sired you? That's absurd!"

He loosed her and fell mute, thoughts a-jumble, chaotic.

"I'm sorry, I didn't mean it like that, but... Tokela, I didn't mean anything to do with Chepiś. I meant River. No Chepiś could have given Her to you. Chepiś twist things. River... it's obvious even to me that She's... yours."

"And if I give in, She will see me outcast! No People, no Clan, nothing!"

"Perhaps you need to make your own, Clan, then."

This seemed incomprehensible. "Make my—"

"What you have is a gift!" Anahli insisted, her eyes a-glitter. "Our People once had such things, and they called them gifts, talents, blessings! Don't you know that? In my tribe we tell the stories. We don't forget, even if we snug too close to memory's cautions. Do those a'Naišwyrh fear the Elementals so much that they've purged even the memories of what once was?"

"Memory"—soft, yet tugging-strong as undertow; was it his voice?—"depends upon the one recalling it, doesn't it?"

"Don't let them take this from you, Tokela. Maybe you can go away, should go away. Go with Našobok. Be Riverwalker. He's of River; he can take you away from here."

"I thought you hated him."

Anahli sobered. "He... it hurt me when he left us. He was my father, my uncle, and I... I didn't realise. How strong an Elemental can be. Until you showed me. Tokela, if I had what you had, I'd let no one take such a thing from me!"

"You don't... understand." Tokela tried to say it, couldn't bring it to life through voice. *I won't be that. I don't want it. I want to be here, of my tribe, belonging!*

"I'm trying to." It was like shade from hot Sun, or a roof against hard Rain.

Trying. To understand.

With a half smile, Anahli leaned forward and touched her forehead to his. Then she turned and left him there, with Rain and River and...

Ilhukaia, lying in deeper water, bobbing gentle in the current.

Tokela watched Anahli go.

For long, halted breaths, he thought to follow her.

Instead he dropped his blanket on the strand and raised his bare face to Rain. He toed from his boots, started to shuck from his leggings and tunic, left off. He was sopping; it didn't matter. As he walked forwards, River tickled his bare toes, made many promises, swore cool, clear bond.

Riverwalkers have scant ties with any but their own kind—and even that lies questionable.

He didn't want to remember Inhya's talk, but it rose behind his eyes and hissed at him like venomous, tiny avatars of serpentKin. "Shut it." The growl went deep, shivered back upwards. "I will not hear you."

Their own kind.

A'io. Better to be outlier. Outcast.

Better than being Other.

Tokela took several running steps and dove forwards.

Well used to the undertows and currents lying beneath Her surface, Tokela was pleasantly surprised by River's accord. He swam, fleet and nigh-silent upon Her undertow, and reached *Ilhukaia* with ease. The trading galley rose over him, wet and sleek as a breaching Sea-wolf, her sides too slick to scale. Lapping *Ilhukaia*'s circumference, he found a length of rope knotted into a ladder.

River clung to him as he rose from Her, tonguing his spine like a lover; Tokela gritted his teeth, shuddered against the rope. "I'll be back," he whispered.

It seemed, to his overwrought senses, She answered. *I know. Still, you are missed.*

A shudder, an exhaust of heated breath, and Tokela resumed his climb hand over hand. The rope made a soft creak in his palms. Reaching the railing, he quickly scaled it, coming to a soundless crouch on the deck.

The clouds parted for several breaths, allowing a rising Brother Moon to reflect against the wet decks, with His siblings to add a skim of bronze and blood to bright silver. Tokela padded across, dripping, his feet leaving wavering outlines on the wooden planking. Rain also left patterns, small circles of strike melting into gloss. Other than his own breaths and the wet patter, *Ilhukaia* lay quiet.

Too quiet. Deserted, almost. Surely some of her crew would have returned by now? And the old one, Našobok called him uncle... Munro was his name. Surely he would be here, at least. But Tokela saw no one.

Našobok had forgotten.

That's what it was, and all it was, and with the realisation came a drowning misery as merciless as River. Tokela wanted to kick the railing, hiss curses, weep with frustration.

My own. So clear, vibrating, a rush of hum and heat that skimmed his skin and stoppered his breath. *Do you truly believe you are so easily forgotten?*

Tokela whirled about. No one was there.

Clouds cloaked the Moons. Tokela paced over to the railing, quiet but worried—*hurried*—and looked down. Still no one. A sharp call echoed from a neighbouring craft against the cliff face, was muted beneath a sudden gust of Wind and wet. The deck rose and fell beneath Tokela, River slapping and tossing against *Ilhukaia*'s hull. It sounded like... laughter.

"I..." A hoarse whisper as he tottered back. "I don't—!"

He bumped against something. Tokela tried to shove it away; instead strong hands laid upon him. Reaction came instinctive

and instantaneous; he twisted, and when the hands didn't let go
he writhed downwards. His feet slipped on the decking as he
lurched sideways, trying to yank free. The grip tightened, shook,
and finally shoved Tokela up against a bulkhead.

Tokela panicked, letting fly with a hard kick. It made solid impact. His attacker staggered hard against him and cursed
roundly in Našobok's voice.

"Yai!" Pain, and real aggravation. "What *ails* you, Tokela?"

The breath slipped from his lungs in a long sigh of relief.
"You're here."

"She's my craft; where else would I be?" Nigh wet as Tokela,
Našobok grimaced, bending down to rub at his right shin. "You
kick like a mare defending a new-dropped foal—whatever have I
done now?" Našobok's glanced sideways, eyes glossed by a torch
held against the murk. "You're right, Uncle, you heard someone.
Only this one was actually invited."

Old Munro, bald, tattooed scalp glistening beneath the torch
he held, padded up beside Našobok. He'd a thick spear in his
other gnarled hand. "Then next time offer the oških a canoe,
'stead of him sneaking up smooth as otterKin and nearly getting
spitted by an old Riverwalker." He spoke Rivertalk, with all the
slurs and stops.

It had been overlong since Tokela had heard such. It gave him
focus upon something other than Rain on his skin and River filling his heart.

Munro peered at him, face cragged further in a frown.
Našobok said something Tokela didn't understand—perhaps
couldn't, because his own senses were set to overflow—and
Munro shrugged, turned, ambled away.

"...is it?" Našobok's voice overrode the hum and heat. Tokela
slumped against the wall. "You're white-eyed as if shadowlings
are after you."

You're not far wrong. Hysteria narrowed itself into a hiccup of
not-quite-laughter; once again Tokela tossed the sodden hair
from his eyes. "I thought—" It was a croak; he tried again. "I
didn't mean to kick you."

Našobok propped one hand just above his shoulder. Belatedly,
Tokela realised they were against the front wall of the den lead-
ing belowdecks. "When I said you were welcome on *Ilhukaia*,"
Našobok chided, fond, "I didn't mean you had to swim here."

"I... I like swimming. I didn't mean to... to intrude."

"You aren't. Don't mind Munro—he's had a few try climbing
aboard without an invitation. He's quite good with his spear, is
the old one; gave them a poke. Not quite the same sort of poke or
spear, mind, as you and I've shared." The sly smile made total
robbery of Tokela's ability to answer. "I was about to paddle
ashore and wait for you on the strand. But I'd hoped Rain would
ease up even a little." Našobok grimaced as, in seeming answer,

the wet just got wetter "No such luck." He hesitated, peered closer. "You thought I forgot you, didn't you?"

Again, talk lay useless. "I... It was—"

"Ai, do you really believe I'd forget you, Star Eyes?"

Do you really believe you are so easily forgotten?

I'm no one. Tokela's teeth were abruptly chattering. *I'm no one. There's nothing in me.*

Našobok leaned in close, body blocking the pelting Rain. His deep voice and presence seemed a refuge from any voice, internal or... Other.

Shelter from whatever storms would rise. The only haven. The only sanctuary.

Go with him. Run away. Make your own Clan...

Tokela reached up, fingers clutching at damp leather. "Našobok?" It was a choke.

Another frown. Našobok leaned closer, put his forehead against Tokela's. "I gave you a start, didn't I? I didn't mean to."

"Našobok."

"What?" Našobok's breath wafting soft across Tokela's cheeks, spiced sweet-sharp—he'd been drinking. His hair fell over one tattooed cheekbone, his tunic gaped unlaced beneath his longcoat, his leggings slung low about his hipbones and barely held to propriety by clout and shell-and-lanyard belt... everything about Našobok including the lithe, well-lubricated bonelessness of his pose spoke to possibilities, abandon. Shivering, Tokela found his gaze following a long stream of wet dripping from Našobok's turquoise-feather chieftain's lock and onto his collarbone, trailing down his breastbone and disappearing sideways. Blood pounded in Tokela's temples, accompaniment to the sticky singsong of panic still lingering in the pit of his belly, trying to overcome the not-quite-whispers of unknown/unknowable urging him just to let go, give in, *dive* in.

"I didn't mean to, either," Tokela blurted thickly. "I didn't mean it."

"You didn't mean to kick me? I know. You said."

"I didn't mean it." Tokela's fists tightened, squeaking against wet leather and fabric. The not-whispers were even louder.

"I know. It is well."

Leaning forwards, Tokela put his lower lip to the runnel of wet on Našobok's chest, caught it with his tongue. Našobok made a small, startled sound, and his hands tightened on Tokela's arms. With nary a wince, Tokela followed that tiny line of wet down and over muscle-sprung ribs.

They expanded with a sucked-in, sharp breath. The not-whispers curled into sighs.

Fingers tightened at Tokela's nape as he suckled Rainwater and damp, risen flesh, then tightened, pulling him away.

"Tokela, I—" Našobok said—or started to say, for when

Tokela's eyes met his, Našobok left off the talk as if someone had taken his tongue.

Half-afraid of what might be limning his eyes, Tokela ducked forwards once more, this time reaching for the neck cords lying beneath the sopping braidlock of feathers and hair below Našobok's left earlobe. The pulse beneath doubled as Tokela latched his teeth there.

Našobok juddered, hissed, "Sa yuškammanukfila ikšo!"

Rut me stupid? Ai, Našobok didn't know the half of it. Because too much was rising within Tokela, and he wanted it tamed and trammelled. Like thisSun's rising, when he'd lingered beneath the wykupeh with Našobok, having been rutted just that deliriously, deliciously stupid. That sated. That silent. That *real*: flesh and heat, bone and blood and the pounding of a heart drum against his own. Power headier than any inward whisper or presence. This. *This.*

Našobok pulled back. Tokela uttered a protesting murmur but Našobok touched his fingers to Tokela's chin and raised his face up into Rain.

There were Stars above, peeking through Wind-torn clouds... or there were Stars behind his eyes, Tokela wasn't sure any more, and he had fallen into Fire's grip and come away unburned.

He wanted the burning, now.

Tokela pulled Našobok against him, and there was no hesitation at his importunity, only a return ferocity that melted his bones to butter. He growled into Našobok's neck as Našobok tightened his arms, picked Tokela up as negligently as one of the feathers at his temple, and shoved him against the wall.

Rain came harder, seeking them. Wind gusted, swelling River beneath them, sending *Ilhukaia* rocking. Našobok didn't so much as grab for balance; Tokela found his by clenching his knees tighter into Našobok's hips. Muscle, sinew, and bone moulded close. No more whispers. Instead Wind flexed His wings, River foamed, *Ilhukaia* shuddered.

"I want—"

"I know what you want." A purr against Tokela's throat, and hands nimble at his clout. "For being such an undemonstrative sort, you certainly have an opinion on *this*, don't you?"

The ship lurched beneath them, River slapping her sideways. Našobok rode her easily, lifted Tokela higher against the wall. Taking one of Tokela's hands, Našobok guided it up, curled it about a thick wooden spar. In answer Tokela tightened his knees and snaked his other arm upwards, grabbing the spar with both hands, rolling his hips forwards. Našobok growled low in his throat and thrust up against him, driving a small cry from Tokela's lips.

"Again," Tokela pleaded. "Harder. Here."

Here. Wet locks spidering, hard flesh straining, damp leathers creaking, the fur and silk and taut aching pulse captured between them, trailing slick tears and tangling, belly to belly. Tokela's heart pulsed deep into his toes and back up against his temples, a passionate drumming to drown out the rhythm inside, to echo the driving of water, Wind and wood. Rain spattered against his exposed throat, to be lapped up by warm breath and even warmer tongue. Shadows, water, the roaring nearness, the voices of both washing whispers into sighs and silence. He could drown in it, in the sound and the pitch, the sweet-hot skin against his own, the rhythm of heart and breath knocking in and against his breast... and only thisNow, this breath and beat to drum it outside, away...

"Take it from me," Tokela whimpered against Našobok's temple. "Take it... take me. *Please.*"

Našobok caressed him, rough and tender, and Tokela clutched to it, writhed against it, buried body and voice and heart into wet hair and flesh. His fingers tingled upon the wooden spar, his arms quivered, his thighs shook. They were literally steaming as Rain's caress, commingled with sweat and saliva, heated gasps fogging about them. The wood scraping against his back, *Il-hukaia's* rhythm an ever-present reverberation against his spine. Tokela's voice rising, begging, as Našobok thrust against him with a shudder and a hoarse sigh, as Tokela's own voice choked, as it all flared and finished within them.

Retreat, then. A slow seepage that left him enervated, as if someone had slit him stem to stern and emptied him out onto the Rain-soaked decking. Strong hands holding him, fingers trailing from his lips to his nape, muscles shivering yet firm against his own. Whispers, again—but these couched in Našobok's soft voice, murmuring endearments against Tokela's hair. The creak of wood, his own hoarse gasps. Sky dark, rumbling against the trees as they swayed, moaned. Spirits, true, but manifested outside, voices soothing, voices welcome.

Voices, sated. Silent.

"Better, now?" was the soft murmur against his cheek. Tokela tried to answer and couldn't. He felt hollowed out, replete, floating. Untouchable.

"Tokela." Insistent.

"I'm... here," Tokela answered, somewhat less than truthful as his head lolled sideways.

"Believe me, I'm well aware of y..." The fond voice trailed off as Tokela staggered. Našobok leaned closer; a slat of Moonslight escaped the cloud cover and pinpointed his pupils, dousing their glow yet clearly illuminating a sudden frown. "Ai, Star Eyes. Are you well?"

"I'm—"

"I didn't hurt you? You seemed to want—"

"You didn't. I wanted it. Wanted you to..." With a bit of effort

Tokela made himself focus. "It was really good. I just feel a little, uhn, light-headed."

Našobok seemed unconvinced. An uncomfortable twinge fluttered in the pit of Tokela's belly and he looked away.

"I am well!"

"Of course you are." Našobok's retort held a bit of acid. He bent to scoop up their discarded clothing. "But Wind's picking up, and both of us standing here soaked with a bare rudder. Come down to my hold. We'll dry off, get warm."

Tokela nodded, leaned back against the wall and closed his eyes.

Dark. Quiet. Nothing Danced there, light or dark or shadowling not-whisper...

"Tokela."

He opened his eyes just as Našobok leaned close and nuzzled Tokela's temple, lingered there, then pulled him close against his chest. Tokela hung there with a delicious shiver.

"Don't make me go back," he whispered, sudden, against Našobok's shoulder. "When you go, take me with you. *Please*."

◊ ◊ ◊

18
SON OF THE LOST

"She said you... sensed things. In her son."

A thrill of alarm ran through Palatan. He had never spoken of what had passed between him and Lakisa. A quick glance showed Aylaniś, too, apprehensive.

Inhya seemed to realise anew the repercussions of an additional presence. "I... This matter, it must stay between us, within this tipo."

She spoke the talk a'Šaákfo, not merely courtesy, but because it had language for concepts dawnLands had long ago sloughed as dangerous.

"You know it will not pass my lips." Aylaniś reached down, clasped Palatan's and Inhya's joined hands, and rose. "I'll pour fresh tea while you tell Alekšu what you must."

The familiar, ritual motions of guest-welcome reassured, but didn't lessen the jangle of Palatan's nerves.

Lakisa had insisted upon the tradition of bringing her infant son to her grandmother's Clan. NameKeepers were different along River's thighs; her dam-right to have her child's name Dreamt by the matriarchs of her birthing-tribe. Only both her mother and grandmother were dead, and Palatan closest in dam-line, so Lakisa had begged Palatan to Dream the infant's Naming.

He'd protested. While Dreaming with Smoke or peya was far from forbidden even along River, he knew it would be considered an affront to his Alekšu. But Lakisa's protests had silenced his own: Chogah had turned from Lakisa, claiming she had tainted herself with Chepiś and deserved whatever it brought her.

That last had made Palatan relent—he was newly a sire himself, found it monstrous to punish a babe for any transgressions real or believed. And Chogah, upon finding out, had been at first furious then oddly complacent.

They'd never spoken of it since. Palatan could still remember the... the taste of a Spirit literally unravelling from within. As if carrying the babe had frayed vital threads, and the birthing had snapped and broken them.

Lakisa had been too far within that... that *place*, and Palatan himself unsure how to broach it and stay whole. Even thisnow.

And thisnow he balanced the Spirit-wealth of an entire tribal alliance upon his shoulders. He could no longer afford rash actions.

"What things, sister?" His prompt was soft, careful. "What talk did Lakisa a'iliq make to this?"

A tremor twitched Inhya's hands as he spoke the name, even with the pardoning suffix, but then, Inhya had been long a'Naišwyrh. She mouthed a tiny orison and continued.

"In truth there was little. Only that his name disturbed her even as she decided he must keep it."

Inyha was hiding something. Perhaps an oath bound her as well. Perhaps one twined with the manner of Lakisa's death.

"Our dam spoke to me of it, later. Suleweya worried after you, said you were strange for Moons after," Inhya clarified as Palatan frowned. Her talk began tripping over itself. "My brother, we all remember what it was like for you. Before. Had I known what La—what my lovemate meant to ask of you, I would have dissuaded her. You were so susceptible as oških, and the danger pervasive. So many Spirits can lie in wait, even beneath the guidance of Smoke or peya."

Smoke actually quieted ša's brethren Elementals, while the peya could make them wild. The one time Palatan had been given the latter...

Chogah had told his family it was to banish the Spirits. She had whispered to Palatan that it was a testing.

And you, my eldest sister, stood amongst the ones who watched as she gave it to me.

The resentment lingered, as did the aftermath of the drug's effects: a faulty latticework with fragments still missing. It made Palatan brusque, somewhat heedless of his tongue. "And now you fear the same affliction visits the son she gave you. You come here and ask me to torture another."

Inhya blinked. "I never wanted them to hurt you. I don't want Tokela hurt. I swore an oath, to protect him even as his dam would have."

"But?" He tried to blunt his talk, couldn't. Inhya frowned, her confusion surely reasonable. As a hand laid upon Palatan's shoulder he stiffened, then relaxed into Aylaniś's touch. It transferred a soft-deep strength, and one that didn't come from pain or rage.

Palatan closed his eyes, gentled, and rested his cheek against his chieftain's fingers. Repeated, "But?"

Inhya's gaze dropped, then her head followed suit, forehead resting upon their clasped hands for long breaths. Then she told him what she had witnessed in the Council den, alone with Tokela.

As she spoke, Aylaniś's fingers nipped, hard. With a tiny, choked noise, she moved away. Beyond Inhya's view, beneath the pretence of pouring tea, her eyes sought Palatan's, dark with disquiet.

Tokela sketching Chepiś faces he'd never seen. Tokela drawn to Našobok, to River. Mordeleg's claim of sorcery—and Inhya's worries that it could well be true. The Šilombiš'okpulo, where Lakisa had gone and Tokela had followed... and perhaps, as Mordeleg had claimed, used the Shaper's well to defend himself.

Not only Inhya's, but Palatan's own thoughts running apace: Anahli stricken afterwards, hints of interference surfacing. Her change thereafter, asking her dam about Našobok, and River.

Had she lied in Arbitration? Why would she?

And now, it seemed Tokela could hold Fire as well as River?

His thumbs stroking at Inhya's temples, Palatan winged a silent question towards the hearth. *Why did you protect Tokela?*

Fire gave no answer, Sent or Sensed.

"Something must be done, Palatan. I swore to shelter him, to raise him as my own, yet at every opportunity he but proves he's not... not..." The talk throttled into clenched fists; she'd revealed more than she felt wise. "I fear to even speak it, but I more fear..."

"You fear," said Palatan, "rumour could be truth. That your son is not your son, but a'Chepiś."

Inhya mouthed a negation, muted, and he could feel the underpinnings sending waves of chill over his scalp and down his nape.

She doesn't fear. She knows.

"You are Alekšu." Inhya raised her head, eyes glimmering. "You are now the one who, alone of all our People, has Grandmother's leave to... to intervene. You can help him as Chogah helped you!"

Chogah did not help me. Chogah hoped I'd not survive. Again, Palatan met Aylaniś's gaze; again, hers lay dark—this time with sorrow.

Yet another reason such secrets shouldn't be easily shared. The toll lay heaviest upon those forced to bear their weight as mere witness.

"I know you say torture," Inhya pleaded, "and I know she hurt you, and I felt my own Spirit dying with every scream you uttered. But you were freed, brother, freed of what Spirits would take you. There was purpose to it, you know there was, for now you can aid others! You've walked their path, you know the horror of it!"

You have, he whispered silent against her hair, *no idea.* Then, full of pity, *Ai, Tokela.*

"You know what he could face. The only reason they never banished La—my lovemate—was because she showed nothing like to... that. She was merely lost, Spirit-lost. It holds shame, but such things are pitied, cared for, released if necessary. It is not... not true possession. And it isn't Other. Isn't *Shaping.*" Inhya gulped a harsh breath, tried to regain some control. "If Tokela is what I fear, if it is laid upon him, if the rumours are proven... I have done everything I can to protect him, to stop it. I have, I swear, but if we cannot stop it, expel what possesses him—"

Cannot, she says. Ai, she knows this is not of us, knows it is truly Other.

I can gather one a'Alekšuáhoklawyhahín. Indeed, I must. There is no choice; so few of us remain. Yet what do I do with one who is but half our kind? I cannot bring Chepiś sorcery into the beating heart of our most sacred places!

"—there will be nothing more I can do. He will be made outlier, walk nameless and clanless." Inhya lifted her head, met Palatan's eyes. "There is none else before whom I can lay this. You must help my eldest son, Alekšu."

Palatan raised Inhya's fingers to his forehead, where the scarified, ebon-and-white Mark still bore a tiny, new-made itch. Then he rose and walked over to the hearth.

He could feel Inhya's eyes follow him, and those of Aylaniś, but he didn't respond, staring instead into Fire's depths.

"Alekšu." It trembled, false force. "Palatan. *Brother.*"

Still, no response. Rain poured, outside. Fire remained placid, as if Ša asked no more than to sear meat and give warmth. Was such refusal its own answer?

Or was it that there could be no answers here?

Aylaniś began to serve the bark tea. Palatan took his and did not drink, mouthing the warm clay of the cup and staring into Fire's eyes.

Turned. "He is only just oških, I know, but how long is it since his voice deepened?"

"Two winterings. He had... an...an ill reaction to the Dreaming, and the Seer said he wasn't ready. Breaking has come late to him."

"You have only seen small signs recently."

"A'io. And not all at once. In... surges."

Palatan nodded. "This is normal."

"*Normal?*" Inhya's voice rose, almost shrill.

Another knife cut, shallow and stinging. Palatan smiled at it, bitter, and gave emotionless explanation. "It means we yet have time."

◊ ◊ ◊

"Rain's stopped," Tokela half-whispered.

Našobok turned from draping their wet clothing over a line of twisted hemp in the corner of his hold. Tiny hisses issued as he did, the garb dripping upon uncovered pots of gleaming-stones. Set below on gimbals, they gave off as much warmth as light—a luxury Našobok was glad to invest in. Their clothing would be mostly dry by Sun's rising.

Tokela stood by the aft lookout, staring out into the darkness. He swayed ever so slightly, not only from *Ilhukaia*'s motion, but some vibration deep within.

Frowning, Našobok snatched up a length of fine-split doehide from a hook and padded over, draping it across Tokela's bare shoulders. Tokela shivered, still swaying, and Našobok leaned forwards.

"What do you See, Eyes of Stars?" he murmured, realising the horsetalker inflection even as he uttered it.

"Everything." A bare whisper, the like language parried quick as a spear. Then another shiver and louder, in dawnLands talk, Tokela murmured, "Nothing. Rain. Dark."

"Mmm." Našobok started to rub the hide over Tokela's shoulders, since it was obvious Tokela'd no interest in doing so. "Sometimes on River, if She's flat calm and Sky is clear, you feel as if you're swimming in Stars."

"Really?" So small, the voice. So remote.

Našobok focused on scouring Tokela's backbone. "Really. All you see is deep black and pinpoints of light, all you hear is water skimming against the hull. You're flying in indigo dark, hung in another... now."

"Another now. I think I'd like that."

Našobok tipped Tokela's chin, but those eyes evaded his, vulnerability skidding behind a cool, thick skim. They gleamed in the dark—no Seeing but nightsight, fled of the random flits and sparks like... like...

Stars. Stars and clouds filled with Rain, and the deep, wild indigo of the dark Mare's belly over us, never-ending...

All of it left Našobok hollowed and breathless and twisted—and, somehow, in need of cover. Ducking his head, Našobok knelt and began to dry Tokela's ankles and feet.

Tokela submitted to the attentions. Then, with a sudden shy grin, "I like that, too. I didn't think..."

Našobok smoothed his fingers over one instep, gave an upwards smirk at what was stirring, obvious response to the caress, amidst the sparse, dark fur conjoining Tokela's thighs.

"I never thought those two things would ever be that connected."

Regaining both his feet and his equilibrium, Našobok laughed. "At your age, everything's connected to your rudder."

Grinning wider, Tokela scratched behind one ear. Našobok traced one indigo-Marked cheek then the other, and once more Tokela's eyes chased away. This time, however, from self-conscious delight. Another chuckle rumbling in his chest, Našobok threw the hide over his own head and started in on his sodden hair.

Soothing, familiar: the tiny hisses of their clothes dripping, of River lapping against the wood hull. Then another soft rhythm, first in question, then increasing both pace and volume. Našobok closed his eyes with a smile. The muted beat of the drum—and the hands coaxing it—were as familiar to Našobok as his own heartbeat.

"Is it Munro?" Tokela moved across the small hold to the map hung upon the back wall. River, from Her starting place amongst the Rumbling Ice Mountains, and down to Sea.

"A'io." Našobok slung the hide over the drying line and grabbed up a blanket. He didn't miss Tokela's eyes, hungry upon the charts scattered and piled across the table beneath the hanging map—or his hands clasped behind his back.

"Riverwalkers... sketch."

"I'm not very good at it, to Munro's chagrin. Says it's my upbringing." Našobok reached over and twitched at one of the charts. "This one is of the estuaries downRiver. Where River folds into Sea. The chart has depths and soundings and... it's all right, you can touch it. It's meant to be touched."

Though perhaps not with the reverence that Tokela gave it, light fingers a-quiver, tracing the lines. "They wouldn't let you, either."

"Wouldn't let me...? Huh. Sketch, you mean. Well, you know our birthing-tribe." Našobok couldn't help the quirk of brow. "Do you sketch, then?"

Tokela's eyes were narrowed, gauging. "Sometimes."

"Then you should make more talk with Munro. I think he tires of his wyrhmates's clumsiness with such things."

Still stroking the chart, Tokela fell silent. There was tension beneath, rising, and Našobok knew why. He hadn't answered the asking:

Take me with you.

It wasn't a journey Našobok intended to make thisdark. He needed rest. He needed contemplation.

He needed to decide what it had meant when Tokela had said *Take me with you* and he'd found himself, against any logic or sense, thinking *Of course I will.*

So Našobok curled close to Tokela, wrapping both arms snug. Against his forearms, slender ribs expanded as Našobok snaked one hand around and down; a quick breath escaped in a decided whimper as Našobok took him in hand and nuzzled the damp hair from Tokela's nape.

Nipped, and said, "Come to my furs."

Tokela wasn't the only one practiced in evasion's Dance.

This was how an elder fem with the joint-ill must feel.

Anahli's hands and shoulders ached. Her eyes burned and wouldn't stop weeping. Her apron—thankfully it was an apron, and not her leathers!—smelled abominably. Her hands stung, and she'd several shallow cuts where the obsidian had decided cutting fishKin-flesh wasn't enough; that ša wanted Anahli-flesh as well.

She never wanted to eat silvers ever again, much less have to spend another miserable halfDark in the lean-tos, fileting and salting, or hanging the catch for Smoke's care. And there were rumours of another run coming upRiver!

Surely she wasn't the only one who hoped it would wait until after First Running's final Dark, with a great bonFire to greet Summering's beginnings. Even if she'd absolutely no longings towards Dancing. All she wanted was a hot soak and several darks' worth of sleep.

Unfortunately, the plethora of hot pools fed by a caldera were a ride of three Suns distant. At least there were bathing dens here, hide and bough wikupehs set up beside River, steam escaping the corners, shared bloodwood tubs warmed by gleamingstones. As Anahli headed towards them, Rain felt good upon her upturned face, cool blessing upon sooty, weepy eyelids.

The oških fems had decided to forgive her transgressions of Dance, making friendly talk with her in the lean-tos instead of radiating chill and silent disapproval. Čayku had even lent her the apron, and made a few promises of the fun they'd have in the baths later...

Soft, her dam would say. *Hot water is for wintering; summerings are spent on the plain, with no real abundance of water, let alone heated!*

All right then, soft, but Anahli craved hot water. Particularly thisnow, in the damp and chill of dawnLands, with bits of fishKin under her fingernails.

First, she had to retrieve a few things she'd left in her family's tipo. It rose before her in the gloaming, wide bulk below and poles splaying like steepled fingers reaching for Sky. A thin trail of Smoke tangled with the "fingers", and as Anahli came closer she could hear murmurs. Her sire's voice, rising and falling, making terse talk with...

Chogah?

Her breath behind her teeth, Anahli crept closer. Her sire kept company with Chogah only when he was forced to.

"—not so simple!" Chogah hissed. "Being Alekšu means not only responsibility to our People, but ourselves."

"And well you know the latter!" Palatan's voice, hushed, snapped like a braided quirt. "I'm still cleaning up the remnants of your *self-interest!*"

"I told you, when you were Marked child-no-longer, that you would need me."

"I'd little choice, as you were then Alekšu."

"With the obligation—n'da, the *right*"—mockery ran like silkweave along Chogah's voice—"to make the cure for those possessed of Elementals. I could have done so with you. Instead, in secrecy, I blooded you to Lapis Council and owlClan."

Lapis Council, Anahli knew. Those were the elders of the duskLands tribes, their gatherings every third Moons. But owlClan? She'd heard nothing of such lineage.

"I told them I hadn't seen a talent like to yours in many turnings. Then you squandered it, running wild with that Riverwalker outcast, not learning at my side as you should."

"Some things"—a hiss—"cannot be taught."

A pause. "Do you smell fishKin?"

Anahli froze.

"Don't change the subject, old one; the entire compound reeks of silvers."

Chogah laughed, soft and mocking. "Yet you insist on letting these hidebound fishmongers throw away more... uhn... unteachable things. Despite that your Riverwalker lovemate has found another of shamanKin to cosset and ruin, an oških that bides even more powerful than you. And you would merely watch as your Riverwalker takes him from us?"

"What choice do I have? You know as well as I, he is not of us. His Spirit is tainted by Chepiś, forbidden."

Anahli's eyes widened. *Tainted by Chepiś* roiled itself under by *another of shamanKin...*

But their like were long gone. Purged.

"So it's said. And enough that many deem him ehšehklan— even his own hearth-mother!" Chogah shifted, a creak of leathers, and her next words proved to Anahli of whom they spoke: Tokela. "Hunh! Inhya always was a heart-blind fool, believing what Lakisa'ailiq cobbled out of Spirit-lost dreams."

"I need your experience, not your bile. Only cowards mock another's pain. My sister is afraid."

"And she should be. But not for what reasons she thinks. Call upon your heart and your Spirits, Palatančokašanli." Anahli had never heard Chogah say her sire's blessing-name in such a tone. "Realise the possibilities."

"Possibilities."

"One of shamanKin, and Shaped by Chepiś! Tell me, Alekšu, that you don't wonder at it. Did Lakisa'ailiq lie with one? She lost every other child of Talorgan's; how did this one survive? How did Chepiś taint Tohwakeli'fitčiluka, eh? How has he survived it? His mother didn't."

"He still might not." Bleak. "I wish we knew more of how it happened. All those who know the truth are dead."

"Galenu knows."

Palatan snorted, and Anahli had to agree with the assessment. That old midLander knew more about his own visage in a clear pool!

"He knows what happened, I tell you." Chogah's voice lowered, venomous. "It is not the only secret he holds that belongs to owl-Clan."

A rustling from within the tipo; Palatan rising and brushing at his leather leggings. "You say I cast away unteachable things—you fixate on impossible things. Galenu has nothing of yours. His dam—your sister—told you things to torment you. That practice runs deep, it seems, in your lineage."

"Hunh. I believe, now, that Anahli also knows."

This did suck Anahli's breath from between her teeth.

No more rustling. Only silence, holding for so long that Anahli leaned sideways—carefully, more carefully—to peek through a crack in the door flap.

Chogah sat on the ground, stirring at a pot of steaming spice-bark. Her sire stood rigid; the only thing moving were his hands, clenching and releasing by his hips as if they longed to be about Chogah's throat.

"You," he finally said, hoarse, "twist your talk as it suits you."

"Huh. As does your spouse's eldest. You have a blind spot two Suns running about Anahli. Yet you've wondered why she covered for Tokela at arbitration, haven't you? I've no doubts the River outlier did—that one's always thought with his bits when it comes to pretty boys with Fire behind their eyes. Only this one has River as well... Two Elementals, Alekšu. Two co-tenants in one host. Isn't that another pretty puzzle?"

"This," Palatan gritted, "is no mere puzzle. And what do you know of Anahli?"

"How do such as we know anything?" Scornful. "I know she saw Tokela use his Power. She was ill in your tipo after the incident with the midLander oških, who just happens to claim, nextSun, that Tokela tried to use 'witchcraft' against him. Why Anahli decided to shield Tokela, who knows? But I do believe something tried to wake in her, then. You felt it too. Didn't you?"

"A mere whisper." Palatan's hands were tightened, tendons and bone sallow beneath bronze. "Sluggish, feverish. A passing thing."

"Like a breeze faltering in the heat."

"A breeze." His whisper came faint. "A swarm of bees, with the Wind of their wings cooling a hive."

Wings. Wind. Waking. Feel. Fevered breeze, rippling River as She washed through dreams not Anahli's own, calling not her but Tokela. Calling Našobok. River's voice like Wind in the trees, whispering:

Eyes meet eyes, to waken Spirit.

Spirit wakens our Mother's heart...

A breeze played with the ends of Anahli's braids, rattled Rain against the hide flaps. Anahli blinked, refocused upon the odd tableau within.

"But nothing, now," Palatan murmured.

Chogah hummed agreement. "I thought I'd imagined it, too." A snort. "No doubt you sired *her*; both of you can cloud your eyes as easily as breathing."

"Insult me as you like, Chogah, but leave Anahli alone. Why do you think she's here? To be away from *you*."

Aylaniś had said it, more than once: *Predator and prey is the way of things. Eventually, all of us are hunted in some fashion. Yet I do not have to allow it in my tipo, with my children as prey.*

"Another pretty problem, *Alekśu*, and this one yours in particular. To need your predecessor, all the while wishing you could see the end of them."

"Or your successor." Pointed.

"Ai, we are bound too close by too many things." Chogah snorted. "Listen. Deep in her heart, Anahli knows what Tokela is. Perhaps more than we can. And"—this with a soft sneer—"she's listening to us right now, outside the tipo."

"I won't say anything. I *swear* it."

"If you do," Chogah said, mixing up another cup of spicebark, "we'll make sure you are unable to bring forth even the memories." She held out the cup.

For a half breath Anahli wondered if she intended to carry out the threat here and now. Chogah kenned the suspicion. As if in challenge, she kept holding out the cup.

Eyes narrowing, Anahli crossed her arms.

"Ai, if both of you were any more stiff-necked, I could break you with a slap!" Palatan growled and, snatching the cup from Chogah, downed it in one gulp. "Take mine. I wouldn't bother poisoning you! I'd rather drag you behind my horse!"

Ai, he was angry, no question. "I didn't intend any—"

"Didn't you? You didn't walk away, kept listening. More fool me for closing my nose and ears, and for making open talk of such things. While Chogah bides thrice the fool for knowing you were there, yet going on—"

"By the time I knew she was there, it was too late—"

"Wait!" Anahli protested. "Are there are still shamanKin? Are—?"

Palatan's fingers slapped against Anali's lip, held firm. "Understand this, ehši. I will alter your memory if I must."

"We might anyway," Chogah grumbled.

Palatan shot her a foul glare, turned it upon Anahli, and only then took his fingers away.

"But..." Anahli saw his hand twitch again, changed what she had been about to say. "Yeka, what do I know?"

"And that is the question of thisSun's rising." Chogah, sarcastic.

"Until you do know, you cannot ask," Palatan raised one finger, this time, pressed firm against Anahli's mouth as she started to protest. "It's not only what you might know. It's also what that knowledge will do to Tokela."

Any talk died in Anahli's throat. Palatan nodded, his gaze hardened into malachite. Suddenly Anahli wondered why she'd never, until then, noticed the tiny blue-to-orange ombre of flames behind. "Anahli. Do you understand?"

Ai, she was afraid she did.

"Ask no further questions." Those eyes softened, and Palatan dropped his chiding hand, turning away. He looked... ai, weary. Old, somehow.

"Chogah, leave me. I've decisions to make, and you make me tired even when I don't. Aylaniś should be back shortly, and..." His nose wrinkled. "You, too, daughter. Go. We'll speak later. After you wash; you reek of fish."

Dawn came in, soft but inexorable, chasing dark to the corners of Sky's realm. Munro's drum had long since gone quiet, the old one retired to his hammock. Even Wind lay still, napping in dawn's embrace as ša often did.

And like some avatar of Wind, Tokela also lay sleeping, swathed in the furs and Našobok's blanket.

Našobok had stood at the flung-back flap of his hold stair, He'd watched the Moons set, first Brother then His siblings, each behind the trees, as Sky turned from indigo, to murky Smoke, then to coals as Sun rose. Let Wind waft over his bare skin. Taken Smoke from his treasured pipe.

And watched Tokela sleep.

Sprawled on the pallet below, Tokela muttered and cast one arm upwards, twitching and lost in some other place—no doubt more astride dark's Mare than any sweet and steaming ośkih dreams. It shot a pang through Našobok so jagged, it was a wonder it didn't draw blood.

Take me with you.

Amongst wyrhling and yakhling lay the favoured cache for undesirables: outliers often came from the forbidden. For as long as Našobok could remember, River had surged through his veins, driven him, and while what possessed him merely glimmered in comparison to what burned, hot and high, within Palatan, still Našobok's blood flowed with an undertow for which he had given... everything.

Thankfully, the undertow threatening to swamp Tokela had been sated. For now, anyway.

Sometimes an Elemental just has to... fix to something. Be consumed by what is here, and present. Smoke, or sex, or Dance... like tinder to Fire's touch. The flare and burn, then the ash.

Našobok had learned such things—first by accident then by practice, in myriad and intimate ways. He'd held Palatan during long, Spirit-ridden Moons passages, teased him back into this-now with well-timed caresses. Had watched Lakisa change from indulgent, merry aunt to time-raddled shade. Had held his sire down on a dark, storm-slick deck when Nechtoun, his Spirit lost in exposure and grief, had tried to do them both harm.

Either Tokela would ripen like to Palatan, throwback to Power most had no idea still existed—or, like Nechtoun, like Lakisa, Tokela's Spirit would buckle beneath such promise and flee, leaving behind an emptiness no Power could fill. Until then would the dual edges remain: passion, expression, *giving*... withdrawal, hiding, *panic*.

Našobok had wondered; now he knew.

His heart kenned his own kind. He could not overtly wield Her Power, but he had learned to listen. To observe. To accept.

Beneath *Take me with you* lay another, deeper plea: *Listen. Please. And accept what I, all too soon, will have to.*

A light tap sounded upon the open hatch of his hold. Našobok started, spared a glance for Tokela and found him unmoved—no surprise there. Palatan too would sleep like the dead after such upheaval. With age and experience came self-possession; still, the Elementals were very Power-full.

Našobok wrapped in a blanket, and mounted the steep stair to find one of his wyrhmates waiting above.

"Kalisom," Našobok smiled. "You're back early. I expected to find Munro."

"Ran out of gambling tender." Kalisom gave a lift of his massive, bare shoulders and grinned. "And the playmate I chose was not so fair upon dawn as dark."

With a chuckle, Našobok came on deck and folded shut the hold door behind.

"I left Munro to sleep. Wasn't going to disturb you, either, but"—Kalisom jerked his ebon head, sending snugged-back twistlocks to jerk and dance—"you've a visitor up aft, wyrhchieftain."

Našobok followed the gesture to see Aylaniś, leathers covered by a colourful blanket, her arms crossed and profile tilted duskwards, backlit by Sun's rising. Odd, that she was here. Or perhaps not; as he saw her, Našobok knew what he had to do. And he'd long ago decided that coincidences to do with his lovemates often weren't that at all.

"She hailed me as I boarded the raft, came across with me." Kalisom seemed uneasy as Našobok turned back to him.

"What has your clout knotted, wyrhmate? You've seen Aylaniś horse-chieftain before."

"She is spouse to Alekšu, now." Kalisom made a warding gesture.

"Hunh!" Našobok cuffed him, half joke and half chide. "You sound a superstitious landwalker. Be easy, she won't bite." He smirked. "Hard, anyway."

A return smile teased at Kalisom's lip. "Well, the others will be back soon, wyrh-chieftain."

"See if you can round them up sooner. Start preparing for a journey. We've rich cargo in the offering."

"That's good news!"

"To put food in our hold is always good," Našobok agreed, and added, "I've a playmate in my own hold. So if a dark-haired oških comes updeck whilst I'm gone, don't cut him, thinking him a thief."

Kalisom's eyes lit up, tease and respect. "In your hold? He must be quite a special lover."

Našobok chuckled. "He is that. You would not know him; a cousin a'Naišwyrh, new to his indigo. He's called Tokela."

"Lucky oških, then!" Kalisom smirked and gave a suggestive lift of his eyebrows. "It's well known our wyrh-chieftain has many skills to share."

"Ai, flattery will have you."

"Already it's had me," Kalisom complained, "and enough for one port! It's well we've a rich cargo; I've not your luck at the gaming."

Našobok laughed, and watched his wyrhmate retreat across the deck. Then he leapt up to *Ilhukaia*'s topmost deck.

"We can't seem to catch any luck between the furs on Earth's skin, Aylaniś horse-chieftain!" he hailed. "Have you come to remedy that?"

A snort, and a toss of her braids. "You think I'd cadge a ride from one of your wyrhmates merely to drag you back to my furs? You border on insufferable, Našobok wyrh-chieftain."

"Only border? I must be slipping." He took her hand and placed it against his breastbone.

"Palatan has talk to make with you," Aylaniś said, her fingers stroking, light.

"As it happens, I've the need for talk with him, as well. Do you now run errands for Alekšu, horse-chieftain?"

"When it involves River instead of Earth beneath his feet, I do," she countered, serious. "He went on ahead, said I was to give you a good mount, should you be able to meet him at Stonebridge." One eyebrow arced upwards as she eyed him, up and down. "I would suggest you dress first. That blanket is quite fancy, but it won't protect your haunches."

Našobok could ride when he had to, and since Stonebridge was a good several leagues upRiver, it would be best if he did.

Sun's journey limned the damp trees, promised a good ending

to First Running. Soon his lovemates would make their journey as well, back towards Dusk and away from River.

They'd not had enough time together. They never did.

Našobok smelled Smoke before he saw ša curling up the lee side of the bridge, and a'io, there Palatan was, lounging on his horse blanket in the grass, puffing at his pipe. Arrow, of course, lay curled beside, and lifted his long head to determine whether this newest arrival made friend or foe. Palatan's mare, her black hide still riffled with drying sweat, looked content from a run and now grazed with white-blanketed haunches turned towards the coppery dust of the Riverside track. As Našobok cantered up, the mare's head lifted and, ears pricked, she nickered greeting through a mouthful of grass. The bay answered. Našobok slipped the bridle, let him go on to graze with his herdmate.

Palatan didn't rise; merely extended the pipe.

Našobok accepted, taking a deep drag. He sat, one knee brushing Palatan's.

Palatan seemed preoccupied but nudged Našobok, accompanied by a sly smile. "You'd company lastdark, I understand. Was it good?"

Arrow, in abandon of his normal aloof courtesy, moved his head to lay upon Našobok's thigh. Našobok fondled the old fleethound's ears, then returned Palatan's nudge and let Smoke curl from his nostrils. "Tokela is... enthusiastic."

"And owes me a return debt, now. As well as Aylaniś. Our lastdark would have been better by one addition." Palatan leaned closer and nuzzled Našobok's neck.

Našobok went abruptly cross-eyed with the sudden thought of how his own Moons passage would have benefited with the addition of Palatan, then smirked at himself.

That just might be entirely too much of a good thing.

"How does it feel to be such in demand, Riverwalker? But I mustn't be selfish," Palatan admitted. "I think Tokela needs you more at present."

Našobok frowned; something odd ran beneath the tease.

"I ride towards duskLands thisSun," Palatan ventured.

Disappointment was a poor companion for Smoke. Našobok let the latter curl out his nostrils, wished the former could do likewise. "Now?"

"A'io. I plan to go and come back as quickly as I can. I'd hoped you'd come with me."

A sigh, and Našobok closed his eyes.

"You can't." More disappointment.

"I want to." Nasobok passed the pipe back. "And would, if I hadn't contracted with Galenu to carry a shipment. It's a rich deal, and we need to take it. With all the difficulties outLand, our lines of trade are suffering. Even outliers have to make a living."

Arrow got up, stretched, and wandered over to a path of

Sun-filled grass. There he dove one shoulder down and rolled over, scratching his back.

"Surely Munro could make the run?" Transparent as the Smoke Palatan exhaled, and hopeful; it made denial all the more painful.

"Munro knows the way, but he's not getting any younger. I can't ask him to take full responsibility for a running that's danger nose to tail. We'll be heading downRiver past the estuaries and into outLands atolls. Galenu offered the chance because he knows my People have done it more than once, in and out with none the wiser."

"You'll tweak danger's nose once too often, my heart." Soft, underlain with worry.

"Hunh. Life is risk. What's the point otherwise?"

Palatan had no argument for that. Instead they both fell silent, bound by Smoke and regrets. The black mare wandered over, rolling air through her nostrils at Arrow, who gave a chiding nip to her nose and got up, offended. Not so offended, of course, that he wouldn't come back and plop half-in and -out of Palatan's lap. Palatan chuckled, gave Arrow an absent scratch, and passed the pipe.

"A quick trip." Našobok took several puffs. "Why go and return? I thought you only meant to stay a few Suns past First Running."

"I thought so, too. Is Tokela still on *Ilhukaia*?"

Našobok didn't possess the same abstruse skill set, so he often found himself left behind when Palatan's thoughts winged ahead. This time he soared with them, catching the draft. "A'io. Perhaps he should go with you in my stead." The thought, still forming as Našobok voiced it, seemed the ideal solution.

Yet Palatan's face had closed, his body still, rigid.

"You're Alekšu." Našobok paused, glanced around. Said, very quiet, "And Tokela is River's."

Smoke escaped Palatan's nostrils; otherwise there was no response.

"It's akin to what I've seen in you, but not," Našobok furthered. "More... elusive, like trying to capture Her in my fingers. Or the Sunwise prickling along my scalp and spine when green SkyFire comes, but there's no ache in my bones to say a storm's coming, and Sky is clear thisdawn—hunh!" He couldn't help the self-deprecating snort; surely Palatan wasn't helping. "Perhaps I'm mad as the legendary Tsinoé, trying to climb Nanihloyeh to reach his Brother Moons... but I do know this much: this storm lingers in my gut, is sleeping in my hold, is wrapped in my blanket."

Palatan still kept looking away, Smoke wreathing the tiny rows of braids at his temple.

"Do you doubt me?"

Still, Palatan did not answer. Puzzled, affronted, Našobok started to rise.

Palatan started, snatched a hand out and took hold of Našobok's longcoat "N'da. I'm sorry, I don't doubt anything you've said. You're Hers; you would recognise one of Hers. But..." He seemed to be searching... n'da, not searching. Picking, choosing, as if he was unsure what talk was truthful, or even prudent.

"Oathbrother..."

Palatan pulled upwards and drew close, their foreheads touching, his talk barely a whisper. "A'io, oathbrother, and I've already had one lessoning thisSun on the ways and wheres to discuss such things."

They were not in the caldera a'Šaákfo, where secrets faded into endless caverns, smothered by the weight of Fire and Earth. Neither were they riding the wide steppes of duskLands where Wind would sing them silent.

River had many reflections, and only one place of silence: beneath her surface. What could People do but mimic the Power of their places?

"It's why I wanted to meet with you here, oathbrother. I wanted—n'da, needed—to know what you'd seen in Tokela. As Chogah said, Anahli wasn't the only one covering for him at arbitration."

"Wait. Anahli?"

"What were they doing when you saw them together?"

"I thought..." Našobok hesitated, then admitted, "At first I thought they were well along on their way to making play together. Then I saw that rotted Mordeleg lying there, and... well. I wasn't too gentle with either of them. Anahli knows just what to say to jab me, and after everything that had happened during Spear Dance—"

"No blame to you there. What else?"

"Nothing, not then. Both of them seemed odd, but I figured it to be embarrassment. Tokela wanted a lover, not another reprimand. It wasn't until he came to *Ilhukaia* that... well. It became more than obvious."

"Again, no blame to you. It seems he's been concealing it quite well. Too well for my liking, but soon he'll be unable to hide from anyone."

"Then take him with you!"

"Našo—"

"At least until I return from this run. He wants out. He knows he's in trouble. He wants to come with me, and I'm prepared to take him. But not for this run; it's too dangerous for anyone new."

A slight smile chased about Palatan's lips. "Ai, you *are* in deep."

"And getting deeper, I'm afraid. Take him with you."

"Našobok." It was soft, weighty. Grim. "This is... difficult. Complicated."

Always between them; oaths sworn but oft torn by two Elementals: Našobok with River at his back, and Palatan with Fire behind his eyes.

"You are Alekšu," Našobok repeated and added, somewhat desperate, "with everything it means, fair or foul. If you can't help Tokela, who can?"

"I don't know, oathbrother." Palatan's eyes were gilt lanterns beneath Sun. "But I intend to find out."

$$\oint \quad \oint \quad \oint$$

19
WYRHLING

He woke in a strange place, with strange smells, strange sounds...

Voices.

Tokela lurched up to a crouch, furs and woollens flung aside, then winced as the movement pulled at bits that should not be sore, surely.

A lurch of the wooden floor beneath him nearly sent him sprawling, and then...

He remembered. All of it: hard rain and misted breath, skin upon skin. And when a silly smirk tilted his lip, he couldn't find it in himself to care.

Tokela sat back on his haunches, looking about to find himself alone in Našobok's hold. The voices he'd heard weren't... within. They carried from without, swallowed occasionally by fitful gusts of Wind. Sun wafted in through open lookouts, and River slapped against the ship's hull, causing *Ilhukaia* to rock fiercer than even lastdark. Tokela's fingers and toes clutched, seeking balance in the movement.

He heard his name.

Every sense flared, every bit of nerve or courage he possessed fled. He flattened on the decking like rodentkin beneath raptor shadow, his hands cupped at his nape, waiting.

They've come for me. Inhya's told Sarinak what she saw, and he's come for me, to cast me out...

His imagination, flaring panic in uncountable directions, nevertheless was not up to this. What would they do?

What was he waiting for?

Why was he cowering on the decking like a beaten dog?

Tokela shoved up from the hard wood, scowling, and crouched there with head cocking back and forth. The talk had gone silent, covered by the thumps of many feet upon the decking. He rose and crept naked to the port opening, peered out.

A set of feet passed by, hesitated, then thumped back. "Wind's grace upon you, lucky oških!" a cheerful voice greeted. A broad, brown Riverwalker with a riot of twistlocks pinned at his nape knelt into view. "There's food on deck if you're hungry. Wyrh-chieftain had to leave, but he'll be returning soon."

"The rainbows come; I can feel it in my bones."

"We'd best be away before then. They cloud River more than any silvers."

"We'll be out of here by evening drumtalk, if wyrh-chieftain has his way."

"A pity to miss the lastDark bonFires."

"We'll greet summering as Riverwalkers should, riding down-River with lanterns upon our bow!"

Laughter greeted this last, and the fem who'd made it—Odina—obviously in charge second only to old Munro: short, stout, and fierce-looking, her hair braided back from a moon-round face tattooed, as they all were, with wyrhling Marks. Sun-bronzed arms bare and rippling with muscle, she was shortest and darkest of all the River People, though her bearing made her seem tall as Matwau.

Like Maloh, Tokela mused, and took a drink with the rest. The liquor burned a sweet trail down his throat. He'd liked Maloh, even though he knew he shouldn't.

He hadn't realised *Ilhukaia* was leaving so soon. He'd said "Take me with you" amidst fright and dread, without contemplating the consequences of leaving.

Madoc, who likely was now even more angry with him. Inhya and Sarinak, who had loved him as their own—until he wasn't. Nechtoun, his Clan, his Tribe, his People. The oških den that he hadn't yet occupied since painting the indigo upon his cheeks. The Great Mound looming over *Ilhukaia*'s bow, a seat of security, stability. The Great Mound was the only home he'd ever known, and perhaps he'd miss the lastDark of First Running...

Wyrhlings had long grown used to leaving such things behind, but would he ever see them again?

Of course, did he have a choice?

Did Našobok even mean to take him, at that? He'd not agreed, not said he would.

Tokela blinked the heat from his eyes, let them cool into something more akin to River stone. Perhaps with a sharp edge of obsidian should any venture too close. It seemed he was going to need it.

Munro offered Tokela more meat. He took it with a grateful gesture, and the elder smiled.

All of them, really, had made him so welcome.

Suddenly, the male who'd knelt at the porthole—Kalisom, he'd said his name was—leapt up and gave a long, piercing whistle. An answer shrilled from just off the bow. The wyrhlings all leapt to their feet, lively with greeting.

"Ai, River-chieftain!

"Našobok, you're back!"

"Is it time to set to?"

"We've your cousin here, safe and fed!" Kalisom called down, and Našobok's voice answered from below:

"Good! Where is he?"

"I'm here," Tokela answered, clutching to the railing and looking down to see Našobok alone in the canoe, pulling close to the rope fenders of *Ilhukaia*.

Našobok wouldn't meet his eyes. "Come down, then! I'll ferry you myself."

"I can't go back."

"A'io, you can."

"You don't understan—"

"I do." The canoe bobbed, gentle, midway to the shore. The oar clacked against the sides, and callused hands gripped Tokela's shoulders, tried to turn him around. "And you have to understand, too."

Ai, Tokela understood, all right. And had no right to expect anything else.

"N'da," Našobok growled, "you really don't." His hands tightened, gave another shake. "Tokela!"

It was gentler than the fierce grip. Tokela made sure his gaze told nothing of what he was thinking, and turned around.

Only he hadn't prepared himself for Našobok's expression—gentle as the shake, as his voice. "Listen, Tokela. There are many things to be considered. There are difficulties."

"There are always... difficulties."

"There are," Našobok concurred. "One being you aren't listening."

"When bodytalk gives answer, what's the point of talk?" It might have been set in stone. Ai, Sarinak would have been proud.

Našobok was not. A puzzled frown gathered his brows, shivering a fissure through what Tokela had so carefully set in place.

It cracked, bled. "If I can't go with you, then... I don't... know where..." Tokela choked off, humiliated, tried to turn away.

He'd forgotten how strong Našobok was; those broad hands denied any movement. "I know, Tokela. I *know*."

You don't know, not really! It almost came tumbling out, then: what Inhya had seen, what he himself had done. Just in time Tokela clapped his hands over his mouth. Usually his tongue would tangle, foul what he wanted to speak—why now did it seem to spew?

"If I didn't have this commission from the old khatak, it would be done. You would stay, and shadowlings take the consequence."

Tokela was frozen in place, hands still over his mouth, staring at Našobok with his thoughts all garbled. There was fear. Despair. And, the ultimate cruelty, hope.

"But there is not just you and I in this Dance we contemplate. This will be a dangerous sail—"

Tokela shook his head, opened his fingers enough to say, "I'm not afraid!"

"And that," Našobok shook him, gently, "is why you can't go. *I'm* afraid of this one. You're not one of my Wyrhmates. Yet." A half grin, a promise swelling hope just that much higher. "You don't know enough for this journey, and that might get you or one of my People killed. The landwalkers like to say wyrhling have no home, no Clan, but they're wrong. My Wyrhmates are my Clan. I don't hold their lives cheaply. Or yours."

Taking a deep breath, Tokela nodded, looked down.

"You have choices, my heart. Perhaps more than coming with me. Perhaps better ones."

"Better?" It tore from Tokela's chest.

"Listen. Whatever has happened"—Našobok's grip tightened, then loosed—"whatever happens, you must consider what comes from this heartbeat. You are not powerless."

You have no idea how 'not powerless' I seem to be. Tokela closed his eyes, gritted his teeth. There seemed more consequences than any choices.

And found himself thinking again, sudden-sharp, upon Madoc.

Consequences.

If I was to go away, go to River, be outlier—wyrhling—what would you do then?

But choices?

"Why did they name you after Her, River Wolf?"

The question was hoarse, and startled Tokela no less than, it seemed, Našobok. Taking up the oar once again, Našobok started to row. When it came, the answer was quiet.

"No doubt the same reason they named you Eyes of Stars. It's what the nameKeeper saw in me."

Beneath them, as if showing off for a paramour, River lurched the canoe frontwards, then back. Našobok took the motion with careless ease, while Tokela had to grab for the closest beam, chasing both balance and subject matter.

"And that's why you kept it? Why your sire refuses to speak it?"

"That, amongst other things." Našobok shrugged and half-turned. "It's one of the things you must consider. If you came with me, the time will come when they no longer voice your name. Though"—another shrug—"you are oških, after all. You've the right to test many waters without irredeemable shame."

"I am not shamed of you!"

"You never have been. It's not a gift I take lightly, Star Eyes."

Silence, as strangely comfortable as the eyes-meeting-eyes. River lapped beside them, Her recognition, once again, almost a vibration between them.

Tokela blinked, shook his head slightly, dropped his gaze.

"There are always consequences. Have scant worry over mine. Those a'Naišwyrh can do nothing to this outlier they haven't already done. But you? Ai, you must think of yourself, Tokela. Perhaps you should ask: what are the consequences? If you leave, or if you stay? Have you thought upon this? Or did you come to me lastDark with a fear upon you that made you ask for shelter? Have you faced that fear, made sure it has merit? That there is no help for you amidst your People?"

It struck deep.

Našobok took the paddle in one hand, reached out with the other and tapped at Tokela's chin. "Palatan left for a'Šaákfo earlier thisSun. He told me to tell you this: he means to return with answers for you. He has vowed this as Alekšu."

It should ease Tokela; clearly Našobok thought it would. But it didn't. It meant Alekšu knew, but also that Alekšu had no answers yet. And...

Don't trust Alekšu.

And *Make your own Clan.*

And *You are not the only one who has seen Other!*

What did Inhya know? What did Anahli?

"I'll be back, Star Eyes."

Tokela slid his gaze to Našobok, whose Smoke-coloured eyes had creased, a smile lingering in tip-tilted corners.

"I'll be back before the Brother Moon completes His turn, a little more or less. If you still want it, you have a place with me. With the wyrhling." Našobok reached out, caressed Tokela's face. "That is my vow, to you."

Drums announced it. Not the huge bass voices of the talking drums, but a light and solitary beat echoing against the cliffs and downRiver. Then other sounds: first a deep-throated call sending shivers down the spine of anyone hearing it; then, one by one, others joining in descant.

Ilhukaia's crew, singing her ready to depart.

Tokela had crept up Overlook after Našobok had set him ashore, and stayed. The ledge was barren of any others; he was glad. For one so skilled at making himself invisible, over the past few Suns he'd been far too evident for his liking. He leaned into the warm stones of his chosen, solitary perch, propped his chin into his elbows, and watched.

There had been some commotion earlier. Wind had shifted

from dawnwards to downRiver, causing a flurry of activity. Old Munro had quickly rowed across, with Kalisom, to meet Galenu upon the strand. Several pouches changed hands almost too quickly to follow, and were ferried back over. The two wyrhlings made it back aboard just as the moorings were untied. The front crimson squaresail billowed loose, quickly manoeuvred and set. Once they'd drifted well into River's main, the settee mainsail was tilted. Catching Wind's breath, both resembled more the fine, bright-hued lace of insect wings than the tightspun fabric they truly were.

And Našobok, of course, a familiar lion stalking the deck, mane flying in what breath filled the sails. The same breath that even now tugged at Tokela's hair, beckoning him to follow.

Not yet, he promised Wind, and River. *Soon.*

He had to hope it would come true. Had to. Otherwise...

His eyes stung; he pretended it was Wind's disappointment.

On the strand below, movement beckoned. Galenu was still there; he'd spotted Tokela, was waving greeting. Tokela returned it, somewhat half-hearted, only to have that heart lurch and beat as strong as Munro's drum as his eyes returned to *Ilhukaia*'s deck, and Našobok flung his fist from heart and outwards, towards Overlook.

He'd known Tokela watched. A foolish, faithless hope filled Tokela's chest, meeting and matching the drum of his heart.

Galenu retreated. Tokela didn't move, watching until *Ilhukaia* disappeared upRiver in a chiaroscuro of trees and Sun. Kept watching until his eyes burned.

Only then did he hear the light pace climbing the last steps to the Overlook. For a heartbeat he wondered if Galenu had actually climbed up here to speak with him; he quickly abandoned that, not only because it was absurd Galenu should have done, but because he recognised the step. Tokela's heart hammered fiercer— this time with active panic.

Truly faithless, hope, for he had implored it to let him avoid this very instance. Somehow, though he knew it had to come. Tokela didn't turn, merely hunched his shoulder and gritted his teeth. Waited.

"There are nets to mend," Inhya said. She was somewhat out of breath, had obviously made the climb nonstop. "The next running comes all too soon."

Tokela frowned. The breath he'd sucked in and held escaped him in a nigh-silent cough. Still, he didn't move.

"Now the wyrhling is gone, you will pay more attention to your share of work, a'io?"

It was so normal as to be inconceivable. Tokela wasn't sure what else to do, so he half-turned.

Inhya stood a little distance away, arms crossed and tangled in the shawl fallen about her elbows, bright-wrapped head cocked, thoughtful brows a-quirk. Again, normal. Inhya looked not much different from any other time when Tokela was in for it.

Save her eyes. They were guarded, much more than normal. Not just wary. Afraid.

The shame and sting of it seared Tokela's heart. But a tiny, venomous place in his Spirit found a fierce—and repellent—glee.

Inhya's expression hardened, as if sensing it, and she tucked her chin, mouth set. "Aylaniś has taken both Madoc and Kuli for another hunt. It would be a prudent time to remove your things from the ahlóssa den."

This was even more inconceivable. Tokela turned fully about, stammered, "Wh-what d-did you say?"

Inhya showed no exasperation at such obtuseness, merely repeated, "The little ones are with Aylaniś. You should remove your things now. It'll be easier for everyone, particularly Madoc."

"But... you..." His tongue kept proving itself traitor, stammering protest. "You were... What happened was—"

"What happened, Tokela?" Inhya seemed deep-rooted as a tree—though much less pliable, more insurmountable. Akin to the cliffs beneath their feet.

Tokela envied her. "In the Council den." Carrion-eaters take him and shred his bones, why could he not *shut it*? "What happened with—"

She clucked, a dismissal, nothing less.

Still, he couldn't let it go. "At the hearth! You *saw*. My arm. Fire."

"What do you think I saw, Tokela a'Naišwyrh?" Her eyes wavered, ever so slight.

And finally—*finally*—his tongue stilled.

"Sarinak is waiting for you at the ahlóssa den," Inhya continued, looking away. "You will do your duty, and he will do his: cleanse and smudge you as is proper, take you to your new place." A pause, then, "You will not speak of any foolishness to him. You know what it means if you do. You will not approach Madoc with such things—or, indeed, with anything else."

Tokela's eyes slid upwards, thankfully hidden by his forelock, for he could only imagine what was in them. So. "This is how it will be, then?"

"Given the past few Suns, did you expect otherwise?" Her riposte was calm, eminently reasonable. "You are oških now, and he is ahlóssa. It's unseemly for you to be with him so much."

I won't let you do this. You'll be sorry.

Wind twisted about them, a sudden chill gust filling Tokela's gaping mouth, tugging at his hair and whipping Inhya's shawl nigh from her grasp. She backed a step, eyes wide, made as if to retreat. Paused, eyes narrowing into knife edges, her talk coming just as sharp.

"You'll not have to be burdened here overlong. There's been talk made of a hearth-place for you. And when my brother returns..." For the first time, Inhya seemed to diminish, uncertain. "Alekšu will return soon, and have cause to... to speak with you."

"Alekšu." It was wooden.

"A'io. You will listen, and he'll aid you."

"How will he aid me? I thought nothing hap—"

"You ask too many questions." Again, a snap. "We'll say nothing more to any of this at present. Mound-chieftain waits, and you—"

"What a climb!"

Breathless, the talk a'Naišwyrh had a peculiar accent. Both Inhya and Tokela turned to see a brightly clad, somewhat portly figure treading the topmost step.

"Your pardon!" Galenu exclaimed. "The climb up always takes me by surprise and I have to stop midway. I didn't mean to startle anyone; I merely came to watch the wyrhcraft set off. Not unlike young Tokela here." A smile flashed, fading as Galenu addressed Inhya. "I didn't realise there was... council being held atop the overlook."

Didn't realise? Yet Galenu's manner suggested otherwise, making Tokela wonder how much the elder had heard.

"No council thisnow, stone-chieftain," Inhya returned, serene and formal. "You merely witness my son finishing his oških Journey. Sarinak awaits him. Come, Tokela."

"If you please?" Galenu held up a hand, gave a charming smile. "I've talk to make to your son regarding Mordeleg's offences—amongst other things—and I've had small chance so far to do so." The smile turned to Tokela, kinder and less calculating. "Might we speak now, oških? You've been"—the smile turned sly—"well, a bit preoccupied these past few Suns."

It ticced a return smile at Tokela's lip.

Inhya found no similar mirth in Galenu's talk, but remained silent. Comprehension struck Tokela; his right now, not hers, to agree to Galenu's request. He was oških.

"My mother, I will come to Sarinak immediately after this."

Inhya's face darkened, but she gave way with some grace. "Not overlong. He waits, with other duties before him."

Galenu watched her descend the stair. Tokela eyed him, somewhat wary now they'd come to it. What did Galenu want?

Neither did he look at Tokela, but everywhere else—Forest's surround, the driftwood railings, the rocks, River. For someone who wanted talk, Galenu lingered remarkably silent. Tokela shifted from one foot to the other, put his own face to River, found calm there.

He could outwait this. He could wait forever.

"Are you comfortable enough with making midLands talk?" Galenu finally asked in that dialect.

Tokela tilted his chin in the affirmative.

Again, a pause. Then, "You're not very happy living here, are you?"

It was the last question Tokela had expected. For a half heartbeat he was unsure he'd heard correctly. But there was no mistake—in talk or the humiliation it rendered. Could everyone see this? Was it written so plain on his face?

Tokela took rabid hold of himself, forced his voice light. "I don't know what you mean."

Galenu fell quiet again. Tokela usually found security in silence; often friend, sometimes a comfortable weapon. Yet he barely lasted two fours of his own heart's beating. Tokela knew, because he counted.

"I am with my mother's family, Galenu a'Hassun. I'm grateful they—"

"Gratitude can be very discomfiting. On both sides."

Tokela had no idea of how to answer this.

"You were ill-treated by a member of my tribe," Galenu continued. "I can only excuse his behaviour in that he feels threatened by you."

"Threatened? By me?"

"Mordeleg thinks you're more closely related to me than he is. He's right, of course."

"I don't understand."

Galenu frowned, then shrugged. "Of course, you wouldn't. In midLands, our moiety is hereditary, through many and varied Hoops of powerful leaders. Here in duskLands the chieftains are ones who can speak the most persuasively, trade effectively and hold back the outLanders; a'Šaákfo the way of leading is matriarchal, held by wit and horse-wealth and the resultant raiding games; in dryLands, Water-tapper is leader; in upLands the one who finds the herds and keeps their people fed when the light leaves in wintering..." He shrugged again. "Well. Mordeleg thinks you threaten his chance to hold our territory."

This was altogether much to take in.

"Either way, Tokela, son of my nephew, I wish to make amends."

"Arbitration demanded and settled restitution; it is done."

"A'io, and fairly done. But there are other matters. Ones for which I'd offer personal restitution." Galenu paced across the parapet and came to stand beside Tokela, looking out.

Tokela kept his spine to the stones and his eyes upon Galenu, curious. Chary. The old chieftain remained silent, as if merely enjoying the view. Altogether curious, with his grey hair in an elaborate knot, his lightweave leggings, long, sashed tunic, and opentoed sandals appended only by a thick blanket shawl.

What did he want? There was no doubt in Tokela's mind but Galenu wanted something.

"Ai, but Wind's breath is heavy, here, filling your lungs with the wet. Your sire thrived here, but I must confess a preference for midLands, dry and crisp—and hot come summering. Did you know Talorgan, Sun and sweet water light his Spirit, grew up only a level below my own sett?"

Hearing his sire's name so boldly spoken took Tokela aback. All he could do was tilt his head, curious.

"We call our lodgings setts. Like badgerKin we dug our homes into the rocky flathills, such as the place where I am chieftain. Not unlike here, where the Mound and Her cliffs have been hollowed out for habitation. It's why we're Hassun, stoneClan—surely you know that? But of course you do. Nechtoun tells me you're intelligent—too smart for your own good, he adds, though I don't see why intelligence needs such critical measure. Ai, well. Those a'Naišwyrh are set in their ways."

His cheeks hot in a reaction somewhere between pleasure and insult, Tokela returned the shrug.

"It can be hard to live in a place where folk insist on keeping their sights trammelled to Earth. Particularly if you have eyes that seek Sky."

That last twisted sharp beneath Galenu's tongue, enough like to Tokela's own name to be no accident. Neither did it contain the normal humour of such puns. Unsure how to answer, Tokela gave another shrug.

"You don't make much talk, do you?" One arm braced against the driftwood railing set into Tokela's support, Galenu lifted one eyebrow. "Hunh. You're very like to your sire, you know."

Again, a complex and conflicted reaction of emotions—first, Galenu had seen something in Tokela of Talorgan, then the realisation that it was a lie, all of it. Talorgan had not sired him—and where no shame should remain in his dam's choice of who would sire her child, there *was* shame in this instance. Shame, and danger in *what* had sired Tokela. He was half of Other. The proof seethed within, rising unbidden as any storm.

Even Alekšu had ridden away with unanswered questions...

"Tokela. You're the only son of my sister's son. You are of an age to gain sire-knowledge. I would offer my hearth to you, if you'd come to midLands."

Not a surprise, exactly, since he'd eavesdropped on Council... had it truly been merely three Suns ago? Tokela looked down at the arm Fire had taken in, still unscorched, unscarred.

Thought: *If you knew, you wouldn't want me either.*

Said: "There is another I'm sworn to."

If it wasn't exactly true, it wasn't false, either.

But what if Našobok knew the whole of it? Insidious, the doubt.

Galenu was frowning. "But horse-chieftain hasn't spoken yet, though I'm sure she... Ai. I see. Našobok." An odd, perturbed expression crawled over his seamed face. Then he chuckled, rueful. "Those eyes of yours indeed look beyond the horizons here. Small wonder they don't know what to do with you."

Tokela looked away.

"Hunh. I don't retract my offer. I think there might be depths to you that Našobok's... simpler means cannot fill."

From embarrassment to affront, the flames of it warmed, cheek to neck and nape. Tokela turned to Galenu, challenging.

"I mean no insult," Galenu held up his hands, spread in apology. "Only truth. The wyrhling will satisfy your body well enough. But what about your mind, Tokela?"

Tokela realised he had opened his mouth merely to have whatever he meant to say abandon him. What did Galenu mean, his "mind"? He knew the word, of course, recognised it as another term for the brain housed within his skull. But the only meaning it could have in the given context was what outLand people defined as intellect, despite the fact everyone knew one's intellect was in the heart, in the knowing, in the instincts and the *feeling*.

"Travel and an undomesticated playmate. It all sounds very exciting. I understand, believe me. It's true, nephew, you won't find such things in my sett. But I hold latches to many other doors; other kinds of excitement. We live not just in thisLand but upon a *world*, Tokela—a'io, a strange word, of outLand use but altogether true—and our world both shrinks and expands with every Sunrise. I've tried to make the ways of stoneClan broader in my time. I don't want my People to only pay heed to the Earth beneath our toes, but also other places and peoples. As I shared it with your dam, I'd share it with you: there's so much more than stubborn, fierce dawnLands can ever hope to hold. And..." Galenu trailed off, then continued, very soft, "I owe fealty to your dam's Spirit, Tokela. I would repay it."

Tokela's heart had begun to drum, hard against his chest, with Galenu's strange talk of places and Sunrisings and... *Worlds*. But at the last it stuttered, went back to the mere *lut-lub* of blood and muscle, shivered as if in pain. Tokela didn't even know why, until he found himself answering, talk a'Hassun dropping, each syllable, like stones into River.

"There are many who would owe my dam. There seem to be very few who would give such regard to *me*."

Galenu's nostrils flared. All this while he'd not been peering directly at Tokela. His eyes suddenly rose, met, held. "I see."

N'da, you really don't. Which is just as well.

Tokela didn't drop his gaze. Galenu finally sighed and shrugged.

"I meant what I said, Tokela. I meant all of it. You've a place with me, should you choose."

Then Galenu touched his fingertips to his own heart and head, reached out to give a gentle push against Tokela's breastbone. Turning, he retreated down the stair.

Tokela watched him go, then slid down the stones to his haunches. He stared out across the compound, past the drum heights and to the thick trees beyond.

Perhaps even all the way to a darkling *t'rešalt* and a Forest forbidden.

He never imagined his heart could be more filled—more *found*—than when he rode beneath Sky's vast arch, across high-Land Forests or lowLand plain, companioned only by four-leggeds and his thoughts.

But here. Ai, here.

Palatan walked the caverns in ecstatic silence. He carried a small, pitch-fuelled torch, for there was no natural light, however faint, for darksight to glean. Every now and then he would raise a hand to lightly trace the rough, ebon surface, hewn by countless Hoops of molten trails. In response Palatan's own skin would twitch, as if he were one of horseKin shuddering a fly. It was not rebuff; it was assimilation. Sensation sparked along his nerves, exchanging Fire without for Fire within.

It was a trail cold to any save those Blooded to it. Many had lost their way—and their lives. They would wander in endless darkness or be cozened by molten runoff—so solid in appearance but in reality a treacherous, deadly cousin to River. Palatan, however, knew this path as intimately as his own heartbeat. The caverns above were deserted save for two vital presences: his best mare, happy with the fodder he'd brought, and Arrow, who waited obedient but disgruntled whenever his two-legged companion descended into a place he could not follow.

The hum of his People also remained with him, vibrating like a faint heartbeat in the volcanic stones above.

The snows were retreating. It was almost time to leave the caverns. Almost time to wander the summering plains.

Palatan kept going deeper. The corridors spiralling before and beyond—beneath—immeasurable trails into an abyss vibrant with Power. He descended unafraid, light of tread but heavy with his own appeals and questions.

Is he ours?

What mystery lies upon him?

What must I do?

At first there was no answer. But the deeper and deeper his descent, the more silence gave way to a tickle at his nape, a touch rousing and soothing and humbling, all at once.

He is ours. More than you can possibly know in thisnow.

Then he belongs here. I'll bring him to us.

But?

I fear he won't come willing.

And you know better than to merely wield a weapon, like outLanders who consider nothing but thisnow.

Palatan considered the heated dark for long breaths. *Yet those outLanders grow bold, restless. I would save our People, whatever it takes.*

The sharpest obsidian will shatter if wielded unwisely.

Again, Palatan closed his eyes and contemplated the skim of Fire & Other always there, ghosting Sight.

Help him, son of my daughters. Show him a little of what lies in thisLand.

And then?

Let him choose.

$$\phi \quad \phi \quad \phi$$

20
FALLING WEIR

"Tokela! Anahli! Akumeh!" Sarinak's voice boomed out above the stream's rush. "Go with these ahlóssa and help them!"

Tokela looked up from the net he and three others were shaking clean and pulling onto the ricks for drying. First Running was over; the nets had to be overhauled before the next fishKin run, and Sarinak had been overseeing the process. Now, with broad feet braced upon the sentry stone, Sarinak was accompanied by Madoc, Kuli and Kuli's friend Laocha. All three ahlóssa were sopping wet and panting from their run downstream.

For the past six Sunrises, Madoc had not approached Tokela. Neither had Tokela the right to approach Madoc; Inhya had made that altogether clear. Sarinak sending him anywhere with Madoc was unexpected.

Or perhaps not, in this strange place they'd all found themselves. Inhya hadn't told Sarinak anything of what had happened; otherwise, Tokela would be outlier instead of retrieving nets with his tribe. Neither had Palatan returned. Aylaniś seemed unworried about this—three Suns there and the same to return, after all. Tokela nevertheless had the impression she was watching him, waiting. Anahli also watched him, but she seemed to have had some change in her heart; she no longer quipped dire warnings about her sire. Galenu hadn't left, either, but seemed pleased to visit Nechtoun until Wind Moons came; he smiled at Tokela when they did meet, and seemed to be waiting no less than Aylaniś.

Even River had gone quiet. It was as if the *t'rešalt* had never touched them.

"The weir at Falling Water is stuck fast. The ahlóssa can't raise it on their own," Sarinak was explaining as Tokela relinquished his task to another and sloshed for the bank.

"Come, Otter!" Waist-deep in River's shallows, Akumeh's elation was infectious: wild water and tangled nets meant excitement, danger, a chance for one more proof of prowess to add to his looming adult status. But Akumeh was still oških, still honouring lowForest obligation to the fishing and, while he was here and oških, he'd made it plain he didn't need the promise of Spear Dance to fancy Tokela.

Tokela had been just as ripe for Akumeh as Našobok. The first Sunrises of the oških den, waking and making his way beside ones who either paid no heed or actively avoided The Half-Breed, separated from everything Tokela had come to—admit it—rely upon, including the young ones who didn't care what he was as long as he gave them stories and entertained them.

He wanted Našobok. He missed Madoc's company. Aloof pride was an unsatisfactory companion, and Akumeh was as skilled as he'd promised. Perhaps not as skilled as Našobok, nor, thankfully, accompanied by the heart-lurch that seemed to hollow Tokela every time he thought of Našobok. There was no lovemate waiting in Akumeh. Instead there was plenty of play—and more, it dulled the keen edge of Other hovering at Tokela's nape.

And there was Anahli.

"Do we have to take Dancer?" Akumeh twisted his eyebrows at Tokela, levelling a wry smirk at Anahli as she strode up. He still hadn't—quite—forgiven her for humiliating him so—despite the fond familiarity of address.

Anahli tossed a fishing spear lengthwise at Akumeh; he caught it one-handed and twirled it, tucked it under one arm. She grinned, fully aware of his annoyance and seeming, somehow, to revel in it. Sauntering over, she linked arms with Tokela and offered the other to Akumeh. With a roll of eyes, he took it.

Tokela rather suspected he admired 'Dancer'.

Madoc, on the other hand, flicked Tokela a sullen glance from where he stood on the bank next to his sire. As if to make up for that, Kuli came running past Sarinak and flung himself at Tokela and Anahli, chattering all the while.

"Ai, I'm glad you're coming with us, Tokela!" The reedy shout could, of course, be heard downRiver. Undeterred by Madoc's loud groan, Kuli climbed Tokela like a favourite tree. More from self-defence than anything, Tokela snatched and swung Kuli around to his back. Akumeh was grinning. Anahli gave Kuli's hind end a shove as he slipped mid-climb.

"You're slippery as an eel, little Fox!"

"Madoc's been grumbling like an empty belly, but the rest of us have missed you, haven't we, Laocha?"

Laocha was in full agreement, hugging Tokela's waist. Her curly black hair stuck out in wet spirals, her thick ahlóssa braid the only part of it lying tame, sodden-flat against her skull. "Will you tell us a story after we're finished?"

Their enthusiasm warmed despite the chill of Madoc's mood. "Perhaps."

"Ai," Akumeh said, "I didn't know you were a StoryKeeper."

"I'm not, really—"

"He should be!" Kuli insisted, and this time Tokela didn't demur.

Akumeh's smile had tilted from indulgence into blatant admiration. Anahli's smirk grew to laughter as Tokela yipped. Kuli had grabbed hold of his hair.

"Perhaps I'm glad"—Akumeh gave wry consideration to Kuli's progress—"I've no stories in my heart after all."

"Didn't you, Madoc?" Kuli pressed. "Miss Tokela?"

"Of course." Madoc's gaze said otherwise. "When I have thought of him."

A shadowling answer from behind Tokela's eyes snarled back, just as thoughtless and cruel. Instead, with utmost self-composure, Tokela answered, "I'm sure Madoc has more important things to occupy him. Like hanging onto Aška's skirts."

Anahli nudged Tokela with an amused snort. Kuli giggled from the security of his perch on Tokela's back, clearly not remembering his own tearful hanging-on to his dam's belt when she'd first left him there before the wintering.

Madoc tossed his head and growled—seemingly to his sire but peering at Tokela the entire while, "Perhaps these oških aren't the ones to help. All *they* ever do is swagger and throw their spears at each other."

"Do you question me, son?" Sarinak smacked the back of the bright head. "Can you can swim better than Tokela? Have you somehow grown stronger than Akumeh? Or quicker than Anahli? Perhaps I should do as your oških brother suggests and send your bold tongue back to your dam's kirtles!"

Madoc's face flamed.

Sarinak beckoned Tokela. "You know falling weir best. You will lead." Sufferance had been bought, it seemed, with Tokela's removal to the oških den. "You little ones, mind him well, and all of you keep your eyes sharp along the trail. Several wily bearKin chance that place." With a curt nod, Sarinak motioned them on.

Tokela put it from his mind as Akumeh snatched their remaining spears from the bank. "You take the little ones, Otter. I'll ride herd on *this* mouth." Akumeh suited actions to talk and grabbed at Madoc's ahlóssa braid, hauling him towards the path. Anahli and Laocha followed suit.

"Tokela is *Tokela*, not Otter!" Kuli took umbrage from his perch on Tokela's back, then grabbed hold with a little yip as Tokela trotted after.

"Oh, I know his name. But Otter suits him." Undeterred, Akumeh threw back a grin.

"Well," Kuli considered, "perhaps it does make sense. Uncle Sarinak is right—Tokela does swim better than any of us."

"How nice," Tokela exchanged the grin with Akumeh, "that you make sense."

"Hunh. I wasn't talking about your *swimming,* playmate."

Tokela's ears heated. His grin, however, widened.

Anahli nudged him again, eyes dancing.

"I think Tokela swims like otterKin, too." Laocha put her bid in, taking Anahli's hand and skipping along beside.

Madoc, unwilling to risk another swat by squirming from Akumeh's grip, let himself be propelled along. But the fond play between the oških increased his grumbles.

"I can swim, too. Not as good as you, Tokela. Or Madoc"—Kuli pacified as Madoc shot him a glare—"but well enough."

The dull rumble of the waterfall had begun to touch their ears.

"What has happened with falling weir, chieftain-pup?" Anahli asked Madoc, who was indeed beginning to sound like growling young wolfKin.

Well, and Madoc had always liked Anahli. Enough to stop growling and answer, "It's stuck again. I was going to free it, but Laocha and the Spawn said they'd tell if I did."

"A good thing, too," Tokela retorted.

"And if you call my little brother 'Spawn' one more time, I'll end you," Anahli furthered.

While Madoc was thinking up a suitable comeback, Akumeh swatted him. "Anahli speaks truth. And ahlóssa have no business moving weirs alone. You should know that more than most, chieftain-pup."

"I'm no pup!" Madoc protested. "And I wasn't afraid!"

"To have no fear isn't brave, just stupid," Anahli pointed out.

Tokela said nothing. He knew it would be fat to Fire. But Anahli was right. Falling weir was particularly treacherous, beneath a waterfall cascading from a stony promontory to the deep sink below. The fall of water was a prime "ladder" for the fish to use to the upper pools, and therefore also prime territory to set one of the largest weirs: a cunningly laced contraption of weeping-tree staves and netting, easily moveable.

The path grew chancy, winding up a woody bluff. The fall's rumble was increasing into a roar. As Tokela swung his passenger down, Kuli ran forwards, dogging Madoc's heels.

"Did you spot any bearKin lingering?" Anahli asked. Madoc's negative was muffled as they climbed deeper, upon the narrowing trail laid by both four- and two-leggeds.

"Which of you ahlóssa swims the best?" Akumeh prompted.

"Me!" Kuli boasted, then "Ai-ye!" as Laocha whacked his arm and protested. "It's true!"

She glared at him, then shrugged at her elders. "It is true. But he's too prideful."

Akumeh gave a fond tug at her ahlóssa braid. Anahli smirked at Tokela and slipped her hand into his.

This much still lingered:

Eyes meet eyes to waken Spirit. Spirit wakens our Mother's heart, and Her heart wakens...

"I remember." Anahli gave a tiny shiver, then as if to deny it squeezed Tokela's hand and released him. "Is it well?"

He nodded, self-conscious.

"Good."

And the vista opened out beneath them.

So many places held beauty upon River and Her children, but this particular fall was spectacular. Whether Sun shone or not, the fall foamed and sparkled, a multihued Skybow of fury—and justly so, with Earth and stone attempting to trammel Her. Mists soared upwards, snagging in the dense evergreens, lingering heavy-sweet in the lungs, and laying a dense fuzz upon hair and skin, to lave thick-wet trails when smoothed.

"Is it possible to grow accustomed to this?" Anahli's murmur was almost lost in the roar and tumble of the fall. "I miss my plains, but this is beautiful, too."

"I hope not," Tokela answered. River's beauty filled his heart and stung his eyes with heat, shivered across his skin and juddered at his heartbeat. There were... melodies, thick and noisome, a clash of not-voices, overwhelming with silent *sound*.

Anahli walked the edge unafraid, her downwards gaze full of wonder, her steps nimble despite the maze of tree roots fingering and burrowing into bare rock. Akumeh released Madoc and went over to the traces holding the weir. Tokela looked down into the fall, where the weir lay submerged in foam and boil, and took the opportunity to lean his palms hard against his thighs, take a deep breath and clench his teeth, eyes shut.

Not thisnow. Not. Thisnow...

As Tokela opened his eyes again, he found Madoc watching him. Tokela peered back, flat, until Madoc's gaze flickered aside. Fingers and toes finding purchase on the moss-slick rocks, Tokela crouched, eyes following the play of the well-waxed lines from River to where they were set into the cliff. Akumeh had knelt at the latter, muscles bunching and sliding beneath his skin as he worked the wooden pulleys, assuring their soundness. Tokela let himself enjoy the sight.

"I already checked the traces!" Madoc's shout was necessary, here atop the falls, but it was definitely aggrieved. "I'm not stupid!"

Akumeh's only response was a grunt. Tokela didn't do even that.

"What does She say to you?"

The query gave a painful jolt of surprise. Tokela sloughed his gaze sideways, found that Kuli had come up silent as his foxKin namesake. Squatting on the bank beside Tokela with one thumb between his teeth, he stared down into the water.

"Sometimes," Kuli said, unusually soft, "I think I can hear Her. River, I mean. It's almost like She's singing, isn't it?"

Memory crashed with thisnow, and if Tokela closed his eyes he could see another ahlóssa with another elder cousin...

That's Sea's voice you hear. More powerful than River, even.

Does She whisper your name, too?

Sometimes... sometimes, I think She does. Našobok's face had been so wistful, as if he knew exactly what he was saying... and as if he wanted it more than anything.

Why would anyone *want* this?

"Tokela!" Akumeh's shout carried above the roar. "Do you see anything?"

Tokela tilted his chin in acknowledgment, contemplating the great rush of water. He could—just barely—see part of the weir. It looked to be angled wrong. Perhaps.

His fingertips brushed the cliff, tiny patterns in the damp as the notion came, swift as wingedKin. What if—what if?—he could somehow *listen* to the fall, try to ken what was wrong? Make this experience safer for everyone?

It thrilled—then chilled. Perhaps that was how Chepiś abominations had begun.

But a'io, River sang. Tokela had, particularly as of late, grown so accustomed to setting the pitch of Her out from his notice. Kuli's description pulled Her back into awareness.

"Do you hear Her, Tokela?" Kuli said, still soft. "You do, don't you?"

"Leave Tokela alone, little brother." Anahli took hold of Kuli's shoulder and pulled him back. "He's trying to figure out what we must do."

Tokela put flattened palms to the edge and leaned out over the roiling water. Here and there flashes of colour emerged—the last of this run of fishKin writhing and surging upwards, climbing their ladder of stone and splash. The sight blurred before his eyes, accompanied by the clashing echo of River's violence, thrumming through his skull... N'da, through his *blood*, like a second, spastic heartbeat.

She sounded... odd. Something was wrong below.

A hand latched onto his knife-harness, jolting Tokela back *here*. "Pay attention, Otter!"

"I am, believe me." It was wry. He turned to Akumeh, overly mindful of the concerned grip, of Anahli's keen lookout, of Kuli's acceptance and Laocha's puzzlement and Madoc's relentless, critical gaze. "It has to be in the netting itself. I'll go down."

"Hunh. Pay attention," Akumeh repeated, with a shake of his hand. Then it softened, ran down to linger at Tokela's nape. "River is running higher than usual this breadth of Hoop, so heed Her well."

As if he'd any choice. Tokela slid his chin towards the ahlóssa. "Mind *them* well, ai?"

"A'io," Akumeh said, and Anahli affirmed it with her own tilt of chin.

Tokela took the few steps to the edge and dove.

He knew this fall well, gauged his descent carefully. Still, he expected his hands to make some sort of contact with bottom silt and stone. River indeed ran high thisnow. At least the currents buffeting him were familiar. They met and matched the noise behind his eyes, as if they made flirting talk, back and forth.

Tokela had to kick down against the current to find bottom, open his eyes to take his bearings, and... and he *relished* it. Coppery foam swirled about him, smoothing his skin, lit with bright flits of fishKin and light streams. Several of the former bumped against him, blind with an intensity that threatened to reach out, take him, too.

Did River speak to all her creatures so, in the spawn and near the end? Fill their Spirits and blind their eyes so nothing remained, in the end, but Her?

Tokela snarled against the swirling water, an uncompromising biddance: *Not in thisnow. Be still thisnow.*

She obeyed.

Somehow, he realised, They had always obeyed.

The breath rushed from him in a burst of bubbles, reaction swift as a blow against his ribs. They? Always. *Obeyed?* What?

He breached the surface like a gasping water horse, paddled there in shock for several heartbeats.

"All right?" Akumeh called down.

Tokela peered up from mists and foam and saw his playmate taking a wrap on the traces, just in case. Four other sets of wide eyes peered down—even Madoc, trying his best to seem disinterested.

Tokela made a knocking motion with his fist—an affirmative—then took Wind into his lungs and dove deeper. His teeth bared, resolute, and he forced his heart to clarity, listening to River with open eyes and wide-spread fingers.

He found the weir. It wasn't where it should be. A new-broken outthrust of stone had trapped the weir in an underwater slide—as well as the large catch of fishKin that would die for no good reason unless Tokela freed them.

It took several tries, and several upwards breaches to take air, but he managed to coax most of the debris away. Milt and mud, gravel and the smaller of the stones—none of those overlarge, and the tumbling water assisting him, carrying away what he cleared. Several hand signals enlisted Akumeh's strong arms on the traces to help shift a few stubborn stones. A tilt here, a tug at the line for Akumeh to pull, a push during those pulls. All of it showered silt over the netted fishKin.

Yet still, the weir wouldn't come loose. Wind growing stale in his lungs, Tokela twisted and reached, felt the trapped fishKin flutter against his forearms, felt the nettings against his fingers... but he could only go so far. His hands had broadened since last Hoop's spawning. They wouldn't fit.

Finally he broke the surface, motioning for the climbing rope.

Anahli already had it secured to a tree with a neat horsetalker knot akin to the ones used upon River. She tossed it down and, grabbing hold, Tokela made his way upwards. Akumeh grabbed Tokela's knife harness and hauled him the rest of the way atop the bluff.

"Did you free it?" Kuli asked.

"Quiet, ahlóssa," Akumeh chided, putting an arm about Tokela. "Even Otters must be allowed to catch their breath after a long dive."

Panting, Tokela scrubbed the wet locks from his face and let Akumeh support him. It was rather nice.

It was also a distinct pleasure to see Madoc puffing up like a mad watercock. But not as fierce as the knowledge they were all, in this heartbeat, deferring to him. It cleared his thoughts; freed the talk that oft would tangle in his throat.

"The weir's still trapped somehow," Tokela sat up. "The rocks pinning it are all gone, yet it won't come free. I can't reach any farther to find the cause; my hands are too big. Madoc, yours too. Laocha, I know you swim very well. Was Kuli boasting overmuch, or does he truly swim better than you?"

Kuli was starting to grin; it was Madoc, this time, who flipped a smack to the back of the cinnabar head.

"Ai, he does," Laocha admitted. "He might be a'Šaákfo, but River carries him as Her own."

"My hands are small," Anahli said, holding one up, splayed in the mist. Tokela laid his against hers as measure—he'd not realised it, she was slim as he, but taller, made of all muscle and sinew—but her hands indeed were narrow, with short palms and long fingers. She laced those fingers with his, eyeing him. "I swim as well as Kuli, better perhaps."

"Aww," Kuli began to whinge. Tokela gave him a stern look.

"Enough," Anahli told her brother. "It's decided."

Akumeh rose, offering Tokela an arm up. "Madoc, you'll see to the lines with me. Laocha, Kuli, we'll need your sharp eyes to watch out for Tokela and Anahli."

Anahli started for the edge.

Tokela halted her. "You'll climb down. You don't know this fall as I do."

She started to protest, instead smiled, lifted her chin, and straddled the rope.

The weir was *heavy*. And the falls tried to toss and spin her like a feather upon Wind.

Glad her assessment of her swimming ability hadn't been any idle boast, Anahli followed Tokela, watching the tilt of his head, hands, and the direction of the indigo eyes a-gleam in the murk.

Twice more they surfaced, exchanging signalled directions and gathering enough of Wind's breath to keep them, then went deeper, circling the trapped weir. Tokela snatched at the ropes and then Anahli as a strong current buffeted them sideways. Anahli climbed his arm, grabbed the ropes and hung on.

They crawled hand over hand towards the weir, Anahli creeping into place where Tokela motioned. Once they got past the initial drop of the fall, the lull of pressure and current was astounding: the water drifting in an almost-lazy spiral just above the weir. Anahli reached in, past the wriggling fishKin and farther, to the tangle of line and webbing that disappeared into silt and stones. She pushed back, motioned to Tokela. He jerked his head, and she followed him up and over the weir, surfaced behind the falls. A mist-filled alcove lay there—an amazing place, both shelter and council. The falls' roar was only slightly muted; nevertheless, the alcove seemed quiet.

"I felt it!" she panted. Her voice echoed huge in the small space, bouncing off water and stone. "The back of the weir's stove in. The line's all tangled with the netting, and there's more debris holding it there."

"Can you free it?"

"It's very tight. Even an ahlóssa would have trouble."

Tokela's brows squinched into a frown; he blew and thought for several heartbeats. "What if Akumeh takes up on the lines to pull it upward? I can hold it steady or sway it back and forth as you need. Use your feet to signal me—a tap that tells me which way to lean, and a kick to stop me." He grinned. "You should enjoy the latter."

She snorted, flinging the wet hair from her eyes. "Madoc might enjoy it more, the brat."

His brows squinched tighter; it bothered him. But obviously not that much as he thought it over. His lip twitched, then gave into a full-blown smile. "You know, I think he would."

"And you're reasonably pretty when you smile. You should do it more." And ai, but half the fun was watching him blink, like landed fishKin.

"Only reasonably?" he finally answered, and smiled even broader. "Wait here. Catch your breath. I'll signal Akumeh, then we'll dive again."

"Do you see them?" Madoc had to ask twice; the first didn't come out loud enough to be heard.

Laocha shook her head.

"Me, neither," Kuli added, frowning. "They've been down a long time."

"We should do something." Madoc turned to Akumeh.

Akumeh plainly disagreed. "There are shadows behind the fall."

Madoc tried to look past the watery curtain, but saw nothing. He shouldn't be this concerned. He told himself it was about Anahli, not Tokela.

Laocha had no reason to hide any worries. "But Akumeh, what if—!"

"Both of you, be still." Akumeh ordered. "I said there are shadows behind the fall, two of them. Tokela mentioned a small lee place there. Likely they're taking a breath."

Madoc frowned and stared at the falls. He still couldn't see anything. With a gusty sigh, he kept dogged hold on his part of the traces and hoped with all his heart Akumeh was right.

He was. Not two heartbeats later, a dark head parted the falls and Tokela leapt through, coming against the banks to tread water and peer upwards. Madoc sagged against the ropes in relief, and was abruptly furious with himself.

With quick hand signals, Tokela detailed what was to be done: keep a steady haul on the ropes so they could squeeze in and free the weir. Madoc wished he was down there instead of Anahli. He knew these falls better than any horsetalker.

Akumeh signalled understanding, and with a pumped fist of acknowledgement, Tokela dove once more beneath the surface.

"Keep your eyes upon the fall; if there's trouble, sing out," Akumeh told Laocha and Kuli, then turned to Madoc. "You know what we must do. Take the near trace. Pull until your gut says quit, and then keep pulling."

Madoc obeyed, taking the trace. Following Akumeh's lead, he wrapped the waxy-rough hemp about his palms, realised those palms were sweating. Madoc gritted his teeth.

All right, then. Perhaps when this was done, he should forgive Tokela after all.

◊ ◊ ◊

"Forgive me! Oh, good Rivermaster, forgive my clumsiness!" The scrawny Matwau aimed again for his precarious seat on the stool beside the wide board. He'd missed the first time, nearly upending not only the board, but the small circle laid with carved wooden discs. "But I know... I know, y' see."

Old Munro sighed. The yakhling seated across from Našobok snarled a question, rising in threat. Našobok held up a staying hand, then leaned against the board and growled at the Matwau, "What can you possibly know that is worth interrupting my game?"

No need to advertise that he was looking for anything, much less information. Našobok came here seldom. It was just one more port with houses dug temporarily into the banks, held up with spit and shit and straw—until the next flood, of course, when they'd move, wait it out, then come back and try again. But he knew Kaaven—the yakhling—fairly well, had willingly agreed to a game and a drink and an exchange of news, keeping his ears open to everything about him.

The Matwau laid a finger against one side of his nose, trying to look canny. But the finger trembled, ruining any illusions save that of too much drink, or dreaming dust, or any of myriad escapist vices that crowded into portside villages the farther downRiver one travelled.

Not that Našobok blamed any of them. Life was hard; harder still when you'd no place or People to call your own. Everyone had to belong somewhere, somehow. Even outliers. Even out-Landers.

"It's your people, aye? You little people. They're looking for your kind. You should take care, Rivermaster. Go back home."

"River-chieftain," Munro growled.

Našobok agreed. One didn't master River; one prayed She carried her People gentle.

"Wha'ever," the Matwau said. "There's slavers hereabouts. I know the *sgralka* Rivermas... well, you... takes 'em down as you can."

As he could, was right. A drop in a very large cauldron, the slavers Našobok had sent to River as sacrifice. He could spend his whole life and never get them all.

The Matwau edged closer, whispered in Rivertalk, "Randan said ye was headed this way. Said t' find ye."

Munro slid his eyes to Našobok. Randan was one of many names for an acquaintance who lived in the estuaries.

"Said t' tell ye. Warn ye. The Chepiś are buying *sgralka* slaves."

At this, Munro sat up. Even the dryLander's eyes widened between the folds of his headwrap.

"Chepiś don't buy slaves," Našobok replied, slow.

"They do now."

Našobok frowned, then shrugged at Kaaven. "You and Munro finish the game." He rose and wrapped his blanket about his shoulders. "Come on, Matwau. Let's walk."

"Not just any slaves. They're looking for ones of a certain age, of a certain build." Našobok's voice dropped, barely a breath against the candle in his hold. "Ones who have Power."

It was then he spread out the parchment upon his chart board. And...

Munro's breath sucked in. "It's him."

The parchment crumpled easily in Našobok's fist. Lurching up, he paced back and forth across the dim hold. "Palatan told me. Or good as, not that he says much of anything about these things, but he knew Chepiś had interfered with Tokela. All those rumours, and Tokela's dam stirring them like well-seasoned stew for reasons I can't understand, but there's no way I believed that Chepiś sired him. You can't breed lionKin with wabadeh."

"Maybe *they* can."

"I find it more likely the misbegotten outLanders Shaped him. Somehow."

"And now they want what they Shaped," growled Munro.

"I have to go back. Warn him. Warn Palatan of what's coming... if they come that far... scorch me, but Galenu knows these Chepiś! What if he's... in on it somehow? What if he's offering a hearth just to turn Tokela over to his... friends." A snarl. "River'll have him if that's what he's done!"

Munro looked up from the crumpled sketch, face sorrowful as one of Sarinak's mastiffs, but determined. Support. "Shall we wait here for you?"

"N'da. Keep to the running. We've still trade to do, even if we go no farther than the estuaries. As to Galenu... I might just ram his trade down his throat."

"If he lives so long," Munro said, as Našobok leapt up the stair and into dark's arms.

21
SHAPER

Tokela dove back down to the weir and gave the ropes a tug, waited. Slowly at first, the fibres began to stretch and quiver, streams of tiny bubbles floating upwards from the sodden hemp. He gave another tug—*wait there for now*—then kicked his way through the waterfall to retrieve a waiting Anahli. He held her gaze for a heartbeat. She smiled and tilted her head.

"Let's go, then."

They both dove this time, below the worst of the upper current. The deep undertow swirled, crosscurrents heading more towards the rocks than away. Tokela murmured a silent orison against the roof of his closed mouth, imploring River for whatever help She could give. Anahli grabbed hold of the weir, waiting. Tokela planted both feet hard against the bottom stones, tilting his face down so the roiling upper current wouldn't force up his nose. Then he wove hard fingers into the weir netting, gripped the staves and hauled with all his strength.

River, thisnow, gave them kindness; once the weir swayed forwards, even slight, the undertow curled beneath it and lifted it even more. Quick as the otterKin Akumeh had deemed Tokela, Anahli darted between rocks and weir, knife flashing in one hand.

The rope went taut, shedding water and creaking, then went lax.

"I think it's coming free!" Akumeh gave a fierce, triumphant whistle, then ordered, "Again! One last haul!"

Madoc gave one more fierce heave on the rope, felt shoulders strain and sinews cry mercy, pulled even harder...

And the rope broke.

The recoil flung Akumeh against the tree and sent Madoc sailing backwards. Kuli and Laocha both screamed.

The frayed rope end undulated upwards in a gust of misted Wind, then disappeared over the cliff.

The weir lurched upwards, then sideways, then heaved itself against the rock wall. Tokela was yanked forwards, his shout of denial escaping in bubbles and foam. With a fierce twist and heave, he regained his footing, shoving his feet harder against the rocks, and hauled backwards against water and weir. Thighs straining, feet slipping; his shoulders and arms burned and snagged. His impulse was to gulp more Wind, but River burned his nostrils and he choked, just in time clutched the breath in his throat and let it burn.

The weir repaid Tokela in like force. It launched forwards, slamming into his torso, sending him in a strange and slow-motion sprawl against the bottom. What air remained was forced from him as the jagged bottom stones stabbed and tore at his spine, the weir raked his torso, pinning him down. Crimson began to edge his sight. Lungs burning, he fought, beat against it, kicked...

Mine, River hissed. *Mine*.

The weir lurched loose. Tokela exploded upward; but the weir smashed against his face and sent him back down. He rolled on the bottom, an underwater motion, deliberate and gravid, like one of turtleKin on ša's back. Calm... so calm, even the seizing of his chest didn't touch, couldn't touch him...

N'da. There was something else. Some*one* else.

He twisted, nearly caught hold of the weir as it sped over and past, but treacherous as ever, it evaded him. The last sight Tokela had before the murk covered him was Anahli's long, ebon braids trailing behind her... and behind the weir, as it went careening downRiver.

Madoc went skidding over the precipice, legs dangling; at the last moment he snatched at the tree roots clinging there. They stretched, some breaking, bark shredding through his palms. Nevertheless, he clutched tight, body jerking to a halt, arm and shoulder tendons stabbing; letting out a yelp, Madoc hung on. It was no use. The roots tore from Earth and tree. Madoc dropped like a stone, heard Laocha and Kuli scream, heard Akumeh give a shout just before Madoc hit the water.

A rush of thick, noisy cool enveloped him, cradled him—but not enough. One shoulder smashed into a boulder; one foot dove into a crevice, held there as he was tossed sideways. The crack of bone and tendon followed, with a rip-snap of pain. Madoc's own shriek was swallowed by River's current.

Something brushed against him, and he recoiled, by instinct

striking out with both hands. His fingers tangled in something both solid and soft a scant heartbeat before his eyes flew open.

Tokela, travelling in the current like an up-rent and water-logged thatch of reeds.

A huge shadow falling from above, a *whump* and torrent nearly atop them. Hard fingers clutched in Madoc's ahlóssa braid, pulling him to the surface. Madoc clutched his own hands into fists, slipped on wet skin then found purchase on Tokela's knife harness. He didn't let go, even when Akumeh hauled him into light and Wind, even after he realised Akumeh also held Tokela, dragging them both to the opposite bank.

Akumeh shoved Madoc up on the bank. Tokela seemed a harder burden, somehow. When Akumeh finally managed to toss Tokela onto the rocky bank, it was with a thick, lifeless *thud*.

After, Tokela just lay there, still and pale, arms flung limp over his head. A big gash was laid open across his temple; it bled, freely.

A huge wave of relief nearly blackened Madoc's sight. Akumeh, too, gave a strangled cry of relief and fell to his knees. He bent over and started shoving—hard—against Tokela's breast.

"Akumeh!" It was a cry from overhead: Laocha.

"Madoc, where's Anahli?" This from Kuli, leaning perilously over the edge above. "Anahli!"

Their shrieks echoed, almost swallowed by the churning water. Anahli.

Akumeh didn't stop shoving at Tokela. Madoc tried to move, act. Pain flared through his leg and felled him on the spot. Tokela choked, convulsed, curled sideways. River water spewed, commingling with blood on the stones.

"Tokela!" Madoc grabbed for him, missed.

Either his voice or Akumeh curling bodily behind Tokela and giving one more jerk and heave was the deciding point. Tokela pitched upwards with a muffled shriek, spewing and choking, water pouring from his mouth and nose and down his chest. Akumeh held him through the worst of it, and Madoc couldn't even resent him, much as he wanted to.

Wild-eyed, Tokela fought him, and when he could breathe enough to speak, his first sound was, "Ah... nahli?" It choked, barely audible over the fall.

"It's done, Otter." Akumeh held on. "It's done."

"Where... where is"—Tokela kept coughing, spewing water—"Anahli? Where is she?" It didn't seem possible, but he was gaining free of Akumeh's hold, squirming and sliding from the firm grasp like a greased Dancer. "We have to find her... River *has* her!"

To hear it spoken aloud shoved Madoc back against the ground like a cart-weight of stone, a shiver and stutter of sudden fear loosed and realised.

Tokela had clambered up, staggering, evading Akumeh's every effort to hold him. "We have to find her. We have to!"

Akumeh didn't stop trying, either. "It's over, Otter. It's over. Over." Every repetition piled more weight onto Madoc. He was immobile from it, pressing into Earth and helpless.

"Otter... Hear me. Otter... *Tokela!*" Akumeh finally grabbed one arm, yanked Tokela back around. "It's done, do you hear me?"

"Not over. It can't be. We have to go after her, have to find her, have to..." Tokela was past listening, disoriented. Maddened, with blood and mud and ebon-copper hair runnelling into his face and eyes—and those eyes were white-wild, with shadows like clouds, and sparks like ice falling from wintering Sky.

Madoc tried to lurch upwards again; again, he fell back with a pained shout.

The two other ahlóssa kept keening on the clifftop, clutching to each other.

"Listen!" Akumeh grabbed Tokela's other arm, yanked him close, shook him. "She's *gone.*"

A soft negation whimpered from some deep place in Madoc's chest, but neither of the oških paid any heed.

"*You* were nearly gone, and she's—"

Tokela turned on Akumeh, shrieked, "*We have to find her!*" It cut even River's sound into tiny shards, echoed upwards and into the trees and hung there, vibrating.

Then he wrung from Akumeh's grip, ran the few steps to River and dove, cutting coppery water like a bone blade, disappearing in the froth.

"Tokela!" Madoc shouted after, and this time he managed to gain his feet—or foot, the other dragged at his side, scraping pain up every nerve he had.

"You can't do anything, not now!" Akumeh growled, shoving him back down. Madoc couldn't help the whimper as his leg went a-Fire with pain. Akumeh shot him a remorseful glance, then shouted upwards. "Go, ahlóssa! Go for Sarinak! Bring help!"

Kuli was no longer there. But Laocha, obedient, whirled and disappeared.

Akumeh took a few running steps, dove after Tokela. Madoc watched, frightened and furious and frustrated, chest heaving like a bellows.

You can't do anything!

Madoc couldn't, but Akumeh would, and Tokela, and Laocha... she would bring help—where was Kuli?—but she had to. These kind of things couldn't truly happen; they were tales to frighten ahlóssa, something only heard about, things that only happened to other people. It didn't happen to your *cousins*, it didn't happen to people you knew. Not like this. It couldn't.

As if a herdbeast had suddenly kicked him in the gut, Madoc

fell back. Lay there, useless and gasping as landed fishKin, memory and reason flooding in where Wind had gone absent.

Couldn't? Ai, but it could. It *had*.

Tokela's sire and dam, after all, had drowned.

Madoc let out a gasp. Wind filled his lungs, an intoxication to match Tokela's display of dizzying strength. All of it made abrupt sense—denial, insistence—and for the first time Madoc became aware of what this one, inconceivable happening would mean to Tokela.

Or at least what Madoc thought it should mean. They'd never spoken of it. They'd shared many things, but not this. Never this. Had Tokela seen his parents drown? Or had it been like with Anahli?—carried away, wrack upon the current, a broken doll tossed upon River...

That hit hardest, racked Madoc over and choked him, making him want to puke until his vision turned to blood-coloured soot. Anahli. Anahli, and Tokela, and...

You can't do anything!

Madoc snarled, then started to crawl towards River.

He didn't need both legs to swim.

I have her.

She means Anahli and he knows it; River is speaking to him... *speaking* to him in thisnow with more than feelings and images crowding in his brain begging interpretation.

It is language. It is talk.

Tokela swims, breasting sleek and fast as any namesake of otterKin. His arms already feel torn from their sockets, his head ringing in the wake of the weir's passage, reason seeping from him as steadily as the blood he leaves behind, a mere darker cloud in already-copper waters. He growls denial of it, breath hitching in the back of his throat.

She cannot take this, too. Does She not already have everything? Has She not already taken everything from him? He is helpless again, helpless before Her as the ahlóssa who found his parents on Her bank...

Not helpless, my own. If you want her, then you must come to Me.

Tokela dives deep even before his thoughts have a chance to surface, following a will that is his, but not.

She has Anahli.

And I will have you. Listen, my own. Listen, and do not shut me away, and I shall tell you all the secrets you have shunned.

He glides through coppery half light as easily if he breathes water instead of air, hears the hollow echoes of his movement, feels crimson-black Power thrumming with his pulse, behind his eyes. Opens those eyes.

Stills.

Listens.

Sees, never witnessed but always known, intimate and deep: how hair floats, carried in the drift; how bodies float, loose-limbed and passive, submitting to the caress of current as if in slumber.

He panics.

In a furious blur of copper froth and weighted, too-slow limbs, Tokela descends upon the weir where it has tangled in bottom sludge and roots. With a heavy-thick slash of knife against entangling rope he frees the unconscious oških and, severed ropes still splaying, bursts upwards to light and life and Sky. Staggers from River's clutch with dead weight in his arms, stumbles as gravel and stones sink him, trip him, fell him to his knees. Falls forwards, his burden flinging out limp and empty beneath him.

Breast heaving in tight-clenched, truncated sobs, eyes dark with a skim of blood and black, he splays trembling fingers over the slack, pale face and down, to query ribs that do not answer to draw breath, that do not quiver, even slight, with the heart's drumtalk.

So cold. So still. So... fragile.

Tokela shakes her. Says her name, first a whisper then a sharp reprimand.

Yet Anahli's head lolls, braids like sodden snakes, joining the matted River-wrack clinging to indigo Marked cheeks and wilted neck.

Don't take her... please, please don't... You can't do this, don't make me live through this again!

In death, lips are the hue of his own gaze, indigo-and-ebon. Tokela knows, because he saw it—saw his parents dead upon Her—and memory seeks him but he cannot bear it, cannot let it ever take him, ducks and dives beneath.

River holds him, curling at his feet, foaming

up the shore to his thighs. She murmurs his name. Whispers Anahli's.

"N'da!" It is a hoarse shriek. "You will not have her, you cannot have her! She isn't yours—I am! Take me instead... me... me..." It wavers into a moan, a frenzied growl/whisper/keen against Anahli's soft, immobile breast as he lies there in the foam and gravel, drenched to skin and steaming, a hum of ebony and indigo filling his burning eyes. Hands splay, plead, clutch...

Take me!

And She does.

A twist within: an answer, a surge to take him under. Curling. Expanding. The water in Anahli's lungs—in his own lungs—sloshes heavy and stifling, and he writhes, whimpers beneath the sodden weight. Retches against it, somehow begins to heave up everything in him, in Anahli, in them. The blood-black skim behind his eyes swells into a crash of copper tide—rushing, pulling back to course through him again, and again, as sobs of denial become a rush of mutters not his own.

Language not his own. Other, filling up every space within, twisting and shrieking through his Spirit, changing, Shaping.

Because everything changes. An entire existence can change in the span of a heart's beating.

Sudden droplets patter against the still and sunken chest: like Rain, like the last seep of life from game hung to bleed out. Each one has a sound as it impacts. Each one leaves a tiny smear of impossible hue—not crystalline tears, not carmine blood, but thin indigo, as if Tokela's oških Marks are leeching beneath the scorch of his tears. Each one pools then runs over and down Anahli's throat, indigo runnelling across sienna. Each one reverberates through Tokela: spilling from his nose and eyes; hitting acrid-thick against the back of his throat; filling his ears and heart to finally burst, the heat/relief/agony of a septic wound being lanced.

No longer himself but more in himself than he has ever been, bound to everything and nothing, drowning and tangled and sinking even faster, and he will not let this happen, will not bend to death just as he has become alive.

Alive.

The chill leather beneath his fingers gives a quiver. Surges, a wave against a shoreline. Chokes, then retches, as if echoing Tokela's force. Convulses, curls, pukes water and bile and more water. Falls back, gasping in huge gouts.
Breathing...

"Otter?" A breath, choked into stillness, faint and nearly lost beneath River's rush within Tokela's ears and heart. "Squander and sc... Tokela?"

For a heartbeat Tokela didn't see—couldn't see—what was standing, shadowed, above him. Slowly his pupils narrowed from black skim to Sun's light-Shapings. They limned a tall, sturdy oških, his half-shaven head with black twistlocks plastered sodden to one pectoral, catching in a knife harness. One arm extended, the fingers splayed as if in warding; legs spread as if he'd sprinted so far then halted half-stride.

Fear, raw, in his face.

Tokela blinked, then blinked again. Recognition set in.

Akumeh. And, behind him...

Madoc.

Sopping wet, sprawled half in the water's roil and half onto the bank, braced on his arms. His tangled, sodden forelock could not curtain the alarm, wide-white, about his Earth-copper eyes.

He was staring at Tokela. At Anahli, lying still and pale and streaked with indigo. Then back again.

Kuli stumbled up, then, and said, "Anahli? Tokela?"

Tokela?

It echoes into the neverending, thrums with the drum of his heart, echoes in his skull but not upon his ears. No talk, only hoarse, waterlogged pants in the stillness, but nevertheless Anahli *speaks:*

Tohwakelifitčiluka. My heart Sees you, oathbrother.

And her eyes open, dark as drowning kelp, and River is there, reflecting a copper haze that gives way, curls back, parts before thick grey mists blown before Wind.

Eyes meet eyes to waken Spirit...

Yet none of that matters. What matters is the horror of what still stains her throat; what slides down her now-heaving ribcage, warm and thick; what drips from Tokela's face even as he watches, to fall upon Anahli's cheek like a tear. It smears upon the fingers Tokela puts to his face then extends before him with sick, detached curiosity. It smells like blood, somewhat;

he can taste the hot melt upon his tongue. But it doesn't look like blood.

It looks like *indigo*.

The keen spills from his throat. Voices have become a voice: his own, a strangled scream ripping into Forest's sudden-odd silence.

It takes him, then, tumbles him into River and spins him into Her depths.

Tokela knelt... n'da, he half-lay, prostrate upon Anahli's body. Like the mourners Madoc had seen upon their dead, swaying, denying what Fire would consume into ash for River... for they all went to Her in the end, didn't they?

Anahli was so still. She'd left them, walked on, gone to River already without waiting for Fire or ash. Tokela was proof of that, quaking like a tree in Wind's fury, shaking his head and making soft, broken sounds. Denial. Fury. The sounds of a heart cracked and split with grief. It tore into Madoc's own breast, wrenched a sharp, springing sob in his throat and a hollow in his gut, deep and sharp and unstoppable.

Madoc had to turn away—he couldn't bear it, couldn't watch anymore—and only then did he see Akumeh standing on the bank, as stilled, as unwilling to intrude into a grief he didn't thoroughly understand.

Tokela pushed upwards, shoving against Anahli's chest as if he still would deny, still not believe. Akumeh shook his head, said, puzzled, "Otter?"

Madoc envied Akumeh; as for himself, he couldn't speak if he'd had to.

"Anahli! Tokela!" A cry from Kuli, who'd sped down here as if he'd wings instead of feet, flying forwards as if to throw himself upon his sister's body.

Akumeh grabbed Kuli up. Held him, too, even when the ahlóssa growled, struggled, even bit to get free.

A strangling sound—choke and mewl and heave all at once—came from Tokela... n'da, from Anahli. Tokela shuddered. Anahli twitched, then convulsed, then turned sideways and heaved up more water than anyone should be able to hold and live.

Akumeh stepped closer, once again spoke—only this time it held more horror than pity. He staggered back as Tokela whipped around from Anahli's body, snarling not unlike one of lionKin defending a kill. Madoc didn't blame Akumeh. Tokela's face was pale as Brother Moon, his eyes nigh black, lit only by faint and frantic glimmers of what must be darksight but seemed even... more, somehow. Blood streamed from a long gash upon his forehead, rivulets streaking his face; it had gathered in his eyes like tears, and a thin stream of it from his nose.

Only, Madoc realised with a jolt, it wasn't. Blood. It ran thick like blood, pooled around Tokela's eyes and nostrils and dripped, slow onto Anahli's breast, but it wasn't. Blood. Was it?

Tokela seemed to notice, then. His sudden cry sent Akumeh staggering back, and the second, more a keen, raked cold claws down Madoc's spine, trying to pull him down.

Yet when Tokela's third scream choked into silence and he fell, senseless, across Anahli's coughing form—even as Akumeh turned to Madoc with active terror scrawled over his expression—the same terror did not take Madoc. Even though part of him wanted it to.

Instead he propped himself higher, half in and out of the water. Ordered, "Go! Bring my sire!"

Akumeh hesitated. Ai, Madoc was chieftain-son, but he was also the same ahlóssa Akumeh had dragged by his plait to this very fall.

"Go on!" Madoc snapped.

Akumeh's response made cold measure of his apprehension. He loosed Kuli without a word, turned, and dove into the water. Not long after, he waded out the other side, disappearing into the trees at a mad run.

Tokela lay on the bank, as unmoving as Anahli had been not so long ago.

Kuli sprinted to his sister's side, crying her name through tears as she tottered up to her elbows.

Anahli had been dead. Dead. Tokela had saved Anahli's life, somehow, and Tokela all bloody from it... only it wasn't blood, couldn't be blood. It seemed more like the tales of the creatures of Šilombiš'okpulo, Shaped things with ichor in their veins hued akin to lapis and indigo.

How could this be happening?

If I was... gone, like Nechtoun. If I was to go away, go to River, be outlier... would you love me then?

Madoc had been insulted by the question. Then.

Making someone outcast because they do something, hear something, feel something—that's right? Is that the sort of leader you want to be?

This was it. Answer, question, all of it circling. Into *this*.

If I was... gone...

Madoc wanted to run. He wanted to growl curses, scream denials, swim away and never look back.

Instead, he heaved himself, both arms and one good leg, through the shallows.

It took forever. It took a span of heartbeats. It roiled pain up his swollen ankle and into his hip, and Wind made chill the wet upon his flesh. Madoc ignored all of it, making stolid progress to gain Tokela's side.

Anahli still coughed, pale and sodden, trying to wriggle out from beneath Tokela; trying to unwrap Kuli's tight grip around her ribcage. Dismal, the failure to do either.

Madoc ended up rolling Tokela over with a great heave and grit of chattering teeth, lost hold; he was limp and lifeless as Anahli had been mere heartbeats earlier. Madoc dragged closer, watching for some sign of life. Anahli heaved herself—and thusly a weeping Kuli—closer, merely to collapse against Tokela's shoulder.

It seemed all ceased until a breath—ragged, hoarse—finally lifted Tokela's chest. Madoc extended trembling fingers to the leached, indigo-streaked throat; it pulsed erratic, but strong. Found himself charmed with a horror he could not voice, with which he could not react. Not now.

How many orisons had he offered up for answers to Tokela's oddities? He'd railed and wanted to strike out, to hurt Tokela for the lack of those answers, furious in the wake of wanting. Now Madoc had them within reach, and he was not going to let such a capricious thing as fear take them from him.

Mine, he growled. *Mine.*

Anahli reached up a hand to Kuli's face and smiled, tried to speak. Instead she sank back down against Tokela, unconscious.

"She's still breathing," Kuli said, all quavery, then scooted over to Madoc. "But... Tokela? What's wrong with Tokela?" It came out as a growly hiccup. "What's on his face? It's on Anahli, too." Still gravelly, but curious. There was no fear, even as Kuli peered at the indigo on his hands. "And me, now."

"To have no fear isn't brave, just stupid."

Then both of them were stupid, it seemed. There was no fear, only what had to be done. Madoc turned, put his hands, one then the other, to Kuli's face and held it. Said, quiet and deliberate, "We have to wash it away, all of it. Wash it from Tokela, and Anahli, and the rest from us. Take care!" he snapped as Kuli moved to obey. "Tokela went to all this trouble to help Anahli, so if you drown, I won't let him save you."

The grass-hued eyes seemed to glimmer—like River, like dull copper flecked with hectic verdigris. They slid to take in Tokela's prone form then dimmed, glossed with uncertainty as they turned back to Madoc. It gave Madoc a sudden, inexplicable shiver—he shook it away.

"We have to do it, Kuli. Now. They'll be coming, and we have to wash it away before anyone comes."

As Kuli obeyed, looking for something to use as an impromptu bowl, Madoc reached out and snatched up a hank of grass from near the bank. It was damp from splash; nevertheless he dunked it in the water and leaned over Tokela, used the grass quid to scrub at the strange indigo substance. It had begun to congeal, sticky. It had the taste of metal and moss, like to blood. Yet it couldn't be blood. Blood was what still oozed upon Tokela's forehead. That was...

Natural.

Gritting his teeth, Madoc kept scrubbing.

"Here." A subdued Kuli knelt and handed Madoc a discarded shell filled with water. "What *is* that stuff?"

Madoc didn't answer. Surprisingly, Kuli didn't press. Even River seemed restrained. FishKin kept running, but not so frantic. They had come some ways from the fall, though it still rumbled upstream.

A shout rang into stillness, thin with distance, then several more.

"They're coming." Kuli sounded worried.

Madoc answered, firm. "His indigo ran. It's new laid, and he must've mixed it wrong. That's what it was and nothing more."

Kuli didn't question, for once. He stayed so quiet that Madoc slid a glance towards him.

Demanded, "Do you understand me?"

The shouts were drawing nearer.

"I understand." Kuli's narrow face was set. "Some things cannot be spoken."

Wind deserted Madoc, then, making his hands shake. "Here," he said to cover it, "you've missed some on your face." He used the grass to scour Kuli's chin.

The uncanny quiet retreated, leaving behind a ahlóssa of eight summerings with new tears spilling over the face Madoc had just cleaned. "Tokela saved Anahli's life. But..." A huge swallow. "Tokela's sick, isn't he?"

"A'io," Madoc growled. "And no one can ever, ever know."

◊ ◊ ◊

22
FATES & DREAMINGS

Asleep...

He is asleep, but he is aware. His eyes are closed, but he sees what she does. He dreams, but he knows her. His breathing re-sounds in the quiet, but it is she who swallows jagged inhalations, moving slowly over to where he lies in his narrow, soft-draped bed. One of flyingKin starts warbling outside, heralding dawn; it is she who quickly lowers the hide over the narrow opening to mute the bird's call, it is she who steps back to the bedside, picking up a thick woollen blanket that has fallen onto the floor.

She hugs it to her breast, stares at him, and he sees himself through her eyes, her sight. "There will never be a better time." Her spouse, thinking her asleep as well, has gone to see to the ewes; he's not left her alone lately, particu-larly with their son. Talorgan is, somehow, afraid.

But that fear is nothing to hers. She is indeed afraid; not of her son but for him.

He is asleep, but Tokela senses it—senses her—as if within his own heart. He has never known such fear and longing and sorrow. She will not see him come of age, she will lose him before she even comes to know him, and he will lose... he will lose...

Everything.

Asleep. He needs to wake. He tries to wake, but cannot, though he must, if he wants to stop it.

"Be still, my own." Lakisa's voice sighs like Sea and Wind in a curved shell. "Soon it will be done, it will be over."

He doesn't want that. Something tells him what it could mean.

"We'll Dance into the Starlight, my son, my Eyes of Stars. You will be where you belong. Where we all belong, before they took Them from us, disallowed our Dreamings..."

This is Dreaming. And therefore real.

Fear and fate, sound and sight, all opened and turned inside out. Sun settling across River, a shining, glittering Hoop. Wind in the darkness, born of Earth and cast in Fire, a mystery graved deep within his being, in what he has been, what he will be.

Lakisa Sees it, whispers to herself, to the golden FireHoop, to the ahlóssa asleep in his cot. "I gave you life, to end in <u>this</u>? It cannot be. I shall not let it be!!"

Yet he cannot know this, cannot remember this. He is hearing voices... he is hearing *her* voices, the possession that took her... how is it possible?

She steps closer, still holding the blanket, tears streaming down her cheeks, heart hammering in her ears. Lakisa bends over her son, the blanket clutched to her breast and her fingers going to his head, lacing into his hair. The song within her heart, fear and longing and fate.

Put a stop to it. You know what will happen to him. You know what they'll do to him. Don't let them hurt him. Stop it. Now.

Now, Tokela pleads, soundless.

Tears and touches laid upon his brow. Warmed yeast and Rainwater, the wool of the blanket whisper-soft in her fingers. Cloth folds over his face, into his mouth and nose; her voice folds about him, and he realises—*I... can't breathe...*

Asleep. Dreaming. Stars and Fire, Wind and Water and Earth, singing Truth to the drumming of his heart.

"I have to stop it, my heart." Lakisa's whisper chokes with tears, her heart beating as if to burst—as if his own, as if he still lies enwombed beneath it—and she trembles, a-Fire with horror and purpose. Fixed, in sway of that purpose, she holds him as she has done only once before: when he was... was *made.*

"Just lie you quiet"—her murmur is a mourning—"and it will be over."

He shifts beneath her, a small sound looses itself from his throat. He nestles closer, nuzzles her arm. It freezes her, breath rattling in her throat at his trust of her touch.

N'da, she cannot quail, not now! She has given everything for him—can she not give this last? A kindness, really, it would be. Never would this changing take him, ruin him—never would he have to suffer!

Never either would he live, or love, or see Moons, or Stars, or Sun.

Slowly, inevitably, she draws the blanket aside. Her son takes a deep, soft breath, mutters, a frown twitching at his brow as if his dreams are unquiet, and she knows. She knows she hasn't the courage, she cannot do this.

And she turns to see Talorgan blocking the door, brown face sepulchral even in the warm candlelight.

"Lakisa," he whispers in numb, almost fascinated horror.

The blanket drops from nerveless fingers to the floor. She sees a reflection of herself in his eyes—as if she Sees *through* his eyes: half-dressed, wild-eyed, her hand snarled in her slumbering son's hair, pulling his head back as if baring it to the knife.

"Lakisa." Talorgan's eyes are black and half lit, even nightsight shadowed, unreadable. His voice twists from horror to accusation. "What are you doing?"

Dreams. Truths...
Apparitions.

With a choked cry, Lakisa runs. Talorgan grabs hold of her, shakes her. His eyes are shadowed, panicked—it feeds her own panic, gives her strength beyond her means. She yanks away, flees from the wykupeh and outwards. The branches snag at her hair. Sobs hitch at her ribs as she runs; they nearly fell her but she keeps going.

River winds before her, a ribbon set ablaze in the last rays of dusk. Fire rises into the morning, circling above her. A shining, glittering Hoop of air and darkness, glittering gold and malice, a ring of death and madness...

And Dreaming... shifts.

Snatches Tokela back in his own heart, his own body, and he sees—though his eyes are closed, his body asleep, how can he see?—he sees his father standing above him. And in that instant he realises what his father *was*.

A buffer of sanity. Of silence. Of blessed, blessed stillness.

Talorgan's eyes are dark, unfathomable with emotions he finds uneasily admitted, and now the pain of holding them within is a scream within Tokela's memory. Shaking fingers touch Tokela's lips, trace down his throat. A sigh, almost a sob, escapes Talorgan as he discovers the pulse beating there, strong and steady.

Then he reaches down, brushes his son's forehead with gentle fingers, then bolts out the door after Lakisa.

no, don't go, don't go, don't...

Fire sucks him back, blazing in his heart, rising into the morning, circling above him... above her the glittering Hoop of Stars and darkness wheels, cast from Earth and born in River. For she is trapped and so he is trapped, and it is, in the end, the same, with only one way to extinguish the conflagration within their mind...

River is chill; the shock forces the breath from Lakisa in a clutch of bubbles, scoops her deep. Without air she sinks, and a copper cloud rises about her, silt wafting upwards through her hair, obscuring her vision, quieting her heart.

Stillness. Peace.

Something tugs at her hair. She struggles but it's strong, snarling tight to drag her away from the soft, dark cocoon. She twists, weightless, gains her freedom but the damage is done and she shoots back up like an arrow.

Talorgan is there, ungainly and frightened, leaning too far over in the small dugout and calling her name. He cannot swim; to come out in the boat at all shows how desperate and afraid he is. He might have been drinking but neither is he drunk—he is more sober than she has seen him in months, and there is a knowing in his eyes. Knowing, and other things that she has no name for, things that rouse the ever-present panic.

In this Dream, thisnow, Tokela can name them—he knows them, all too well.
Fear. Devotion. Surrender.
He knows what his father, cornered and driven past any reason, did—and will do.

But Tokela didn't/doesn't want to know. He didn't/doesn't want to be held within this sway of memory/Dreamings, doesn't want to be there, again, as it happens. Yet he is dragged along in his dam's wake, as it has been since he was Shaped within her womb—*don't let my son die, I cannot bear to lose another*—tangled and twined fast in a song of Other.

Though he tries to break away, tries to stop it, stop it, stop it. As his world heaves about him and the Dreaming takes him back, as

Talorgan snatches at Lakisa, voice harsh and shrill with fear, as he lunges too far and the dugout tips. Falling atop her, suddenly and painfully, driving the breath from her lungs as he slams into her then struggles underwater, his body heavy with wet and flesh, flailing and clutching to her, trying to help and merely sinking them further. For precious seconds she feels air upon her fingers, touches the wood of the boat, clutches at it as

in a narrow bedshelf her son lies, eyes closed against Stars, his heart a-blaze and dawn-hot wings snarled by cloying, gossamer threads. In unconscious reaction he reaches out to stop the pain, as

a broad, strong hand clamps to her wrist and seizes. Lakisa tries to take them up but instead is dragged down, down, into the silt and the inky shadows. Talorgan is gone and in his place is an empty shell of sinking stone, taking her with the undertow, taking them *all* into the copper-cool depths until the Dreamings die and Tokela tears free from the awareness—stops it, silences it—and their Fire is smothered with Rain and Earth, shut away with only the faintest glimmer of Sun fading into the river bottoms, and

it is like giving birth again, only this time her son is truly gone, separate in soul as well as flesh, all strands of contact severed by a knife of thought, a terrified act of pure survival. He is separate, he is safe.

Suddenly River is warm—inexplicably so—upon her eyelids. So warm, so welcome, this current and this soft hum and this shadow, and it is peaceful, so peaceful... The curious promise claims her, and finally she submits, opening her mouth and her eyes and her lungs to the heat of Her finality, and

he is alone, alone as he has never been but it is worth it—his wings are broken and web-tangled, but they will dry and heal and he is *free*. Tokela gasps and somehow it is Wind, not River, that fills his lungs. But nevertheless it is dark, and peaceful, and he is here.

Here.

He is now, and instance, and impulse. He knows nothing else, feels nothing else, has somehow been emptied of all save the simplest and most basic drum of life:

Survival.

Dreaming. Asleep. Oblivious. The strange foresight, the Star-voices, the crippling awareness, all of it he locks away. All of it he makes still, silenced, never to be wielded again, never to emerge again...
Until now.

"I have no reason to lie, Mound-chieftain. He was my play-mate. I mean him no harm. But I saw what I saw."

Akumeh was scared.

His honest fright skittered into Inhya's own breast. It twisted chill about the thick, turbulent knot that had lain there, tight-spun, since Laocha had come running to the main fishing grounds with news of tumult at falling weir. Then Akumeh—steady, cheerful Akumeh—had come as well, babbling of drownings and madness and blood that was not.

They had descended upon the Fall with ropes and slings and plenty of strong backs, and brought their children home.

"I know you're not lying, Akumeh," Sarinak reassured, walking across the chieftain's gathering den. Akumeh knelt on the rug in its centre, eyes steady upon Sarinak as he laid a hand upon Akumeh's shoulder, then his head. "I do not question your honour. I don't doubt what you saw. I merely question your interpretation of it."

"Mound-chieftain, I—"

"You were, all of you, pushed past any reasonable limits. I'm thankful all of you are alive."

All of them. Anahli, swathed in furs in her dam's tipo, with Kuli and Aylaniś in constant attendance. Madoc, sitting proud and propped on a narrow shelf, watching Akumeh with narrowed eyes. The ankle was swollen, to be sure, and painful, but instead of a bone snapped, it had been the ligaments that had torn; longer healing, perhaps, but less chance of deadly infection.

Tokela, on the other hand...

He'd been unconscious from the time Sarinak had hefted him, limp, over one shoulder and carried him across on the barge they'd brought. He'd remained unaware when Sarinak lowered him—remarkably gentle—onto a rush-stuffed pallet on the floor of their bedding den.

"You are troubled." Sarinak took a few paces sideways, eyes upon Akumeh. "Still."

Akumeh looked over, spoke to Madoc in a voice that quavered. "You were there, after. Tell him what you saw. Tell *me*"—a plea—"what it was. It looked like he was bleeding. Bleeding from his nose and eyes, only it wasn't. Blood."

The chill ran up Inhya's spine and lodged between her shoulder blades.

"That is true. It wasn't blood." Madoc met Akumeh's gaze with a composure quite unlike his normal fierce defensiveness. "Tokela was already bleeding, didn't you see the gash on his head?"

"A'io. The weir must have hit him." Akumeh took a breath, let it out slowly. "I pulled you both from beneath the fall. Tokela almost submitted to River, but we made him breathe. It was truly blood, then. But after?"

"We were all... not ourselves," Madoc agreed, very soft. "It... It made me think wild things, too. But when you ran for help, I tended to Tokela myself," Madoc said. "What you saw was not blood. It was the colour of indigo. It was indigo."

"He had newly laid more," Akumeh agreed, but it came chancy.

"It mixed with the blood running down his face, nothing more."

It was unnerving, how well Madoc spoke the lie. His sincerity made Sarinak grunt with satisfaction, made Akumeh's confusion settle further into willing disbelief.

But Inhya had already seen the truth.

Either Madoc had not been careful enough, or the strange bleeding had started again. For when Inhya dried and tucked her eldest son into a mound of furs in the chieftain's bedding den, she had seen the traces. A small skim, in Tokela's ears and nostrils, of a substance she'd seen but once before—the colour of lapis, of indigo stain.

Lakisa's birthing-blood.

Shaper blood.

Chepiŝ blood.

This was no mere River Spirit. This was nothing that Palatan could help, no matter how he might try.

"Perhaps River hadn't washed away all the dried matter, and the indigo smeared and mixed with the blood from his head wound," Sarinak offered. "Be easy. It is good you came to me with this, good to fear something Other. But it is dangerous to make assumptions, also."

"I would not hurt him," Akumeh insisted. "But neither could I remain silent if—"

"'If'," Inhya put in, "is just that."

As one, the three males looked at her. Madoc alone seemed wary. Sarinak was relieved, and also Akumeh, though still anxious.

Sarinak took note of it, repeated, "Be easy. Your actions thisSun were honourable. You saved lives. You spoke with frankness despite your feelings, ensured dawnLands remains untainted by any sorcery. Your people will know of your bravery, and surely you'll be given leave to take your adult's path after this. You have earned it, Akumeh."

More relief as Akumeh nodded, started to turn. Then, hesitant, "What of Otter? Tokela, I mean. Will he...?" Again, the hesitation. Sarinak threw a troubled frown Inhya's way. "My chieftain has drummed for my return," Akumeh continued, "and I... I..."

"We shall tell Tokela what you seem unwilling to," Inhya replied, blunt.

Akumeh flushed and retreated from the den.

Madoc growled something beneath his breath; Sarinak gave a hiss of disapproval and Madoc subsided, looked away.

For some time there was only the crackle and sizzle of the chieftain's hearth, and the ever present lap and surge of River.

"This," Sarinak finally voiced, "means trouble. Forestlodge is made of chatter. Seguin will welcome it."

Inhya couldn't disagree, but jerked her chin towards Madoc, meaning plain in her expression.

"Akumeh imagined it!" Madoc challenged.

Inhya set her mouth firm. There was strength—and then there was belligerence.

"And that will make its own talk, ai?" Sarinak's tone was wry, unthreatened.

"There was nothing to make talk about!"

"Before this is done, there will be. Such already follows your brother like flies to sweat."

"There's nothing wrong with Tokela!" Madoc protested.

"I seem to remember, not even several Suns ago, you were crying to brother Moon over how Tokela had wronged you and everyone a'Naišwyrh," Sarinak growled.

It gave Madoc pause, but didn't stop him. "But this time he did something *right*. He saved Anahli's life! Don't you even care that he saved Anahli's life?"

"Of course we—"

"I've never seen him like that," Madoc continued, soft. "Never seen him so... He found them, didn't he? Tokela found his parents after they drowned."

Inhya made a small, choked sound.

"He did, didn't he? He never told me. Yet I heard he was there. That you thought he'd drowned with them, until you found him under their wykupeh."

Underneath, gone to ground like any small, wounded animal, fingers grimed with dirt and blood where he'd dug in, frantic. It had been normal. Ever since his birth, his blood had been normal, so much Inhya had doubted what she had once seen.

And now, this. How? *Why?*

"You didn't see him. He was so upset. I think he would have done anything to bring Anahli back to lif..." Madoc's talk, rushing together, suddenly choked, wavered silent.

"Bring Anahli *back* to... life?" Sarinak's voice was soft, but it seared through Madoc's outrage like a hot blade to fat.

"We... we thought she'd drowned. Tokela thought she'd drowned. But she... hadn't."

Sarinak kept peering at him. Madoc looked away.

Silence. Then,

"Come with me, spouse."

"Sarinak—"

"With me."

Without a word, but not without a warning glance to Madoc's sudden-pale face, Inhya followed as Sarinak strode into their private den and gave an enraged flip of the hide to cover the entry.

Whatever was said, did Madoc hear, he would be constrained from any mention by the mere lowering of the thick hide. Not that Inhya believed for a heartbeat Madoc would restrain himself from listening.

But Sarinak used Hunting-talk, aware of both their sons—one without, one within, lying bundled in the next alcove near the wide hearth filled with gleaming-stones.

This. It was accompanied by a low growl, a flit of his eyes to-wards Tokela's senseless form. *We cannot look aside from this.*

Inhya didn't know how—what—to answer.

What has he done, Inhya? What else might he do? Sarinak moved closer. *What else does our son—our blooded son!—hide?*

Inhya looked down, making her own silence within his talk—until he strode over and took her arm, hissed, "And what do *you* hide?"

She raised her gaze, met his. Signed, *I swore oath to Lakisa!* The name, even if not spoken aloud, still had the power to back him, if slight. *Do my oaths mean nothing?*

"Your oath cannot displace the good of our tribe, and you know it!" Sub-vocal, yet still betraying his agitation. "You heard Akumeh, claiming he saw the blood of Shaped things. You heard our son! Even, rot him, Mordeleg made claims I scarce wanted to believe, yet... all these winterings, all the rumours... are they true, Inhya? Have we sheltered a creature in our dens all this time? Does he have the ability to Shape, even life from death?"

Inhya put her face in her hands.

"Are the rumours *true*, Inhya?"

Jerking her head back and forth, Inhya spoke into her hands, hoarse. "I have already spoken to Palatan."

"Palatan!" It rang against the curved walls.

Over in the tiny alcove, limned faint, Tokela murmured, tossed amidst the furs. They both froze, watching white-eyed as any prey animal. Only when Tokela stirred no more did Sarinak take in a deep breath. Tightening his grip, he pulled Inhya away from the alcove, but did not allow any agitation to colour his voice, once again dipping nigh-silent.

"Your brother—"

"Is Alekšu," Inhya returned, just as soft. "You know such things are his dominion. His right, even here in duskLands. His duty, to stand against such sorceries."

"Then why has he left?"

"He said he will return. Perhaps to help Tokela—"

"Perhaps! And what are we to do until then? Keep that one"—Sarinak threw a hand in Tokela's direction—"drugged sense-less?"

"If we must."

"If we can."

Inhya let out a sob, echoing hoarse into the den. "Palatan will return, and help him. He is our *son*, Sarinak!"

"And if Alekšu has no Power over half-bred creatures?"

"*Sarinak!*" It was a choke.

He loosed her, began pacing, resorting, once more, to signs. *The rumours. All the rumours, at which I scoffed, while you kn—*

I knew nothing for certain.

You suspected, then. And said nothing.

My—

Your oath. I know. He kept pacing, muttering curses.

"Sarinak, heed me. I beg you. Such things happen, but they can be cured. It happened with my brother. He was possessed when he was younger than Tokela. Chogah cast it from him."

Sarinak halted, peered at her. "I'd heard he was sickly. I didn't know... this. Of course"—he shrugged, as if trying to shed his disquiet, and padded closer—"such things would not be openly discussed. But it is there, in the blood, this... this madness. Those a'Šaákfo carry it, insidious, like invisible Marks. It lingers, displays fangs in unlikely ways. My sire, his sister... even Galenu is, in his own way, mad." Sarinak shook his bright-wrapped head, talismans and tokens rattling. "Perhaps we should let Galenu take him back to his own kind."

"We are his kind!" Inhya protested, faint.

"Are we?"

"He is of our blood. Spirit-madness is not the same as being Shaper!"

"And what if, in him, it is? Rumour has become truth—has perhaps always been truth. Tokela's dam let herself be cozened by outLand sorcerers, and *that*"—another gesture towards Tokela—"is what has come of it!"

Their murmurings were barely audible, but emotion had its own life, roiling about the den. It roused Tokela, slight; with a twitch, he curled deeper into the furs.

He did not even have the wet, rasping quality to his breath one nigh-drowned should have, would have. His inhalations were taken with eerie peace.

"Inhya. As much as our two peoples are joined, dawn to dusk, Naišwyrh'uq cannot lie so easily with such things. You are of thisClan, now. Your birthing-tribe chooses to tread a risky path, one as dangerous as courageous, but we cannot countenance such things here. DawnLands was nigh destroyed by Other. Those who lived along River bore the brunt of the devastation. You *know* this!"

Inhya kept watching Tokela. Said, through her teeth, desperate, "He saved Anahli."

"And what if Anahli wasn't meant to be saved?"

"And what if she was?"

"I cannot believe you're asking such questions." Sarinak gripped Inhya's shoulders, shook. "This... *thing* has taken all wisdom from your sight. You've let your mourning of Lakisa'ailiq lead you too far astray. Inhya, you swore an oath that protected the get of *Shapers*."

"I swore to protect Lakisa's son!" She didn't use the suffix, and it hit them both like a blow. "An *infant*. You would return to the old ways of child killing, of witch hunting?"

Sarinak released her. His eyes went dark, then hooded as they slid sideways, taking in the still, fur-wrapped form in the alcove. "That was an evil time." He shook his head, paced over to their bedshelf, lowered himself to sit on the edge with another shake of his head. "But Inhya, what has happened thisnow, the doubt of it will grow, and splinter. Such a weakness—disease—of Spirit has nearly felled us more than once. Lakisa'ailicq's Spirit-madness, my own father's weakness when my mother was taken, Našobok's defection—"

"Sarinak—"

"I watched, and wasn't allowed to so much as weep as my brother was rived from us! As my dam, her heart wrung but her eyes dry, watched her youngest hung from the poles for two Suns, then watched agains as he was forced to run the gauntlet, beaten and debased and cast from our lodging to become less than nothing! Little *he* cared, but it killed us all! And then, so soon after, my sire's decline—you remember how it was, tšukasi. In the end, I had to go to Council, conspire to his replacement."

"You took nothing that wasn't yours," she whispered.

"Inhya, you know we always bide unsure. With all that's happened in our family—all the weakness, the sickness—the tribes were well within their rights to not accept me."

"But they did."

"A"io. They won't accept *this*." Sarinak jerked his chin towards where Tokela lay. "All the speculation damaged *his* standing—so much that there was never a breath of hope that he would be trained to perhaps hold Mound-chieftain's staff. And it was his right to try; Tokela is eldest of our Clan after me! But now? Rumour will burn through our Land like flames. You know our tribal law, my heart: those possessed of an Elemental must be cast out! Shapers are never allowed in our territory. We hold duskLands, you and I, and we must hold to the law or be set aside."

"I know." Almost a moan. "Yet if we do what you say must be done, my oaths lie broken. One I swore to protect shall hang from the poles and run the gauntlet, never to return, and our... our blood son will... ai. Madoc will never forgive us."

Sarinak let out a vile curse, turned away. "Would you have me keep Other in our midst, just so our son will love us? I can't do that, Inhya. And it hurts my heart to think you would ask it of me."

"That isn't what I—"

"I know you loved my father's sister. I know what she meant to you. I didn't understand, then. I had playmates, of course. I eased the heat in my blood amongst my own, as proper for oških. But I never had a lovemate, never an oathbrother. I scorned my brother's ways, his insistence upon rutting males even past his oških summerings. I was contemptuous of what he had with your brother. I didn't understand such love. Not until I found *you*."

Inhya came over, knelt before Sarinak and laid her head upon his knees. His fingers, strong and callused from spear and fishing-net, stroked her hair with the gentleness he gave only to her. She closed her eyes, took a deep breath, peered up at her spouse. "There must be something to be done, other than..." Her voice choked. "Sarinak, he's our *son*."

Sarinak crumpled, then, as if the strong cliff stones that had made him and borne him were shivering into sand around their feet. "He *was* our son." It quivered, thick with tears. "But that time, beloved, is long past. And we've been deluding ourselves to imagine otherwise."

"How is she?"

Aylaniś turned from the furs, looked outwards to Inhya's silhouette within the opened tipo door.

"She sleeps, peaceably." A smile, shared between two mothers. "She's alive, thanks to your sons. Both of them."

Inhya's gaze flickered, and she entered, her voice strong-seeming. "If there is anything... well. You must take care she doesn't fall prey to the lung-sick. It happens here, often, when someone has nigh drowned."

"There are times advice is maddening as blackbuzz in summering," Chogah growled from where she'd squatted in beside the hearth. "We know better how to care for her than even one as exalted as you."

Inhya slid a dark glare Chogah's way, said to Aylaniś, "Do you have any more of the sleep stink?"

Chogah made a disagreeable noise.

Aylaniś slid her a quieting gaze, little hoping for its success, and peered at Inyha. "For Tokela."

"I must."

"We've enough ourselves for now." A well-filled pouch came sailing from Chogah's direction. "A'io, drug him. What else can you do? Unless you plan on smothering him middark."

Inhya still didn't answer Chogah, but she tied the pouch at her belt.

From the Bowl, drums announced midSun meal. Aylaniś reached out where Kuli lay, curled up in the furs against Anahli's sleeping form. He'd remained there all thisSun, quieter than Aylaniś had ever seen him. "Wake up, son."

Kuli always woke quickly and this was no exception; he sat upright, his wavy hair scrunched in several directions. "Aška?"

"I need you to go with your aunt Inhya, Kuli."

"But Anahli—"

"She won't wake yet." Aylaniś peered at Inhya, though her

talk remained for Kuli. "You have time to eat with your friends, and perhaps help Aunt Inyha, a'io?"

Inhya's eyes held to hers, acknowledged the plea. "I truly could use your help with a few things, Little Fox."

Kuli rolled from the furs, shook himself with a sleepy shiver, then grinned at Inyha and sped out of the tipo. Inhya started to follow.

Aylaniś touched her sleeve, murmured, "We must leave, soon."

Inyha clearly hadn't expected this. Her eyes chased away—the way Kuli had gone.

"He will stay through summering at least. I like that he's learning different ways here."

"Perhaps we will trade Kuli's further hearthing for Tokela," Chogah drawled. "It would, after all, be better than smothering him."

Aylaniś shot Chogah a quelling glance.

But the statement, outwardly ignored, had raised hope in Ihyha's gaze. Aylaniś didn't know how to answer it, had to look away.

Inyha's voices followed her, though. "Will Palatan return soon?"

And neither could she answer that. *I grieve with you. But I don't know. Don't know if he can help Tokela.* Her gaze moved to Anahli, met Chogah's over the small hearth, then slid to Anahli, drugged as surely as... *What has Tokela done to her? Made?*

Shaped?

Finally, Aylaniś answered, "I'm sorry, but I cannot say any more to this. We're not Alekšu. It isn't our place."

Inhya took in a long, quavering breath, then nodded. Retreated.

Aylaniś watched her go, eyes stinging, wanting to speak, go after.

"We should take the lost one's son with us, my chieftain." It was respectful. Ai, Chogah could pull respect from her tail split when she had to.

"It is not a decision we can make. Neither of us is Alekšu." A keen cut, no matter how much Aylaniś tried to blunt it—too many paths had been walked down to trust this elder.

"The Power does not leave with the title. Do you think I don't See what is happening?" A jerk of chin towards Anahli. "He has changed something in her. He has awakened something that we thought would never rise. We should take Tokela with us.

"So he can... infect more of our People?"

"You sound like a dawnLander, horse-chieftain."

"And you seem to forget what your own purpose is!" Aylaniś hissed back. "To protect our Grandmother from Other!"

Strange, how she was the one spitting and hissing, and Chogah so fiercely calm.

And her gaze, fixed upon Aylaniś. "That is not our only purpose, my chieftain."

Aylaniś closed her eyes, took in breath for another heated reply. *How do you expect me to know that, when all of you hold your secrets close as skin?* Instead it changed within her; what came out upon the exhale was the beginnings of song. She turned away with another breath, and from deep in her throat the warbling Moons prayer came, soft as the damp cloths she bent to rinse in the basket then replace upon her daughter's forehead.

Anahli was too warm; the Medicine had that effect. But sleep was preferable to waking, now and here.

"You'll need another dose of the sleep stink for her, soon enough," Chogah murmured.

"I have plenty."

"She can't stay here. Not now."

"I know."

"Hunh. It is time. I know you thought thisnow would never come, but it has. She must come home, and take wing with the night flyers."

Aylaniś nodded, and kept singing, soft but carrying.

It is time. I have waited long enough.

He is underwater, currents folding busily about him. But River is strangely still upon his skin, calmed as far as his arms can reach, as if he can contain Her.

Why do you think you are here? You have given yourself to me, and this time, I will not let you go.

But I am not... His throat closes, instinct, mere pressure trying to halt the not-talk. There has never been need for talk in thisnow. *I have... changed things. I... Anahli...*

Have you? Are you sure that what you wakened was not already there?

My mother... my... father. I...

You survived. You showed mercy, for they were already Mine.

I... am... Other.

You are of Us, and what you bear within you makes you more of Us.

Us?

We have waited long. You are no longer an infant sucked into a spiral of ignorance. You must take possession of what is yours. You must awaken what is not. It is past time for the teind to be counted: in blood, for blood. The not-voice is strong, ringing inside his skull, inescapable. Pulling him deep into the dive.

He puts hands to his temples, as if to knead the pressure away. *Teind? You have my parents!*

And you gave them to Me, Eyes of Stars. What else will you give Me, merely to evade what you are?

Tokela came bolt upright.

The den was empty and dark. His choking breaths tore the stillness, overloud.

This had happened before. The Dreams, the waking into an empty room, his lungs filled with water and his bedding soaked with River brack, his cry ringing into the wikupeh to those who would never again answer...

Happenstance fled, a shadowling skittering from illumination, a dark shroud...

The furs were wet. Heavy. Clinging. Tokela kicked them away and crawled closer to the hearth, shivering and damp. Another blanket lay close by; he snatched it up, curled into the nubbly dry warmth, and laid his head to his knees.

And Fire stayed merely that: warmth, comfort.

Soon his shudders eased, heat beginning to steal through skin and bone. Thoughts stole, also, in flits and starts. What had happened. What would happen.

The rush of blood in his skull, the drumbeat of his heart, echoing the Spirits whispering behind his eyes and creeping through his veins.

His veins. If he was to open them, now, what would he find?

Tokela held out his arm, pondered the knotwork of indigo tracing the length of it... and there was the conundrum. How veins seemed indigo, or even sometimes the hue of moss and mould, but when spilled... changed.

Should he empty his veins onto the stones, would he be found cold and limp within a darkening pool of indigo, or carmine?

He was naked of everything but the tiny eating knife that still hung from the thong at his throat. Unsheathing it, he quite methodically put the keen edge to the underside of his forearm and against the thickest vein, indigo pulsing—

"Tokela?" It was thin, wavering. "What are you doing?"

Tokela's heart lurched up into his throat, descended and hammered like a too-tight drum. "Seeing if I'm still alive," he told Kuli, and ran the blade along his forearm.

Shallow. Not enough to spurt and fell him before it could be staunched. Only enough to watch the blood well, and to find his breath come easier as it dripped down tawny flesh: sanguine, thick... *normal.*

"Are you?" Kuli's voice was small. "Still alive?"

Am I? Is Anahli?

But ai, he knew. Could feel her heart beating, and her breath smooth, in and out, like Wind.

Like she was beside him. Inside him. Part of him.

Wind and Water. Fire and Earth and Spirit and...

Eyes meet eyes.

Is this how Chepiś felt when they Shaped me? Made me?

"You saved Anahli from River." Kuli padded across the floor both silent and subdued. "She's still sleeping. Both of you, sleeping so long... it's already well past midSun meal. Almost dusk."

Why was Kuli here? He'd seen what had happened. Madoc had seen, and Akumeh had. Likely the tale had been told of what they'd witnessed. He'd seen the fear and loathing in their faces. Surely no one would leave Kuli alone here, with a half... creature.

More likely Kuli had snuck in.

Kuli confirmed this in the next breath. "I was helping Aunt Inhya fold blankets, but she was called away. So I came in to see you."

"You shouldn't be here." It was a growl.

Kuli merely folded down onto hands and knees beside Tokela and began to crawl into his lap.

Tokela should shove him away. Chase him out. River's voice rushed through Tokela's own heart, a merciless background descant to his heartbeat, a blood heat sure to drown anything.

If only he had drowned instead of Anahli.

Instead Tokela quivered like a hart in a meadow who listened for the predator's second step. Found himself leaning against his tiny cousin, letting Kuli wrap skinny arms about him, rock him as if Tokela were the younger. Tried to halt himself as he snaked his arms about Kuli; instead felt the sting of weakness as he buried burning eyes into cinnabar hair and tried to forget the questions:

What is happening? What have I done?

What could I do, given the chance?

None of them mattered. Only the kinship, and comfort, and silence.

Into that silence, Kuli spoke. "You saved my sister. You almost drowned to save her."

"I... suppose so."

"I owe you blood debt. That makes us oathbrothers."

Tokela wanted to laugh in the face of such youthful seriousness—but that same thing sobered him. "When you're old enough."

Silence, with Kuli holding to him, wrapped close. Then, "Are you cold, Tokela?"

Gritting his teeth, Tokela bade his shudders to stillness. That stillness merely opened him further to every other movement: Kuli's heated, wiry frame and quick, shallow breaths, the brine and sweat lingering in his tangled hair, the tingling behind Tokela's own eyes rising like a water-horse to heat and light and air, eager for River's call.

"Perhaps," Kuli considered, "it would be warmer if you had a story for me."

This did break a laugh from Tokela, though also a half sob. He tried to speak; it truncated into a whisper, "I'm sorry. I've no stories in my heart thisnow."

What have I done? To Anahli? To my parents?

What could *I do?*

Kuli peered up at him, RainForest eyes wide and unquestioning.

"You must go," Tokela growled. "They can't find you here. They can't know what I've done, or..." *or they'll take your sister from you.*

Kuli suddenly burrowed against Tokela's shoulder, no longer comforter, but one in desperate need of comfort. "I think they're going to send you away, Tokela."

With shaking fingers, Tokela smoothed the snarled, cinnabar locks, said nothing.

I think they should send me away. Far away.

It smelled... strange.

It gave Madoc a sparking, throbbing pain behind his eyes.

He'd woken, off and on, though he wasn't sure how many Suns had passed... and now he feigned sleep, eyes narrowed to bare slits, watching as his dam woke and begun tending the smelly clay pot with bits of leaves and bark from a pouch at her hip belt. It was well known that Inyha had brought her birthing-tribe's herblore to dawnLands, had grown as expert in River and Forest plants. Even the old herbKeeper used Inyha's tinctures. But this, escaping around the edges of the pulled down flap, was something Madoc had never smelled before. It must be from duskLands.

Memories sparked, a telling of passage. His sire coming in, grimacing at the scent. How they wouldn't let Madoc move about the few times he'd woke, just lie there with his foot propped and swaddled. How Inhya occasionally rubbed it with smelly, sticky unguents or bathed in salts and herbs. How his sire carried him to the bodysoil trenches. How Madoc had tried to hear what his parents had said that first dark when Madoc had blurted what he never should have, both closed up in their sleeping den, but his leg had foiled him from sneaking close enough.

He knew it couldn't be good.

They were so... subdued. It worried Madoc all the more. After the intensity of... whatever, whenever... it seemed as if everything had closed down into a small and tight space.

With a huff, Inhya dipped a cup into the pot, wiped its rim on a cloth, and took it over to the window ledge. To cool, Madoc figured—the breeze coming in was misty with falling Rain.

He hoped it wasn't some concoction he would have to drink—if the smell of it gave him a headache, he could only imagine what the taste would do.

Small noises, coming from the bedding den. Madoc's nape hairs vibrated as recognition set in: Tokela. Only, not.

Inhya stilled. Then she snatched up the cup from the window and hurried into the bedding den.

Tokela was there, Madoc knew it.

More sounds—not speech, not at all, but more like an animal's whimpering. Then a silence, enduring so long Madoc thought his nerves would snap.

Inhya came from within, the empty cup dangling from nerveless fingers.

Madoc couldn't stay quiet, not any more. "What did you give him? What is that stuff?"

Inhya started, as if her heart had been leagues absent, and turned. Her eyes shone brilliant in the dim with some emotion Madoc couldn't comprehend. Then she seemed to shake herself, and padded over to sit beside him. "Everything is well, son."

Madoc didn't believe her. He realised suddenly, when it came to this one thing, he'd not believed her in some time.

And it *hurt*.

"I want to see him."

"Madoc—" Fingers covered his lips.

"I want to know he's all right." He wanted to be strong, angry—instead his voice betrayed him, slipped up high and wavering.

Inhya peered at him for long heartbeats, then tilted her head, relented. She helped him rise, let him lean heavily against her as he limped into the tiny alcove. Pain shot up and down his leg; Madoc was glad when they stopped at the lowered hide covering the alcove's opening. Inhya reached out, pulled it aside.

Acrid smoke fingered out, drawn to the larger space: a bowl of dried resin smouldering just inside. Beyond it, on a pallet of rushes and furs, Tokela lay stretched out, twitching in some senseless reaction, arms thrown up over his head and hair flung over his eyes. Inhya hooked the door hide then ambled over and bent down, fingering the dark forelock back. Tokela frowned, drew up an arm as if shielding his face. He didn't wake. Madoc's breath caught in his throat. Tokela looked nothing like himself; not the brother Madoc had run wild through woods and fields with, wrestled with, argued with.

It seemed Tokela had gone away to somewhere far and unwelcoming. What had returned, Madoc didn't know.

Suddenly Tokela went lax, arm falling back. Madoc's breath squeaked and hung; his dam took his arm as he leaned forwards.

Pain shot up his leg once more, and with clearer eyes Madoc saw the pulse, steady-strong, in his cousin's throat.

"See," Inhya murmured. "He's sleeping, nothing more. I gave him a strong draught. It's like what I give to your grandsire at times; to let him rest without—" She took in a breath as if to bite back her talk, and Madoc felt his stomach sink.

She knew. Somehow, she *knew*.

Madoc refused to say the first, or even the second thing demanding voice. But what did come out surprised him. "You can't."

It was louder than he intended, into the close den, but Tokela didn't hear. Didn't stir. Nevertheless, Inhya put gentle fingers once again to Madoc's lips, helped him limp, slowly and awkwardly, over to their bedshelf. To his surprise, she flung back the furs, nodded him in.

"You can stay here. For a little while. You can let me know if he gets restless again." Inhya shrugged. "But he shouldn't."

"You can't," Madoc repeated.

"I can't what?"

"Send Tokela away. You're going to send him away, aren't you?"

She finished tucking him in, knelt beside the bedshelf and put her chin upon her folded hands. "You know we must."

"I don't know that! I don't want to!"

Inhya reached out, gave a gentle, intimate tug to Madoc's braidlock. He wanted to jerk away, rebuff her; he couldn't.

"Ai, Madoc." A sigh, resolved. Weary. "Denial won't help any of us anymore."

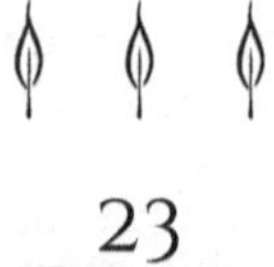

23
EXILE

It was a tiny and private gathering, held in a small alcove off the great Council den. Usually such things were taken care of in Council, in public, but all things considered...

Galenu was not surprised.

He kept still until Sarinak finished speaking, and knew all along there was more, much more, than Mound-chieftain let on—or likely ever would. But what was said told enough. Galenu let Sarinak's voice ring into silence, let Inhya pour him another cup of copperbark tea. Took a great draught, tasted sharp green needles and sweet honey, and stared at the curve of rock overhead.

"So," he finally said, "you think Tokela is mad."

With one hand Sarinak made a quick, sideways gesture, ward and negation.

"Isn't that what you're saying, avoid the topic as you may? You're keeping him drugged and locked away, as if he were some dog with the foaming sickness!"

"He has a Spirit ill." Short, from behind Inhya's clenched teeth. "You should know, Galenu—son to Mituna ailiq a'Šaákfo—the healing ways of duskLands. Draughts and resin are best for such things."

"Ai, and a brother of such Smoke is often used to quiet hiveKin, when one thinks to steal what is theirs," Galenu riposted. "You're not Alekšu, yet you think to use such strong Medicine?"

"Alekšu is not here," Sarinak broke in, a clear threat within it. "Aylaniś and Chogah gave us the draught. Not that I must explain anything to one who has raised no offspring nor cared for Spirit ill. You've no rights to criticize anything my spouse must do."

"I'm afraid I've every right, since you seem bent upon tossing me the mess you've made!"

"We," Inhya rocked forwards, "have not made this situation, Galenu a'Hassun."

"I think I could speak to many who would disagree. Našobok saw it. Your brother saw it. Nechtoun has shared his heart to me on this one thing of import: that you, Inhya, and Tokela, were bent upon colliding. We can debate the making of this situation as you will, but you've certainly put a finish to it!"

Sarinak lurched to his feet and strode forwards, burly but graceful in his anger. Galenu gained his feet, both defence and vehemence. Inhya also had angled forwards, fists clenched.

All right, perhaps Galenu had gone a bit too far.

And ai, but Sarinak was all a'Naišwyrh, and they were *big*.

"How dare you come to my place and speak to me so? If any 'finish' could be said to have been made, you and your outLand *friends* have more to do with that than any could boast!"

"You and Inhya would blame a clouded Moons' rising upon Chepiś!"

"What blame I lay is justified!" Sarinak retorted furiously. "I remember what they did to Tokela's dam."

"And you know so much of what they 'did' to her, do you?"

"They killed her as surely as if they had put her to River themselves!" Inhya hissed. "And *you* know *that*."

"You're so certain," Galenu said, very soft, "of what I know."

"You have always claimed to 'not know'. You, who claims to be storyKeeper; you, who claims friends in outLands! Which merely means you know just enough to slither past responsibility."

That one clung, stung. "If I'm so irresponsible, however can you trust me with a young oških?" Galenu snorted disgust. "Ai, that's right. It's either me, or the gauntlet and exile, since your precious brother Alekšu has quit the field."

"You have no—"

"But you expect me to take an oških you've treated as some disobedient bondling!"

"Unlike stoneClan, a'Naišwyrh do not bond or beat *children*!" Inhya snapped. Before her, looming altogether too close to Galenu, Sarinak's stance promised he held few such compunctions against coldcocking an adult. Even if he was an elder.

Galenu refused to back down. There was a reason to this, one lying beneath all the ones layered atop, and he would find it, know it. "That oških is no longer a child, and I've eyes in my head. Fear is what he has here, nothing more."

"Not fear but contempt is what that one holds for us—and you think we would *choose* that?" Sarinak snapped. "Tokela has never invited me to so much as lay a hand on his shoulder. *Never*. I learned long ago not to even try."

"Preposterous!"

"Hunh. You stand in my place, an old khatak thinking to tell us how to raise a child? Pity you didn't give as much as a thought before now!"

"Perhaps I would have, if—"

"Rot!" Sarinak spat. "You'd all but forgotten he was alive, I'll warrant, until you saw him during First Running and decided,

based on a Sun's passage of acquaintance, you had found someone to understand *your* madness! Well, perhaps you're correct
there, stoneChieftain. What goes on in that one's heart is not
normal, and you've your own responsibility to claim there!"

The force of the outburst stilled Galenu's tongue. Inhya also
hung back; silent, almost wary.

"Don't play innocent, Galenu, it ill suits you. You know what
responsibility I speak of. You were in it up to your so-charming
chin!" The low ceiling rang with the power of Sarinak's voice.
"You're cursed lucky my sire loves you and never blamed you for
any of what happened with his sister. You're doubly lucky his sister's spouse refused to call his mother's brother out, make you
answer for even one solitary rumour!"

"I take your meanings," Galenu ventured, "and your warnings, insulting and oblique though they be."

"Ai, spare me!" Sarinak snarled. "I didn't think it was even
possible to insult you! We've made it plain as we can. What happened to the dam is visiting the son. Alekšu hopes to help, but he
is away. Tokela can't stay here with what has been proven. This
is no simple matter of purge or gauntlet. You know these... creatures. It is possible they can aid him. We cannot." His eyes slid to
Inyha, dark. "No longer."

Galenu narrowed his eyes, watching. Had Inhya known? Her
avoidance of Sarinak's gaze seemed to further the possibility; her
next words made it clearer.

"Ghost Eyes leave grieving in their wake, always, and we have
all paid the price." Inhya took several steps towards Galenu,
hands balled into fists, her upper lip curling. "All of us. Save *you*.
And it is long—ai, it is *long* past time you paid *your* due."

Galenu peered at Inhya as if he were seeing her for the first
time. Perhaps he was. If what happened to Lakisa was revisiting
her son, fear had completed the cycle more than any Chepiś-invoked madness! Mismanagement, nothing but; traditional hard-
headedness on every front. They'd blown circumstance out of
proportion. If the oških indeed had some ancient Elemental gift,
better he should be away from here, where they wouldn't even
let him sketch pictures for fear he was conjuring up ghosts—or
"Ghost Eyes"! How could young Tokela turn out balanced, when
he'd paid for the slightest oddity with every breath?

And ai'o, Galenu knew he owed this much to Lakisa's son. Inhya was right about that if little else: Galenu had brought Lakisa
to Chepiś, though he never would have dreamed what she would
ask and what it cost her. If—if!—Tokela had some Chepiś-invoked
madness, then Galenu was the best one to help. If nothing else,
he could take Tokela to them. Somehow.

"He can't stay here one Sun longer," Sarinak rumbled. "You
will take him, or I will take his name. I have nothing more to
say."

And he turned away, ambling over to the hearth, to slowly kneel beside it, Fire turning his broad profile all the more to stone.

Galenu slid a look towards Inhya. She was solely focused upon Sarinak, dark eyes glimmering. She seemed to have forgotten Galenu was there.

She hadn't. "For once in your life, Galenu, try to heed something other than what *you* want. This is about Tokela, not you. You owe Lakisa 'a'iliq that much."

Galenu took in a breath, let it out, slow. "And what if he doesn't want to come?"

"He will." Inhya didn't take her eyes from Sarinak.

"If so," Galenu said, quiet, "then surely I'll take him."

Inhya rounded on him, eyes still glimmering. No darksight, no anger. Merely defeat. "Just take care of him, Galenu."

"I—"

"There is," she interrupted, and turned away, "nothing more to be said."

The smell is thick, sick-sweet, curling over him. *Smoke*, something within him recognises, and as a hand curls familiarly at his nape and raises his head to a bowl that smells dull, and dead, a tiny, gibber of panic wants to claim him. *Fight*, it says, and Fire would rise only Ša is not here, and *not yet, not yet*, River soothes...

He drinks. It sets him mercifully dull. The deep ache in his heart lies numb, the shards in his Spirit still cut, but their edge is blunted. Everything is... diminished.

His eyes open, take in Inhya. Perhaps it should make him feel something, but nothing rises. Or speaks, as he closes his eyes and goes... *away.*

Quiet, in this far-flung not-place. No whispers, no senses vibrating undeniably as a beaten drum, no breath against his ear, no rush and soundless hum behind his eyes.

No remembrance.

And he wonders—*is this death?*—even as something in him disagrees, tries to rise and speak. But he submits, closes his heart, refuses any wonder, bespelled beneath the silence.

Then, as if his name has been spoken—a chord of silver song into the silence—he wakes.

Quiet, still. Tokela smells spicebark tea, and Rain, and River.

Galenu a'Hassun is sitting next to the hearth, sipping at a cup and watching him.

Madoc woke, startled, wondered if Tokela had shouted in sleep. He peered across, toward the sleeping den, merely to find the hide was flung back. And the den beyond looked...

Empty.

He lurched up, kicking aside what furs didn't fall away, and made the mistake of kicking with his injured leg. A shrill yip escaped, and an oath for which his aška would've dunked his head in the washing basket.

Only she didn't. She merely watched him from the carven-smooth entry to her bedding den. "Tokela's gone, Madoc."

He stared at her. For a half heartbeat he thought she meant Tokela was dead—but for the fact she'd named him. Panic skittered away, to be replaced with dread. "Gone? Gone where?"

"Galenu stone-chieftain has taken him to his hearth." Inhya's talk came slow; she seemed more intent upon his reaction.

Only Madoc wasn't sure how to react. Only... "He... he wouldn't have left! He wouldn't! Not without..." His eyes were stinging-hot, his voice tight, stammering though he tried to halt it. "W-without saying goodbye."

Inhya came over to the bedshelf, placed her hand on his chest. Something rolled beneath her palm, and she murmured, "He left this for you." As she pulled her hand away, a small parchment roll wobbled on Madoc's breastbone. Leaning over, Inhya laid her forehead against his and furthered, even softer, "See it for what it is, son. I shouldn't need to tell you to take care with it."

Then she was gliding from the alcove into the main den, her voice normal. Sarinak's answer sounded satisfied.

Madoc sat up, concealing the parchment between the fold of his knees—just in case—and unrolled it.

See it for what it is.

A sketch, obviously recent, of Madoc; a hasty sepia profile that nevertheless mirrored what Madoc saw in a still pool.

Eyes stinging, Madoc rolled the parchment closed, and tucked it in his tunic sleeve.

Sharp, the smells, but familiar: the contained burn of dried greensap and leaf in a pipe bowl, exhaled across her cheeks like the brush of feathers; charcoal, vermilion, and indigo for the Marking; a thin, sharp-acrid taste of blood and sweat; the blessing Smoke of sweetsage and braided grasses; ground šinc'teh and pollen mealy-sweet at throat and hips and feet; woven blankets lain with dried petals and seedpods.

Underneath that, the sounds: a tenor thrum of a small drum singing to the ash and blood between her eyes, upon her palms, her insteps. The rhythm—four-and-one, four-and-one—to bring the body waking from the Elemental thrall...

Anahli woke.

She was home. She lay in the Breaking Ground, hair unbound and a white blanket across her torso. The Ground was deserted, save for Sun's light, and the drum Chogah caressed, and...

Here, beside Anahli, *with her*, bending over her, fanning her with a beaded owl-feather fan, and garbed in white regalia edged with the lapis of a falling-leaves Sky. Her sire was here, but not only that. He was Alekšu, here, the Smoke and smudge wafting about them like mist as he painted the white blanket with indigo and Sun-hued streaks. Singing her, with a soft tenor so like to the drum.

"One of us, now, you are one of us, now, Lapis Walker, Owl Sister, you are one of us. Sing the Wind, protect our Earth..."

Palatan finished the song, leaned over Anahli, and put a thumb to her forehead. "Once," he whispered, so soft, "I was told that no child I sired upon my chieftain would follow me to this place." He cupped her face, smoothed fingers over her cheeks. "They were wrong."

The cart was small and sturdy; the pony equally so. Galenu had spent much of the journey making cheery talk; Tokela found that he needn't reply much, or often. The talk was all over, from assurances that Mordeleg would be sent to relative upLands, to stories about the flatstone hills, where Galenu's tribe lived and farmed. Their šinc'teh grew short but powerful, and their weavings some of the best, traded all over...

Tokela was watching Land's scape change, from thick trees to less, then less still, smaller and sunk into sandy hills. Sun came from behind her cloud veil, and River faded, too, until She was a mere, thin whisper behind his eyes. He wasn't sure he cared about that, either.

Maybe it was the drug, still runnelling through his veins, dulling everything.

Maybe it was better this way.

Lost in the pressure of Galenu's chatter and the heavier weight of his heart, Tokela didn't hear the galloping hoofs until they were nearly upon them.

The cart creaked to a halt. Galenu stood up with a glad shout: "Back already, River-chieftain? Do you have my cargo?"

River-chieftain? Tokela spun about as Našobok charged to the side of the cart and round the front. His horse halted, dancing.

"Rot your cargo!" Našobok snapped back. "Where are you taking him?"

Galenu blinked at the first, and at the second. Našobok leaned in; he looked furious, ready to leap over the cart and atop Galenu. It made no sense.

So Tokela answered, "Galenu's offered me his hearth. There was... well, it was decided—"

"You're pie-eyed as a downdocks outlier," Našobok interrupted. "What have they...? N'da, it doesn't matter. What matters is I went to Naišwyrh'uq looking for you, and they said Galenu had taken you—" He interrupted himself this time, demanded, "Old one, are you taking him to the stone hills? Or to Chepiś?"

"Why would he take me to—" Tokela started, but Galenu tilted his chin and puffed his chest.

"I'm taking him home, of course. But if my Chepiś friends could help him, then of course I'd—"

"Get off the cart, Tokela."

It didn't quite connect. Tokela stared at Galenu. "Chepiś? You'd take me—"

"If they can help you, of course I would."

"Just like you took his dam to them for help? Get off the cart, Tokela."

Tokela didn't budge. It still wasn't quite making sense, and this last... He stared at Galenu. "You... you were the one who... You took my mother... to Chepiś?"

"A story for another time, and I'll be glad to tell it to you some—Let go of my horse, Našobok! Shade and sweet water, are you mad?"

And truly, the look in Našobok's eyes was enough for worry. "Not mad," he growled. "But angry enough to drag you behind this cart... are *you* mad? Your friends, you said. Your Chepiś *friends*, and you'd just hand him over to them?"

"You make it sound like some sort of... portside deal. No doubt you'd know a lot of those, but come now, you know me well enough—"

"I don't think I know you at all, old one. Not if you'd be party to this."

Tokela kept opening his mouth, kept closing it, but any good sense was dribbling out his ears at the realisation:

Našobok had come for him. Had ridden, from the look of him, through lastDark and thisSun to find him.

"Get off the cart, Tokela. I'm taking you back to River, with me. Where you *belong*."

"How romantic," Galenu scoffed.

Našobok ignored it. "Do you want to go with Galenu? Are you willing to have him take you to Chepiś? Willing for them to do more than he's already seen them do? I told you, you've choices—and I aim to see you keep them!"

"What choice would you offer, wyrhling?" Galenu's tone quelled, sarcastic. "Outcast upon a leaky craft, no home, no true place... save in your bunk, perhaps?"

This time Našobok did strike. He leapt across Tokela and grabbed Galenu by his tunic. Would have yanked him off the cart, no doubt, if Tokela hadn't smacked at his head. Pure instinct, not even hard, but it broke the inexplicable rage. Našobok blinked, looked at Tokela for a long breath, then let Galenu back down. Slowly.

"Portside deals!" Našobok spat. "There's plenty of those to be had, to be sure, where I run—but there's ones even I won't touch!" He turned to Tokela. "That's why I'm here. They're looking for you, my heart. Making deals in those portside villages. Sending their Matwau pets after you, prowling the slave markets up and down River, putting a reasonable likeness of you into the hands of whoever might be able to take you to them!"

"They wouldn't!" Galenu put a hand to his hung-open mouth, and leaned back against the cart bench.

"This isn't sneaking around to pay you a clandestine visit, or doing trade for *glašg* eyes. Your *friends*, Galenu, are making hostile incursion. Openly breaking a truce that's lasted generations."

Tokela dropped his gaze to his hands, didn't see them. "To get at me." It was hoarse, and the drum of his heart slowing, thick beneath Sun's glare. His temples pounded.

Choices. Was there such a thing?

Našobok merely leaned over and laid his hands over Tokela's. "And you know why. Don't you?"

Tokela raised his head and peered into the storm-hued eyes. Nodded.

"Then nowhere's safe!" Galenu blurted.

Našobok kept looking at Tokela. Waiting, buoying.

"River," Tokela said. "River will see me safe."

$$\phi \quad \phi \quad \phi$$

24
HUNTED

Massively unpleasant, this part of the big island. Even in the earliest phases of morning, it dried one's nostrils and drifted through one's lungs, leaving only a taut rasp of dust and heat behind.

No doubt should Sivan hint at any discomfort, her brother would explain in gravid detail how they were in a rain shadow, and how the western mountain range would, the more they left the southeastern estuaries behind, inspire not merely dry plains, but pockets of desert. Well, and Sivan knew that, and Jorda knew she knew it, but his nerves were strung in a different place than her own. Jorda prattled against Sivan's quiet.

Maloh, on the other hand, would just roll dark eyes and smirk. This was her element. Even now she strode out, the sun glinting against her short halo of crimped sienna hair, her muscled arms bare to welcome the coming sun. Of course, Maloh's people, like most of the planet's natives, had adequate melanin. Furthermore, they did judicious trade with this continent's stunted, if canny, denizens. Maloh had little reason for concealment, be it from a stint of solar rays or a breached truce.

Jorda was already cloaked and veiled. It was a reminder that Sivan should draw her own and pull the goggles over her eyes.

They shouldn't *be* here.

"You're sure they'll come this way?" Maloh was scanning the horizon with dark brows quirked. "There aren't many who venture near this part of the desert. Only the nomads, and they don't stay in one place long. Hard enough for even their like to eke a living hereabouts, but the proximity to the vortex should make it all the more off limits."

"I'm sure of nothing at present." Jorda stumbled in a drift of sand; Sivan reached out to steady him. "Not until the satellites rise. I touched him briefly last night, but the connexion was... blurred. Faulty. As if he were drugged."

No doubt *proximity to the vortex* also plagued decent reception. That or this rotting planet itself, shifting beneath their feet, keeping a baleful eye upon everything they would try to do.

They kept walking. Not even a burden beast had been allowed them. No easy journey, no light visit. Get in, get it done, get out. Capture the native boy and bring him before the Domina, both psi-powers and limbs trussed and gagged akin to the temple offerings of Maloh's people.

Former people. Sivan wondered if she herself would have been brave enough to follow heart instead of identity. Though Maloh had been saved any decision by her people's edict: working for aliens was one thing, a matter of expediency and survival. But taking one of them as lover?

Unforgivable. Maloh could not go back.

But then could anyone, ever?

"What is the boy like?" Jorda's voice quavered with a faint thread: wonder, it sounded like.

Sivan shrugged. "I've told you several times."

"I know. I wish I'd been with you."

"I wish I'd never seen him. I wish you'd never seen his mother. So much trouble, from one foolish—"

"It wasn't foolish. He would have died, had I not acted."

"He well could die now. Or worse."

"Lack of compassion bears no truth," Maloh threw back over one shoulder.

"Compassion." Jorda repeated. "What was I supposed to do? She was a friend, in need. She'd already miscarried four other kits."

"The Accord says 'no interference with the northern island's natives', and censure those who do so."

"Yet now our superiors send us and pay no heed to—"

"They pay heed. They must." Maloh stayed a stride ahead of them, her sandals fording the variables of sand and shale with only an occasional slip. "The little natives know when they don't, eh?"

"And how do they know?"

"You're the one with all the answers, Jorda."

His eyes sought Maloh's, tinted amber behind the lenses, pale nose and cheeks sunburnt from several sols of open-air travel. "You're the one who first pointed out how this mission went against Accord."

"And see how far that got us." Maloh's gesture took in the entire desert: mesas, draws, washes, and beyond, a backdrop of purplish mountains. "We're here, aren't we? We have our orders. Your Domina wants the boy and will break truce to have him. Only she doesn't seem to understand how his People won't take this lying down. They're not animals to be caged."

"Sometimes things must be contained for their own safety," Sivan murmured. "And ours."

"You don't believe that." The disappointment in Maloh's brown eyes scored a stinging furrow in Sivan's composure.

"What I believe is irrelevant at present," Sivan retorted. "History has proven it, over and over. What if the Dominus hadn't been confined?"

Jorda grimaced.

"If he had been left to go on as he was, both your people and mine would be no more than another extinct myth told around the fires of little Tokela's people! If *they* even managed to survive!"

Jorda stumbled again, this time went to his knees. With a shudder, he rocked onto his palms.

Maloh turned, started to help Sivan haul him to his feet. Jorda backed from beneath their grip, yanked the goggles from his eyes and the gloves from his hands.

"There's something. Something—"

"The vortex is but a sol's walk away," Maloh pointed out.

"Something else."

"*Jorda.*" Sivan gritted out. "Are you sure it isn't interference?"

"I don't know! Let me find out!"

It took time. The sun advanced, slow and shimmering against the hot sand where Jorda's pale fingers dug, searching.

This close to the vortex, what inklings of psi connexion her brother possessed with the boy might be more pliable, easier to splice and follow.

Or not. The island's vortices were thankfully small, but also, one and all, violent. Unpredictable.

Jorda raised his head, eyes going pitch-black from corner to corner, lighting with the silvery star-trails of connexion. It was easier for those of their people who had been born on this world to link into the framework. Still, it wasn't easy.

Finally Jorda looked up, gaze fading to pale grey and blinking beneath the strong sunlight. "They're heading this way."

Sky was boundless in dryLands, and beautiful for the travelling. Našobok had never thought to regret fine weather on any voyage.

But now he did. And kept whispering: "Here. I'm here."

As invocations went, it made little impression.

Tokela propped hands to either side of Našobok's ribcage. Neck cords bulged. Teeth gleamed, a snarl. Našobok tangled his fingers in thick chestnut and pulled. Hard. Tokela's elbows wobbled then gave, and Našobok muscled him close, wrapping arms and legs tight.

No passionate embrace. Scarce time for that, now.

"Tokela!" It cracked like a quirt, a rough shake as punctuation. "You waste what strength you've left, fighting me as well as—"

"It won't... stop. It... I... Bring me... *keep me...*"

"I'm here. You're here."

"Here." A snarl. "I can... will do this."

"I know you can. I have you. You're with me."

"N'da, not just... with!" From faint sough to grating desperation; but ai, better to give it voice than sink into a silence that had, finally, toppled Tokela from their mount's back.

Našobok set his teeth, hung on. Wondered if he held one of serpentKin instead of a nigh-grown oških he outweighed nearly twice over. Kept murmuring reassurances as one whipcord arm snaked itself free, and braced himself for the ill-considered blow or three—ai, his Tokela could punch with the best.

Instead Tokela slammed his palm against his own head, fingers clawing, small furrows blooding their wake.

He'd already torn his lip in an earlier self-inflicted bout. Našobok had been too late to prevent that one. Granted, it had shattered the first Dreaming-hold, but...

Enough.

Našobok flung Tokela onto his back, hard, and Tokela huffed a choking gasp, ribs expanding like a bellows' breath. Sure enough, the IceFire sparks behind Tokela's eyes scattered, dimmed. But Našobok didn't loosen his grip.

He was learning.

"Leave off!" he growled. "Pain might break whatever's taking you from your body, but all blood will do is attract predators."

"I must," Tokela panted, "make it stop. Stars are *theirs*. What if they can... hear?"

Ai, that wasn't something Našobok had considered. "We'll be to River before they even know where we are."

He hoped it wasn't a lie. Their path hadn't lain altogether easy, though so far dark's basket had scooped up Rain clouds instead of Stars. They'd made progress—albeit slow, and that more from weather than any wandering of Tokela's Spirit. Thunder had swooped down, chasing them across the dryLands with spear-shards of light and rain-torrent wings. A flash flood had sent them to higher ground, the aftermath slowing them even more, their mount sliding and skating across muddy flats. They'd given up, spent the rest of thatSun's passage and the following dark in wait beneath a sandstone overhang, all the while listening for the whispered telltale of the sodden cliff perhaps sliding down upon them.

Finally Thunder had furled ša's jagged pinions and drawn the clouds away, bringing Sun to dry wet garb and warm their skins. But with it had come their first clear dark. With it, Stars.

Našobok hadn't known, then.

To Tokela's credit, he'd lasted some time. Perhaps such fortitude had miscarried, merely allowed this... whatever-it-was to build. Or perhaps the drug that had made Tokela so pie-eyed on Galenu's cart had lasted just long enough and no more.

Had Našobok realised, he'd have found some before they ventured the dryLands plain. For now, he could only hope they'd run into a yakhling caravan.

"Better here," Tokela husked. "Grandmother at my back. You as shelter. Always, you try to shelter. Only this time you can't. I'm so sorry." He let his eyes close, lashes inky shadows amongst the fading, indigo-and-clay Marks stippling his cheekbones. "Are you?"

"Am I what?"

"Sorry." The forlorn twist beneath snarled the breath in Našobok's lungs, sent his heart into small, shattered pieces. "That you came for me."

"Never. I'm here. We're both here. You're not alone." He meant it, yet couldn't help the tiny thrill fissuring up his spine as Tokela gave another shudder, eyes rolling. No longer *his*—or perhaps his in a twisted, extraordinary way—a gaze of white squall, light and murk shifting and twisting, Stars reflecting ever on, down and in.

At times like this, it was easy to believe Tokela had been sired by Chepiś.

Našobok tightened his grip and bent closer, shadowing those eyes from Starlight with his body and the long, ebon fall of his hair. "Make talk with me, Tokela. Stay with me."

"Can't." It was a gasp.

"Then"—Našobok bent closer, breathed the talk against Tokela's neck—"ask me."

"Won't." It was faint within the dubious shadows of sanctuary. "Not a... good place."

So Tokela wasn't as far gone as all that. "Indeed, a poor choice, but here we are, a'io?—and better the distractions of pleasure than pain. You don't have to face this alone."

"Alone." Harsh, like sand in a grain mortar. "What happens"—another shudder and gasp—"when we get to your ship?"

Ai, this was a different thing altogether than bringing amongst his crew one possessed by Elementals... and who also, it seemed, heard the Void-within-Stars long ago loosed upon this-Land by Chepiś.

No wonder Sarinak and Inhya had resorted to drugs. It was startling that they'd let him go with Galenu. More, why had Palatan left him there? And what of Aylaniś?

What had *happened*?

Time for that later. For now? "Cast it from your heart. We'll know what to do when River is beside us, a'io?"

"*I* knew what to do. I didn't listen. Didn't want. But River would sing my name, tell me how..." Another shudder and the eerie, inwards turn of focus that Našobok had come to realise was Tokela... *listening*. "She's faint, here, so faint... but She can swallow even Stars, reflect them back, away. She'll hide us."

"A'io. I believe you. But first we have to get there."

And they'd a ways to go. At least another Sun's passage before they even saw Her marshes and bottomlands. Another dark of naked Stars.

Not counting, of course, however long after that it would take them to catch up with *Ilhukaia*, making her steady way down-River. But there they'd have trees, and River.

The Moons' combined light pulled crimson from Tokela's hair, slatted across his forehead to spear one eye. The pupil contracted, as if in answer.

"Can't... let it." Small flickers waged war behind Tokela's visage; more of Sky's realm than any of Earth's scape, and Thunder sending shards of lightning across to warn: *I come with storms upon my tail, take care.* Našobok shifted to block the changing light—shield and thrown shadow, spreading the tail of his leather longcoat behind him to cover as much of Tokela's legs as possible.

Somehow, it worked. As if Stars were indeed eyes, and Našobok set upon keeping their gaze from the one They hunted.

"Ask," he whispered, cupping his hands about Tokela's face.

"N'da. Can do it. Will..." Finally, the Stars in Tokela's eyes dimmed, one by one. Then those eyes closed and, still twitching and shivering, Tokela went limp.

Sleep, escape, it didn't matter. Našobok pushed up to hands and knees, dubious of their situation.

It most certainly wasn't a good place: the middle of dryLands, in a wash muddy from Rainfall, amidst meagre protections of scrub and brush. Chepiś sorcerers with their odd singing-net of Stars weren't the only predators to worry over. They couldn't stay here overlong.

The spotted bay mare who'd carried them was nibbling, matter-of-fact, at what sparse forage she could find: sweetsage and needlecreeper, mostly. Našobok chirruped to her and she raised her head, ears pricked. He preferred riding River's back to any Kin upon thisLand, but he'd learned a few horsetalker ways in his time.

"My tail is killing me, old friend," he murmured, half-silent as his gaze lowered to Tokela. "But my Spirit wails harder. Ai, Palatan, if only you were here."

Tokela remained quiet beneath him, twitching and sweating despite the chill. Našobok gave the soft, carrying trill that meant "come here" and the mare obeyed.

It took more innovative encouragement to convince her to lie down, propped over Tokela as he was. But her training had been thorough—even the castoffs from duskLands superior to any others. Našobok kept clucking and persistently tapping behind her knee; with a resigned sigh, the mare at last lowered herself with a *whump* and a sprinkling of sand. Her recumbent body would offer some protection, with Našobok's longcoat serving as the rest while he set up a lean-to. And invoked Fire's protection. He'd heard the rumbling cough of lionKin more than once.

It didn't take long. He squandered some time attempting to find sticks long enough for shelter poles, and that a flat failure. The tallest scrub barely reached his hip. Instead Našobok resorted to one of the bows and several arrows as props to the skin tarpaulin no traveller was ever without. His longcoat he left wrapped about Tokela whilst unrolling his sleeping blanket: long enough for a makeshift roof. He flipped the blanket over the poles, covering Tokela, and chirruped the mare to rise.

Coaxing her nigh to the circle he was preparing for Fire's dwelling, he made talk with her, rubbing a chalk-dusted thumb upon her wide forehead, promising no ties or hobbles in case she had to defend herself. She shared his breath and lipped his hair, understanding. Content.

But as he turned away she pinned her ears and rolled air through her nostrils. He heard it, too: a low sough echoing from a distant ridge. A bark followed after, farther away. Našobok muttered an inventive curse. He'd hoped to be on the move during thisdark's passage, not tethered in one spot asking to be eaten.

At least there was enough dead, dry brush to make a fair blaze. Fire crackling new and hungry beside them, Našobok gathered more fuel, scanning the cliffs and angles of the wash. He didn't wander far and, upon returning, thrust his longspear close to hand in the sand, double-checked his knives, and made sure of his pack of necessities: water, food, and the pipe and bag of leaf he was never without. Digging into the latter, he took out a pinch and tossed the leaf into the tiny breath Wind blew across his cheeks: an offering, a plea, any help would be welcomed. Then he let out a snort at the vagaries of his kind. Mere tiny motes striding Grandmother's broad belly, ever-insistent upon the coercion of hope. As if any Spirit, Elemental or otherwise, would consider varying a long-charted course to heed the plea of one outcast Riverwalker.

Yet...

He peered at Tokela, stretched out and hopefully senseless.

Something had varied its course towards this oških, heeded his fate. Had done, in truth, from their beginnings, claiming some and passing others by, an infrequent Dance forbidden and all but forgotten. And to what purpose?

Ai, but Našobok was full of questions, ones not his to ask nor tell. It wouldn't help them now. Nothing could help, not some vagary called fate by outLanders, not all the forbidden puissance seething within Tokela's overwhelmed Spirit, not an absent oathbrother...

It wasn't the first time Našobok had wondered: should they be heading to dawnLands, to Palatan? Could he help?

But Palatan had left Tokela there, in dawnLands where to hold a co-tenant was to court banishment. And Aylaniś, despite her promise to stay until Palatan had returned, had packed up and gone, with only the flattened-dry circle of grass where their tipo had been.

It made no sense. What had happened? When Našobok had petitioned his former Clan for answers, they'd told him nothing other than Tokela had been sent away with Galenu. But he could guess at some of it.

Either way, Chepiś were after them. After Tokela. And Našobok hadn't the right to lead any outLanders into duskLands and the sacred—secret—heart of Grandmother.

No choice, thisnow, but to head back duskwards. Perhaps Tokela, without River's grace, lay more vulnerable to this uncanny Star hold.

Našobok knelt and breathed across Tokela's forehead.

"Ai, Star Eyes." The intimacy barely stirred Tokela's thick, dark hair. "You spoke true. This is *not* good."

It was good to retreat inwards when Frost Moons began to display a bite; even better to sit about the hearth, blow Smoke and hear the old storyKeepers lead the old Songs. But it was just as good to ride and greet dawn across the baking warmth of open plateaus. Beyond good to feel Wind's full force, and the lurch and slide of muscles between his thighs. Bliss, to revel in the shared strength and communion between four- and two-legged— *horsetalker*—to hunt and howl and lean against warm hide and roll naked in the grass. To ride beneath Sky's great basket, beneath the light of Moons and Stars spilled from that basket into endless ebon and indigo.

To wander.

For wandering season was upon them. Even now the gathered People of the Horse were moving from the caverns and out over the wide grazing plains. Palatan loved the deep, volcanic caverns, revered them for their legacy and their protection of all firstPeople, but he craved open territory with every fibre of his heart. Wandering first alone, then with a playmate who had, over turnings, become lovemate then oathbrother, then with his chieftain who had become his spouse...

And now, with a daughter.

None of the children you sire upon your spouse will quicken to an Elemental's call.

Yet now Anahli rode beside him, her face into Wind and her heart flying with Ša's breath.

This trip was yet another transformation. They'd barely moved onto the plains down from their caverns before Palatan had headed dawnwards. Into midLands, where Aylaniś said they'd sent Tokela.

Anahli, barely from her Breaking into owlClan, had insisted they go.

The turnabout was still difficult. No matter the assurances of She Who Guarded the Deep Places, to bring one touched with Other into Her heart...

Anahli drew rein. Her mount crabstepped, uneasy beneath her rider's sudden tension, and blew a challenge into Wind's breath.

Palatan, brow quirking, did likewise. "What is it?" Getting used to a new co-tenant often held more challenge than refuge. Wind, more than most, bided rootless and edgy. It took some strength of will to resist Ša's instincts.

"I don't know." Anahli shook her head—to clear her vision, no doubt, and thumped at her chest. *Here. I am here.*

"A predator, perhaps. Scented upon Wind's breath." Palatan's suggestion was soft, asking.

At their heels, three fleethounds peered upwards, gazes quizzical. Their leader, Arrow, lay down, willing to the wait. Between Palatan's hide-wrapped knees, his chestnut mare pricked her ears, searching for what had claimed her pasture-mate's attention.

"Predators," Anahli answered, slow. Her eyes gleamed, not merely co-tenanted, not merely darksight, but also the faintest and eeriest whiff of Starlight. Tokela had awakened that, too.

Palatan soon heard it—Sensed it, a vibration against his breastbone. A song, a story, a rhythm like to any drum, in truth, setting a-quiver the great Starry basket. And others answered, sought to join it... unwelcome, off-key and asyncopated, brittle ice reaching, seeking...

Hunting.

Beneath Palatan's haunches the chestnut began to prance in place. Arrow growled, rolling to his feet, and the younger ones followed suit, silky hair shivering erect. Palatan swayed beneath the force of it, for a lingering breath taken in the Dance.

"Yeka?"

Palatan couldn't answer. The ice shivered and cracked, warming, and with no more than a waft upon Anahli's Wind, the new and homely voice whispered along the soft, Starlit grass. Beloved and ai-so-familiar, carrying a wish—

If only you were here

—fading as quickly as it had approached.

"Gone." Anahli's gaze, turning to him, had dimmed, any hint of Starlight fading, revealing that her connexion with Tokela had dissolved. "He's not in midLands, Yeka. Where is he?"

Where is he?

If only you were here.

Possibilities lingered, burrowed deep into Palatan's Spirit, and began to gnaw.

$$\phi \quad \phi \quad \phi$$

"Tokela?"

A familiar voice broke the quiet, but he didn't want to acknowledge it. Wanted to just burrow down, curl up in the sudden surcease of everything...

"Cousin?" Insistent, and a hand lighted upon his arm, gave a brief, firm shake. "Tokela. Wake."

N'da, he wanted to growl, but even that would make noise, and it was so welcome, so foreign, so... *silent.*

"*Tohwakelifitčiluka!*" That got his attention even as the grip upon his shoulder pinched, shook.

Slowly—unwillingly—Tokela opened gluey eyes. A familiar, broad figure knelt besides, hair shining mahogany, for Fire lay just beyond, stirring upwards sparks and demanding notice.

Yet still, the quiet.

Tokela blinked, rolled onto his back. A blanket arched overhead, shielding him. But spilling over Našobok's sleek hair and wide shoulders, the void of adamantine neverending shone. Stars reached for him, glimmered. Tokela squeezed his eyes shut.

"Come, my heart." Našobok shook him again, his voice purling soft but grim. "I need you alert. We have company."

Company. It shivered cold into even Našobok's endearment, stirred the possibility: had the tall ones had found them after all? But n'da, nothing lingered. The icy presences remained distant, sniffing around the internal barricades he'd erected.

At that last, thankfully, he was very, very practised.

Tokela heaved himself upwards, shivering beneath the blanket, trying to read their surroundings. There was a makeshift lean-to beneath which he lay; Našobok crouched beside him with longspear and hunting knife crossed ready; the mare snorted defiance just past, weaving back and forth. Fire flickered, catching reflections. Luminous pinpoints blinked in the dark, wary. Tokela shielded his eyes from Fire and squinted across the plain. Darksight betrayed furry, brindled bodies pacing, making the Dance of prowlingKin.

"I suppose," Našobok drawled, "we should thank Grandmother they are Kin, and not cursed Chepiś."

A grin quirked at Tokela's lip. "How...?" It wavered; he sucked in a shaky breath, held it, let it out. "How many, do you think?"

"Six at least. Maybe more." Našobok rose from his crouch, let out a growl that carried outwards. The wild dogs whined and gave ground, but didn't retreat.

"They know I'm down," Tokela reached for his own hunting knife, found it gone. Našobok saw the motion, for without taking his eyes off the pack of predators, he drew a knife from his belt and threw. It sculpted a copper arc against Fire's light to bury itself in the sand beside Tokela's knee.

"I wasn't keen leaving it close, earlier. Now?" Našobok shrugged, eyes flickering upon every direction. "You're right, long as you're down they'll think to chance it. Even with your elder cousin growling at them in their own talk and a pissing-mad mare ready to kick shit from anything that moves. Are you with me?"

Tokela took knife in hand, started to rise.

A quick smile, and Našobok bent down, still not taking his eyes from the half-circled predators. He took the bow from its place as hide prop, proffered it.

Tokela came forwards...

Staggered as, from the black, silence broke into screams. Shrilling, beckoning, Stars flicked an icy-bright touch over his face, ran cold-flame fingers through his hair, grabbed hold...

But others also raised a chorus... closer, expressions and forms, stray images, patterns that drummed as they wove and unwove, attempting translation. As if some ancient, nimble-fingered weaver plaited connexions into the loom of his Spirit, his heart opened and gave voice:

Stop them. Tame them. You must keep Stars in check; I can help if you can listen. The sand beneath his feet bore him up, kept him upright.

Do not give. Fire insisted. *You must be sharp, have foc—*

Staggered again, as something thwacked into his solar plexus, huffing his breath and sparking pain across his ribs. Starlight broke into small scatters just beyond his vision. Tokela shuddered beneath the relief of it, eyes clearing to see Našobok with bow raised, ready to whack him again.

"Stay with me, now," Našobok warned. "Better bruises than our blood on the sand, eh? If you can't pull your bow then take *this.*" He tossed the spear; Tokela managed to catch it, hefted it as Našobok strung his bow. A brace of arrows were already stuck in the sand beside him.

The points of light began to glide closer.

The surcease of breathlessness and pain was subsiding; brilliant shards were starting to flash and regather behind Tokela's sight. He gritted his teeth, let one sharp canine score his tongue.

Intent upon the predators' advance, Našobok also kept an eye upon Tokela. "Perhaps you can make their talk better than my feeble attempts?"

Make their talk? Wasn't he there enough to contend with, with Elementals nattering and complaining and singing—Ai, shrieking—in his Spirit? As well as Stars?

Stars...

This time Našobok brought the bow against the small of Tokela's back.

This time it *really* hurt. With the pain came clarity, and anger. "Yuškammanukfila ikšo!" The epithet snarled and snapped. "Reason with hungry prowlingKin? Are you mad?"

Is it so different? Another Voice, dispersing Starlight. River, then Fire; now the sand beneath his feet echoed Grandmother. *Are you not all kindred and my children?*

"Ai, there you are," Našobok flashed his teeth—smile or return snarl, Tokela wasn't sure. Perhaps both, knowing Našobok. "I'm not the one balancing upon an unsteady spar, little brother."

It drawled soft into condescension. Ire was almost as good as pain, sifting through the internal bedlam and lulling it quiet.

"I need you at my back, *in* yourself. It isn't my intent for either of us to die hamstrung by prowlingKin—"

"Našo—!"

With a whirl and push against the bow, Našobok's arrow released, found its target with a sullen thud and a shrill yelp.

Chaos erupted beside them. The mare leapt, twisted and bucked, kicked out with a furious, hoarse grunt. Another *ki-yi*. A shadow rippled to Tokela's knife hand; he spun, flung his spear. A third shriek answered his aim.

Našobok took down another. Several more pairs of glowing orbs joined those waiting on the fringe.

The speared dog was trying to drag itself away. Tokela followed, whispered apology for not making a clean kill even as he grabbed the spear shaft and twisted, sharp, hopping sideways to avoid the dying snap.

Front hoofs striking and great teeth flashing, the mare squealed as one of the predators leapt for her. She grabbed ša by the nape, shook with an audible crunch, then flung ša aside. Another lunged into the lit circle; Tokela leapt forwards and pinned ša to the ground with his spear, finished the job with his knife.

The pack ringed tighter. There were more than had started. The mare drew closer to her companions, snorting low in her chest.

Stars throbbed dull behind Tokela's eyes. He bit his tongue until he tasted blood. They receded.

"Tokela?"

"I'm *here*."

Našobok's gaze flickered back and forth, troubled. "This isn't good. There are"—he loosed another arrow, and the predators scattered as one fell—"too many. I thought to save you from the tall ones, and instead..."

It was hard to stay angry at Našobok for long when such raw concern broke his talk.

"I think you have to try. Influence them. Not with outLand witchery, but your Elemental's aid."

"I can't *hear* Her, don't you under—"

She is not here, true. But She is not the only one who will stand in you, little brother. The diminutive curled fond-quiet, no insult. Earth, rippling beneath Tokela's feet. Fire, tongued with a faint breath of Wind...

Eyes no longer his. Or reflexes. With a negligent flip of spear, Tokela strode towards the waiting predators.

"Tokela—!" Našobok tried to snatch at him, but missed, as if the swift motion had been done underwater.

No worry, Tokela wanted to whisper, he wasn't about to walk into the waiting jaws; thankfully his body obeyed, halting beside the makeshift hearth. Another flip of spear, the bloodied point swinging downwards.

Sparks leapt. As if the spear were a conduit, a gust of smoke and flame roiled up. Našobok cursed and tottered back; Tokela didn't move as heat glossed his eyes, flared up about him.

The mare snorted, popped a front hoof towards the flames but stood fast.

Yelping panic, the predators scuttled back.

Fire surrounded him, touched him, filled him. *Opened* him—

Panic rose. *Let me go. Please don't, let me go—*

—but didn't burn, held firm.

And from searing edges whispered a soft not-voice. *Some things needn't be done alone, cousin. Better, though, if you learned to ask before you reached and nigh yanked me from my horse.*

Gnawing worry grew sharper teeth, bit down.

Untutored. Strong. Overwhelming, if Palatan hadn't his own strengths.

Anahli gasped. Her horse tried to take off; she held her, held on. Palatan's own mare shied sideways, and the same muscles his daughter had just used—trained since before either of them could walk—also kept him a-horse: thighs against hide, fingers laced into ebon mane.

It took some doing, but Palatan retrieved control over what had been snatched from him—

before you nigh yanked me from my horse—

—and slid off his mount, teeth and fists clenched. Turned towards dawn, where the horizon was beginning to light itself silver-grey as the fleethounds, panting and watching. Anahli had also dismounted, grasped both sets of reins, awaiting his lead. Her eyes once again whirled with faintest Starlight; Wind breathed from the coming dawn, lifted strands of hair about her cheeks, and Fire kindled upon a horizon...

Where a wilding talent groped unaware for whatever help ša could find, surrounded by predators in the desert.

Palatan smiled, spread his feet upon Grandmother's grassy

flank. He extended one hand, felt Anahli's fingers lace snugly into his, and... *reached.*

It should be difficult, at this distance. It wasn't. Fire reached back, welcomed and spun Palatan into contact, would have locked him tight-bound into the Sharing. But Palatan kept his own control firm, snugged Anahli at his side, and spun out what Spirit he could...

Not without a fond whisper for an absent oathbrother who willingly Walked with shamanKin.

Not just Fire, but Earth and Wind, a longing, faraway whisper from River, and...

Stars. A scream of Ice and Fire and *Other* set upon taking, to capture a changeling boy and whatever he had touched, Shaped. Anahli leaned forwards, wilful mutiny; Palatan denied the wilding Power, slamming his own shields down just in time.

"Yeka!" Anahli protested, "we can't just—"

"We have given him what we can! This... this is a Chepiś thing!" Palatan snapped back. "It is the one thing we cannot join with—"

"Tokela has, and won!"

"So far," he whispered, looking to the horizon.

Anahli untangled her hand from his. Defeat lingered about them, skimming the back of Palatan's tongue like soured mare's milk.

Scavengers. Not Kin. Nonetheless the lingering wait dissolved; filling the space was an oddling approach, careful-slow.

"It's them, isn't it?" Anahli breathed. "Chepiś. They... hunt him."

No need to ask which "him".

Hunting. Against the truce. Against...

"Follow!" Palatan leapt on his horse, whirled her on her muscular, spotted haunches, and galloped back the way he'd come.

Anahli, after a breath of hesitation and a glance towards the horizon, followed.

The disengagement, so abrupt, nearly felled Tokela. Only then did he realise he'd sought the contact, unaware of what, or how.

"Tokela?" An odd mix of apprehension and composure laced Našobok's voice.

Fire had opened the way. Fire was Palatan's... co-tenant, that was Ša's calling, gleaned from faraway embers of memory and experience. And though Palatan had closed the opened place— fear? horror? revulsion?—Fire hadn't subsided, Ša's Spirit waiting, beckoning, and Wind wafting Tokela's hair, faint.

Stars had tried to overtake, *use* him—Tokela wasn't certain the opposite was possible, even now felt it anathema, evil. But the Spirit-presence bound down to Grandmother's soil, the flames behind his eyes; those were welcoming-warm, buffering infinite chill. Tokela sucked in a breath and opened his eyes wide, letting the coppery light within. Without.

He raised the spear. Flames twisted upwards about the shaft, hissing in sheer delight as the edge traced patterns in the dark.

"Tokela!"

"I am well." The talk lingered, grew into a snarl. Like, yet unlike Našobok's attempt, the not-voices reached outwards. His dam's horsetalker blood uncoiled beneath his tongue, adding layers heard as well as unheard. Shapes flowed up the spear and into Tokela's chest, smoke and heat and Spirit all a vortex of wilding flame. Fear and desperation were moulded into a spear of command and thrown, unerring, to the target's heart.

Within one heartbeat, the pack was steadily advancing with one objective, one heart. In the next they were broken; separate and cowed individuals scattering and slinking away, melting into all corners of the desert.

Gone.

Slowly, Tokela became aware that he had stepped forwards, over the flames and towards the pack. The -tracings hung in the air, faded and disappeared. He still gripped the spear in his hands, corposant...

Burning.

Tokela dropped it on the ground, stared disbelieving at his undamaged palms.

The flames upon the spear writhed, lighting the sandy pan with indigo and silver. They flickered, guttered, then sucked away, leaving merely a sturdy, unremarkable spear, its bronze head a dull gleam, gut lacings and wooden shaft not even scorched.

Tokela staggered, unsure what he had just done. Unsure, in fact, of where he was, only that he was suddenly burning from inside out, shivering and sweating and filled at fever pitch.

Reality came to him, strong and solid, in a firm handclasp pulling him close. He wanted to give to it; reason fought instinct and dictated otherwise, sparked recoil.

Even Palatan had done.

"Not now. Don't... don't touch me."

But Našobok didn't retreat—more, didn't let Tokela retreat and pulled him even closer. "This is me, remember?" he whispered against Tokela's cheek. "I can touch you. You cannot hurt or change me."

Ai, it was true: Našobok was a worthy wall to batter against. A rock in the rapids to hold to; someone to remind Tokela he was... here.

Even when he wasn't.

A teasing murmur in his ear, a nip to that same ear. "Rut me stupid, but you are the most amazing and beautiful thing I've laid eyes on in a while."

It sent Tokela further sideways—an utter mystery that Našobok did, somehow, actually think him lovely, didn't shun or fear this... this whatever it was, lying within him. Another draught of reality, shivering his body from the strange hold/ trance.

Yet it remained, heart-deep, waiting white-hot behind the eyes he clenched so tightly. "I think that's a good thing. Because we're safe for the moment and I think..." His voice creaked; a faithless reality tried to pull itself out from under him again.

Arms caught him, held him—real, and solid, and *here*, as present as Našobok's breath heating his temple. "I think," it was wry, "that you need to stop thinking, and start asking."

Tokela twisted about and practically climbed Našobok's muscular frame, breathed his breath and shut his own eyes. Asked.

Begged.

25
SHAMAN KIN

"Alekšu? What is—?"
"Let the drums talk!" In one smooth motion, Palatan dismounted and slipped the rope from his mount's nose. "Lapis Council convenes soon!"

The drumKeeper was seated on the edge of camp, greeting the fingerlings of Sun's rising. She stroked the taut, wide skin with callused fingers, whispering a query; the talking drum hissed and vibrated like a wakened, wise serpent. She smiled at Anahli, eyes following Palatan as he ran off in the direction of the chieftain's tipo. Then she started to drum.

The rhythm pounded within Anahli's breast, thick comfort, as she released her own mare and followed.

A horse waited, ground-tied just outside the chieftain's tipo. Anahli's youngest sister, Vinka, was grooming the horse's sweaty, dusty hide. The other two were eating, dipping flatbread into the large pot upon the outside cook. Cavern or tipo, the stone kettle was always heating with good things.

"I thought you were both gone for—?" Samke's query trailed away beneath the drum-talk. "Yeka's called Lapis council. What's happened?"

"Let her eat, first." Nishe handed Anahli a rolled-up piece of flatbread, soft and warm. Anahli took it and bit down gratefully. She was famished.

"Whose horse?"

"A message-talker just arrived," Vinka said, in rhythm with her strokes—and the drum. "From midLands, and the old khatak."

"Vinka!"

"Well, that's what Aška calls him."

"No drumtalk?"

"Private." Samke shrugged. "Aska and Yeka are both in there, so we're stuck outside."

"At least it isn't pouring," Nishe reminded.

"Ai, but we need Rain."

"Anahli?" Aylaniś pulled back the door flap. "Your sire wants you."

With a shrug, Nishe passed over another piece of hot flatbread. Anahli grinned thanks.

The message-talker was rising from a guest blanket; clearly he'd finished his errand. Palatan stood in a shadowed curve, frowning thoughtfully whilst Aylaniś told the message-talker, "Please. Eat at our hearth until you're ready to depart. My daughters will see to your comforts."

"My thanks, horse-chieftain," the message-talker said, and with a polite gesture, slid out past Anahli.

"Galenu sends word," Palatan spoke quietly. "Našobok has taken Tokela to River. The outLanders are hunting him."

Anahli shifted uncomfortably. It merely confirmed what they had already found, upon the connexion of Elementals.

"I'm glad Galenu thought to warn us," Aylaniś said, bending to roll up the guest blanket.

"His mother was of the night flyers, once," Palatan replied, soft.

"Surely Galenu knows nothing!"

"He knows less than nothing. Nevertheless, it's enough to look outside his own concerns upon such things. He knows it's a matter for Lapis council to decide upon."

"Despite thinking he could take Tokela to Chepiś!" Aylaniś snorted like an angry mare, resumed rolling the blanket in a tight-taut fashion that suggested she wished Galenu within it.

Anahli felt likewise. "Has Galenu gone mad?"

"He was sure," Palatan growled, "that Chepiś could help Tokela."

"He's wrong!"

"Maybe he is, my Dancer. Maybe he isn't. What matters is we were right, you and I. What we felt on the plain. The Chepiś aren't making small incursions or trading forays; they're sending groups of their own all over thisLand. They've broken truce. They're hunting Tokela." Forest-hued eyes slid to Anahli. "And maybe you as well, daughter."

Aylaniś faltered in her motions, unrolled the blanket just that far then snugged it close. Rising, she placed it in a hanging net. "What will Lapis Council do?"

"I don't know."

"I can't come, can I?" Anahli said, downing the rest of her bread.

"N'da. You haven't been accepted in Lapis, yet."

She was beginning to understand some of what Tokela felt.

If they don't accept us, oathbrother, we'll make our own Clan. Somehow.

"Ai, Tokela, that smells wonderful."

Dawn was in full regalia, finger-painting Sky all gilt and copper. Smoke lifted a misty scrim upwards and between as roiled, sated, beneath a steaming basket.

Sated indeed. Tokela wondered if he would ever get used to the shivery wonder that clenched his heart whenever he realised he himself had put that indolence into his playmate's voice. Perhaps such things should never be taken for granted—or perhaps he was all too new to the courting. Raising his head from where he knelt beside the hot rocks, he let wonder trace itself into a small smile as Našobok stretched, like a waking lion.

"Stew made from the grain and dried meat in our pouches." Tokela leaned forwards, gave the small basket another stir with his knife. "I watered Lioness, too." He jerked his chin towards their mount, nibbling here and there to top off the handful of dates he'd found in another pouch.

"Enough small things make a feast. Lioness, you say?"

"She was brave enough to earn the name during Moons passage."

"Hunh." Našobok grinned, then rubbed hands over his sleep-scrunched face. "You should have woken me. How long have you been awake?"

Tokela shrugged, unsure he'd means to describe what had kept him awake. The *release*; not just after the rutting but from what had happened before. The utter, blissful *silence* that remained, long after the Elementals had burned through him. And in the silence, the ability to contemplate what else had burned through him. Answers, winnowed from Stars...

Winnowing. It gave him a shiver, and he shrugged the blanket closer about his shoulders. Instead he motioned a spear's throw away, where scavenger birds were skirmishing over the bodies from lastdark's stand. "The meat was already turning with the heat, so I left it. Instead I used some of your leaf to give our foes due honour whilst retrieving our arrows. But I used sand to clean the points; we've only the one skin of water remaining."

"I hadn't planned on so many things going wrong, and..." Našobok trailed off. The subject matter was less than comfortable.

Tokela also fell silent.

Then: "Našo—"

"Toke—"

Their voices met and collided, broke into a short, shared laugh. Našobok scooted closer and brought his fist to lips then breast, gestured outward: *Say what is in your heart.*

Easy enough to ask, not so to do. Tokela tried to find talk, finally settled on the one thing that did come more readily into voice.

"Do you think they would help me?"

Našobok frowned. "I never said the tall ones would help—"

"Not Chepiś." A shudder. "After what I felt lastdark... they don't want to help, believe me. I mean the duskLands shamans."

The frown deepened, and Tokela continued, quickly, "It is what they call themselves amongst themselves, a'io?"

"How can you know what...?" Starting in confusion, it trailed away.

"Lastdark, I touched Fire, and *he* was there, just for a few breaths."

"He?"

"Alekšu. Palatan."

Našobok's lips formed the latter.

"Fire pulled him in to help me, lastdark. But in the end he... retreated."

The storm-hued eyes flickered, lowered.

They have an oath, the Wolf and his brother Warrior, one that reaches far beyond lovemates, Tokela reminded himself. *Yet, he knows something! He knows!* clamoured fiercer.

"Anahli was with him, and..." Tokela hesitated as Našobok frowned. Of course, he didn't know. Couldn't know; he'd been downRiver.

So Tokela told him what had happened. All of it.

"You... *wakened* Anahli." It was a dry whisper, Našobok's eyes lighting as he met Tokela's gaze. "Do you realise what this means? If you can waken powers long thought dead... ai, Star Eyes, no wonder they hunt you."

"It wasn't just Palatan. Not just Anahli. There were more... more shamanKin. I... I felt them, couldn't help but have done. In my heart, a presence treading upon Spirit's hem, like how River fills me. But it was with voices, instead of an Elemental's silent not-talk. Not many, but..." Tokela paused, then whispered, a savour upon his tongue. "They were *there*. That's why Anahli is with them. With her sire, after she told me to stay clear, else he might rip from me what is rightfully mine... Anahli is there, and her Power bides with her."

Našobok had lowered his eyes.

"Našobok, please believe me."

"I believe you." It was wooden.

"All our lives we've been told: to manipulate the Elementals is forbidden. To be possessed of one is unthinkable. Inhya wanted to send me to Alekšu, because she think he—"

"Cures the possessed or proclaims them incurable." Našobok finished, but still his eyes remained downcast. "Chogah said I was incurable. She was glad to make of me outcast. I was glad, too, in the end."

"But now Palatan is Alekšu, and what becomes of those who have been... dispossessed? They never answer that, do they?— but I Saw it. They bide there, in secret, with others. There are other Shapers!"

"Tokela, there are no more Shapers. Save Chepiś."

"And me." He couldn't help the waver of his voice, nor the bitter edge.

Našobok's gaze rose, startled.

"So, those who have kept Grandmother protected since Winnowing are named Shaman. Not Shaper. And it's different, isn't it?"

Those storm-hued eyes widened, then narrowed. Gauging.

"Different because Winnowing was an evil time." Tokela leaned forwards, stirred at the stew again, heard Fire whispering, sated. "Chepiś twisted Grandmother, and the creatures birthed—formed—still exist. In Šilombiš'okpulo. In other places, scattered over Grandmother's belly. And here. Even now we draw closer to one of those mis-Shapen places, hoping its twisted nature will twist their hunt 'round. Don't we?"

Našobok blinked, surprised. "I didn't say..." Then shrugged. "Ai, only what I deserve, courting the likes of you. Of course you know."

"I didn't, before last night. I... it was like the Star-basket, pouring into me."

"Then you know more than I ever have. And what knowledge I do have, I gave oath. Can you understand? It will never pass my lips."

"Then I'll say it. And I do understand, now. It's because of the wreckage Grandmother endured that our ancestors decided Shapers must be purged from thisLand. Even those who were our own. So"—his eyes slid upwards, met Našobok's—"any who would defy that, even to use such things for our good and protection? Ai, they would do well to hide, lest we eliminate them, too. Hide, beneath the truth."

"What if everything is truth, Tohwakelifitčiluka?"

"Then, Našoboka'qékla, we've nothing to hide."

"I cannot speak to what's not mine to tell."

"Then speak to what is yours. Did shamanKin offer you a place? When they couldn't"—so long ago—n'da, merely a waning of Moon ago—he'd wanted it; now Tokela could barely voice it— "purge River from you."

"I wield nothing; I'm merely an outcast tainted with River's possession." So careful, the talk. Našobok was trying.

"Can Alekšu help one who is tainted by Chepiś?"

"There is no taint in y—"

"Isn't there? When you came for me..." Tokela's thoughts ran apace with his heart, hammering swift. "You said you wouldn't take me there, to duskLands. That we *couldn't* go there. It's because Grandmother's true Spirit hides in duskLands caverns, a'io? And Chepiś mustn't know or come near."

"Neither"—Našobok reached out, gave Tokela's arm a slight shake—"must they come near you. Tokela, belay these questions for another Sun's rising, and for one who can answer. One who knows the answers."

But even that was an answer. "It's just... there are others. I'm not alone. There are *others*, but..." Cheeks stinging, Tokela dropped his eyes. "They still aren't like me, are they?"

"You aren't alone. I'm here. We have this much of an oath between us: while I breathe, you are not alone."

And me. It came, faint, upon Wind. *I'm like you.*

Anahli.

If they don't accept us, oathbrother, we'll make our own Clan. Somehow.

Eyes stinging now, as well as cheeks. Tokela shook his head and shrugged from the blanket. "I don't know if I'll ever understand. You've never turned away. You don't care what I am. What they're hunting—"

"Who. Who they're hunting. You aren't a thing."

Not a thing. At his toes, Fire hissed content.

Tokela stared.

You are not a thing. I'm glad you finally hear me in thisnow.

Why haven't I heard you before? Tokela pitched the not-talk just as silent, just as if he'd always known how.

Perhaps you haven't wanted to listen. You are River's, true enough, but you are also child to all of Us, little brother. You remember My co-tenant, first of shamanKin, but do you not remember how you opened to Us, let light into the darkness to Dance with you?

Tokela reached out, stroked fingers over the heat. It was somehow just as perilous—just as wrong—to not acknowledge the presence as it was to cede to it.

You let Us take you, little brother. Even as you took the wilding River-brother after, in another lovely Dance through which River spoke, washed calm through you both with the pounding heat of seed and heart-blood.

A steady hand gripped Tokela's chin. "Come back, tšukasi."

The endearment warmed. "I wasn't far." As he spoke, Tokela realised its veracity. The Elementals had quieted somehow, commingling within his heart. Not out of control, like Stars always were, like Fire had been lastdark beneath Them—*Reaching* Them, that was the way—a transfer carried on rough, hot Wind for perilous heartbeats. "I just... I need to know. Could shamanKin help me? Would they?"

"I swear to you, I don't know. I think Palatan means to find a way, but things aren't so simple. Ai, well." Našobok grinned. "Nothing is, with you."

Tokela couldn't help a return smile; it laced his voice, wry. "But I'm not merely one who hears Elementals. I'm enemy. Shaper. Part... Other."

"You're not an enemy."

"But still, we're heading away from duskLands."

A shrug, then Našobok sniffed at the cooking basket and tsked approval. "This much I do know. The shapingWells are wild, beyond even the control of what Chepiś made them. The one we approach might subvert their sorcery, help hide us. You might be conversant with other Elementals"—this with a twist of brow, more puzzlement—"and how *that's* possible I don't know, because my heart recognises you as River's. I didn't think it was possible to be held by more than one. Either way, you say She will hide you, and I believe you. Still, our fight is to get there." Testing with his fingers, he found their meal cool enough to eat and dug in.

Our fight. Tokela wasn't sure he could fully express the emotions rising within his own Spirit, let alone in outwards voice. "But you're worried."

"Of course I'm worried!" Našobok pushed the warm porridge towards him. "You had me scared to leaking. I don't like being that helpless, I don't want either of us to be in that place again, and I'm not so thick as to think we'll have smooth sailing just because the waters have calmed beneath Sun's gaze."

The confession lay between them, oddly reassuring.

"Eat," Našobok insisted. "I had to sleep, but we need to get some lengths behind us before Sun's heat forces us to halt. Are you able for some hard riding?"

Tokela nodded. Našobok smiled, brief but wide, and began eating. Between bites, he hummed a travelling orison beneath his breath. Tokela tasted the stew; at first unwilling, then ravenous.

Perhaps it was why, at first, he shrugged away the odd lightness of his hands and head. He didn't know enough about what his Spirit made of him, but it did make him hungry.

But as he stood, he knew.

Like fog creeping over River's lowlands—yet in the same breath nothing like—it crept forwards. Intent.

"We have to go," Tokela said. "They know where we are."

"Here? The Chepiś dare to hunt across our Lands?"

"We were fools to think they would honour truce."

"The reports have come, more and more, of their transgressions. A visit here, a hunting party there, and Matwau traders accompany them—"

"Matwau traders! Traitors, more like!"

"A curse upon Matwau! I'm more worried about what Chepiś want!"

"But taking slaves! Sending their like into our territory, hunting our People?"

"What is their plan?"

"Who can know the heart of such creatures? If they honoured Grandmother they wouldn't have crawled over her, infecting her like body insects—"

"Enough!" Lomuyiho's face was lined with the wisdom of many Hoops walked, her eyes clouded as milk. Still, she eyed up her companions one by one, "seeing" them plain. "To chatter like fearful burrow-pups serves us nothing!" Tucking further into her blanket, she held out weathered hands to Fire and prompted, "Alekšu. You didn't say whether you sensed the tall ones through your co-tenant, or through the ehšehklan."

An ugly, midLander name, meaning amongst other things, "half-breed". One Palatan should protest. But truth had stood him down, out there beneath the mountains and on the plain. He had Seen into young Tokela's heart, Sensed the Void-within-Stars swirling within. The Power that Chepiś had stolen long ago. The Power only they could wield.

"The tall ones look for him," Palatan admitted. "We knew this might happen. It's why I asked to bring him here."

"And it's why he cannot be allowed here!" another growled. He was a brace of summerings Palatan's younger—late come to his co-tenant, and gifted, but still uneasy.

So few, Palatan mused, looking over the small group that had gathered in the caverns, hearthFire flickering over their faces. Lapis Council had once filled this cavern, so Lumiyiho taleKeeper claimed. Thisnow gathered only nine including himself, with fewer born each turning of Hoop.

Their society had begun in secrecy; at this rate they well could end in extinction.

"You show disrespect," chided Lomuhiyo, and several others murmured agreement.

"Yet he speaks with some truth," another pointed out. "Bring the ehšehklan here, to our most sacred place? When it's likely he is a beacon set in our midst to betray us?"

Palatan was glad he'd not allowed Anahli to come. He knew she longed to participate, but... n'da. Not yet.

"His dam broke truce, and wandered the forbidden territories. In consequence the Chepiś bewitched her, Shaped her to hold their seed."

"That is a lie." The voice filled a shadowed side alcove and extended into the chamber, low and hoarse and strangely musical.

Palatan's protest whistled out, muted, between his teeth.

The voice continued. "May the oških's dam Dance with the ancestors; the Lost One was daughter to my sister. She was born amongst People a'Naisqwyr, not here in horsetalker Lands, but even upon River's thighs do People mate by choice. The Lost One was overfamiliar with things she shouldn't have touched, but she did not despoil herself upon any Chepiś creature."

It was surprising enough that Chogah had agreed to accompany him. But even more surprising was that her silence should be broken in Tokela's defence.

No doubt she waited, like Weaver in ša's web, to spin a trick-trap none could yet see.

"You cannot deny the oških has been Shaped," another protested.

"That," Chogah drawled, "is obvious. You forget, I knew my sister's daughter. I touched the child when he was still en-wombed. Shaped, a'io—but get of Chepiś?" A derisive snort.

"So he is alien, and presents a danger to us!"

"A half-grown oških? He hasn't even earned status enough to claim a spouse!"

"Naišwyrh'uq cast him out."

"Ai, and Naišwyrh'uq is so known for their flexible ways." Again, Chogah's sarcasm withered any opposition. "They would cast out a dog if ša showed the least hint of possession. Our own Alekšu has an absent lovemate for whom River's Spirit showed too much love—it mattered not that he was chieftain-son."

Leave Našobok out of this. Palatan clenched his teeth as, from the shadows, Chogah slid a glance towards him and smiled. Pretty—and petty.

"Our dawnLands cousins have been damaged by Winnowing," Lumihiyo's voice was flat. "As have we all. It's not ours to judge how others must survive, O'yotalichogah Alekšu tuk."

Also Alekšu tuk—before Chogah—Lumihiyo remained one of the few who could silence her.

"What possesses Tokela is not half-grown," Lumiyiho continued. "Our chieftain-daughter was brought back to life by him. The Lost One's son took River from Anahli, gave Wind to her. Now we have a new member to owlClan."

"Then was she not Shaped surely as the ehšehklan?" the youngest protested. "Are such things not then forbidden?"

"You speak in absolutes," Lumihiyo chided. "We do not deal in those here."

"Yet one thing is absolute," another elder said. "We must pro-tect. The Shapers must be kept out."

Silence followed this.

"Are we Lapis Council, or pecked hens?" Chogah added, with a sneer for the youngest though her gaze held to Palatan's. "Are we shamans who guard the sacred places, medicineKeepers who soothe thisLand's outraged Spirit? Or cowards and whelps?"

"I wasn't the one who suggested we shun the oških," said Palatan into the sudden quiet.

"Neither," Chogah's eyes glinted upon him, "was I."

"We're near it. The Shaper's well."

"Not that near." Našobok frowned, checked his bearings. "I've made sure to skirt the cursed place, though even this close should confound any Chepiś. You mean you feel it?"

Tokela nodded. "It's like... the tickling legs of crawlingKin. You know, when they explore a slick surface? They touch then back away, test then feint forwards."

The black mare picked an equally dainty and surefooted way across a sandy expanse of small dunes. DownLand's horizon, wafting in a mix of heat and cloud, would every now and then betray faraway smudges. Not the flat tops of tabled hills, either.

"Trees. Close enough we should find water soon." Našobok nudged the water skin that held a few remaining swallows. "Perhaps even a River-daughter to bless us."

"Or more Rain." Tokela gave the gathering clouds a tiny smile, and Našobok found himself wondering if he'd anything to do with that weather.

Already Našobok had second- and third-guessed his decision to head for River, was working on a fourth. He was out of his depth here, in more ways than one.

"They're waiting out there. Somewhere." Tokela tangled fingers in Lioness's mane, and the little mare stretched her neck, happy with the caress.

"You said they can't hear you unless—"

"They don't need Stars to glean where we're going." It was cold, oddly accepting. But a nigh-imperceptible shiver ran across Tokela's shoulders.

Našobok leaned forwards, gave his hair an affectionate tug. "Then perhaps we'll be able to stop long enough for a wash, eh? In that little River-daughter we hope for. You smell of horse."

"There are worse things to smell of. You aren't so sweet yourself."

"Was that an insult?"

"Insult, promise, your choice." Indigo eyes, thankfully clear and uncomplicated at present, slanted his way.

Ai, this was more like it. Našobok snugged a little closer, ensured it with a murmured, "I'd like nothing better than to have a swim with you. Dunk you in River's curves, haul you up sleek as a Sea-pup, drops of water shining in that dark hair like Stars."

Such talk did as he'd intended: Tokela's shiver held more pleasure than uncertainty. Still...

"I used to play beneath Stars." Tokela's voice dipped low. "They were... friends. When I was old enough, I would go with my father, check the herds his brother kept for him in midLands. Sky was wide, there—not like here, but more than within the trees spreading across River's flanks. I'd curl up with him and we'd lie awake, watching Stars while he would tell me their names." A soft intake of breath, then another shudder. A grit of teeth.

A reminder past any diversion: the hunters were still hunting.

Našobok didn't want to contemplate the strength it must take for one oških to deny them. After all, taleKeepers spun fables of an ancient and united front, an entire tribe of shamanKin standing firm upon the boundaries of Grandmother, locking their Spirits into Her defence.

Only it hadn't been forever, had it? Perhaps it hadn't been that many shamans, either.

"Našobok." It wavered, unsure. "*Was he my father?*"

"Of course he was, in any way such things matter. I remember him well, Tokela. He and your mother were kind to a young troublemaker. He even tried to make of me a herder." Našobok grinned. "It didn't go well."

Tokela snorted. "That takes no guessing."

"Ai, well."

"It seems you've always been around. Always"—a smile—"here."

"Hunh. Some things sing long before we understand their songs."

"You were there when River took my parents. It was before you were outcast, but you didn't truly belong a'Naišwyrh, so you told me. You knew you'd have to leave, find another place. Still, you sat with me, told me stories."

"I did." Našobok remembered that child sitting lone and lost in the dusky light beside River, tears tracing his cheeks.

"But was he my sire, Wolf?"

"Ai, but since when do such things matter?"

"This time, it matters."

"Perhaps it does and perhaps it doesn't, but what sire has any rights to claim any child other than by a dam's grace? You are your dam's son, and of our People."

Tokela was silent, and Našobok realised common sense had its own flaws, here. Tokela's dam had been the one to insist, after all, that her child was of two sires.

Of course, her Spirit had long since wandered, then.

"Either way, it doesn't matter, Tokela. Not to me."

A half turn, and a wry smile. "Perhaps one day it won't matter to me—!" It lurched upwards into a yip.

The mare stumbled and lurched, went to her knees. Tokela grabbed mane and stayed on, barely. Našobok pitched sideways into the sand.

Only it wasn't just sand. It slithered, shifted like a living thing. The mare clambered sideways, heaving herself out from under Tokela and onto more solid ground, whilst beside them another cry echoed—it sounded like Tokela's name—before the sand sucked them both down and into a shuddering of dust and black.

"As usual, they do nothing."

Palatan thought he was alone. He would have sworn that even Chogah had left the chamber, it seemed that empty.

Yet, here she was.

So he answered, polite, "I can't blame them. Their hands are tied by ways older than any of us."

"Even me?"

"You are indeed old, aunt, but not that old."

"And you're young enough to give me their arguments, nephew. What of your own?" Chogah leaned, heavy, upon her staff. Her dark gaze refused direct contact with Fire's light, leery of the co-tenant Spirit that had snatched another, more powerful staff from her. "If not for the first of medicineKeepers flaunting that same law, neither you nor I should be here, debating what is and what will be."

"There is nothing to debate. The Council has spoken, and they have the right to—"

"To make more cowardly mistakes?"

"I'm just glad they haven't refused Anahli's right of place." Palatan closed his eyes.

"Yet. She is Power-full. Even moreso than you once she finds her way. Tokela, even moreso. And Galenu would have given him to Chepiś!"

"He knows no better."

"Just enough to be dangerous. And foolish. The Chepiś want Tokela for his Power."

"Našobok will keep him safe."

Chogah snorted. "I asked you once before how such things have come to pass. What if *we* acted, not Chepiś? What if *we* considered how that power could benefit us, not the tall ones?"

"You walk forbidden paths, Chogah."

"As do all, Palatan, who would tread in the steps a'Alekšu'ín." She angled forwards, hands taut upon her support as if to choke the horse heads carved there. "What did our Mother tell you, down in the deepest places?"

He froze. "You have no right to make talk of that. Not anymore. Nor do you have the right to ask—"

"What did She say?"

He remained silent, remembering.

"She claimed him. Didn't She?"

Still, he didn't speak.

Finally, Chogah turned away with a grumbling sigh. "Then what you and I—Alekšu and Alekšu tuk—must ask ourselves is this: Do we let Chepiś have the oških, and perhaps, in the having, take and use the shamanKin heart within him? Perhaps against us? Or do we take him in and...?" She fell silent, eyes meeting his.

He couldn't deny it, finished the thought with a hiss into the cavern, "And in doing so, have what Chepiś weaponry he carries."

26
VORTEX

A deep-soft drone: teasing, tickling, making promises with a tongue he can't understand, but well could know.

It remembers...

And returns to the one instinct that never leaves him long: fight.

With a cry, Tokela rolled and snatched for the knife at his calf, found nothing. Instead his knife hand was grabbed, and an equally large, well-muscled arm chuffed the breath from his lungs. He was hoisted upwards and held in a vice grip, feet dangling. There was absolutely nothing he could do about it.

So he started wriggling and kicking.

A curse—surely it was a curse, then a familiar voice said, in the talk of his People, "You little... Stop... aah! Stop *kicking* me, Tokela!"

He stilled, and all his senses began working. Maloh's scent and voice were unmistakable.

"That's better."

This voice, however, wasn't. Maloh's companion moved into view, wrapped in layer upon layer, as if afraid of Sun. The hood was pulled back, revealing a sharp, milk-pale face... only its eyes were wrapped, small and blinking behind some sort of amber-hued *glašg* held by a harness. Its hands were covered, too, with some stuff that looked like hide, yet didn't smell right. "Listen to her, little one, or we'll be forced to knock you as senseless as your companion."

We. Your companion. Quicksand...

Našobok!

Sky curved overhead, clear brilliance, yet Sun had retreated, shadows fingering sideways from an upthrust, striated tower of a cliff. Tokela felt—smelt—Našobok's presence before his eyes adjusted, and relief juddered him as he sensed the breath rising, the heart pounding strong in the pulse of Našobok's throat. Sand-encrusted from scalp to worn boot soles, Našobok had been dragged into the cliff's shadows and flung there.

The sand pit that had taken them both was some distance beyond. Surely heat gave the illusion of movement—such things couldn't travel, they were Earth-bound. Fire had been kindled close... or was He, truly, Fire, with such a strange and pallid presence? Unspeaking, Ša didn't Dance. A strangely jointed bowl had been nestled within Ša's coals. Surely such a thing couldn't hold water?—but a wisp of mist shivered Tokela's nostrils with moisture.

Našobok groaned, twitched, and Tokela lurched forwards.

Maloh didn't let him. "Be easy. I pulled you both out, your companion is well enough. When he wakes, we've water and bark tea for you both, but I fear your pony ran, and who can blame it?"

She loosened her grip, allowing another to move into view. This one also yanked a thick hood back, revealing pale hair slicked back, doubled, and nape-knotted like to the folk of mid-Lands. More cloth concealed its neck and chin almost to those amber eyepieces, which the creature shoved up onto its high forehead. Another shiver raced up Tokela's spine—there was silver glimmering in the round eyes, a slurry of Starlight, and recognition...

"You," he said.

"It is a ways from the forests," Sivan said in dawnLands talk. "We're both far from home."

"Wh-why are you hunting us?" Tokela stammered.

"I was under the impression we'd saved you. From the vortex."

"Be easy," the other Chepiś said, just as faltering and broken. "Done is done. As Sivan says, the vortex tried to take you, but you're safe."

Voohr-tekhs? What was that?

No matter. They lied. He wasn't safe. Našobok lay senseless, and they were surrounded. Perhaps Sivan had even set this... this *voohr-tecks* upon them.

Perhaps they meant the sand trap.

Which had moved. Somehow. Either that, or Tokela had misplaced his memory...

N'da, he hadn't. Even as he watched, the sand trap seemed to... to writhe, and spasm, and shift sideways.

Closer.

It rose his gorge to keep looking at the thing, but he gritted his teeth, made sure it didn't go anywhere near Našobok. Thankfully, it didn't.

But his cousin's breathing had steadied. Našobok was awake.

None of their captors seemed to notice any of this. In fact, Sivan and the other Chepiś seemed to be... smiling?

Sivan knelt, peering upwards at Maloh, who lowered Tokela so that his feet once more touched the sand.

"He has freckles," the other Chepiś said, slow and faltering. "Like his dam."

Like his... dam? "How do you—?" Tokela choked it back as the Chepiś reached out and down, stroking two cautious fingers across Tokela's cheekbones. The urge to flee throbbed strong, but Tokela held his ground, unwilling to admit the weakness.

The Chepiś's touch was cold, the gloves flat but pliable, and rank-smelling. "And these pictographs on his cheeks, like to hers, but less permanent." The Chepiś leaned closer, still with that odd not-quite-smile. "Was it your dam who called you Star—"

"Tokela," he interrupted, then peered at Sivan. "Please. Let us go."

The Chepiś mouthed the name curiously.

The bigger they are, a soft voice teased at his consciousness, *the longer and more fatal the drop.*

It seemed to come from Fire. Which made no sense. This hearth was Shaped; it wasn't, truly, of Fire.

"Jorda, we don't have time for this now," Sivan said, albeit gently, and pointed.

The Chepiś—Jooohr-da—followed the gesture, as did Tokela. The sand trap had moved again. And again, thankfully, it wasn't towards Našobok, who was aware, perhaps listening, with fingers a-twitch and eyelids quivering.

Don't move, Tokela implored.

Sivan shot a spate of syllables at Maloh who, still watching the sand trap, pulled Tokela slightly to one side.

"We cannot let you go, little one." Sivan's answer was quiet. Behind her the other two began to murmur in their own talk, back and forth. "I'm sorry. But if you cooperate, we will release your companion." Her gaze flickered that way—n'da, towards the oddling sand trap. The shadows were lengthening further, and the trap had also moved: closer to them, not Našobok.

Jorda eyed it with no little concern, said something in Chepiś talk. Maloh's grip had loosened upon Tokela; she, too, was speaking to Sivan, her tone anxious.

One of Našobok's eyes gleamed, a knife-edge opening merely enough to focus. Beside him, Fire appeared less contrivance and more natural in aspect.

Help me emerge, Fire said, *and I can help you. Their efforts will lie thin, here on the edges of the Shaping well.*

There was an echo of... Palatan? And upon the breeze that rose, slight, to tug at Našobok's long hair...

Anahli.

Tokela was afraid to answer. The Chepiś would hear.

They won't hear.

They are—he didn't want to say it but had to—*part of me! In my Spirit!*

If you are one with us, they can't hear you. They can't hear any Elemental, only try to chain Us—Shape Us—to their will. And you—Fire tried to Dance, warm-bright ochre within muted silver—are altogether skilled at keeping them out. Do you not realise? It's what you've done for most of your life.

"We have to leave. Soon." Jorda had paced closer, after a smattering of unfamiliar talk choosing to speak to Tokela directly. He seemed more nervous about the sand's strange behaviour than any other possibilities. "We can't be here after dark, this close to the vortex. Do you understand me?"

Tokela believed he finally did. Old tales ran true; the thing these Chepiś called *voohr-tekhs* was a Shaping well. Like Šilom-biš'okpulo, only wilder. Angrier.

Not only that. In this place where their own sorcery had run amok, the Chepiś seemed warier than even firstPeople.

"We'll answer any questions you have on our way," Sivan continued. "We'll see your companion safe, but you must come with us."

You must not go. They would make of you a weapon.

How can a person be a weapon? Like a spear, or a knife?

Believe me, little brother, you have seen no weapons akin to what these outLanders could summon through you and your kind.

My... kind? I have none.

You do.

That last was definitely Anahli. Tokela almost smiled.

But Sivan still knelt before him, watching him. Her thin, pale brows twisted, almost a question.

So Tokela asked, "What do you want with me?"

Našobok watched, too. One sand-dusted hand moved, ever so slight. Hunting-talk. *Keep on. Occupy them.*

"Make talk" with prowlingKin. "Occupy" Chepiś. Našobok's confidence was daunting, sometimes.

"If it were my choice," Sivan answered, "I would leave you to your own place."

"It isn't your choice?" Tokela stepped to one side. It was slight, but three sets of small, round eyes gave it notice, tracked it.

"It is the will of our... ah"—Jorda fumbled, tried again—"do you have a word for someone who is leader?"

Tokela frowned, tilted his head. "We have many leaders in many traditions; which do you mean?"

Sivan seemed confused, but gave it a go. "You must have one who holds power over all. One who gives directions and must be obeyed."

"How could there be one leader over all tribes and clans?" This was an easy answer. "One born and bred upon River's thighs wouldn't know enough of life upon the duskLands grass to lead anyone. Our leaders guide others with their skills and wisdom, each to their own purpose and ability, but we've none who hold the kind of power you speak of."

This was met by bewilderment. Even the Matwau seemed surprised—which just proved outLanders understood firstPeople even less than firstPeople kenned outLanders. Tokela took the opportunity; more query as distraction. "Does your leader never let others guide them? Do they never make mistakes?"

Ah... confusion was being replaced by disquiet, varying degrees. Reassuring, that even these outLander faces were easily read despite their alien cast.

"Our leader wishes to help you." Jorda's answer was too firm, too rote. "She's interested in you. What you are."

"What I... am?"

Maloh slanted dark eyes first to Jorda, then Sivan, then back to Tokela, who'd already decided the Matwau to be the most dangerous of the three.

"You are unique, Tokela," Maloh replied, wry. "It seems our leader wishes to keep it that way."

Keep it that way.

If you can waken powers long thought dead... Ai, Star Eyes, no wonder they hunt you.

The sand trap was on the move again. Maloh's gaze flickered that way.

Now behind them, Našobok rose quiet as huntingKin, searching for a suitable weapon.

"Did you know my dam?" It wasn't anything Tokela had truly meant to ask.

Silence.

Jorda broke it. "She was my friend. I helped when she asked."

"Help her? Like you would help me by taking me from here? What do you want with me? What did you want with my dam?"

Occupy them. And here Tokela was, more occupied with obtaining answers than covering an escape.

"It was a mistake, to interfere. But now we can make it right." Jorda's bodytalk, though, read uncertain. "Perhaps we can mend you."

Only a half-circuit of Moons ago he would have leapt at the opportunity. Now... "Perhaps. You don't know."

"How can we make things right by taking the little one from his people?" Maloh crossed her arms, shaking her head. "Such things should not be done without consent. The price is high."

She sounded like someone who knew.

Našobok crept closer. He'd a large stone in one hand.

"Then I do not," Tokela started to back away, "consent."

Fire exploded upwards, knocking the water bowl sideways. As one the tall ones turned.

A stone hit Jorda in the temple. He dropped.

Tokela also dropped, but to purpose. He ducked and rolled, snatched up his knife from Jorda's limp, thin fingers, and leapt to his feet as Našobok let fly a second stone. Našobok didn't wait to see if he'd downed another target. Instead he headed for Tokela, who'd also started running.

They barely made two fours of strides. Another shallow pit shimmered then yawned before them, runnelling outwards then back before it spurted upwards into a fountain of sand and dust.

Našobok grabbed Tokela's arm, hauling him sideways just as the sand went soft at their feet. They dodged sideways merely to find another, then another...

Stopped.

"It was a good try," Našobok shrugged and turned about to face their enemy, chin lowered.

This time it was Tokela's to lunge sideways and yank his cousin from another dust spume, pull him forwards.

And knew, with the inwards Other that crept like weavingKin along a web, what the Shaping place sought.

Not them. Not even Maloh. It was after the Chepiś.

Našobok's aim had been true. Jorda's head was splashed with an ichor of indigo. He lay senseless. Sivan and Maloh were trying to wake him, even as the first sand well curled and shifted towards them. As other wells seemed to stir, wake.

"Come!" Našobok grabbed Tokela's arm, tugged. "Let's go!"

Let us have them, Fire urged.

Spoiled and shifting, Earth held full agreement. *For what they have made of us—made of you!—let us have them.*

Instead, Tokela headed for the downed Chepiś.

They were surrounded. The Shaping place had leaked outwards, not in water but sand and rock—heaving, spouting, *moving*—and far too quickly for any escape. Nevertheless, the tall ones sought that escape. Maloh bent down, flung Jorda over one broad shoulder. Beside her, Sivan cast a hand towards it almost wildly. Thinking to control the sand-pits? How?

You know how.

Našobok followed—though he rumbled Rivertalk curses with every stride. "Tokela, what are you *doing?*"

Tokela wasn't sure he knew, but instinct proved, once again, a boon. The curling, heaving sands let him pass. Let Našobok pass, albeit on Tokela's heels, to slide to a halt beside the tall ones.

"Are you out of your mind?" Sivan demanded. "Go! Get out!"

Tokela peered at her for a breath, then turned towards the Shaping well and knelt. His hair stung his cheeks, whipping in the wind. Sand fuzzed his sight, watering his eyes and nose, but he ignored all of it.

Splaying his fingers in the sand, he took in a long breath. His fingers, as if of their own accord, began tracing pictures, shapes. Drums and dancing figures. Clouds and wind-swept trees. Things he didn't have names for, abstract, abstruse. When the breath escaped him, it was soft, a whisper, a rhythm. "Peace. Peace. Sleep, o wounded Grandmother. Sleep."

Našobok didn't turn his back on the tall ones, eyeing them with wary, storm-dark eyes. One hand did reach out to touch Tokela's shoulder. It trembled.

"Earth won't take us," Tokela whispered assurance. "Not thisSun."

"Either way," Našobok's voice tremored like his hand, "I'm watching *these*."

"These" were talking, rapid back-and-forth full of disbelief. But they made no move, and Tokela knew why. In thisnow, he was somehow the only thing to save them from what they had made.

Grandmother's face was twisted, here, angry. Ill and mad, twitching as if from fever. Nevertheless, as he sketched indescribable images in the dirt, whispered Her name, She retreated. Slow, and obstinate—but in the end, unwilling to retaliate if it meant taking Her own.

Her own. See? Fire, down to sand-blown coals. *You are Ours, Star Eyes. You belong to Us. You are not alone.*

Wind died to a soft breath. Earth smoothed, went still.

Silence.

Tokela stood and wiped the dust from his face, turned around.

Našobok stood, knife in hand, daring the tall ones. Maloh still had Jorda across her shoulders, and Sivan had drawn close. As Tokela turned, she stepped towards him.

Halted with a sideways glance as Našobok's knife gleamed, and merely asked, "Why?"

"Did you do this?" Tokela gestured towards the Shaper's well.

Sivan frowned, shook her head. "This was done long before I was born."

"And him." Tokela angled his chin towards Jorda. "He's my sire. Isn't he?"

Maloh muttered something. Behind the amber lenses, Sivan's eyes had gone wide, yellowed-white. "It isn't," she finally answered, "so simple."

"He saved your scrawny pale necks." Našobok stiffened, ready to pounce. "You owe him more than that."

"The Spirits here said your people made them," Tokela persisted. "Even as you made me."

"He... He did make you what you are. I'm not sure your language has a way to tell you how—"

"You assume," Našobok growled, "a lot."

"—any more than you can tell me how your... Spirits work in *my* tongue."

Tokela slid a quelling gaze at Našobok, who grumbled a sigh.

"If you're asking if he physically copulated with your mother, then, no. But still he... made you, Eyes of Stars, more than any other. You would not be alive, had Jorda not Shaped your living."

There was no meaning to it, compared to one truth. But upon another, it made horrific and heavy sense.

"It's the truth," Maloh put in. "I swear it upon my mother's bones."

Našobok blinked, eyed Maloh then Tokela. Said, "She's Matwau, but I believe her."

"Go." Sivan's directive came abrupt and almost fierce. "It was never right, our coming here to take you. Go. And don't look back. Leave now, because they'll know what we've done."

"They?" Tokela repeated.

"Our leaders. You must hide yourself, because I warn you, in the end our leader will come for you herself. She sees you as a threat to us. She chained her own when they became a threat to us."

"And what of your threat to *us*?" Našobok snarled.

"Neither of us can do anything about that." Sivan shook her head, started backing away. "Go. Now. Run."

A'io, Fire hissed. Run. *Keep running, and do not stop until you reach River. She alone can help you now.*

The caverns dripped, cool and close.

Palatan sucked in a single, harsh breath, and loosened his grip, opened his eyes.

Fire flickered, spastic warmth, over joined hands. Chogah had slumped forwards, shivering, murmuring to herself. She was too old for this... but she had insisted.

Palatan was beginning to like her despite himself.

And the other, also sometimes unlikable, but always loved. Anahli sighed, rolled her head on her shoulders, and opened her eyes.

There were Stars there, faint, behind clouds tossed by Wind. "Yeka."

"Ehši." Fond, quavery, but exhausted. This was the sort of work that needed many.

"We did it."

"You did much of it. You are the connexion."

"He's my oathbrother."

Palatan lifted his chin. He understood.

"If only we can convince owlClan of the same."

River was close. He could smell Her, *feel* Her...

Tokela wasn't sure he cared. Lioness surely didn't; walking head down, muddy to the thighs from slogging nonstop through leagues of chancy ground. Her riders weren't much better; they'd taken turns walking and riding to spare her, were woozy with lack of sleep, nervy and keen from constantly looking over their shoulders.

They'd found the mare not far from the Shaping well, grazing in a wallow that had seen recent Rain and sprouted new grass. Lioness had been glad to see them, then. Now, perhaps not so much.

How odd that they should finally reach River, merely to have her lie so quiet, so unobtrusive. She'd none of the brash cheek of Fire, none of Wind's insistence; even Earth's firm waiting seemed more something both outside and within, whereas River...

River's voice filled him like a hand in a fine-stitched glove, lulled and stroked him like the soothing patter of Rain upon Her skin.

Tokela nearly ran into Našobok, who'd slowed.

Beyond, an upright row of lodgepoles seemed inconsistently moored: a barrier of tall posts decorated with mixed intentions, plus a thick layer of mossy growth. A tree-lined road led through and past, fading into thick mist. Even the scents were muted: Smoke, food, people.

There was a town somewhere near.

Našobok gave a mutter as several figures appeared in a curl and waft of damp. Cloaks shiny with Rain's breath, their challenge apparent; this town had entry guardians. Tokela didn't recognise the talk—perhaps a word, here and there—but Našobok obviously did. He brought both fists to his heart and dipped his chin in greeting, his eyes never dropping, his answers fluent.

While they spoke, another lift and sideways hitch of mist revealed a squat hut, mossy to its leewards side, hunched beside the barrier wall. A steady flicker dipped and beckoned within; Fire greeted Tokela with a promise of warmth. He'd no coherent answer, merely response, taking several unsteady steps towards the hut with Lioness in his wake.

The guardians—there were three of them, swart and broad as breeding bulls—broke off conversation and rounded on Tokela. The warning was plain.

Našobok quickly spoke and ambled over, his hand seeking Tokela's shoulder. Its lightness was deceptive; Našobok's fingers pinched, hard, and Tokela gave a small start, brought back within himself.

If only *back within himself* didn't mean being so wet and chilled. And hungry, he realised. Whatever meals they'd shared had been from dwindling stocks of trail food, eaten on the run.

They'll know what we've done. They'll send others. You must hide.

And the only place left to hide was River. They hoped.

Našobok's hand didn't leave Tokela's shoulder. After a few mollified exchanges and a gesture upwards beyond the road, the guardians retreated.

"Just so you know," Našobok led them on, voice pitched for Tokela's ears alone, "hereabouts, to peer into someone's home without their leave is asking for trouble."

"You said this was a major trading outpost—"

"A'io, and the welcome is fierce. But customs are even more so. We both came of age in such a place; follow my lead, and you won't find more trouble than you can take."

"The hearth," Tokela muttered, trying to explain, and Našobok's grip turned into a caress, moved up to stroke at his cheek.

"We'll have that, soon enough. This way, tšukasi." Našobok pressed on, Tokela and the little mare at his heels.

The sodden road wound up a steep hill. Našobok took it with a hobbling roll unlike his normal gait; it reminded Tokela how gimpy he, too, was. His thigh muscles began to pull even more, sending aching twinges from knees to groin. The discomfort re-aligned what sparse mental clarity he possessed; until that heart-beat, Tokela hadn't appreciated how much he'd just set himself, leaden and grim, to endure.

They trudged upwards, accompanied by the draggy *cup-thup* of Lioness's hoofs. Bottom mists gave way with an abrupt change of light, and Našobok gave a happy sigh. Tokela saw why: the hill crested into a long, level clearing, where several good-sized lodges spread, one open and airy for animalKin, and beyond, a well-thatched longhouse fit for two-legged sensibilities.

They saw to Lioness first—of course—and then retreated to the well-lit longhouse.

It was cozier than anything Tokela thought the scrubby, damp town capable of. Smells rose, delicious-thick, hanging in the rafters like a warm blanket. People from every curve of Grandmother's belly gathered, eating, laughing, and making talk. One couple they passed had the broader, well-fleshed fea-tures of dwellers from snowy upLands; another small group had the flattened foreheads and notched ears of those who dwelt within the mesas downLand of the desert Našobok and Tokela had crossed several Suns previous; another group held close in a far corner, colourful scarves covering their heads even indoors and proclaiming them as a Clan of upper midLands herders.

Tokela kept his eyes cast down and stuck to Našobok like a seed in a dog's ruff. Not many bothered to turn and notice two more stragglers.

The hostel's caretaker, however, noticed them, with cheery downRiver talk. "Našobok Riverwalker! It is a joy to see you in my lodge!"

The name was recognised: with welcome smiles or a disinter-ested shrug, some inquisitive... and a few, Tokela noted, with trepidation.

He hung back as Našobok strode on. The place was altogether close, Fire leaping upwards in several places as if demanding recognition. Tokela clenched his teeth and shuttered his eyes. Enemies might lurk here. He could show nothing untowards.

And as if She understood, River calmed Fire's abandon.

"Šaya a'Cassauk!" Našobok was returning the caretaker's ges-ture—both hands instead of one clenched at his chest—his teeth flashing in a broad smile. "A joy to see you—*hunh!*"

This as the fem gave Našobok a bone-cracking hug. Šaya was well-suited for her line of work: strong, well padded, and exuberantly handsome. Našobok returned the embrace, more proof of longstanding acquaintance.

"Grandmother's toes, Riverwalker, you resemble something a barn cat wouldn't drag over my doorstep! And face fur? That's a look I've not seen upon you in ages."

"We were travelling a bit rough." Našobok rubbed a hand over his face, grimaced. Tokela realised how detached he had really been; he hadn't even noticed Našobok's scruffiness. Putting a hand to his own chin in mere impulse, he blinked. Felt again.

He hadn't thought he could even *grow* face fur yet. Most males didn't—not until nigh onto their adult's Journey and many not at all—yet there it was, a tiny slick of down along his jaw.

Most, River purled, *are not Mine.*

"—and what are you doing Earthbound?" Šaya was demanding. "On a *horse*?"

"I had cargo to gather upLands."

"UpLands!" someone hooted from a corner. "That's a ways to go for cargo!"

"Ai, but it was very special cargo." Našobok threw a wink at Tokela, who couldn't help but smile into his hand.

Šaya snorted up a laugh. "Was this your cargo, then?" she demanded, giving Tokela a cheerful repeat of Našobok's greeting, including the fierce hug, after which she pushed him back, eyeing him. "N'da, you've the Marks of the Great Mound. New crew, or visitor?"

"New crew," Našobok answered. "This is Tokela, son to my sire's sister."

"Ai, that's why he's so young. I imagine he's pretty under all that mud—I know you, after all—but I haven't seen you court an oških this young since you *were* that young!"

"I've seen nearly twenty winterings," Tokela put in. Perhaps face fur would be a good thing, after all. "I'm not *that* young."

"Well, believe me you'll have more liking for those youthful looks when you're older." Grinning, Šaya bellowed several commands that carried to the outwards reaches of the hostel.

In short order they were lounged in one of the largest bark-and-stave tubs Tokela had ever seen, with their mud-spattered, sodden clothing and furs whisked away to be brushed clean and spread to dry by the huge hearths in the far alcoves. Šaya even offered Našobok a shave. He politely declined, saying it was more likely he'd fall asleep in the process and end up with a cut throat instead of a smooth cheek.

Finally, back in the main den of the longhouse, hide scrubbed a-tingle and hair let loose to dry, Tokela found himself cross-legged across from Našobok and focusing on his first real meal in some Suns. Tubers, roasted meats, fresh bread, and a side bowl

brimming with cracked šinc'teh parboiled in bone broth. The Elementals had subsided beneath River's gentle croon. Between
the relief of that and the meal, Tokela was nodding off. For the
second time, he barely saved himself from landing face-first into
his well-scraped plate. Across the board, Našobok was dozing—
snoring, even. Somehow he hadn't yet fallen over. Tokela
smirked, leaned over and gave him a push. Našobok woke up just
in time to topple over, legs still crossed.

Fire hissed approval. Tokela chuckled.

Šaya led them to a huge pallet, a privileged one right beside
the largest of the hearths, wide enough for a tangle of four and
piled high with colourful midLands blankets. Tokela willingly
shed his borrowed robe and burrowed in. The blanket threads
were worn soft, sliding thick comfort against his skin and wafting delicious spice past his nostrils.

Našobok crawled in beside and gathered him up. But not even
the sensate enticement of that hard, heated body sculpting close
could keep Tokela awake any longer.

The grotto was dark, seeming uninhabited.

The Domina was present, nevertheless. Her anger sparked reflections, trailed luminescence in her wake. *They have failed.*

"The vortex—"

Was merely a factor. Did you think I wouldn't track them?

"I assumed you would." Cavodu crossed his arms, waited.

Sure enough, *You sent the wrong ones for the job.*

"Under your orders, Domina," he reminded. "They know this
world better than most."

*Which means they are tied to it. To the world, and moreover, its peo-
ple.* White fury underlaced it. *And so they let the little savage go, for
no more than some unfathomable... ephemeral reason!*

"The fault is mine, Domina."

Yes, it is.

Silence. Then, just as Cavodu was about to turn away and head
from the grotto, the silent threat whispered from the brine.

Well. Better to take care of it oneself, after all.

Tokela woke to the smell of burning leaf. Našobok sat, a
bronzed silhouette drawing Smoke from a beautifully carven
pipe.

Lying on his side, Tokela peered at the pipe for some time,
eyes following the lines of leaping Seawolf chasing smiling fish,
watching the shells dangling from the bowl dance and shiver.

Rain pattered on the thatch, a relief. No clear skies thisdark, no Stars. Only the echo that had, since the desert, been ever-present but bearable. Tempting, to let ša lull him back into slumber; instead Tokela sat up and scooted close to Našobok. Opening the blanket he wore across his shoulders, Našobok gathered Tokela in.

The longhouse lay so quiet. For a displaced brace of heartbeats Tokela was confused, almost reached out to see if... well, if They were even there. He had slept hard—his first real bed in some Sundowns probably had much to do with that—and bit by bit the uneven tenor of his dreams came back to him. That awareness made him doubly conscious of the unfathomable echo humming just beyond true hearing, of the more Earth-bound presences conjoining within his Spirit...

Of River, keeping all submerged. Contained.

Even outwards, though, silence broke itself, here and there. Muted noises came from the alcoves that held the cookFires. No stirrings from their sleeping neighbours, bundled in various cloaks, blankets and furs... Ai, perhaps one. A movement flickered from the corner of his eye and Tokela turned to see one of the herdClan females shifting in her blankets, putting an infant to nurse. She flitted her eyes up at the movement, and Tokela smiled. She returned the smile, then settled her attention back upon the infant.

She had met his gaze. What was humming within must not be evidencing itself without.

Perhaps... if he loosed himself into their Dance would it be easier? Maybe he should go to the shamans, learn the way. Earth seemed willing to the try, Fire importunate as always and Wind whistling about the eaves, filling his chest and...

No more pain, My own, only the undertow of dreamings to wash them clean. An ache in his heart and a shiver through his limbs, River's presence a tandem comfort as Našobok's hand settled over his. It displaced an unthinking yearning, bringing Tokela back into reality.

Našobok was reality: sound, strong, *sane.*

"Did you sleep well?" Našobok murmured, subvocal huntingtalk that carried only to the closest set of ears.

Tokela answered in like fashion. "Well enough. Better than I should, perhaps. How long have you been up?"

Našobok shrugged, offered a puff of the pipe. It was tempting, but Spirits were soft enough so that Tokela could waft on the waves of them. He was still unsure about Smoke's effects. Shaking his head, Tokela kept up the nigh-silent conversation.

"I hope sleep comes easier to you on board *Ilhukaia.*"

"It always does." There was a buoyancy underlying Našobok's voice that had been absent during their journey. Tokela understood. His own heart had lightened as River's voice had strengthened within him. Despite misgivings of what could happen, he could hardly wait to ride Her again.

As to riding... "What shall we do with Lioness?"

"I thought of sending her to Inhya. She was born of horseClan, you remember. It would be a more certain future for a worthy travelling companion than just trading her here. And fair enough exchange for stealing you."

"You stole nothing! They didn't want me. And my body and heart are mine to give."

"Ai, sharpen your horns." Našobok turned a half smirk upon Tokela. "When I was oskih I too chafed at restrictions." The expression widened. "But was very glad of the freedoms, at that."

Good humour restored, Tokela reached up and traced his fingers along the thin fur on Našobok's cheek and throat and back through the thick length of bistre hair beneath the blanket.

"Hunh! One dark of rest and the rutty oških returns." Našobok inclined his head against Tokela's for a heartbeat. "Do you... well. Sense anything? Except for sleeping—and you needed it—I've seen you watching out. Waiting. Listening?"

Tokela shrugged and didn't take his head from Našobok's shoulder. Instead he looked into Fire's eyes, breathed lightly the smouldering leaf, felt two voices swirl in his head, mixing as surely as heat and Smoke.

Soothing. Not wakening.

"And what, then, do you hear?"

"Very little. Stars are covered, River is close. I sense nothing. Yet."

"Yet." Našobok nodded. "A'io."

They will know what we've done. She will send others.

She. Spoken with such fearful regard by all of them, but particularly the one who had claimed but denied Tokela, who had spoken of "mending" him as if he were a pot that had somehow broken.

What is broken? Fire again, speaking with Palatan's voice; as if he lingered with them, curled up beside Našobok. *So many meanings, but what meaning for the likes of you? Damaged, but not past reason. Wrecked like a craft on a sandbar, disconnected—and that the worst of all, for you keep turning away from ones who could help you.*

Help? More like danger for others, Tokela replied, swift as an arrow's flight. *Your... co-tenant touched me, and almost couldn't retreat.*

From hold of Stars, not you.

They are in me, somehow. Danger lies in the very smell of my blood.

And that blood drawn forth by shards of breakage; by shattering of what promise is yours: a promise that now bleeds unclean and pools fallow in your Spirit. This spoke deep beneath Tokela's feet, speaking with a twinned aspect of both Earth and River. *To deny that promise is to refuse what you truly are.*

Refusal, a'io. And also pure survival. He had spent so much of his existence asking—disputing. Spent even a normal maturity, he realised, shoring up closer to Našobok, in staving off and sequestering any hint of Spirit into a small knot of denial.

It had saved him. Until it no longer had.

Back to the same tangled pathways, only this time Tokela could actually See where they might take him, where they had taken him.

I know that what I am has hurt others.

It has also saved others. Would you sit in judgement upon your own actions? Do you even have that right?

A gentle hand took his chin, tilted it up; he found himself peering into Našobok's storm-hued eyes, heard others stirring, saw dawn breaking into the far windows of the hostel. All of it telling Tokela he'd been... gone.

"Hunh. I thought as much. Come back to me, Star Eyes... what is this, eh?" Našobok's fingers stroked along the fine, soft fur on Tokela's jaw. "You're getting awfully well grown, I see; from late bloom to full fruit. Your grandsire would have said an animal Spirit was rising too strongly through you."

"Is that such a bad thing?" Tokela matched Našobok's sudden grin with his own, albeit a self-conscious one. "Did he say that to you, then?"

"Often. As to bad? N'da, not bad, but you know our birthing-tribe. They'd call it presumptive, more like, taking upon ourselves what Spirit rightfully belongs to our animal brothers and sisters. I also grew my face fur early—like a half-wild horsetalker, Grandsire always groused. I finally told him he'd married into horseClans, so he had seeded my animal Spirit."

"Did it make him angry?" Their mutual grandsire's temper was legendary; Tokela had never felt the edge of it himself.

"To the contrary. He always respected strength, even if it rose as precociousness."

Tokela laughed.

"I rather like yours, too."

"Mine?"

"Strength." The grin widened. "Precociousness. And I definitely fancy the look of *this*." Našobok fluffed at Tokela's jaw once more; that and the tone of voice tingled heat into the pit of Tokela's belly. "But back to present matters." Našobok's voice lowered once more into hunting-talk. "You were... away. This won't serve you well on any craft. Do the tall ones lurk? Or the Spirits? I thought River's voice would aid—"

"It wasn't Chepiś. Nor any of the Elementals... well, not exactly," Tokela amended, thinking of the Fire-filled voice.

Našobok's brows were twisting, almost comically so. Plain as plain his thoughts: *Grandmother's toes, what* now?

"It's... Palatan. He wants me to go there, to him."

The breath leaked from Našobok in a long, low whistle.

"I'm not... Oh, Wolf, I'm not sure I can."

$$\phi \quad \phi \quad \phi$$

27
EYES OF STARS

They broke their fast and, while Našobok was chatting up the hostel's caretaker—something about a very big fish—Tokela slipped out to see to Lioness.

Simple. No voices, no hovering anything wanting... well, whatever. Only the soothing sound of animalKin breathing and sighing over breakfast with flat molars crunching cured grasses; only the smell of horsehide as Tokela brushed Lioness until she gleamed. Dawn slid through the barn, sending motes of dust dancing upwards into the roof timbers. The little mare lipped his hair, stood soft-eyed and rapt as he shared breath with her.

After the fifth such interchange, Tokela heard a chuckle, looked up to see Našobok leaning against the doorway, grinning.

"Ai, animalKin See you, no question." His grin widened, and he hefted the rucksack higher over one shoulder. "I've news. A trade vessel has been spotted upRiver."

"Yours?"

"Likely. They were due here two darks ago. Come."

They strode down the hill. It was a much different place with Sun cresting the trees, spilling brilliance across the settlement. There was mud, to be sure—always mud this turn of Hoop in duskLands—but the dwellings seemed less forlorn, the tall, carven lodgepole fortifications with their watcher's hut less forbidding and more sensible.

A shout rose from the tall stands of still-misted conifers ahead; Našobok alerted, threw the rucksack over one shoulder, said again, "Come!" and skipped into a run, light-hearted as a ahlóssa.

Tokela followed into the towering trees; thick, then thinning, then a brilliant flash against his eyes nigh to match the one in his Spirit: River's reflection, outer and inner. Still steaming around the corners, fog burning away but still hiding Her other flank, Her coppery waters lapped at the quays and shorehouses, tilting the small craft tethered there. A large promontory was beginning to peek through just upRiver, a protective jut of ochre stone and conifers. Nothing to be seen past that, but sounds travelled:

a slap and slide of water against a great wood hull, voices floating, seemingly, in another place. People were emerging from the trees beside and behind Tokela, waving and calling out, running to eagerly line the largest and most deepset of the quays.

Našobok halted. Still grinning, he put thumb and fingers to his mouth, and let out a piercing whistle.

It was answered from the mists beyond the promontory, carrying high in Wind's nigh-stillness. A span of drawn-out heartbeats passed. Then a tall mast burst from the mists and rounded the promontory, oars working.

Shorn of the grace of her winged lateen sails, the craft lay down in the water, broad and working-like with cargo, but Tokela felt his breath catch in his throat as she hove to, parting coppery water in search of the outer quay. In thisnow *Ilhukaia* was, inexplicably, one of the most beautiful things he'd ever seen.

Riverwalker, she called to him with River's voice.

"She does it to me too." Našobok's voice was a mere whisper, and as Tokela turned, he saw River glint in the storm-hued eyes.

Heard, in a sudden scree of warning: *Riverwalker. Beware!*

Scented a tang, high upon a slight, dry breath of Wind.

Then, from the water, they came.

The colour of silt and kelp and bitter poison, exploding from River like water-horses. Yet they were nothing like. These were unnatural, Shaped *things*: bipedal creatures with fins, and claws, and one bulbous, lidless eye above a lipless mouth. Gashes gaped upon their swollen, misShapen necks, raw and open and fluttering.

They fell upon *Ilhukaia*.

And River... *screamed*.

The not-sound plunged into Tokela's heart like a dual-edged blade, ripped sideways, and took him to his knees.

Panicky cries rose, bouncing off the fog and surrounding trees. The current was against Našobok—not River's, but the onlookers in flight. Našobok leapt forwards nevertheless, his passage a cresting wave, heading for *Ilhukaia* and shoving aside those who didn't give way.

His crew was fighting for their lives. Munro hung to the tiller by sheer will, while a pair of oarmates fended off the invaders snatching at their oars. *Ilhukaia* gybed, a dip and swerve that sent everyone sliding. Only seven of them, against...

Monsters.

They screamed, a low-level keen that dug behind Našobok's eyeballs and burned.

"Well," he let the word drawl into a sneer. "The tall softlings must now make creatures to do their bidding?" He slowed but once, and that to shrug the shortbow from his shoulders and string it. He shot a glance backwards to ensure Tokela had heard...

Tokela hadn't. He had fallen, sprawled facedown on the hard planks of the quay. One of the cursed creatures was squirming out of the water and towards him—too close for Našobok's liking.

Fisting several arrows, he bent the bow, nocked and loosed,; gave a grunt of satisfaction as the creature collapsed into River. Shouted, "Get up, Tokela!"

But Tokela didn't respond. perhaps the creatures' screams were doing something Other to him, perhaps whatever had flung him down had also flung him... *away*, as if Sun had become Stars to incapacitate him.

His crew fought on, some hand to hand, others with whatever weapons could be snatched up and wielded. There was something hanging nigh to the furled sail... perhaps not... but a'io, it was there, fading like wings against bright Sunlight.

More, it seemed to focus back. Not with eyes, nor with any identifiable feature or expression. Nevertheless, its reality and intent hung there, Shaping the will of its creatures with...

What? It didn't matter. Našobok snarled and shot. Waste of a good arrow. The hovering thing merely faded then reShaped itself, like some sick incarnation of clouds beneath Thunder's wings.

Tokela suddenly twitched, lurched upwards, and let out a hoarse shout—a warning? Našobok's body obeyed before he thought, whirled. One of the creatures, two arrows in its neck, skidded past him and rammed headlong into another. The things moved blind, clumsy, but when they went down they didn't stay down. Even with missing limbs, or mortal wounds bleeding a thick, blue-black ichor, they kept coming.

And his crew kept fighting. Two were back-to-back, shadowing first mate Odina, who was beating off several of the things with her spear—and losing. Another was being dragged across the planking by the hair. Half were downed.

Several more of the creatures leapt out of the water; one headed for him and the other for Tokela. Našobok took them out, one after another, and laughed as two more scrabbled up onto the quay. He grabbed for the quiver at his hip...

Laughed again, this without humour, as he found it empty.

And three of the screaming creatures fell upon Našobok, sending him sliding across the slick-wet quay and into River.

He had seen such creatures before, smelt the ichor of their blood, seen the Void-within-Stars kindling behind their eyes. But

these creatures were twisted beyond any recognition. Their eyes
roiled with inky shadows and ice-white flashes, mouths gushing
blood, neither the indigo ink of outLand things nor the crimson
of Grandmother's Kin, but a black that rejected both. Even its
skin pulsed, as if it were still, somehow, changing, body insects
crawling a corpse, Shaped with outLand sorcery.

Not that Tokela could see, eyes and skull aflame from the
keening not-sound. He kept dragging himself along the quay towards Našobok.

Ilhukaia crawled with the creatures. The Riverwalkers re-
sisted takeover with everything they'd to hand. But there were
too many of the things, overwhelming strong fighters as if they
were children. And the *screaming*—scraping from inside out, raking Fire down his spine.

N'da, not *Fire*.

It wasn't just the things that let out those horrific shrieks, but
River, whose cries had turned to pain as the Shaped creatures
swarmed, swam, *infested...*

A thick snarl clotting his throat, Tokela crawled on his belly
over the quay. Even as every instinct buttressed his heart with
horror and rage, the horrific not-sound still had the power to
stagger him, make him slip.

He couldn't slip. He couldn't stand by while these things had
their way, couldn't let them catch him, couldn't allow the horrific noise to blind him, snare him.

There was another way.

The creatures, diverted, swarmed over the quay and pulled
Tokela into River.

And Tokela let them, slipping into Her like swimmingKin,
sinking like a stone.

◊ ◊ ◊

River took Našobok in a crash and swirl of foam. Furious,
stinging claws tore at him, slimy limbs choked as the creatures
pressed him. Twisting, stealing the breath from his lungs, pulling
him down into the deeps. And the more they descended, the
more of them came.

Deeper still. Pressure, and his ears pulsing thick, and what
Wind he'd taken with that last gasp and laugh was failing. A hum
rose behind wide-open eyes, foam, and murk, and Shaped creatures choking the life from him, and Našobok pondered it—all of
it—within the span of one heartbeat. It seemed River would claim
him at the last, and he could only hope Sea would bless this last
dalliance with Her sister.

Palatan, he whispered, as a carmine haze began to bleed over
his vision. *Aylaniś.* His next thought was both surprise and solace:
Tokela. Ai, I'm so sorry. I tried.

A flurry in the water, then. Fury and panic, shrieks and grunts, clicks and whistles; all echoing over him, through him. The claws loosed him, stripes of pain raking in their wake. Something struck him in the belly, nigh folding him in half. The rest of his used-up breath escaped, a final gout of bubbles, and the water filled his mouth with salt and his own blood.

He was moving, flying backwards through the water with a passive violence that rolled him then, impossibly, impelled him into the light. Našobok broke the surface with a choke and cough. Wind filled his aching lungs and he clutched outwards, a spastic judder like to the instincts of a dropped newborn. One hand struck wet wood, the other moulded with the skin of his torso against something alive: wide, and slick, and cool.

For the longest heartbeats of his life he couldn't see, could only clutch to *Ilhukaia*'s hull with one hand and the slick-wet hide of his saviour/captor with the other, could only puke River and gasp Wind until, finally, he was able to go slack, panting. Slowly, Našobok opened his eyes.

Another eye regarded him—lidless, the colour of shallow Sea and wet kelp. His fingers twitched against skin mottled pink and grey, glossy with wet and smoother than duskLands leather.

The smiling fish blew, sucked in clean Wind. The spray misted Našobok's face, reeking of brack and fish, then the smiling fish made a string of ša's creaking, squeaking talk, which cut off with a piercing whistle, before ša swerved and dove sideways, away.

River was filled with ša's kin, pods leaping and thrashing, squealing and clicking. Not just the smiling fish, but swimmingKin of every description—fish, reptiles, even the flyingKin obliged to River's bounty were diving from the sky. The oddly rhythmic chaos darted over and around his craft, as if the perpetrators were out for a lark.

Beneath, however, lurked serious intent. A bare length from him, a pair of smiling fish dove into one of the Shaped creatures, their high-pitched talk drowning its cries even as they took it under.

Ichor rose in ebon puffs, and flyingKin dove, literally picking up the pieces.

My people! Tokela!

Shaking away both revulsion and fascination, Našobok remanded himself to thisnow. He inched sideways, one callused hand unsheathing the dagger at his calf, the other caressing *Ilhukaia*'s hull until he found a dangling rope. Knife in teeth, he hauled away and landed upon the deck, dripping and ready for anything.

Anything, perhaps, but what he found.

Below, River churned in copper chaos, twisted predators becoming prey. The deck lay oddly quiet, almost peaceful. The... things were gone, only ichor and slime left upon the wet, smooth deck. His crew stood, still and shaken but all accounted for, even the steerKeeper clinging to his tiller with several of the younger ones who'd kept fierce guard over their elder.

Yet none paid any heed, staring towards the bow.

Našobok followed their gazes. Saw what the others did, balanced on *Ilhukaia*'s front sprit, feet bare and wet to skin, eyes filled black and pocked with Stars.

Wings. The Power that would call monsters had wings, ones spread to cover the Sun, calling a StarVoid to Shape a cage.

Tokela dove through River towards *Ilhukaia*'s hull and climbed to meet the thing. He knew he wasn't alone, not thisnow, perhaps never again.

And when he called, They came—not just the Elementals, but the co-tenants who were claimed by them, Spirit and flesh.

Little brother, We are here.

Fire was first—of course—running Star-cast sparks that struck, searing. Wind carried them, frothing River into tide-swollen glory. Earth grounded *Ilhukaia*'s bow, so that those who belonged to Her wouldn't suffer, then sent tendrils of green and mud to foul those who leapt back into River.

And River...

River burst from confinement like a soul freed of flesh; a water-horse leaping, a song from many throats to fill a cast net of Stars and burst it with Sun's rays.

Free. They were, all of them—*all!*—freed and just as incomprehensibly bound together. Tokela had no need to require or even ask. Just *Reach*, then release.

And when the Chepiś ghost with darkling wings sought to beat him back, foul his own Elemental flight, River safeguarded him, filled him when Her People quailed beneath the Void. River drowned conjured Starlight with a thick *hiss*, slicking against Tokela's skin and pounding behind his ears in the flow of his own blood, salt-silt and coppery-warm.

Mine, She told him. *You were Mine, first.*

With eyes reflecting Starlight upon water, Tokela met the alien eyes both there and not-there, felt the net falter, and the fabric of the Shaping start to fray.

"I won't come with you. This is my place, and my People," Tokela said, in a voice that filled the estuary like River at full tide. "You will not come here again."

And with a great booming rush of wings, the thing escaped.

The cleanup was foul. Without the Spirit that had animated them, the misShapen creatures began to bloat and rot.

Fire was happy to consume them. Tokela suspected Palatan approved.

But it wasn't only the smell of the things burning that kept the villagers circling the one who'd vanquished them. They also gave Tokela a circuit as wide as Sun dipping towards Dusk. Even Našobok's crew were eyeing him warily.

You were alone before you took this path. It was River. *It was unhealthy. Now, you are alone no longer.*

No longer, echoed, fainter. ShamanKin, fading into dusk.

"Ai, it is a mercy." Našobok refused avoidance. He came over, threw an arm across Tokela's shoulders, and snugged him close. "These... things. Once they were Kin."

Tokela nodded, and ducked his cheek against Našobok's arm. *So was I.*

So you are, River chided. *My Kin. My son, returned to Me and Mine.*

"Huh." Našobok nuzzled his hair. "Good luck, old Munro says, to have shamanKin aboard."

"But I'm not—"

"Aren't you?" Našobok gestured all about them: the burning creatures, the villagers lingering with food and drink and awed murmurs, the wide expanse of water that lay calm once more. "The stories will be told for many Hoops. How the Spirits of long-gone shamans joined with an oških's latent power to help a village beleaguered. How that oških, with his own Spirits, drove back an invasion of Shaped creatures." His voice dipped into a whisper. "Can I help it if shamans are still about?"

"Ai, River Wolf!" Odina addressed Našobok with familiarity—and respect. "Our craft is clean. The village's trade has been carried and counted. Do we stay, or move on?"

"We move on. Prepare our craft."

Odina gave a respectful tilt of chin, first to her chieftain, then to Tokela. Turning on one heel, she marched down the quay.

Našobok watched her go, then turned back to Tokela, serious—and sudden. "So. We have come to the turning place. We go forwards, or back. What is your wish?"

What is your wish? An echo in thisnow, but faint behind Tokela's sight, Fire was a soft presence surrounded by moisture. No desert heat, no burning Sun, no white-hot Stars to sear a seeking Alekšu. Instead there were soundless depths to immerse abandon—*his* depths, Spirit and body and breath.

This was his... and his co-tenant's... place.

Come to us. We would help you. Protect you. Teach you.

He was no longer sure which voice was which. Their intent floated upon the mists and melted together upon River's coppery surface, mirrored. Whilst She waited, secure enough to be silent—wherever Tokela went, She would hold him; but here, upon this craft so aptly named *Surrender*...

Našobok misread the hesitation. "I will take you to Palatan." Slow, almost unwilling, did Tokela dare think it regret? "If he will give you sanctuary. If you wish to go."

"If he wills. If I wish."

Našobok took Tokela's shoulders in gentle hands, broke the whisper with a quick shake and said, just as gentle, "What *do* you want?"

"I want to be with you. With River." It tumbled out. "What I don't want is to be used."

"I would never—"

"I know. I know. But the others... I'm not so sure."

"No more than you should be. Even those outLanders in the desert can't be trusted. They seek to use you."

"Not just the outLanders. Našobok. I don't want to be a weapon used by my own People against the Chepiś any more than I want the Chepiś to use me against my own People."

Našobok was quiet for so long Tokela was sure he'd offended him. Angered him. And no wonder.

"It seems to me you've answered your own question, then," Našobok finally answered.

"You'll let me stay?"

A snort, and Našobok cuffed at his ears. "I asked you what you wanted. You are River's; you belong here. On *Ilhukaia*, in my bedding, at my side for as long as you choose."

Warmth spangled heart-deep and spread.

"But heed me, Tokela. The time may come when the decision will be taken from you."

"Then I'll fight them with their own weapons. Ensure truce is kept." Tokela looked out across River. "I am Tohwakeli'fitčiluka. Eyes of Stars."

FINIS

WANT TO FIND OUT
WHAT HAPPENS NEXT?

Be notified of the next book in
The Hoop of the Alekšu'in

AND be the first to receive the latest
shared content, sneak peeks, releases, and news!

Join Talulah J. Sullivan's newsletter at:

https://talulahjsullivan.com

You'll even nab yourself a free story!

◊ ◊ ◊

AFTERWORD

I feel as if I've been working on the world of the Alekšu'in for much of my life.

I didn't know it, at first. Or, more likely, just refused to see it. Openly acknowledging one's cultural ties wasn't exactly encouraged where or when I grew up. So the world you've just been introduced to in *Blood Indigo* went through, well, a lot of 'white'-washing at its beginnings. When the story first began to emerge, it had different cultural suggestions—safer, for the mainstream—except there were, always, these indisputable subterranean layers that kept bubbling up, refusing to be ignored.

Listen to us, they said.

Finally, I did.

The world introduced in *Blood Indigo* is speculative, one of magical realism. It might not be ours, and might not be of our future and/or our past. But it is based on experiences in this world—lessons learned, tales shared, a long history of resilience in the face of attempted erasure—and a life lived with, but not bounded by all these things. The journey to understand and reverence my cultures and my ancestors—*all* of them—is ongoing. I often didn't altogether understand what I was living or hearing, but the influence is undeniable.

(Like the language of *Blood Indigo*. Much of it is influenced—heavily—by Choctaw and Chickasaw... but the language and ways of speaking are nevertheless a fantastical one, shaped to another reality.)

Blood Indigo is also one of those books that has been loved by more than a few readers, but has been unable to find a place for a long time. What I myself found comfortable was "well-written, but too... difficult", or "a talented effort, but not mainstream enough". It was "complicated" and "challenging", and required "too much thought".

I found this astounding, particularly coming from the field of speculative fiction.

See, when I read SFF and magical realism, it's because I want to *be* challenged. I want the story to give a damned hard push to my established or habitual patterns.

(It's kind of like travelling—what's the use of going somewhere I've never been merely to eat at McDonald's? Not that I eat there anyway, but you get the drift.)

What I absolutely *don't* want is to read an accepted status quo. And after over fifty years of reading speculative fiction, many of the tropes have long worn thin. Give me real, complicated people of all shades and shapes and sexualities, give me the entire spectrum of queerness, give me diverse systems of belief, and give me cultures that *aren't* the bog-standard same-ol' same-ol'.

We've gotten lazy. For while the speculative reads I had growing up had their problems—some of them big ones, too—there were also reads that blew the mind, opened the heart, and asked Big Questions.

We're finally starting to see more of them again.

I truly believe that *Blood Indigo* is one of them. I hope I've told a story that convinces you likewise.

Peace,

TALULAH

CAST OF CHARACTERS

FirstPeople
From the Wintering Tally of Allied Tribes, gathered by Inhya a'Naišwyrh in the Hoop of the Great Incursion

Anahli	oških a'Šaâkfo, first daughter to Aylaniś
Akumeh	oških a'Nunkáhiti, hearthed a'Naišwyrh
Aylaniś	horse-chieftain a'Šaâkfo, espoused Palatan, dam of Anahli, Nishe, Vinka, Samke, Kuli
Benniic	wyrhmate a'*Ilhukaia*
Bimih	oških a'Naišwyrh
Calidon	(deceased) tyah a'Šaâkfo, sire of Palatan
Čayku	oških a'Naišwyrh
Chogah	(also O'yotali'chogah) elder & Alekšu tuk (Medicine-Keeper) a'Šaâkfo
Galenu	elder & stone-chieftain a'Hassun
Giltha	(deceased) hearth-chieftain a'Naišwyrh, espoused Nechtoun, dam of Sarinak, Našobok
Inhya	(born a'Šaâkfo) hearth-chieftain a'Naišwyrh, espoused Sarinak, dam of Madoc, hearth-mother to Tokela
Kalisom	wyrhmate a'*Ilhukaia*
Kuli	(also Kulahiši) ahlóssa a'Šaâkfo, son of Aylaniś
Lakisa	(deceased) espoused Talorgan, dam of Tokela
Madoc	ahlóssa a'Naišwyrh, chieftain-son to Inhya & Sarinak
Mordeleg	oških a'Hassun, hearthed a'Naišwyrh
Munro	wyrhmate a'*Ilhukaia*, foster-uncle to Našobok
Našobok	(also Nashobok'aqékla, River Wolf) wyrh-chieftain a'*Ilhukaia*, outcast son to Nechton & Giltha
Nechton	once-chieftain a'Naišwyrh of Gilda, sire of Sarinak, Našobok
Nipok	wyrhmate a'*Ilhukaia*, rigger
Nishe	oških a'Šaâkfo, second daughter of Aylanis
Odina	1st wyrhmate a'*Ilhukaia*
Pallaton	Alekšu a'Šaâkfo, tyah horseClan, espoused Alannis, sire of Anahli, Nishe, Vinka, Samke, Kuli
Saltha	oških a'Naišwyrh
Samke	ahlóssa a'Šaâkfo, fourth daughter of Alannis
Sarinak	Mound-chieftain a'Naišwyrh, espoused Inhya, sire of Madoc, uncle to Tokela
Šaya	hosteler a'Cassauk
Seguin	forest-chieftain a'Nunkáhiti
Stannic	taleKeeper a'Šaâkfo, uncle to Pallaton
Talorgan	(deceased) herder a'Hassun, espoused Lakisa, sire of Tokela
Tokela	(also Tohwakeli, Tohwakeli'fitčiluka) oških a'Naišwyrh, son of Lakisa & Talorgan, hearth-son to Inhya
Vinka	oških a'Šaâkfo, third daughter of Aylaniś

OutLanders

Cavodu	Chepiś, High Lord of the Western Temple
Domina	Chepiś, Supreme Empress of the New World
Dominus	Chepiś, ex-Emperor of the New World, Synced, Exiled
Jorda	Chepiś, Lord of the Western Temple, progeny of Cavodu & Ranlaia, twin to Sivan
Maloh	Matwau from the eastern continent, fostered into Chepiś, lover of Sivan
Ranlaia	Chepiś, Lord of the Western Temple, Synced, mother of Jorda & Sivan
Rann	Chepiś, Disciple to the Western Temple
Sivan	Chepiś, Lord of the Western Temple, progeny of Cavodu & Ranlaia, twin to Jorda, lover of Maloh
Vox	Chepiś, Disciple to the Western Temple

About the Author

TALULAH J. SULLIVAN
has been a pro equestrian, a dancer, an actor,
an activist, and a teacher who has learned as much
from her two- and four-legged students as she's ever
shared with them... yet she's never managed to NOT be
a storyteller. Ever.

Being a result of one of the original "hands across the
waters" cross-cultural exchanges—Scots-Irish and
Choctaw/Chickasaw—making a home base in
dampish forest country came quite naturally. Sharing
that home base with a longtime spouse, several four-
legged companions, and a lifetime's collection of books
took a bit more work, of course. And, having also
inherited the itch for travelling from both sides of the
pond, her house has wheels for a reason.

Her works reflect worlds both old and new,
cultures both fantastic and familiar—and
promise an immersive, subversive experience.

More information can be found at her website:

https://talulahjsullivan.com

www.ingramcontent.com/pod-product-compliance
Lightning Source LLC
Chambersburg PA
CBHW051159190726
48288CB00006B/1722